A DATE WITH
DEATH

ALSO BY KELLY CREAGH

The *Nevermore* trilogy

Nevermore

Enshadowed

Oblivion

Phantom Heart

Strange Unearthly Things

A DATE WITH DEATH

KELLY CREAGH

GALLERY BOOKS

NEW YORK AMSTERDAM/ANTWERP LONDON
TORONTO SYDNEY/MELBOURNE NEW DELHI

Gallery Books
An Imprint of Simon & Schuster, LLC
1230 Avenue of the Americas
New York, NY 10020

First Gallery Books trade paperback edition July 2026

Interior design by Hope Herr-Cardillo

Manufactured in the United States of America

10 9 8 7 6 5 4 3 2 1

Library of Congress Control Number: 2026934998

ISBN 978-1-6682-0983-7 (pbk)
ISBN 978-1-6682-0984-4 (ebook)

For Ethan, who said, "What about the Grim Reaper?"
(You know the chapters to avoid.)

1

HELENA

Given that we'd reached mid-October—and, more importantly, Halloween season—I shouldn't have been surprised to find a man dressed up as the Grim Reaper on the balcony of Anatole Manor. Still, the historic Gothic home turned event venue made him look so perfectly *picturesque*, I couldn't resist investigating.

I rapped a knuckle against the sliding glass door, but the impossibly tall, hooded man didn't look up. Instead, he stood in profile at the banister of the stone balcony, lonesome and cutting an ominous image, the handle of his huge scythe propped against his shoulder. Its curved blade gleamed as silver as the slivered moon that floated high above.

Opening the door with my free hand, my other cradling a plastic wine cup, still half full of cheap Chardonnay, I stepped into the night.

I closed the door behind me, muffling the thumping techno remix of "Monster Mash." The music bled from the crowded ballroom that I'd given the slip—right along with my otherwise-occupied date, who hadn't noticed my exit anyway.

As the sound subdued to a fainter heartbeat rhythm, I breathed a sigh of relief.

Was that why Tall, Dark, and Gruesome was out here? Maybe his ears—and nerves—needed a break from the ultra-kitschy spooky-themed tunes, too.

"Wow," I said, turning to my fellow party absconder. "That costume is a ten out of ten on the epic scale."

The figure didn't move. And though he remained still enough to be one of those overpriced-lawn-ornament-type deals, the dramatic brooding act wasn't fooling me. This guy had clearly spent weeks planning this. And no one poured that much time into a costume unless they were dying to show it off.

Not only that, but the man had implemented the special effect of gray fog tendrils curling off the tatty hems of his robes. I wasn't sure how he'd accomplished that, but my educated guess was that he'd sewn dry ice packs into the fabric.

A glowing hourglass hung from his belt, multicolored orbs floating within—another off-the-scale special effect.

"Truly," I said as I approached, the floor-length skirts of my sparkly lemon-yellow taffeta ball gown rustling with my movements, "that look is movie-level authentic. Did you rent those robes? Or maybe you made them. Either way, *please* tell me you're entering the costume contest. I think there's a cash prize. Runner-up gets a spa gift card. I guess you don't have flesh, but you could still get your phalanges done." I wiggled my rainbow-painted nails at him. "You'd certainly get my vote."

He didn't answer. I didn't care.

He didn't own the balcony, and I needed to get away, too.

As the quiet wore on, a pleasantly chilly breeze stirred my wheat-blond hair, which I wore long under my crown. My dress didn't have sleeves, but it had been warm in the manor, and thanks to the wine, I probably had a good ten minutes before I started to shiver.

"Nice and quiet out here," I observed. "Are you waiting for someone?"

Could be he was loitering (sulking?) outdoors because his date had left him alone as well. Mine, an actuary I'd been chatting up on a dating app for weeks, had bailed on me the moment he'd caught the attention of a brunette dressed as a sexy librarian—a costume I wasn't sure if I should be offended by since I actually happened to *be* a librarian.

I stopped next to the enormous looming, dooming Reaper Man, and straightening my spiky crown—spray-painted with love and dunked in gold glitter—I grinned up at him. "It's obvious who you are. But can you guess what *I* am?"

He didn't say anything. He still refused to move, too. But he wasn't running away from me, so why not continue the one-sided conversation? So far, this interaction was still going better than any of my exchanges with Dale, who had already blocked me on the dating app.

I knew because, while I'd been sitting alone at our table, I'd had plenty of time to check my phone.

Maybe I shouldn't have quoted *Hamlet* when he said he didn't believe in ghosts.

Or maybe I should have worn something saucier.

"I'm sunshine!" I spread my arms. Then I snapped my multicolored spandex belt with my free hand. "*And* rainbows."

Next, I lifted the hem of my dress, accented with cotton to simulate clouds, and flashed the rainbow, rhinestone-covered pumps that were officially killing me. "I made and repurposed everything myself. Thanks to my job, I'm pretty crafty. Not to mention thrifty. It was Abigail, one of my regular patrons—I'm a children's librarian—who suggested this concept. She's five." I raised a finger. "And a half. Except, everyone keeps asking me if I'm Belle from *Beauty and the Beast*." I shrugged. "But that's cool, too, so . . . I just say yes."

I took a big swig of the wine, which, to be fair, I'd already had enough of.

When I went back in, I'd call an Uber and scarf down some cheese puffs and bruschetta to counteract the effects of the adult grape juice.

Then I'd go home and do my usual bedtime routine of washing my face, brushing my teeth, and reading about other people falling in love until I fell asleep.

"What do *you* do?" I asked him, but he kept the stoic shtick going.

Either he was annoyed, or he just wanted to stay in character. Possibly both were true.

But I could play along. I literally had a master's in make-believe.

"Dead-silent type, huh?" I asked him with a wink as I gazed out over the grounds, which we hovered two stories above. On either side of the balcony, a set of curving stone steps swept down to meet with a dormant garden, the roses pruned back to near nubs. Quilts of leaves blanketed the rest of the barren beds and the cobblestone walkway, too. "Lonely lonesome loner. I get that."

Plucking a stray golden maple leaf from the stone balcony's cracked banister, I gave it a twirl before sending it floating over the ledge.

Though he still didn't speak, he did move, lifting his head just a bit.

My curiosity exploded, and I craned my neck to gaze into that hood, which framed only blackness.

"Goodness," I said, eyes bugging as I took yet another swig from my wine. "You've really gone all out." I gestured to his lost-to-the-shadows face. "H-how are you doing that?" No sooner had I voiced the question than I held up a halting hand. "You know what? I don't want to know. Honestly, I'm starting to think your way is more fun. Because, no lie, I'm kind of scared right now."

And I was—a little.

"That's what the unknown does to us, right?" I prodded. "That's why you, the Grim Reaper, are so scary. You represent death. The greatest unknown there is. Really, though—and correct me if I'm wrong—I think you're a little misunderstood."

More silence from my menacing cohort, and suddenly I found myself trying to picture what dwelled beyond that solid wall of blackness that lurked within that hood.

Was he cute? He could be.

And was I flirting with him? I could be . . .

Normally, I flailed in that arena.

Something about his silence made being myself easier, though. Because it didn't matter that he wasn't laughing at my jokes, or that he hadn't said anything about my costume. If he was the Grim Reaper, why would he? He wouldn't. Because he was just being himself, too.

"Again," I went on, "correct me if I'm wrong, but I don't think the Grim Reaper *is* death. I think you just . . . collect the souls of the dead and kinda . . . scoot-aloo them along to whatever's next. You're like a modern Charon. You know who that is, right?" I scoffed and shook my head, embarrassed. "Of course, what am I saying? *You* know your roots. That guy's probably your great-great-great-great-great-great-uncle or something. But what I mean is, you're like the ferryman. You just transport souls. It's not like you use the scythe to kill people. You just shave souls off dead husks. Thankless job but somebody's got to do it, right?"

Another nervous laugh escaped me because, now that I thought about it, he *could* be a serial killer. Though he didn't give off the slasher vibe—not that I necessarily had a barometer for detecting murderous intent. But if he was here to hunt for his next victim, why would he be out on the balcony alone?

Then again, I hadn't seen him inside. Maybe I wouldn't have noticed him, but with his height, that scythe, and his literally misting robes, he *did* stand out.

"Anyway," I said, "that's what I think. I think that the archetype you represent is . . . well, unfairly judged. Take the Middle Ages for example." I waved my wine at the moon and the sky, with its slow-moving, tattered-lace clouds. "Death was so rife—indiscriminate, too. Kings and vagabonds alike bit the dust, but that doesn't mean you were the one who brought the plague upon them. The rats did that. You were, and are, just . . . well, I guess you're just the messenger, aren't you? Though, at the same time, you're a little more than that. Or a lot more, I guess. Am I making sense?"

Squinting, my head light and swimming from the wine, I spun to put my back against the banister.

Clasping my almost-empty cup between both hands, I peered down into the sip that remained and waited again for the answer I knew wouldn't come.

"There's probably an art to it," I said. "What you do, I mean. Which is true of anything that requires skill, wouldn't you agree? Anyway, in your case, I can't imagine the responsibility. The workload. The pressure. There's likely little room for error, too. Not at all like my job, which is messy and chaotic—but in a good way. The *best* way. *By* the way, did you know they recently changed the alphabet song so that *LMNOP* no longer runs together all willy-nilly? There's now a pause right before *O*, if you can believe it. It's been an adjustment, I'll say that."

Silence, silence, silence.

I sucked in a breath, and clutching the cup even tighter, I peeked up at him and blurted my next question. "Are you here alone?" My nerves twisted tighter, spitting sparks. "Technically, I'm not but, I mean, I also kind of am. He, my date, wouldn't miss me, I mean. *Isn't* missing me. I know you don't know me, but if . . . if you wanted to get out of here and, I dunno, catch a midnight movie or hit up Wendy's for a pretzel burger, I'd totally be, um, game?"

He turned toward me, and my face, already heated from the alcohol I wasn't used to, caught fire.

"You're married," I guessed. "Aren't you? Everyone's married these days. I mean, *I'm* not. Mom says that, at twenty-nine, I should be—but dating hasn't been going too well. But . . . we're not going to talk about Mom, the careening approach of my thirties, *or* the emotionally unavailable werewolf I came here with. *Or* getting married because, on the off chance that you're not already, where would we find an officiate at this time of night anyway?"

I laughed but then stopped myself and shut my eyes. I gritted my teeth and, frowning, commanded myself to unweird this monologue—stat.

"I'm sorry," I said. "I didn't mean to come out here and pester you like this. Sidenote, now that I think about it, *is* there such a thing as an emotionally available werewolf? Probably not. So, again, *LMNOP*, joke's on me."

Another nervous laugh bubbled out of me, but it died off in the continued and unending silence.

"Listen," I said next, "I'm going to get out of your hair, er, I mean your skull now and head back in. I really *do* like your costume, and I hope you have a nice night."

Why did it never fail? Always in these situations—situations with guys—I did something to make a fool of myself. I said too much. I did too much. I *was* too much.

I drained my wine and, tears already pricking at my eyes, I moved to push off from the banister, mortified.

Before I could get my footing, the stone railing supporting my spine cracked and jolted backward, crumbling. I dropped my plastic cup, which bounced away with quiet taps.

Eyes wide, I toppled with a shriek, following after the chunks that broke free, blond curls rushing ahead of me, screening my view of the hooded man who, instinctively, I reached for.

He moved fast—*too* fast, somehow unfurling into smoke and vapor before rematerializing in front of me to seize the wrist of one outstretched arm with a freezing and *literally* skeletal hand.

"Omigod!" I gasped as he yanked me to him, the fallen chunks of balcony cracking loud as gunshots on the flagstones below.

My feet under me again, I teetered on my two-dollar Goodwill heels, my free hand going to his chest.

Instead of plastering themselves against a solid pectoral, my fingers dipped into the black fabric, curling around . . . *ribs*?

I snapped my hand back as if burned, and swiveling me away from the broken balcony, he released me.

Skittering in reverse with a cry of shock, I lost my balance a second time, my heels snagging in the hem of my dress, and I went spilling onto the stone floor.

I landed on my hip, catching myself with my hands, palms seared by the stone, my crown knocking askew, one knee screaming from the jolt.

But then, I wasn't lying broken and bleeding on the flagstones below, was I?

"H-how?" I managed as I swung my head back toward my rescuer.

Except he was gone. Vanished from the balcony altogether.

But that . . . was impossible.

Behind me, the sliding door shushed open. "Oh my God," fussed a woman, her heels clomping fast as she hurried over to me. "Are you all right?"

"Is she okay?" asked a male voice.

"What happened?" questioned a second feminine voice.

"This door is supposed to be locked," answered the first voice.

People crouched around me, but I couldn't move. Couldn't tear my gaze away from the now-missing portion of the balcony. Because I'd nearly gone with it. Been smashed, too, on the stone below.

Right at that moment, I could have been *dead.*

Right at that moment, I *would* have been.

If not for the man with the skeleton hand.

Except men—people, *living* people—didn't have skeleton hands.

Or touchable ribs.

But the *real* Grim Reaper . . . supposedly did.

2

GRIM

I should not have done that.

I should not. Have. Done. *That.*

Scythe clutched in one hand, glowing hourglass holding the day's collected souls in the other, I stalked down the long hall leading to the Basins, the repository where, every twenty-four hours, I delivered my cache of spirits.

My boots made no sound against the dark marble floors. The quiet that had never bothered me before swelled like a scream, aggravating my thoughts, making my normally calm mind snap and snarl at itself.

As I drew nearer to the open archway leading into the main chamber, the tall walls seemed to cinch tighter. And why did the vaulted ceiling have to resemble the roof of some unending serpent's mouth?

On either side of me, green Soul Flames guttered in their sconces, their quiet wafting like whispers.

Made me nervous. Paranoid. Like their hissing pertained to me. What I'd done. *Hadn't* done . . .

The librarian, my final mark of the night, would have gone so much easier if she hadn't been able to see me. No one ever saw me these days. No one but the kids, and they weren't my sector anyway. Not anymore.

But the librarian worked with children—something I hadn't known. Not that I cared.

But *that* must have been why she'd been able to see me. The influence of her young patrons must help to keep her mind more susceptible to seeing the truth—the reality that everyone else in the world had convinced themselves didn't exist.

"Grim?" called a familiar voice from within the main chamber, his German-accented words echoing out to me. "That you?"

"Who else would it be, Johann?" I droned with my low and caustic reaper's voice as I entered the enormous circular chamber. I'd made this exact entrance countless times over the years—the decades. The centuries. It wasn't so much that I'd lost count. Since this wasn't a gig I was planning on retiring from—ever—I'd just never bothered keeping track of the time in the first place.

Why bother when, for me, this was it?

"Well, let's see," mused Johann even as he kept scribbling away in the pages of his enormous book, feather quill scratching against parchment. "You could have been Flora or Cedric. Could have been one of The Few, too, for all I knew. God forbid you could have been my old friend I wish never to meet again . . ."

A wizened, white-haired man who had also been here for centuries, Johann sat in his usual spot behind the scribe's desk that occupied the center of the circular ballroom-sized chamber. A waterfall of snowy hair flowed down his back, while a mystic's long beard draped his front.

"Demons can't come to the Netherworld, can they?" asked Pluto, Johann's annoying-ass raven, in his smooth and lilting Estuary English accent—the question rhetorical. "That's why we're here."

I glowered at the onyx beast currently perched on his ornate bird stand near Johann's desk, his vapid, brainless head ticking this way and that like he was trying to rattle the two thoughts he had into something *not* clueless.

Good fucking luck.

"True," grunted Johann as he continued to scribble, "the fiend can't enter the Netherworld portals, but that hasn't stopped him from trying, now, has it? And if there's one thing I never say . . . it's never. Aside from that, when it comes to our corner of the universe, does one ever *really* know who or what to expect?"

He had a point. And maybe I'd forgotten how, in so many ways, paranoia *came* with this . . . department.

"He's talking about Mephistopheles," said Pluto, speaking to me.

Like I didn't know. Like I hadn't been here long enough to get the picture better than him. Like I hadn't punched the demon in question square in his fanged face more than once.

"I told you not to say that name!" bellowed Johann, his voice resounding through the chamber.

Pluto puffed on his perch, spiked feathers frilling out. "Shall I call him Phil instead?"

"Haven't you ever heard the saying 'Speak of the devil and the devil shall appear'?" groused Johann. "I can tell you firsthand and perhaps better than anyone . . . it's true."

"But demons can't come to the Netherworld, can they?" asked Pluto.

Again.

At last Johann looked up from his writing to glower at the bird.

"Grim's home," the bird offered.

"He'd be just as useful to you stuffed, you know," I droned to Johann.

"If only that were true," he muttered. "We both know I need all the pairs of eyes I can get."

Johann, once a doctor of alchemy, astrology, magic, and other weird shit, had a famed history with the diabolical. And the very literal demons of his past had led him here.

Tonight, along with robes of red, the doctor wore the fez Flora had brought him from Morocco.

"Quiet night, I hope?" he hedged.

“I had no complaints,” I grumbled, which I supposed was true enough.

Five large and decorative stone vats encircled his station, the swirling, misty, and glowing “waters” of each a different hue.

The Basins served as receptacles to which Flora and I delivered souls.

None of us knew where or what any of them led to. But then, it wasn’t our job to know.

After leaving my scythe to stand on its own in wait for my return, I marched toward the stone Basin with the white iridescent waters.

The hue of summertime clouds, the fluffy, pillowy kind that produced uncanny shapes, the hazy liquid within rotated at a languid pace.

Hovering over the White Basin, I unscrewed the silver raven-shaped lid of the hourglass and tipped the topmost contents into the liquid.

The mixture of sparkling souls, each a different pastel hue—powder blue, pale pink, seafoam green—flowed out, blending easily with the cloudy essence.

Next, I approached the Blue Basin, which radiated a strange coldness. Within this Basin, the liquid stood utterly still, rippling only when I added what was due—three deep sapphire-blue souls. Again, I spared a glance to Johann, who, paying me no mind, continued scribbling along—checking off the names the Basins whispered to him in tones only he could hear.

So far, so good. Meaning he seemed none the wiser that I didn’t have one of the night’s souls with me—the librarian.

Resisting the urge to cross bony fingers, I moved on to the Green Basin, which always maintained a steady swirl, like a slow-moving hurricane. In went the Basin’s matching deep emerald souls, a smaller stream that the vortex sucked up and swallowed.

From there, I moved on to the Red Basin, the murky, blood-hued contents of which flickered with silent bursts of lightning. The deep ruby souls I tipped into this vat never wanted to go in. They went anyway, yanked by a magnetic pull. Brighter bursts of lightning accompanied the influx.

Finally, I arrived at the Black Basin, my least favorite. Not that I had a preference. More like I simply held an aversion to this one. But only because it seemed to hold an affinity for me.

I didn't always have souls for this Basin. But tonight, I had one.

The souls for the Black Basin always sank to the bottom of the hourglass, heavy with burdens and, I suspected, deeds that weighed them down and darkened their essence to the hue of ink.

After rolling back my sleeve, revealing nearly the whole of one bony arm, I extended the canister over the Black Basin.

The vat presented as a smooth onyx mirror, and like any reflective surface, it showed my alternate form—a muscle-corded flesh-and-blood arm riddled with black tattoos.

That form, I never took it anymore. Not unless I absolutely had to. A rare event since I'd become so efficient at what I did. At who—*what*—I was.

Again, I tipped the hourglass, slowly this time. Out rolled the lone onyx soul, which pierced the center of the black liquid like a marble.

Up splashed the murk, which, like whips of tar, wrapped and lashed my bones.

They tugged at me as if wanting to haul me in.

With a muttered curse, I yanked up, breaking the tendrils, which slurped back into the Basin, the contents of which at once went smooth again.

I backed away from the Black Basin, glaring at it while screwing the lid of the now-empty hourglass back into place.

"Well, *that* hasn't happened for a while."

I jumped—actually jumped—and, swinging around, glared down at four-foot-nothing Flora, who had appeared at my side from out of nowhere. She peered up at me, blinking vast green eyes, her red hair done up today in lilies.

An eight-hundred-year-old Scottish fairy, Flora presented as twelvish in human years, with enormous pointed ears, iridescent wings, a sprightly face dusted with freckles, and a gap-toothed smile that even *I* found adorable. Not that I would ever admit as much.

Today, she wore a knee-length forest-green dress cinched at the waist with a leather belt that had a gold leaf latch. Matching bracers cuffed her wrists. Hands on her hips, she wiggled the toes of her bare feet—next to which sat her golden lantern, filled with the glowing firefly- and bumblebee-sized souls of the young.

Never once had I seen her in shoes.

Flora tilted her head at me, batting those large eyes. "Have you thought about asking one of The Few why that Basin does that with you?" Her gossamer wings flickered behind her—a sign of interest.

"*No.*" I latched the empty hourglass to my belt. Then, turning, I marched to my scythe, grabbing it on my way to my look-alike statue, one of the three—one for each of us—that stood sentinel around the perimeter of the room, between open archways leading to other sections of the citadel.

"It never does that with me," Flora called after me in her too-sweet voice. "Look here. Grim, look!"

With a growl, I whirled toward her again. She stopped at the Black Basin and held a small arm out over the reflective void. Keeping eye contact with me, she wiggled her little fingers. "See? Nothin'."

"*Your* soul is still locked in your body," I snarled her way. "So . . . a little less accessible than mine. Aside from that, you never make deliveries to the Black Basin. You want to collect a few of the dark spirits? Then try that again?"

"Sure." She folded her arms. "We could even swap beats for a night."

"Yeah, no thanks," I grumbled as I again turned away.

"Flora's back!" said Pluto. "Gave Grim a heart attack."

"Grim hasn't got a heart," said Flora, who hurried over to stroke the bird's chest with a finger. "Or so he'd like us all to believe," she added under her breath, earning another scowl from me.

"How's me dapper bird boy?" she asked the raven.

"Dunno," said Pluto, blinking at her. "You should ask him."

Flora had come to the Hallowed Halls well after I'd entered this role—when I'd finally asked for help. Flora got the kids now. And that let me concentrate on everybody else.

The dark spirits in particular could be . . . unruly.

"Grim." Johann this time.

Grinding my teeth, I halted again, because could it be he'd already tracked the missing soul?

"Turn around, please," he instructed.

Glaring hard out the impenetrable shadows cast by my hood, I slowly rotated to find the old man squinting at me from behind his round spectacles, his pointy nose out of that book and his long pheasant-feather quill, for once, motionless in his hand.

This was it. He'd noted I was short. Which meant *he* was short.

And none of us who worked here in the Hallowed Halls could afford a single slipup. Not when the alternative was facing the consequences—the *real* consequences—of the actions that had led us each to these . . . roles.

"Something the matter?" I asked the old man.

"The matter," he echoed, rubbing his chin. "Yes. There's something quite the matter, I'm afraid."

I spared a glance at Flora, who only blinked at me, her expression expectant. It was like she'd somehow sniffed out my being short a soul as well and was silently urging me in that goody-two-shoes way of hers to fess up.

"Well, what?" I barked, never one for admitting anything until backed into a corner.

Johann tilted his glasses down, then pointed a crooked finger at me. "There's glitter on your robes."

"Oy, gods!" said Flora, letting the words out as if she'd been holding her breath. "I noticed that, too! Wasn't going to say anything, because it's right funny considering who you are."

Glitter?

I peered down at myself—patting my midnight robes. Which apparently provided the perfect backdrop for the dusting of golden glitter that covered my front.

"*Fuck*," I grunted.

Flora snorted, then burst out laughing. I sent her a glare that, of course, due to my hood—not to mention my lack of a face—she wouldn't see. Then I swiped at the onyx fabric with one bony hand, trying to loosen some of the sparkling dust.

"Pretty!" cried Pluto as a flutter of sparkling motes floated to the floor.

But more remained, the tiny specks embedded in the fibers.

"How in the Hallows did that happen?" asked Johann, and I had to stop myself from admitting I'd bagged a children's librarian dressed as sunshine and rainbows that night because, oh yeah, screw me, *I hadn't.*

"Don't worry about it," I snipped.

"Did somebody keel over in a craft store?" prompted Flora. "Then again, maybe you picked up a go-go dancer." She bounced her brows at me.

Officially, I was done. Turning away again, I stormed to my statue and handed it my scythe, which the effigy clamped its marble skeletal hand around. An instant later, with a low grinding of stone on stone, the sentinel shifted away to reveal the spiral staircase hiding beneath its plinth—stairs that led to my chambers.

"Grim," called Johann again.

"What?"

"Cedric was looking for you earlier."

Fuck. Not *this* old argument.

"I'm tired of repeating myself, Johann," I snapped. "There's nothing Cedric and I need to discuss."

"I'm not getting in the middle of things," Johann said. "I've nearly learned my lesson there. I'm just telling you he had something he wanted to discuss with you."

"I don't give a shit."

"You'd like me to tell him you said so?" asked Johann.

"Unless you'd rather tell him I said to fuck off," I snarled, and past ready to be done with the night, I descended into the gloom.

3

HELENA

"Oh, for the love of all paperbacks," I cursed between my teeth, climbing down from one of the step stools that could be found within the stacks. Because even though the computer system listed the book I was looking for as "IN," it wasn't here. I didn't see it mixed in with its immediate company, either. Probably—horribly—some overly helpful patron had misfiled it somewhere. Or else it had to be on one of the nearby carts, waiting to be shelved. I hadn't checked the return date in the database. What if it came in yesterday? Or even this morning?

With renewed hope, I strolled out of the three hundreds and scanned the aisles until I found Hunter, one of our pages. When it came to library jobs, pages existed on the bottom rung, their central responsibilities being to collect returned books from all bins, organize them on the carts, shelve them, and perform other, random as-needed tasks. Hardly glamorous work, but for the antisocial sort, the position had the built-in perk of being solo and, for the most part, non-people-y. And so, perfect for someone like Hunter.

Soon to be eighteen, he'd just started his senior year at Delmont High. At six foot two, he could reach a lot of the higher shelves without a step stool, and he towered over most of the other employees—

including five-foot-four me. Always dressed in some mixture of black, black, and black, he did a fair job of warding off patrons, too.

Today, he had on a baggy black My Chemical Romance T-shirt layered over a black-and-white-striped long-sleeved shirt and black jeans. Boots, piercings, rings, and floppy dyed black hair that obscured one eye completed his moody Tim Burton–enthusiast look.

Per usual, while shelving, he had his AirPods in, nodding along to the buzzing screaming of some band.

"Hunter?" I called. He didn't respond.

I sidled up to the near-overflowing cart that stood between us, and flicking my gaze between him and its contents, I bent forward and tried to find my prize. Always, the pages organized the carts by Dewey decimal to streamline their process.

This helped me to streamline mine since a quick scan of the cart's bottom shelf came up no dice.

"Holy shit fritters," said Hunter, and I glanced up to find him pressing a palm to his chest. "'Scuse my language, Miss Hart," he said as he pulled out his AirPods, "but you scared the sloth snot outta me."

I twitched a smile, the first I'd managed since the party. Since the . . . incident.

"Sorry," I said. "I'm . . . looking for a book. System says it's in, but it wasn't on the shelf. Thought it might be on your cart."

"What book?" he scoffed. "*How to Scare Friends and Terrify People*? Cheese and crackers, I'll never have the hiccups again, so I can thank your jack-in-the-box ass for that."

Despite his monochrome wardrobe, Hunter had a colorful way with words. And though I was a librarian and therefore a superior, I had nothing to do with the adult department, so he didn't often check himself around me. Which I was fine with. I preferred authenticity. And Hunter's was a particularly special brand.

"Wait," I said, straightening. "Back up. Did you just admit we're friends?"

"Uh," said Hunter, who went back to scanning spines and filing titles, "that's a no-offense negative. When I'm in this crusty, dusty, fusty palace of brain drain, I'm a lone wolf. Stick my steel-toed boot out for nobody."

I folded my arms. "You and Emily seem to get along fine."

Emily was the new part-time clerk for the Hideout, the recently renovated teen area located in the basement. I had to cover that desk for Emily during her lunch. Which, lately, she'd been taking in the break room—with Hunter.

Hunter shifted toward me, and squinting at me, he draped an arm over his cart.

"Are you supposed to be in the adult section of the library?" he challenged. "Last I checked, your corner of the Literary Hunger Games was the kiddie area."

"Are you supposed to be shelving with AirPods in?" I countered. "Last I checked, Rick frowned upon that."

Rick, an adult reference librarian, was Hunter's overzealous and somewhat controlling supervisor—one of them.

"Fine," he said, "we're friends. Which means you can't snitch. Now, what book are you looking for so I can help you find it and get on with my miserable, underpaid, bottom-feeder life as a lowly library serf?"

I bit my bottom lip. "You know, a clerk position *did* just open in the children's department. I'd totally put in a good word for you. I'd be on the interview panel, too."

"There are *so* many words that I'm allergic to in what you just said."

"Pay is better," I offered. "Closer to the Hideout?"

"*Book*, Hart." He gestured to the stacks around us. "You were looking for a book."

I smirked and dropped my gaze again to the cart. I had a hunch Hunter secretly liked his job. He'd been here for two years now. So long as he got to have his AirPods, he didn't seem *too* miserable, at least some of the time.

"It's a book on . . . a myth," I muttered as I scanned his collection of nonfiction again, just in case I'd missed the volume.

"Myth," he repeated. "You know, they came up with a few of those."

I shook my head, embarrassed to say it out loud even though I shouldn't have been. Because Hunter wouldn't know why I was asking for the title.

"It's called *Grim Tidings: The History and Origins of . . . of the Grim Reaper.*"

"Fire," said Hunter, with appreciation. "And low-key unsettling." His eyes darted like he thought there might be someone watching us, or hidden cameras aimed our way. "This for storytime research? I might come to that one. But just for the parents' faces."

My cheeks burned all the hotter, because I hadn't thought of an excuse for why I wanted the book, and I could hardly tell Hunter it was because I'd had a . . . Well, I wasn't sure what to call it. Technically, "near-death experience" applied, but not in the way one might assume.

"It's . . . for a friend of mine," I lied. "I told him I'd pull it and . . . and put it on hold for him."

"He sounds cool," said Hunter, who, without warning, abandoned his cart and stalked out of the aisle.

I blinked and, jarring myself into a scuttle, hurried after him. "Hunter?"

"You might just be in luck, Hart," he called over one shoulder as he made a beeline to one of the tables that flanked the large windows overlooking the street and the trees that lined it, their limbs sleeved in rioting autumn foliage.

Halting at the table, empty of patrons, he aimed a hand at the book someone had left there—the very book I'd been seeking.

"Abra-ala-cadabra," said Hunter. "One Grim Reaper reader with a side of déjà vu."

"Omigosh!" I seized the title, a slim, small, and gray hardback volume with a black silhouette of the Grim Reaper on the cover, the title embossed in silver on the spine. "This is crazy. How'd you know this was here?"

"Yeeeeah," he said, rubbing the back of his neck as he glanced over his shoulder again. "There was a dude. He must have left it. Super-weird guy. He came up to me with the Dewey number asking for help, and I pulled it for him. Like, not even thirty minutes ago."

Oh. That's why Hunter had said it was "unsettling" that I was asking for the title, and why he'd mentioned déjà vu. Not because of the subject matter, but because I'd been the second person to request the title.

I blinked rapidly, trying to absorb this—and not put extra meaning to it.

Hard to do after what happened to me. After what failed to happen to me.

Maybe, if I was lucky, this book would provide some kind of insight as to what had occurred or, at the very least, point me to a source that *could* provide insight.

"Hunter," I said, pulling the book close, "thanks."

He waved me off. "I did it for the plot. Also, if he's researching the Grim Reaper, your friend is metal. And *I'm* metal. Metalheads gotta stick together."

Peeling away, he reinserted his AirPods. Riffing on air guitar, he then vanished between the stacks.

Frowning, I glanced left and right, scanning the reading areas for any sign of the "weird guy" who had requested the book. I didn't see anyone who I thought classified as weird. Just a lady with thick glasses trudging into the eight hundreds, her arms already loaded down with books, and a backpack-wearing college kid headed for the checkout counter, a stack of titles tucked under one arm.

Curious, I made my way down the aisles, checking each as I passed them.

But . . . there wasn't anybody.

I paused to examine the book next, noting something I hadn't before. Someone had bookmarked a set of pages in the middle with a bit of what looked to be . . . parchment?

After taking my reading glasses off the top of my head and sliding them into place, I opened the book to that page to find an etching of a figure in swathing black, scythe gripped in one skeletal hand, an oversized hourglass clutched in the other.

Someone, or something, peered out from the shadows nested within a black hood.

As had been the case at the party, though . . . there was no telling what.

Who?

He *had* been a who to have done what he had, right? Meaning, there was *someone* in that hood. A person. Or a . . . being. A collector of souls who could, himself, even be a soul?

I wanted to believe that was the case.

Especially since the alternative was that I had imagined him, or that I was going batty.

My fingers went to the torn bit of parchment that marked the pages, and pulling the thick and aged paper free, I turned it over.

I gasped to find a message there, which had me dropping the book—and stifling a scream with one hand.

"Yes, Helena," the blue-ink note read in beautiful, scripted handwriting, "he's real."

4

GRIM

The following night, I entered the Basins to find the doctor missing from his station. His witless bird, too.

Except Johann rarely left his desk. When he did, Pluto, the proverbial eyes in the back of his head, went with him.

I abandoned my scythe, which stood waiting for me as it had last night, its cool silver blade reflected in the shining black marble floor.

Slowing my steps as I approached the swirling vats, I glared down Johann's vacant chair.

A missing Johann never failed to make me nervous. Theoretically, he was safe here, in the Netherworld—at least he should be—but that did little to erase the fact that he *did* have a stalker.

A dangerous one.

"Doctor?" I called, but I didn't receive an answer.

A strange and unshakable foreboding needled me as I made my way to the White Basin, unhooking my hourglass from my belt along the way. I unscrewed the lid, and the soft squeaking of metal against metal loud in this chamber that I rarely found myself alone in.

While I poured out the portion of the souls due to the White Basin, I glanced toward Flora's statue, which offered its usual stone lily to some unseen passerby. Whenever Flora was in, her statue's eyes would open. They were closed. Which meant she was still out gathering souls.

As I made my way to the Blue Basin, I checked Johann's statue.

Just as was the case with my scythe, Johann would deposit his quill in the statue's grip to gain access to his chambers. At the moment, the feather quill protruded from the inkwell on his desk. So Johann hadn't retired early. And since he never—ever—left the Netherworld, well, he and his feathered beast had to be around here somewhere.

If I didn't find him before withdrawing for the night myself, I wouldn't be able to concentrate on my music—or anything.

"Old man," I called into the chamber, my voice echoing down the four open archways and halls that led out of the Basins—to the library, the courtyard, the apothecary, and the cloisters.

Again, I received no answer.

"Where did you get off to?" I grumbled before moving on to the Green Basin.

The Red Basin came next, and in went the souls destined for it. Thankfully, tonight, I didn't have any souls for the Black Basin, which meant my shift had reached its end.

At least officially.

"Johann," I called, louder this time.

"He's in the cloisters," came a voice from behind me. A British-accented one that would have made my eye twitch if I didn't have just sockets.

Whirling, I found none other than Cedric, the Hallowed Halls' resident pain-in-the-ass wizard, standing next to my scythe, his fist wrapped around the handle of the tool—which he would not be able to budge since it waited for and responded only to me.

A tall young man with short white-blond hair, a medium build, and a misleadingly boyish, clean-shaven face, he wore his usual modern ensemble of a black suit and tie. A pretentious-as-fuck silver watch chain and fob hung from his waistcoat pocket.

He liked to look important, but he did jack all of significance. Like the rest of us, he'd come to the Halls for refuge. For him, that meant conducting busywork in the archives. Translating old magic texts, organizing volumes, and annotating historical crap or whatever—bullshit kid-in-detention nonsense.

If you asked me, he was a spare part if there ever was one.

Worst thing about him was that he knew it. And it chapped his ass.

Which was why he made it a point to chap mine.

"What is Johann doing in the cloisters?" I asked.

He didn't pay me any mind. Instead, he smirked up at the scythe and put his other hand on his hip as if pretending the instrument belonged to him.

Most likely, that's exactly what he was doing since Cedric had no qualms about making it known to anyone who would listen that he felt more equipped for—and worthy of—my job than me.

"I asked you a question, asshole."

Cedric did a double take at me with those unnerving frost-blue eyes, almost like he'd forgotten I was there. Frowning, he gestured toward me. "Is that . . . glitter on your robes?"

I ground my teeth. Because I thought I'd shaken that shit out.

"*Johann*," I pressed.

Cedric cricked his neck—one of his quirks since he'd once lost his head. He had a grisly scar from it that I often fantasized about reopening. He probably had a bunch of other ones from where he'd died and re-died over the decades. He'd once been shot by Billy the Kid and, before that, turned into a lawn ornament by Vlad the Impaler. If I didn't know for sure they were both dead, I'd start a fucking fan club.

As if it took some effort, Cedric withdrew his hand from my scythe. Then he strode toward me, his expression as pompous and judgmental as ever.

"There was a soul missing," he said. "But no one can say which soul it is or where it's gone."

The shadows of my inner essence contracted in the cavity of my ribs, the murk radiating something akin to fear. That wasn't an emotion I'd encountered in a very, very long time. All the same, did one ever forget such a poisonous sensation?

"That still doesn't answer why Johann is in the—"

"He's in the cloisters talking to one of The Few," Cedric said in that emotionless way of his, gaze set with indifference as he stared straight into my hood. "They're going over all the names from last night, but the name of the missing soul is also missing on the roster. So, again, no one knows which soul is absent, or where it's flittered off to."

One of The fucking Few was here? And Johann was *alone* with them?

I spun away from Cedric, heading down the hall that led to the cloisters.

"Where are you going, Grim?" Cedric asked, my steps soundless while the heels of his polished black dress shoes clicked against the marble.

I didn't answer. The less said to Cedric, the better.

"Is it possible *you* know something?" he asked. "About the missing soul?"

I walked on, the bones of my right hand cracking as I curled it into a fist.

"Did you miss someone, you think?" he ventured.

The shadows in my rib cage dispersed, the essence of my soul shooting through my limbs. The force of my sudden anger had me whirling on Cedric, who I seized by the collar.

His hands went up in surrender, but I still shoved him against the wall, pinning him there.

"You'd love that, wouldn't you?" I ground out.

"I just think it might be evidence—further evidence—that I'm right."

"I never miss anyone. Ever."

"Must have been Johann's mistake, then," he said. "Or perhaps Flora's."

"We don't miss souls," I snarled. "Any of us."

"Noted," said Cedric. "But say, while you're here and I have the rare bestowal of your undivided if prickly attention, I *do* have something I'd like to discuss with you."

Cedric wanted to accompany me on my rounds. Countless times, he'd voiced the unsolicited—and impertinent—opinion that I could benefit from an assistant.

It was his fault he was bored. And, for the most part, useless. Not mine.

I wasn't a babysitter. But that memo—I couldn't seem to get it through his thick and inflated skull. Or Johann's for that matter. Flora wasn't much better.

"The answer is no," I snapped. "It was no when you got here, and it's no still. For as long as I exist in this capacity—which *will* be for fucking ever—it will always *be* no. Do you understand?"

Cedric glared into me hard with that bleak winter stare, frosty eyes searching for the face he would not find. "Yes," he said, his tone even, disconcertingly calm. "Thank you for the clarification. It's honestly exactly what I needed."

I held him pinned for one moment longer, sorely tempted to rip out the soul he still possessed so I could offer it up as the one to replace the librarian's. Since that wouldn't work because he happened to be immortal, and since that action would only give me away as the one responsible for the missing soul, I released him.

"Touch my scythe again," I warned, turning to continue my trek to the cloisters, "and I'll use it to play hockey with your head."

Maybe that was a low blow. None of us knew the details surrounding his decapitation, but it was no secret how touchy he could be about that particular death. The wound would even still bleed if anyone dared to mention it, or even if something heavily upset him—an involuntary reaction that suggested the pain involved wasn't just skin-deep.

But maybe he needed a stronger reminder to get back on his fucking side of the undead fence.

"Incurring your wrath to the point of death," mused Cedric darkly, calling after me. "A preferrable and perhaps less permanent fate than the Black Basin."

I halted again, glancing over my shoulder at him. Because why had that sounded like a threat?

But the wizard had vanished. Back to his worthless collections and writings. What *else* was he going to do with his time? Unlike the rest of us, he didn't have true purpose in the Hallowed Halls. He'd just been sent here because there was nowhere else for him to go.

Unlike us, he could leave if he wanted—go back to the world. Back to life. But he didn't want to go back. He wanted to move on. Specifically, into *my* role.

For some reason, he thought what I did was glamorous. But also, becoming the Grim Reaper would give him the option to do the one thing he could not. Essentially? Die.

It was his hypothesis that moving into my position would allow him to shed his curse since it would require the transformation of his physical form. From there, he planned to harvest souls until the opportunity came to pass along the scythe. Then, at last allowed to perish, he'd go into whichever Basin would have him.

Green, most likely, since that was the color of his soul, which I'd had in my grip a time or two. Just because Cedric was immortal, that didn't mean he couldn't—temporarily—die.

None of us knew quite how long Cedric had lived—only that, somewhere along the way, he'd tampered with the wrong kind of magic. Immortality was a slippery slope. Maybe I'd chosen to dabble in its waters, too. But, for me, the alternative of being bound for the Black Basin made such an arrangement necessary.

Cedric's missteps weren't my problem, though. His delusional machinations weren't my responsibility, either. So he could pine to occupy these robes and wield my scythe all he wanted. I wasn't relinquishing my post ever. Not for anything or anyone. Least of all that arrogant slime bucket.

Point blank, I wasn't going into that Basin.

So an eternity of scything it was.

"There you are, Grim," came Johann's familiar voice, which had me pivoting to find him scuttling toward me, Pluto perched on his shoulder. "I don't know if you heard, but there was a mix-up with a presumed-missing soul."

"Mix-up," I repeated. And *presumed*?

"Yes," said Johann as he shuffled past me, leaving me to glance behind, down the long straight hallway within which stood no one else. "But I told Sir White the mishap wasn't on our end."

"Not us," said Pluto. "Not you. This slipup belongs to The Few."

Sir White. So that was the member of The Few who had come looking for the librarian. That made sense, didn't it? Not that I knew where the White Basin, let alone any of the others, went. But then, the souls relinquished to the white vat always leaped to join those hazy waters. Didn't their pale iridescence and happy springtime colors suggest some measure of serenity, too?

I hadn't had a chance to view the librarian's soul directly given that I hadn't taken it, but there'd been a lightness to her spirit. A heaviness, too. But no darkness. At least, none that I'd been able to detect.

With a long stride, I reclaimed the distance Johann had gained and peered down at the old man, who, tonight, wore sapphire robes and the pointed blue star-and-moon-speckled hat with Mickey Mouse ears that Flora had brought him from Disney World.

Had he really worn that while addressing Sir White? Probably he'd forgotten the ridiculous thing was on his head.

"Grim Grim," said Pluto, fluffing his wings like I made him nervous. "Grim is grim."

"What did you tell him?" I probed.

"What else would I tell him?" asked Johann.

"More than usual," said Pluto. "Grim, I mean."

I glowered at the bird. Because when did *he* become so fucking perceptive?

"I reminded Sir White that we've never had a missing soul," Johann continued, paying no mind to the bird. "Neither you nor Flora miss collecting them, and *I* never miss accounting for them. We are each impeccable in our work. So, I told him this was a him problem, and not an us problem."

"Take that, Sir White," added Pluto.

Johann actually said that to White? And didn't shit himself in the process?

Those words were beyond bold ones to give to one of The Few. And I might have been impressed by his gall, but between the four of us who resided in the Hallowed Halls—five if you counted the damn bird—Johann had the most experience with the grander forces of the hereafter. Aside from that, he had earned my respect long before now.

Not that he needed to know.

"And you're saying White just left . . . and that's it?"

"Of course," said Johann, like I was an idiot for even asking. "Granted, he wasn't very happy. He said that, at the end of the day, the issue is moot since the missing soul is a Fated. He said you or Flora would be sure to capture it in the next day or so. He promised to return for another inquiry if it did show up via your delivery or hers, but I assured him the soul *was* in his realm. Rather insulting, really, for White to jump to conclusions and insinuate an oversight on *our* part."

"Nervy," said Pluto. "Topsy-turvy. Try to make us feel unworthy."

I went silent as we reentered the main chamber that housed the Basins, the murky essence of my spirit gathering behind my sternum before congealing into a vortex.

Johann must have noticed the shift in my demeanor, because he paused to glance up at me again, a weathered hand going to brace that absurd hat.

"It is, isn't it?" Johann asked.

"What?"

"Insulting," he repeated. "For White to suggest any of us would be so careless as to miss a soul? Especially a Fated."

"I didn't miss a soul, if that's what you're asking," I snapped before turning away to trudge for my statue. And that wasn't technically a lie. I hadn't missed a soul. I'd just . . . *salvaged* it.

"That's good," said Johann. "Because if it shows up on our end, White *will* be back."

"Scary Sir White," added Pluto in a singsong voice. "Red eyes. No face. Disappeared without a trace."

That description—too accurate—ratcheted my anxiety to ten.

Still, I played it off.

"Return to your desk, old man," I said, collecting my scythe. "Or we'll be short names tomorrow."

Johann didn't say anything else. But I couldn't fight the needling inkling that he now suspected me.

I had bigger problems, though. He'd just revealed how Sir White knew the missing soul was among the Fated. Something I'd suspected since I'd been drawn to the site of her demise before it could occur. That was always a sign of a preordained death. Part of me had been hoping that, despite getting the call for her, she might, by some stroke of luck, *not* be a Fated.

The fact that she was complicated the situation further because it meant her soul had somewhere else to be. Something else to do.

Whatever that something was, *I* had disrupted it.

Worse, I still couldn't seem to understand *why*.

But the why—that didn't matter anyway. Only the how. As in how I was going to rectify this . . . issue.

Since I'd never missed a soul before—on purpose *or* on accident—I hadn't known until now what would happen if I did. Apparently, I'd get the call for the librarian again.

"Grim Grim, Grim is grim," sang Pluto as I descended the spiral stairs, heading once more into the gloom of my quarters, the solution to this entire quandary seeming simple.

Collect her soul when the time comes and deliver it to the White Basin.

Except then Sir White would know one of us *had* missed a soul.

Since I would never let Flora or Johann take the fall for my indiscretion, I would have to admit to what I'd done.

But saving the life of a Fated and thus tampering with the fabric of the universe as a whole . . .

If that wasn't grounds for dismissal . . . what was?

A flash of the murk of the Black Basin lashing my arm had those bones resonating with the remembered sensation.

Cedric's words from earlier came back to haunt me, too.

That Basin. Clearly, if I was dismissed, that *was* where my soul would go.

I knew better than to think its waters led anywhere good. Or even tolerable.

Which meant that, when I *was* summoned back to the librarian to again collect her—and I would be—I was going to have to do something drastic. Even more drastic than before.

Until I could figure out a way to smuggle her soul, undetected, into the beyond, I was going to have to save her.

Again.

5

HELENA

Awkward sauce at uncomfortable o'clock.

That was my thought as the elevator doors screech-slid open to reveal none other than Peter Winston, the library's British archivist. The library's *hot* British archivist.

Relief poured through me, though, at the sight of the red-clad pizza-delivery lady standing next to him toting a fragrant, insulated bag full of pies, her face half lost beneath the visor of her crimson ball cap.

Until she offered me a nod and a ruby-painted smile before abandoning me, heading down the hall.

Probably, if I had to guess, to deliver reward pizzas for the HR office.

The children's department sometimes got parties, too. In lieu, of course, of raises.

Or upgrades.

Or general supplies.

Like glue sticks.

Oh well. So much for having a buffer.

I gritted a smile at Peter, who now stood alone inside the elevator, a stack of tomes tucked under one arm.

He maintained a stiff, close-lipped smile while he pressed the button to hold the door for me.

Then, gripping tighter the pumpkin-orange pastry box I held, I surged forward and onto the elevator. Because how much more awkward would it be if I rerouted to the stairs now? Something I should have done in the first place. Then again, chances were high that I could have run into him there, too.

A head taller than me with glasses, long dark hair worn in a low ponytail, a handsome, clean-shaven face, and a lean but muscular build, he had on his usual ensemble of slacks, black blazer, and white button-down.

Let's just say he rocked the thirtysomething college professor look *very* well—blending chic geek with a touch of dark academia. Like if Dracula decided to teach at Oxford except less pale.

"Miss Hart," he said, and my spirit sank with the cool and too-formal greeting. Especially since it wasn't so long ago that he'd called me "Leaflet," a nickname I'd earned after getting caught in a breeze with a stack of newly printed flyers for the upcoming children's programs. Peter had helped me collect them.

Right before our clandestine first kiss.

My cheeks burned, and I cleared my throat as I turned to face the doors, the soles of my flats scuffing on the flooring, the minor flag in my stride reminding me *why* I hadn't taken the stairs.

I had two VIP-designated Halloween-themed cupcakes from Sugar Rush, the café down the street. One had a chocolate-covered-strawberry witch's hat; the other oozed cherry filling from vampire fang marks. They were so precious, and I could *not* risk these getting smashed. Aside from that, I was already running late to get to the Hideout to relieve Emily for her lunch since the eleven-thirty day care crowd had filed in late for storytime.

"Peter," I said, returning his greeting with a nod as the mirrored doors of the ancient elevator *squueeeeaked* shut. Their squeal seemed extra creaky today, as if they were cringing as hard as I was inside.

As if they *knew* Peter and I had been together for a few weeks and, during that time, found ourselves in a few compromising positions as well.

We'd broken up after discovering neither of us was prepared to leave our roles at the main branch of the Wyvern City Free Public Library.

Well, *Peter* had been the one to call it off back in July. Because, yeah, we *worked together.*

Maybe not in the same department, maybe not on the same floor, but I now had to admit he had a point when he'd brought up the possible . . . complications of dating a coworker.

The same enormous building *could* in fact seem awfully small in select situations. Like this one when my teeth might just crush themselves to powder.

I held my breath, willing the awkward to ebb away like ripples in a pond.

And why *should* this interaction be awkward? Just because our last one had ended in tears—mine—didn't mean this one had to become a smoking tire fire.

"Headed back to the basement?" I asked him as the doors clunked together, sealing us in as they reflected our figures in the faintly gold-tinted glass.

Ugh. *Why* did we have to look so cute together?

"Going up, in fact," he corrected, his London accent, along with that subtle hint of his sophisticated cologne, *doing* things to me the way it always did, tempting my brain out of the realm of work, cupcakes, storytime, and all things G-rated. "To the director's office. Yourself?"

Wait. *Up?*

"Um, down, actually," I said through a nervous laugh, stepping forward to panic-press the darkened "*B* is for 'Basement'" button. "To your neck of the woods. Or the Hideout at least. I've got to relieve Emily for lunch. I wasn't paying attention to the elevator light, though. Didn't realize it was headed up."

"Given that there's only one lift in this archaic time capsule of a civic citadel, I don't think it makes much difference. Aside from that, the up and down lights just stopped being operational anyway. A pity since we are rather not-for-profit, and the facilities budget has no doubt been relegated to triaging the repeated issues tied to this prestigious landmark's prehistoric—not to mention precarious—plumbing."

Dagnabbit. This man's vocabulary had me almost salivating.

Instead of asking him if he ate crossword puzzles for breakfast, I held my tongue and frowned down at the box in my hands, focusing hard on the café's seasonal swirly-lettered and spiderweb-swathed logo as I tried not to wish that Peter and I could still work out. Or at least give it another go.

He'd said I'd have to, at the very least, transfer to another branch for him to even consider it. *He* couldn't leave since there was only one set of archives after all.

Mom had really liked Peter. Which had given me high hopes.

Hopes that had apparently been too high.

"Now that the aroma of marinara and cheese has cleared the air," he said, gesturing to the box I held, "I detect a hint of buttercream. Are you bribing someone with cake? Or perhaps just paying them off."

"Cupcakes for Hunter and Emily," I said. "It's Hunter's birthday. He turns eighteen."

"Hunter," said Peter. "That's the lad with the boots."

I smiled. "He dropped enough books in his first week to realize the wisdom of steel toes. Now they've become his signature."

"I'm thinking of asking him for a bit of sorting help in the archives," he said. "Do you think Rick would loan him out?"

"You could ask," I offered. "If the task is solitary *and* secluded, well, that's Hunter's vibe."

And of course, the *moment* I started to feel a bit easier and like I actually *wouldn't* say something off-putting, cringey, or extra blurt-y, the elevator ground to a clunky halt.

"Cheers," said Peter as he bolted for the doors even as they struggled to wind open. He slid between them, going sideways when the gap became wide enough—like Indiana Jones skirting a booby trap. Like he couldn't wait to get away.

From me.

It was the kind of exodus that made me want to smell my pits.

Instead, as the doors closed again, I locked my jaw and tried to keep from recalling (and overanalyzing) everything I'd ever said to Peter Winston.

Maybe he'd thought the fairy lights in my room were weird. Maybe it was the fact that I'd worn rooster earrings for today's barnyard storytime.

Could be the dad jokes . . .

No. If I had to guess, it was the Hi-C fruit punch I'd spilled on his dress shoes when we'd met at Taco Bell for an on-the-sly lunch that one time.

I sighed—loudly—as the elevator car started down, my face heating at the memory of Peter standing in a bright red pool of sticky juice.

Ca-clunk.

I yelped when the car jolted to a halt, the steady mechanical hum replaced by silence.

Followed by a far-off creaking—as the lights flickered.

"Oh no." I shifted the bakery box to one hand as I hurried forward to press the buttons—all of them. They flickered like so many dazed eyes after a KO punch. "No, no, no, this is so not on my bingo card—ah!"

The lights failed. Darkness consumed me within the blink of an eye while an acrid burning aroma filtered into the car, chasing away the lingering ghost of Peter's cologne.

"*Noooo*," I squealed, free hand searching now for the emergency button—which I couldn't find.

How many times had I been inside this stupid, cranky, crotchety relic of an elevator and never once bothered to locate that lifeline?

The lights flashed, this time revealing how I wasn't alone anymore.

Backpedaling to one corner, which I smashed myself into, I screamed to find *him* now in the car with me.

He loomed in the flickering light like a living nightmare, dark robes spilling to the floor, skeletal hand gripping the staff of that grim scythe. Its curved blade gleamed sharp, a silver grimace in the fluttering dark.

Swirls of the smoke that, at the party, I'd mistaken for dry ice vapor wafted off him, charcoal wisps curling upward before misting away.

"Omigod, it's you," I rasped, my heart rapid-firing, my blood screaming in my veins, shooting primal panic into every inch of my trembling frame.

True to form, he didn't answer, and he didn't move. Not even when the car jolted hard and careened down a good five feet before jarring to a halt a second time.

Bracing myself by gripping the worn banister, I screamed again. This shout, short and sharp, started and stopped with the elevator. Still, I clutched the box of cupcakes in my free hand, its edges now crunched, the cargo within possibly crunched, too.

By all appearances, I was about to join the Crunched Cupcake Club.

He was death after all, wasn't he? At least he was the collector of souls, as the book had said—something I'd assumed already.

Except, what was he doing?

The lights stabilized as, in a careless gesture, he tossed aside the scythe, which misted away to nothing. Then, fast as a darting shadow, he surged forward to tackle the closed doors, the sleeves of his ebony robes falling back to expose skeletal arms as he shoved bone fingers into the crack.

I gaped in horror and awe as he then began forcing the elevator doors open.

They fought him despite his determination, screeching like dueling dragons as he pulled.

Stunned, I could only marvel as his strength prevailed and, by inches, the groaning elevator's doors started to open.

My attention shifted—caught by his reflection in the gold-tinted mirrors.

His arms.

Though the forearms of a skeleton worked to pry those doors apart, the mirror showed those of a man. A *strong* man, his skin covered with small black tattoos, each a different shape—none of which I could discern in the sputtering light.

The car jarred once more, though this time it—*we*—didn't go anywhere.

From above, that ominous creaking grew loud again before devolving into a low whine: something trying—and failing—to hold on.

I clamped down harder on the box of cupcakes, my mouth falling open when that black mist wafting around him gathered to shove its way between the doors, too—working with those arms now to wrench them apart.

The mist lent enough extra oomph and the doors gave. They slid open, revealing how we were caught between floors. The top half of the doorway framed only the smooth concrete wall of the elevator shaft, while the bottom half opened to the ground floor, which waited below at a four-foot drop.

Those bony arms pinning the doors apart, the dark figure turned that hooded head my way, the blackness within concealing, as it had at the Halloween party, any hint of a face.

"*Get out,*" he commanded in a deep and caustic voice—one that was anything but human. Like that of an avenging angel mixed with one of those arcade "Game Over" guys, its soul-shaking tenor rattled my own bones and froze the blood in my veins.

I gulped, my face draining. My hammering heart stopped right then and there, too, stalled by that stare I couldn't see, by that terrifying voice of literal doom.

At least until he jump-started the muscle again by speaking a second time.

"Now!"

I jolted forward. Because that voice. It wasn't one that was meant to be argued with.

Hugging the bakery box like I still had hope of avoiding cupcake casualties, I made a run for that opening, streaming past him and straight through those wisps of smoke.

With as big a jump as I could muster, I leaped from the elevator.

Like the last time we'd been that close together, me and my otherworldly savior, I went sprawling onto another hard surface, my fall not at all cushioned by the cupcakes that I flattened with my impact—box and all.

Still better than my sharing in their fate.

Swiveling my head back and craning my neck, I only caught sight of the top of the elevator as it rushed out of sight, frayed cables singing as they snapped and wriggled in its wake.

Two seconds later, the elevator crashed into the basement with an earsplitting, floor-shaking cacophony of screeching metal, shattering glass, whipping cables, and crumbling mortar.

6

HELENA

Oh God. *Can death die?*

Screams echoed around me in the main lobby, panicked voices reverberating through the cavernous space, bouncing off the cold marble floor that I struggled to rise from.

Smoke and dust plumed out of the gaping mouth of the elevator shaft while the fire alarm blared, its brash bleat pulsing at top volume while emergency lights sparked a blinding white.

Patrons rushed past me, mothers shepherding wailing kids toward the main entrance while Ben, one of our security guards, waved them out.

I shook from head to foot, my mind a scattered mess, my sense of reality numbed. But while I could forsake the flattened cupcakes, I couldn't bring myself to join the flow of bodies now bottlenecking between the tall columns flanking the front doors.

Instead, I whirled and hurried for the stairwell. Grabbing the iron railing, I plunged downward, hurrying to the basement, barreling past the steady stream of those rushing up to get out, noses and mouths shielded by sleeves and shirt collars.

I coughed against the bitter taste of smoke and ducked toward the haze. Then, turning the corner, I sprinted in the direction of the Hideout, which the elevator opened to.

I arrived to find its exterior metal doors still closed, smoke and dust seeping from the busted seam, the bent crack showing only darkness within.

Before I could surge forward to try to wrangle those doors like I'd seen my now-two-time rescuer do, something cold and hard seized me by the upper arm.

Then a second skeletal hand went to cover my mouth before my captor drew me backward, out of the dust clouds, away from the elevator, and into the tall stacks of YA books.

This time, for whatever reason, I didn't scream at being handled by him.

He must have feared I would bolt given the chance, because as soon as he had me between the shelves and out of sight of the figures rushing for the stairs, the bony hand on my arm tightened its grip.

Strangely, I had no urge to scream *or* run—not even with the outline of his bottommost ribs digging into my upper back.

Not that I wasn't afraid. I was.

My heart scampered hard in my chest, and my breath came fast, but my curiosity, which had only been fed and stoked by the information in that book Hunter had found for me, overrode my fear.

Obviously, whoever this being truly was, killing me wasn't in his plans.

Well, at least it wasn't *yet.*

"*What are you doing down here?*" he asked, my whole frame going rigid as that black-as-night voice rumbled *through* me, officially, inexplicably, and somewhat disturbingly, well, apparently . . . turning me on.

"Um," I managed when, with a click of bones—*literal bones*—his hand uncoiled from my mouth.

I blinked several times at that settling and now-thinning screen of dust and debris, the logic department of my brain trying to compute the question he'd asked me while the lizard portion sent a zing of interest through my limbs and, maybe, other places.

Oh, wow. *This* was new.

Probably just a symptom of my nearly getting squashed. Had to be, right?

Except he *had* also kind of just rescued me with tattooed arms?

Focus, Helena. Don't be rude. The nice undead doom-voiced skeleton man asked you a question.

"I came . . . to check on you?" I whispered as, somewhere in the distance, sirens kicked up, their screams joining in with the droning blare of the fire alarm.

"What?"

The faintest of growls underscored that already-gravelly one-word question, his incredulous tone betraying just how stupid he thought my answer was. But how was *I* supposed to know he was okay? Maybe he was the Grim Reaper—the real Grim Reaper—but I didn't know how that worked. In my world, falling elevators smooshed their occupants, no matter who or what those passengers happened to be.

"*Are* you okay?" I pressed.

That hand on my arm flexed just a bit tighter, though only for a second, as if something about my question made him flinch.

He didn't answer, but after a beat, he raised his free hand to point toward the elevator in a gesture reminiscent of Scrooge's Ghost of Christmas Yet to Come, tatty sleeve draping and fuming and everything. "That man. Do you see him?"

I blinked several times. Man?

There—in the clearing smoke—he materialized.

A tall figure garbed in fastidious black strode into the evacuated area. Since he faced the elevator doors, he had his back to us, his white-blond hair just a shade lighter than the haze that enshrouded him.

"I see him," I whispered.

That skeleton hand released me, and he stepped around to my side, an action that had me flattening my spine to those of the books, hands splaying against their plastic-wrapped bindings. Again, he swiveled that hooded gaze my way, the unfathomable darkness within funneling its full attention on me as he raised a bony finger between us.

"Do not let him see you," that voice commanded. "Do not engage with him. And if you see him again . . . *hide.*"

Hide? Why? What in the Hades is going on?

"Wait," I rasped as he turned away, and I actually grasped for his robes. My fingers caught only mist, which dissolved in my grip.

He strode off toward that man, who flung his arms wide. A strange poison-green glow flared along his sleeves, and the elevator's doors tore open—all without his touching them.

While the blond man stepped forward to peer inside the mangled elevator, the Grim Reaper's right hand shot out to the side. Bone fingers closed around the handle of the scythe that reappeared with that motion. The tool, or weapon—I still wasn't sure which—unfurled out of that same undulating and soundless fog that trailed him.

I started forward, my heart thundering at speeds I'd never felt, as Reaper Man gripped the scythe between both hands, raised it, and then brought the now-glowing silver blade screaming down on the unsuspecting man.

That smile of silver soared through the man without cleaving him, ghosting through him instead, leaving no wound or mark. A gasp caught in my throat, though, when the blond man crumpled to the floor, an eerie and crackling spherical green light springing forth from his spine.

The hooded figure seized the fizzing orb in his free fist and then collapsed into the floor, vanishing in an explosion of dark miasma. Its remnants fountained upward before every trace of him, in the next instant, misted away.

"Omigod," I said as, despite the reaper's warning, I pushed off from the books to rush to the blond man's side and crouch next to him.

Turning him over, I found the man—the young man—staring sightlessly upward, his too-blue-to-be-real eyes wide and unseeing.

Shouting voices drifted near, along with tromping boots.

Half a beat later, a brigade of first responders and firefighters descended upon us. One of them tugged me gently back from the man while another knelt to check his pulse and confirm what I already knew.

The man I'd just been warned to stay away from . . . was dead.

7

GRIM

Unfettered rage coursed through me as I stormed down the entrance corridor of the Hallowed Halls, Cedric's sputtering, fritzing, and bucking soul clenched in my grip.

On either side of me, the Soul Flames snuffed themselves as I passed, as if wanting to avoid catching my eye and thus my ire.

I'd never minded the dark, though. And Cedric's smarmy soul, kicking and screaming as it sizzled and sparked in my fist, provided enough pale green light to illuminate the grim trek to the Basins anyway.

I'd warned him, hadn't I? I'd told him to stay out of my business.

And what had he been doing at the library anyway if he hadn't somehow followed me there?

I wasn't naive enough to buy for one second that asking him would get me any truthful answer. Aside from that, he was beyond the point of interrogating now, wasn't he? At least for the time being.

If I released my hold on his soul, he'd fly straight back to his useless carcass, which would reanimate and do more stupid shit to piss me off.

"Grim?" Johann asked as I thundered into the Basins. Glancing up from his scribbling, he lowered his spectacles to take in my state, no doubt also noting the unwieldy soul I carted.

Pluto gave a hoarse caw and took flight from his perch on the ledge of the Black Basin, which he sometimes stared into for hours. He circled above us, frightened—marking my volcanic mood even before Johann.

"Grim Grim! Watch out for him!"

Normally, I stored souls in my hourglass as I collected them. I had no need to stow this one. Aside from having zero intention of hoarding it for *any* length of time, my plans for it amounted to the immediate sort.

"Grim," Johann tried again, a note of alarm rising in his aged voice as he set down his quill, eyes widening on me when I approached the Black Basin. "What are you doing? What—*who* is that?"

I didn't answer the old man. I didn't have to. This was none of his business.

Above us, Pluto continued to caw as he flew panicked laps around the room.

"Grim, stop!" Johann commanded as he scuttled down from his scribe's desk, the yellow beret Flora had brought him from Paris tumbling to the floor in his haste.

Again, I ignored the doctor, making a beeline for that onyx vat that I would, despite the sour-lime hue of Cedric's serpent's soul, *force* him into.

But then, moving with far more speed than I would have thought him capable of, Johann slid to a halt in front of me, spreading his arms wide like some deranged referee calling a foul.

"Is that Cedric?" he demanded, and I gritted my teeth. The soul—it must have spoken its name to him. Something I couldn't have prevented even if I *had* besmirched my hourglass by stuffing the oily son of a bitch inside.

"Grim," said Johann, his expression darkening, "whatever has happened, I must insist that you release Cedric this instant. Like you, like me, he is a tenant of the Hallowed Halls, and a member of our order."

The fuck he was.

"Move," I commanded, "or I will make you move."

"You'll do nothing of the sort," blustered Johann, his hands going to his hips. "You will, instead, unhand Cedric and let him go to find his body. And you'll do that for the benefit of all of us. Including yourself."

"He interfered with my work."

Johann's scowl deepened, and he thrust a knotted, crooked finger toward the Black Basin. "You know as well as I do that Basin is going to kick Cedric back out no sooner than you send him in."

"*Fine*," I snarled, "then Green it is."

I pivoted away from the old man and stalked toward the glowing Green Basin with its swirling vortex. But with slippers squeaking against the polished ebony floor, Johann managed to skitter in front of me a second time, walking backward until his spine collided with the Basin.

"The same thing will happen with this one and you know it," Johann cautioned, actually shaking a finger at me. "His soul is cursed, and sooner or later it *will* come spitting right back out—just like the last time you threw him in there. As is true of the rest of us, Cedric's not going anywhere, Grim, and the last thing any of us need, including you, is for another of The Few to come poking about in the Hallowed Halls. Lady Green was quite cross the last time, you'll recall. Especially since The Few are the ones who cleared Cedric to take asylum here. Are you listening to me, Grim?"

I growled low, the tightness of my obsidian soul, which had coiled around all my bones, giving by a fraction of a centimeter.

Green *had* admonished me not to submit Cedric's soul a second time . . .

I'd once dunked him in the Red Basin, too—which he'd actually stayed in for half a day.

I'd never been angry enough—at least not until now—to kill him myself. *Or* set my sights on tossing him into the Black.

But Johann was right.

Like a bad case of toxic mold, no matter what, Cedric would just come back.

Maybe Johann sensed my reluctance to release Cedric despite his admittedly apt and reasonable warnings, because he continued his tirade.

"I don't know what Cedric's done to anger you this time, but I can gather he pressed one hell of a button. If *you* want him to press it again only harder, by all means, shove him into one of the Basins or try bottling him for a decade. It's not going to work, and it'll just make whatever this is festering between you two all the more unmanageable."

"Stuffing him in a bottle isn't a bad fucking idea!" I bellowed, wrenching that wretched soul tighter in my fist as if I could squeeze the arrogance out of it, my arm tremoring with the effort to deal a hearty dose of pain Cedric wouldn't—couldn't—feel in this form anyway.

"Let him go, Grim," said Johann. "I will talk to him."

"That never does any good!"

"I said, let him go," Johann insisted, starting to shout now himself. "Let him go, and I swear *I* will take personal responsibility for him from this point forward."

Personal responsibility. What did that even mean?

Johann was stuck here. Just like me. Just like Flora. Just like fucking Cedric.

Our lack of personal responsibility was *why* we were here.

"I'm tired of you always covering his ass," I snapped even as, whirling away from Johann, I pitched Cedric's godforsaken spirit toward the hall I'd just traversed.

Loosed, the sphere sparked and sputtered—perhaps spouting a barrage of curse words only Johann could hear before the foul thing pinballed down the hall and zipped out of sight, zooming off to reconnect with the physical form it was forever shackled to, a mangy dog in search of its miscreant master.

"Grim."

I veered on Johann. "What!"

Pluto soared down toward us, and with a flutter of ebony wings, he lighted on Johann's shoulder.

"Grim Grim," the bird said, as though sounding an alarm, his feathers bristling. "Grim is grim."

Even though my rage had now shifted toward Johann, the old man's scowl softened, wiry eyebrows coming together with concern, the collection of deep lines on his weathered face multiplying.

"Pluto's right," Johann said. "This isn't like you."

He waited a beat, pale gray eyes searching the darkness of my hood for the face—the soul—he wouldn't find because I kept it hidden. From everyone. Including and maybe even especially him.

"This is *exactly* like me," I argued. "And Cedric's had this coming."

"This," echoed Johann, his volume dropping. "Don't tell me *you* killed him."

That, I didn't answer. And maybe it messed with me—a little—that I didn't feel even a twinge of shame that reproving tone might have otherwise evoked in me.

Cedric had crossed a line, and Johann had no right to be pissed, shocked, or *whatever* that I'd finally answered that asshole's special brand of chaos with my own.

With a small shake of his head, a flash of fear-mixed wonder in his eyes, Johann spoke again.

"I'll admit that, so long as you've served in this role, I've never seen you this angry. Not even at Cedric. For that reason alone, I can only assume his transgression was a grave one. That said, I'll remind you *why* each of us, including Cedric, is here."

I wasn't the one who forgot.

"Save the lecture," I barked, turning away. "I know why we're here."

"We dabbled in deeds that cannot be undone," he called after me, his voice echoing through the domed chamber, his words—his *worry*—rankling me to the core. "Trifled with forces forbidden. Our fates, we each sealed them with our own wills."

"Your point?" I hurled the question at him from over one shoulder.

"My point," he snapped, his own temper flaring now, "is to remind you how these roles that keep us from much worse fates do not protect us from repeating the transgressions that landed us here in the first place. *Or* the resulting consequences it's doubtful we'll escape a second time."

"It's up to me if I want to take my chances."

Now I was just being obstinate. Taking my frustrations out on Johann instead of Cedric, even if the old man *had* just stopped me from raining trouble—*more* trouble—down on all of us.

With a huff and a dismissive wave, like shouting at me was akin to shouting at a wall, he spun away, grumbling to himself in German as he tromped back toward his desk, though Pluto turned on his shoulder to keep me in his beady, blinky sight.

"Frightful fight," said the bird. "Cedric is deadric. Point to Grim. Don't cross him again."

Couldn't have said it better myself. And how was it that the fucking *bird* got the picture?

I continued my own march toward the exit—because I still had souls to gather.

What was more, because I'd needed to detour to the library, I was late—*and* behind.

More souls than just the librarian's had called to me in the time it had taken me to get her off the elevator. And then Cedric's interloping had complicated everything.

And his presence near the librarian, the fact that he'd searched the demolished elevator for evidence of her death—that alone suggested he knew more than he ought to about the soul I'd failed to deliver.

Perhaps he even knew it was her . . .

That thought. It summoned that tight inner discomfort back to my soul, which gathered itself behind my sternum, a makeshift heart wrenched in the fist of fear.

The emotion had returned, as black, uncomfortable, and uninvited as before.

And what did it say that my thoughts of the librarian had done a quicker and better job of summoning it than Johann's sage—if annoying—cautioning?

It's only because of the Black Basin.

That's what I told myself as I exited the Hallowed Halls for the Netherworld Forest. Endless blue-gray—almost teal—mist curled through rows of ancient trees. Their leafless limbs dripped moss, their thick trunks lashed by vines, their roots sprawling like a graveyard of petrified pythons.

I walked among their ranks, heading down the worn path toward the freestanding stone doorway—the portal.

It would take me out of the silence of this mid-region and back to the roaring world of the living. A place to which I'd once belonged, even if I couldn't recall a single hour of the time, the years, I'd spent there. Or even my name—my real name.

That I'd shed with my skin, my self. Right along with the answer to what I'd done to land myself here in the first place.

And I liked it that way.

Another reason why I was going to have to figure this shit out with the librarian.

Only now, apparently, I was going to have to do that before Cedric could interfere a second time.

The alternative certainly didn't bode well for me.

Or for her . . .

8

HELENA

Seated on my living room couch in my tiny fourth-floor apartment, reading glasses still on, I stared at the slim volume I'd already read cover to cover—twice.

The book stated that, contrary to popular belief, the Grim Reaper didn't end the lives of those whose souls he went to reap. Rather, he was a symbolic figure meant to help explain the mystery of death. A figure who, as I'd hypothesized—to the *actual* Grim Reaper's face—was said to only collect and usher the souls of the dead.

Still, I *had* seen him kill. And the book hadn't been written from a standpoint that presumed the Grim Reaper was, in fact, real. Even if the note that had been stuffed within, addressed to me, claimed exactly that.

Who had written the note, though? And who had the blond man been?

I frowned, hunkering into the cushions, a chill scampering along my arms.

I seized the overlarge, smiling pineapple Squishmallow I'd bought to use as a throw pillow and hugged her close, bringing my knees up.

"That young man," I said through a sigh. "He was probably only a few years older than Hunter. His poor family . . . If they've been notified, they must be devastated."

But whoever he was, what had he been looking for in the elevator?

The doors of which he'd apparently used mystical green mojo to command apart.

And then there was the biggest question of all: Why and how had the Grim Reaper become invested in saving my life rather than letting fate take its course before reaping my soul?

Wasn't that his job? The book confirmed that it was . . .

Maybe, in this one instance, the answers I sought couldn't be found in a book.

I took off my glasses and, frustrated, flopped them onto my notes. Frowning, I stood, and with Maui the ginormous pineapple tucked under one arm, I went to add more "pumpkin spice" oil to my aromatherapy diffuser.

Except the calming scent wasn't calming me.

Then again, I *had* almost died that day. Almost died *again.*

Keeping an eye on that book, which lay in the center of my coffee table next to all the notes I'd scribbled down in hot-pink ink, I paced behind my yellow couch, chewing my thumbnail, Maui cinched in a headlock while I fretted. Because it couldn't be a good sign that the infamous harvester of souls had shown up to rescue me from death a second time. That alone suggested that there could be a third time coming.

I also had no idea *why* any of this was happening, or why my mysterious rescuer had bothered warning me to "not engage with" and to "hide" from someone he'd then proceeded to take out.

Murder?

Maybe he *was* a serial killer . . .

Fighting off another shudder, I shook my head, unable to make sense of anything.

"Even my internet search for people who've encountered the Grim Reaper has come up short," I told the plushie. "Right before leading me down a rabbit hole of Reddit stories that read like fan fiction."

That said, I hadn't worked up enough courage to post my own story. Yet.

"What do *you* think, Maui?" I asked the pineapple, returning her to her usual spot in the crook of the couch's armrest.

Maui smiled her quiet slip of a smile up at me.

"No, I'm *not* obsessing," I told her, folding my arms. "Or . . . maybe I am. But this is kind of obsession-worthy, don't you think? I mean, in the elevator he was all . . ." Widening my stance, I mimed the way he'd pulled apart the doors Incredible Hulk–style. "Then, with the scythe thingy he was all . . ." I grasped the staff of an invisible scythe before taking the same great swipe Reaper Man had taken at the blond man. "And then he just whoooooosh!" I mimed an explosion of smoke with my arms.

Maui said nothing. Though, did her smile seem more knowing than before?

"Don't give me that look," I admonished, hands going to my hips. "It's not like that."

My phone rang, and I startled hard, eyes falling to where the device lay near the book.

I'd already spent two hours on the phone with my mom that day, assuring her that I really was okay. This call, though, wasn't from either of my parents.

Instead, the name on the screen read "Peter."

Peter. Gosh. What was *he* calling for?

Should I answer?

Maybe it was important. Maybe it had something to do with work. Or maybe . . .

"I should answer," I said, speaking maybe to myself, maybe to Maui. "Mom asked about Peter . . ."

Lamented how I was no longer with him. Didn't have anyone here to comfort me . . .

Before I could talk myself out of it, I rounded the couch, plucked up the phone, and accepted the call.

"Hello?"

"Helena," said Peter, his voice warm, his tone concerned. "My goodness, darling. Are you all right?"

For a moment, I didn't answer. I wasn't sure what to say. Aside from the fact that I didn't really know *how* I was, I still couldn't piece together why he was calling me. Or why I'd been "Miss Hart" earlier and now "Helena" again. And not just Helena, but "darling."

No matter what I'd been hoping for, this included, the whiplash stung. And rattled me.

Then again, maybe he was just being kind. There didn't have to be a deeper reason behind Peter's call. Probably best if there wasn't . . .

Since he'd gotten off the elevator moments before it had taken me on a *Final Destination*–style ride, maybe he just wanted to check on me.

"I'm okay," I said. "Just . . . a little shaken."

"A little." He scoffed. "You had quite a fright today. Please tell me you're not alone at home."

I didn't answer. Because I couldn't tell him that I wasn't.

Mom and Dad lived half a state away, along with half my undergrad friends—something he knew. My grad-school friends peppered the United States, and no one lived closer than a few hours' drive.

After earning my MLS, I'd moved to Wyvern to take this job. And even after four years in the city, I still only had a few close friends.

Who were all married now . . .

"I *am* thinking about getting a cat," I said at last. "Does that count?"

"You *are* alone," he murmured.

I scowled. And maybe it was the pity in his downward-inflecting tone that stirred my anger. "I'm not alone, Peter," I blurted out.

"Oh," he said after a beat. "Brooke is there?"

Brooke was my best friend, a fellow librarian in the school system. Who'd gotten hitched earlier that year. And . . . busy.

"Um," I said, gaze sliding back to Maui. "N-no."

Another pause. And then: "Oh."

Silence pulsed from his end of the phone. When he spoke again, his tone was even softer than before. "Well, I won't keep you from your guest. I just . . . There's a rumor swirling about that you were the one to find John Doe."

I flinched as I made my way toward the window overlooking the complex's parking lot.

"The patron who died," I said, "they still don't know who he was?"

I scanned the cars in the parking lot below and the shadowy trees beyond, searching perhaps for evidence of my cloaked follower. Probably a good thing that I didn't see him since he only appeared when I was about to fall to my death.

"There's not been a positive ID that I've heard of," he replied. "They say he was younger than us, but they're citing a heart attack, if you can believe it. But I *am* curious how you got off that elevator before finding your way to the basement of all places."

"Um," I said, fingers trailing down the gossamer fabric of my off-white drapes before I went in search of my tea. "There was . . . a Good Samaritan. He . . . got me out of the elevator. I followed him down to the basement."

All of that *was* the truth, wasn't it?

"Samaritan," Peter repeated. "You're not saying someone boarded the elevator after I disembarked, are you?"

"Disembarked?" I asked through a small huff of a laugh, finding my favorite Stitch mug, the one where the little grinning alien wore a grass skirt and strummed a ukelele. "It was more like you were Double-O-Seven-ing your way out of a viper pit."

Silence again radiated on his end.

"Listen, Peter," I said, "I appreciate your concern. I do. But I'm okay. And I don't need you to check on me. I really am all right."

"I suppose I feel a bit guilty," he said. "That I'd only just left you. I can't help thinking that, if I'd stayed, *I* could have done something. I can only be grateful you had help from a stranger. An angel in the flesh."

I blurted a nervous laugh, which I hoped didn't hurt his ear. I couldn't have helped the half-hysterical sound, though. Not when it had come bolting out of me like someone stepping on a raspy squeak toy.

"Are you sure you're all right?" Peter asked.

No. "Of course."

"Your benefactor," Peter pressed. "Did you happen to catch his name?"

"There was so much going on. I . . . It didn't really come up."

"No, of course it wouldn't."

Silence again emanated from his end. I frowned, staring down into my mug. The citrus tea had lost its steam.

Seemingly just like my interest in Peter.

Which, on the whole, was good information to have.

Apparently, almost dying—twice now—had done something to me. Or maybe the incidents had simply awakened me to the fact that it was folly to want something—someone—who didn't want me back.

There'd been my rescuer, too. I wasn't ready to buy into the idea his plans didn't include reaping my soul at some point in the near future, but then . . . why rescue me in the first place?

And if my time truly *was* limited, then it would be no one's fault but my own if I ended up wasting it pining for someone who couldn't seem to make up his mind regarding how he felt about me.

"I have to go now, Peter," I said to him. "But . . . I'll see you around at work."

"Helena," he said. "Listen, I *am* sorry."

I scowled and, turning, pressed my back to the countertop as I again peered toward my window. There was no telling what he was apologizing for. Was he simply offering empathy for what had happened that day? Or, after months of not so much as a how-do-you-do, was he expressing remorse for the coldness he'd shown me on the heels of so many empty promises . . . and so much heat?

"I appreciate that," I said.

Quiet. And then, "Good night, Helena."

"Cheers," I whispered in response—and ended the call.

9

GRIM

After my unceremonious slaying of Cedric and my subsequent release of his soul, he did not return to the Hallowed Halls.

Had the circumstances been anything other than what they were, his failure to reappear *would* have brought me rare solace. But since I didn't know the extent of his knowledge regarding the librarian, his prolonged absence sent me into an unending state of red alert.

My anxiety over where he had gone and what type of retribution he was planning put me in the habit of checking on the librarian nightly.

Best-case scenario, Cedric had woken up six feet deep in a box or some other precarious state and was now tasked with the tedious assignment of exhuming, extracting, and possibly reassembling himself—something that could potentially keep him busy for a spell.

Worst-case scenario, my knee-jerk wrath had confirmed his suspicions regarding the librarian, and he was now biding his time with a new and more thorough plan to use her to ensnare me.

So far, I had not again felt the pull of her imminent death. Something I kept waiting for: an unstoppable event I simultaneously anticipated and dreaded.

The anticipation part should concern me. So should the dread.

But I refused to let them. Examining the roots of either emotion too closely would just complicate the already-unmitigated clusterfuck I'd found myself in.

So would another non-vital interaction with her. Which was why I kept my distance.

Between making my rounds, I stopped by her building just after midnight every night.

After assuring myself that her car, an offensively yellow Volkswagen Beetle, slumbered in its usual spot, I checked her fourth-floor living room window.

Almost every night since the elevator incident, I'd glimpsed the pale blue flicker of television light flashing between the curtains that she kept parted. As if, perhaps, she sometimes searched for me, too.

Except that was an idiotic thought. On the off chance she *was* searching for me, her terror alone would be the sole motivator behind such an action.

Not that I hoped for a different motivation. I didn't. I sure as fuck wasn't in this job to make friends.

On the rare nights that the television failed to verify her presence, I sent a call to her phone, something that, due to my powers, I needed no device to accomplish.

Always, she answered, her quiet and curious "Hello?" soft as it resonated through my empty skull.

I never said anything in response. Just ended the connection.

One night, when I glimpsed her pacing and talking to some visitor, I floated up to her window, making sure I stayed back so she wouldn't catch sight of me.

She used her hands a lot when she spoke, and whoever she was talking to seemed to be getting quite a story. Hopefully she hadn't told anyone about me. For some reason, I was less worried about that than I was about who she had to be yammering at.

Finally, she turned out the light and left the room, probably to go to bed.

Wait. Was someone staying over? Sleeping on her couch?

Before I knew what I was doing, I unspooled to vapor, then rematerialized in front of her sofa.

And glowered down at . . . a stuffed pineapple?

The fuck?

I tilted my head at the thing, which wore a dopey smile, and I had to resist the urge to tell it I knew of a bird it might get along with.

The shower kicked on. Followed by a radio blasting some folkie, touchy-feely, *Twilight*-soundtrack-sounding, acoustic "Kumbaya" guitar shit.

Ugh. I should get out of here.

But hand tightening on my scythe, I lingered.

Because the librarian started to sing along. To Taylor fucking Swift—of course.

Not like me not to want to cover my nonexistent ears and maybe, I don't know, *melt.*

But . . . the librarian had a good voice. A beautiful voice, actually.

On a nearby armchair, next to a tote stuffed with picture books, sat a ukelele covered in goddamn glittery stickers, one of its strings popped. A packet of unopened replacement strings lay on the coffee table next to a pair of reading glasses.

No. Absolutely fucking not.

The librarian went into the chorus, her voice carrying over the rush of water.

I deliberated.

Because it wasn't like I didn't have time.

She sure didn't.

Damnit.

Grinding my teeth, I left my scythe standing where it was while I went to pluck up the instrument. I examined it, turning it over between bony hands. The other strings seemed okay.

I sat down next to the fucking pineapple, and balancing the ukelele on my knees, I replaced the broken string. I'd snapped enough in my afterlife—more than I could count—that the repair only took a minute.

As the librarian's playlist switched over to some lively and unbearable show tune, I stood and replaced the instrument. Then I returned to collect my scythe.

Glowering down at the pineapple, I aimed a bone finger at it.

"Not a fucking word," I said, before vanishing.

This nightly check-in, touch-and-go setup was hardly ideal. But I was convinced Cedric had somehow deduced the missing soul *was* my doing, and that I was now trying to cover my tracks.

His plan perhaps was to catch me in the act of rescuing the librarian or to somehow capture evidence to present against me, thereby paving the way for him to get rid of me and, at long last, assume my role himself.

If so, that was indeed a surer plan than informing Sir White outright of my impudence.

In that instance, I would at least have the ever-useful tool of plausible deniability on my side. If, however, Cedric managed to produce evidence—or even somehow the missing soul itself? Well, at the very least, he would be providing proof that I'd been willfully derelict in my duties.

All of this increased the pressure to find a way to smuggle the librarian's soul into the White Basin. I dared not remove said soul from its living vessel, though, until I devised a way to deliver her to that Basin undetected. Something I was still working on. Because it would be far worse for me if I was found in possession of the missing soul.

So long as the librarian lived, I could, at the very least and as a last resort, feign ignorance in the event of an inquisition.

When midnight came again, I approached the librarian's apartment building, the glow of too many streetlamps forbidding all but a few patches of shadow for me to hide in should she happen to glance outside.

Per usual, her absurd car dwelled in its designated slot tucked beneath a long port.

But her darkened living room window did not flicker with pale light.

Stationed in the cover of a willow, its curtaining screen of golden leaves half illuminated by the streetlight, I hesitated—then called.

She answered right away, her voice having grown familiar to me—something decidedly *unfamiliar* since I only ever spoke at length with Flora, Johann, and, unless I could avoid it, Cedric.

"Don't hang up," she said, breathless. "Please."

I should end the call. I had the answer I sought. Her car proved she was home. Her voice confirmed she was not in distress. That plea in her tone, though, had me acquiescing to her request despite my better judgment. A judgment I *needed* to start heeding.

Something about her had me throwing every "should" aside.

"I know it's you," she said. "And . . . I think it's time we talked."

Talk? That was not a good idea. *Or* an option. We'd spoken enough, and in that brief conversation, I'd already conveyed to her everything she needed to know about the situation at hand.

"I know you're there," she said. "Who else would always call after midnight with the ID listed as 'Unknown'? Aside from that, I can feel it. And though I don't know how . . . I can feel you."

She should be afraid of me. Everyone was afraid of me. Why wasn't she?

"Say something," she pleaded. "*Please.*"

Why did I want to reply? I couldn't.

"Am I going to die?" she asked when the silence only swelled.

Yes.

That *was* the answer. One that, if she was asking, she likely already suspected. But . . . why couldn't I say it out loud?

"I admit I wasn't sure before," she pressed, her living room light flicking on, "but now I know you *can* talk. Just . . . say something. Ask me if I like scary movies. Or demand a ransom. I'd ask your favorite color, but something tells me it's death-by-scythe black."

I lingered on the line for just a moment longer. Just until she appeared in that window, her visage framed like a figure in a portrait, her form backed by golden light that set her matching hair aglow like a halo.

That light. Oddly, it seemed to be coming . . . *from* her.

"Can you see me?" she asked. "I think you've been watching me. I get this . . . funny feeling sometimes. Something like a spider sense. It's spooky, but . . . kind of nice, too."

Moving of its own accord, my hand went to my ribs, the place her fingers had sunk into that night on the balcony. When she'd fallen against me after I'd yanked her away from that ledge. For reasons I still didn't understand.

An echo of that sensation rippled through me now.

"At least tell me your name," she pleaded. "I . . . don't know what to call you. I'm Helena. If . . . you didn't already know."

Helena. Fittingly, a name one letter more than that of the most beautiful woman in history. The name of a song I'd, years ago, learned to play, too. A song about grieving, yearning, the residue death hefts upon the living . . .

"Thank you, by the way," she said. "For saving me. Both times. And I mean that. Even if . . . you can't keep doing it."

My soul gathered itself into a knot before thudding just once—its essence beating against my sternum, like a banging fist that brought with it the reverberation of some kind of murky remorse.

The emotion—less recognizable than all the others. I didn't like it. I didn't like *this.*

Killing the connection, I unfurled, unwilling to risk catching her eye and confirming what she already grasped. That fate had dealt her a bad beat. That there was nothing that could stop that. That, despite what either of us preferred, I *was* coming for her.

And soon.

10

HELENA

Frustratingly, after I'd tried to talk to him, the calls stopped.

If there was one thing I'd learned about Reaper Man, it was that he wasn't the conversating sort. A fact that led me to question why he bothered calling me in the first place.

But that question. Wasn't it the last one in a long line of too many others left unanswered?

I just wanted to know what in the fiction turned nonfiction was going on. And since it was my keister on the line, didn't I at least deserve that?

Of course, I'd be lying if I said I didn't also long to hear that *voice* again. Buzzing into my ear over the phone. *Or* in person. Bossing me around some more. But maybe *without* the threat of imminent death?

"Any wild party plans for tonight?" asked Cleo, one of my library assistants, the question stirring me from my bordering-on-dirty thoughts.

Together, we descended the steps of the building's main entrance, the brisk and blustery Halloween-night air whipping our hair about.

"No," I admitted, my enormous jack-o'-lantern earrings swaying as I huddled into my matching oversized orange sweater. The early afternoon had been warm enough when I'd arrived that I'd left my jacket in my car. "I already did the costume-party thing. And frankly, ever since then, my October has been scary enough."

"You could say that again," said Cleo, straightening her black-and-pink cat-ear headband. "You doing okay after all that?"

It had been just over a week since the elevator incident, or as Cleo had put it, "all that."

"Glad to be alive," I admitted, though I couldn't keep her eye as I said it. "What about you? Headed out to a big party?"

On weeknights, the library closed at nine, and this year, Halloween fell on a Thursday, one of the two weekdays that Cleo and I were scheduled to work. Not that I'd minded. Living in an apartment meant I didn't get trick-or-treaters. And I'd ditched the dating apps after the epic-fail night with Dale the wandering werewolf, so there weren't any more spooky-themed romantic escapades to be had, either.

And since I'd had my two brushes with death, I'd been resisting the urge to tempt fate by spending my nights holed up at home with vintage cartoons, movie musicals, and Netflix baking competitions.

Tonight, with the exception of some pumpkin-shaped Reese's and maybe a glass of wine, would—fingers crossed—be no different.

"I'm meeting Peter at that new witch-themed bar for some spooky drinks," she answered.

I froze on the last step, my head swinging her way because . . . what?

"Peter," I repeated.

Halting, too, Cleo smirked. Biting her bottom lip, she wagged her brows at me. "Winston," she clarified like I couldn't already guess. Like there'd been any question regarding who she'd meant. "The archivist?"

Anger, more potent than a swig of Fireball whiskey, bolted through my veins, setting my blood ablaze. Words—salty ones about Peter—dogpiled in my mouth, but I pressed my lips into a line, disallowing a single one to slip past.

Obviously, Cleo didn't know Peter and I had dated. How could she when he'd insisted that I keep our every move an absolute secret? Seemed Cleo had received no such gag order. She had no clue, either, that Peter had used the excuse of our working together to end things with me. So how could she know how much it stung that he was apparently now seeing *her*? Someone who worked in the exact same department as me, never mind the same building.

Unless I was overreacting. Unless I had this all wrong—jumping to conclusions and assuming Cleo and Peter were seeing one another when they could just be friends.

Friends could wag eyebrows about friends . . . right?

"You didn't hear this from me," laughed Cleo as she leaped off the bottommost step, "because he doesn't want anyone to know we're dating since we work together or whatever, but if you can get him to shut up, that man is one hell of a kisser."

I scowled, glaring after Cleo. When she turned around, I managed to clear my expression.

"Well," I hedged, "sounds like you've got a spicy night ahead."

"Won't be the first," she said through a grin that befitted her feline makeup, the too-cute whiskers and little pink nose she'd drawn on with greasepaint.

Don't ask, don't ask, don't ask. You don't want to know, don't ask.

"How long have you two been an item?"

Cleo shrugged. "We're more like coworkers with benefits. But we've been on and off since July. Currently on." She winked at me. "Very, very on. Rroow," she added for effect, pawing at me with one hand before turning the gesture into a wave. "See you tomorrow!"

"I'm off," I called after her. "It's my week to work Saturday."

"Ah, well," she said, "then bright and early on Monday. Enjoy your Friday."

Breaking away, she hurried through the parking lot toward her car, a definite skip in her step.

When she was far enough away, I let my smile fall and allowed my glower to take over again. I wasn't jealous so much as I was angry. *Incensed.*

Because what was Peter's deal? Why lie to break up with me?

And had he been *cheating* on me?

I honestly *didn't* want to know.

"Stupid hot accent," I grumbled as I wrestled with the ridiculous faux patent leather pumpkin-shaped purse I'd impulse-bought off Amazon because, for whatever reason, I'd wanted to be festive. Wrenching open the zipper, I then scrounged for my keys. "Dumb pretentious ponytail. *Pompous* blazer with the *absurd* elbow patches!"

Every *p* I spoke got extra emphasis as I hit the button on my key fob to unlock my doors.

Except nothing happened.

I blinked at the fob, and then at my car, searching the interior to make sure I had the right yellow Beetle. And I did. There was my oversized silk sunflower beaming at me from the built-in dashboard vase. Also, lying there unhelpfully in the front passenger seat, the jacket I'd failed to carry in with me because why think ahead? Doing so hadn't exactly worked for me before, had it?

Not when I'd said yes to Peter flipping Winston that day he'd stopped to help me with the book drop so he could ask me out. Certainly not when I'd proposed going on a first date to a Halloween party dressed as rainbows and mother-flipping sunshine just so Dale could write me off and rub himself on some hussy with knee-high socks, a pencil in her updo, and a fake branch-manager badge with the asinine name "Paige Turner." Some vapid, job-appropriating poser who probably had never read a line of Shakespeare in her life, didn't know who Keats was, thought Hemingway was just a type of cat, and had no idea just how horrible of a no good, very bad day poor Alexander had actually had!

"Augh!" I roared at my car, giving the front tire a good hard kick, which, just like every other action I'd taken to try to find a man who wasn't a walking pooper-scooper, did me absolutely no good.

Was *that* why I'd gotten the toe-curl tickles for a literal skeleton? Because while all the other eligible bachelors couldn't be bothered to not make moves on everybody else in my vicinity, *he'd* actually opened a door for me?

And if we wanted to get technical about things, out of everyone, Reaper Man *did* call me.

Maybe it was on *his* bingo card to, at some point, take me out the way he had the blond John Doe, but at least he *did* still call me.

The bar for dating standards. It really was in hell, wasn't it? So doggone low that I had developed the hots for (and maybe was a little sad about not getting to have phone sex with) the. Grim. *Reaper.*

"Unbelievable," I snarled as I shoved my apparently dead key into the lock to manually unlock the door. Except that wasn't working, either. "*Got* to be kidding me," I added through chattering teeth, though it was anyone's guess at this point if I was grousing about the car, Peter, or my possible impending demise.

With a sigh, I cast a glance around the parking lot, scanning for any of the other employees who'd yet to drive off.

Another frigid gale rushed by, sending brittle leaves scampering over the asphalt and the nearly vacant lot.

Cleo's car was gone—something that, even given the circumstances, I had a hard time not being grateful for. I certainly didn't need details about her and Peter, any more than she'd already divulged, which had given birth to enough frolicking brain goblins as it was—happy *frigging* Halloween.

Ben's truck wasn't here, and neither was Peter's Volvo—not that I would have resorted to texting *him* even if he had been working the night shift. At this point, I'd sooner hit up Michael frapping Myers for a ride.

Still, I dug my phone out. Because my options seemed to be calling Roadside Rescue or Uber. Which did I truly need?

I got my answer to that—at least partially—when my car started itself.

"What?"

Blinking, I backed away from the vehicle, which revved loudly as if someone was pumping the gas even though there wasn't anyone in the driver's seat—or any of the seats.

The car jolted forward, an action that sent me skittering in reverse.

Oh God. It was happening again. Except this time, instead of tumbling off a balcony or careening down an elevator shaft, I was about to be run down by my own sunflower-yellow Volkswagen Beetle.

Looping my head through the pumpkin purse's crossbody strap, I bolted, making a break for the building, my keys to the front door gripped hard in one hand, my phone still clutched in the other.

If I went back into the building, I'd trigger the alarm, and the police would come. I could wait inside while—

With a gasp, I fumbled to a stop at the steps leading up to the main entrance.

Garbed in that same impeccable black suit now paired with a matching frock coat, a man stood front and center on the wide stairway, blue eyes blazing an icy stare, white-blond hair stirring in the wind.

The man, one who was supposed to be dead, one who I had *seen* die, stared straight at me, the faintest of up-to-no-good smirks tugging at one corner of his mouth.

All of Reaper Man's warnings came rushing back to me, making far more sense than they had before because he must have known this man would be back.

Blondie had already seen me, though, and with that smirk he was wearing, "engaging" with him was certainly the last thing I wanted to do.

Hide, Reaper Man had told me.

But what if there wasn't anywhere *to* hide?

Not with my car barreling straight at me, headlights blazing.

11

GRIM

"Happy All Hallow's Eve, Grim."

I sighed inwardly as Flora drifted to stand in my periphery, bare toes peeking out over the roof ledge of the New York City high-rise. I'd chosen to brood there after collecting a blue soul from one of its cubicles. Hopefully they would find his vacated shell sooner rather than later, but then, the ones who worked late tended not to have many who would miss them quickly.

Seated on the edge, a hulking stone gargoyle on my left, my boots dangling toward the windows, I glared at the glittering streams of traffic below.

The sour stench of smog swirled with thc far-off hints of food, the conglomeration of scents so different from Helena's warm, citrusy, and faintly floral aroma. Oranges and honeysuckle, with just a hint of vanilla.

Shit. How the fuck did I know how she smelled?

Maybe I'd caught a whiff while holding her hostage in the library basement. Maybe her scent lingered in her apartment, too.

Disturbing that I could list the components. And maybe a little creepy.

Fuck, was I a creep?

"Quiet night for me, too," said Flora. "Hope it lasts . . ."

Far below, horns honked, and sirens wailed, all while the wind rushed past us, sending Flora's fiery tresses into a flurry while it tugged in vain at the hood I never allowed to come down.

"I have to ask," she said. "Are you really not going to speak to Johann again?"

Shifting her cloth satchel into her lap, Flora took a seat beside me, her own legs kicking while she waited for me to answer. When I didn't, she scrounged in her bag.

"Just left Wisconsin," she said. "Lookit what I got him."

With one delicate hand, Flora yanked forth an enormous wedge of fake yellow cheese. Grinning, the fairy popped the foam triangle onto her head, revealing the novelty to be another hat for Johann's growing collection.

"I think he's going to love it," she said, "don't you?"

I didn't say anything. Not because it was in my plan to ignore Flora. Just as was the case with Johann, I didn't know what to say to her.

The truth was . . . I needed help. At the same time, I didn't know how to ask for it.

I wasn't sure I truly wanted it, either.

Because, if I did ask for help, that meant Flora and Johann would get involved—become culpable, just like me. Flora might even have the capacity to collect the librarian's—Helena's—soul herself. Most adult souls proved too strong and cumbersome for her, but Helena's might just go with the fairy.

Over the phone, Helena had said she could "feel" it was me. In a way, I could sense her spirit, too. I got the impression her soul, if handled properly and so long as it wasn't disturbed, would be light and easily transferred, delicate like silk.

Though the idea of it leaving Helena's lifeless body conjured a sick churning in my empty gut.

Maybe that was only because of what would happen after that.

I wouldn't put it past Flora to make the delivery to Sir White personally and try to claim responsibility in an effort to take the heat off me.

The Few—they weren't going to remove Flora from her role. Who would they get to fill it?

Still, Flora's indispensability didn't mean she wouldn't still incur some kind of punishment for conspiring.

Aside from that, I didn't want her to collect Helena's soul. *I* was supposed to do it.

But then, the task wasn't one I wanted to perform, either.

Flora sighed. "You're not going to tell us, either of us, what's really going on, are you?" Tilting her cheese-adorned head at me, she leaned forward to try to catch my uncatchable gaze.

"It's complicated," I admitted.

"Complicated," Flora echoed. "Obviously, it's got something to do with Cedric. And maybe, if I had to guess, that missing soul?"

Mm. Seemed Flora and Johann had conferred to compare some recent notes.

"You know," Flora said, her voice tight and small, like she knew she was about to tread onto paper-thin ice. "You might consider changing tactics with him. Cedric has his flaws. Guess you could say we all do. But Grim. Is there really any harm in allowing him to come with you a time or two? Who knows? Letting him see the grittier side of the job might make him realize it's not for him after all—and then he'll find something else to obsess about."

Anger surged inside me. Rage hadn't done me any good with Johann, though, so I did my best to let it go.

Johann and Flora—they saw something in Cedric that I didn't. Maybe if he wasn't always so keen to usurp me, I'd find some tolerance for him.

"Would you say that if it was you who he was trying to sell out?" I challenged.

"I think Cedric is a big talker," said Flora. "Says he wants your job, but he's so keen on annoying you, I have to wonder if it's your company he's truly after. If you ask me, I think he secretly looks up to you. Must be lonely, too, if you think about it. Being immortal."

Flora and Johann babied Cedric. They saw the best in him because they hadn't provoked his worst.

I provoked it. But just, it seemed, by being.

Regardless, this wasn't an argument I was going to win.

There *was* a battle with Cedric that I still had hopes of defeating him in.

For a long moment, I held my silence, letting it stretch on, biding my time so that I could phrase my next words as carefully as possible.

"I need a favor," I told her.

"If you wear the cheese hat for one whole night," she said, "anything."

Slowly, I turned my glare her way—even if I couldn't, in my current form, technically glare. Still, she would feel the heat of my stare.

"Flora, I'm serious."

She shrugged. "So am I!"

"I'm not wearing that thing."

She smiled at me. "Then I can't make any promises I'm going to be of any use to you."

"I need to know how to get into the realm of the White Basin without . . . going through the Basin. Being detected."

Flora's smile fell. She turned her gaze forward, eyes scouring the cityscape and the Hudson as it shimmered under the moonlight.

"Johann said he thought it might be you," Flora whispered, the mirth gone from her sprightly voice. "With that confirmed, it's not hard now to guess what Cedric's up to, either. He's trying to get you caught, isn't he?"

Now did she see why I hated his ass so much?

"Do you know how to get into Sir White's realm or not?" I asked.

"I don't," said Flora. "But . . . I think I can find out. I have . . . a friend who might know."

"A friend," I repeated. "This a friend who is going to want something in return for your help later?"

Flora smiled again, more mischievous than before as she resumed kicking her bare legs, the cold having no effect on her even though she wore a cream drop-sleeved blouse paired with a green calf-length frock. "I guess I'll have to let you know and pass the bill along if so, huh?"

"I would be indebted to you, too," I intoned.

Again, Flora's smile fell. She blinked at me, taken aback, and then she removed the cheese hat.

"You're not going to tell me about this soul, are you?" she asked.

"Nothing to tell." I drew up my legs and then pushed to my feet.

"Well, that's a big fat lie if I've ever heard one," scoffed the fairy as she rose, too, having to take four steps for every two of mine to keep up with me as I trudged across the rooftop. "And that's even if you happen to believe it. Answer me this, then. Has this bourach you're in got anything to do with that glitter you're still sporting?"

I halted to glare back at Flora, who pointed at my robes. Spreading my arms, I peered down at myself, jaw jutting when I caught the faintest trace of a golden shimmer. I'd even used one of those damn sticky roller things. Did *anything* get this shit out?

"I've got to go," I told her, the hem of my robes snapping in the breeze.

"Where?" she asked, gesturing next to the glowing hourglass on my belt. "I'd say you've already met the night's quota, and as of late, you drop your souls off *before* going on your new mysterious midnight errand."

I ground my teeth. "Didn't realize you kept a flowchart on my habits."

"Only when they change," said Flora. "Which really hasn't ever happened before, has it? And that alone suggests there's cause to worry. And Grim, Johann and I, we *are* worried about you. By the way, before you come home to the Hallowed Halls, I should warn you that Cedric's returned."

"What?" I took a step toward her. "When?"

She blinked at me, startled by the growl in my tone. "Just . . . a bit ago? When Johann asked him what happened, Cedric said it was between you and him. He asked if you were in, but Johann told him you were working, so he left. But not before telling me to, when I saw you, let you know he *would* be picking up that library hold."

I braced a skeletal hand on my forehead. "*Fuck.*"

"Grim?" Flora asked, her expression darkening with a deeper concern even than before. "What is it? Does that mean something bad? He's always after some book or another, so I didn't think much about it."

"What time is it?" I demanded.

"I-I don't know," blustered Flora. "Wee bit after nine? Why?"

I didn't have time to explain.

Possibly I didn't have time at all.

I dissolved to smoke anyway, heading first to the library since Helena worked Thursday nights.

I hadn't felt the pull of her impending death, but I wouldn't since any attack from Cedric wouldn't be a fated event.

If I was lucky—if *she* was—I could still get to her before he did.

12

HELENA

My legs pumped under me hard as I flew past the library, heading as fast as I could away from the curb that my renegade Bug, in its pursuit of me, had already lumbered up and over. I hurtled toward a barrier of bushes that, though they wouldn't stop the car, might just slow it down.

"Help!" I shouted with as much volume as I could muster as I burst through the bushes, though it remained to be seen who *could* help me in this scenario.

One glance behind showed my car struggling to roar over the shrubs. I took the opportunity to fly into Third Street, into the path of a pickup that had to swerve to avoid hitting me.

"Oh God!" I shrieked, scampering to clear the road and climb onto the opposite sidewalk. Just as I shot through the line of darkened cars parked at meters, the vehicles revved to life, their lights springing on.

"Not happening!" I squealed as I diverted course again, shooting straight back across the street, racing away from the row of driverless cars that, one after the other, peeled out of their slots to barrel after me just as my Bug had done.

By some miracle I managed to make it back to the library's side of the street without becoming roadkill, though my Beetle had since vanished from its spot near the bushes.

I bolted down the sidewalk, my flats crunching the crispy leaves that scuttled after me. Pushed by the wind that seemed to be trying to hurry me along, I traded my attention between my phone and the road.

Traffic now split into two raging streams, one consisting of drivers all swerving to avoid the chaos and another consisting of sentient cars bent on flattening me.

"Heeelp!" I screeched again, fumbling to thumb the emergency button on my cell. Then, as I leaped to avoid being bucked by the grille of the driverless Buick that bumped onto the curb, I dropped my phone, its screen cracking on the pavement. I abandoned the device, taking a hard right down the alleyway behind the library.

The narrow road let out onto Second Street, which ran parallel to Third. Except something worse than either my Bug or another car blocked the path to the other side.

Somehow, the library's gargantuan children's bookmobile—the one with the Very Hungry Caterpillar plastered across its side—had made its way into the alley.

The flat, dark face of the enormous and rumbling bus reflected the streetlights in a way that gave the illusion of bright glowing eyes. Its engine revved and roared, and I shrank under its scrutiny, vision burned and blurred by its high beams.

I hesitated, half tempted to charge the thing just to see if I could swing my way into the driver's seat, action-movie style. My odds of infiltrating its prone-to-sticking folding door before the beast could mow me down, though, weren't good, so I turned to again run. But only just in time for my Beetle to appear at the far end of the alley.

"Oh, shut the front cover," I whispered. Though maybe now was as good a time as any to start actually cursing.

With a squeal of tires, the growling bus shot forward. I screamed and charged toward my Bug even as it sped straight toward me, because what other choice did I have?

None. At least not until a tall, hooded, and black-clad figure gripping a scythe materialized before me, his dark form unfurling from plumes of smoke.

With a cry of relief, I ran at him as hard as I could—harder than I'd ever run toward anything in my life.

He stood there—reaching for me with his free arm even while my Volkswagen closed in on him from behind, its headlights outlining his phantasmal shape, their white glare all but blurring that skeleton's hand from sight.

But he didn't seem to care that he'd found himself in the middle of a spectral game of chicken.

He wasn't looking. He was just waiting.

For me.

Reaching him at last, I launched myself at him, throwing both arms around his shoulders, clutching him tight, my crushing embrace finding only bones to hold, my rib cage smashed against his.

That arm closed in around me, gripping me tight in return, clamping me to him before we shot up like a rocket. His robed form carried us above the dueling vehicles and out of harm's way an instant before they collided.

An earsplitting roar of crunching metal and shattering glass ripped through the night. My Bug's horn blared as the bookmobile shoved the car down the alley.

We remained in the air, levitating just below the tops of the surrounding buildings where we weren't likely to be seen.

Unable to help myself as the wind battered us from every side, I buried my face against his shoulder, fingers curling into the coarse fabric of those dark robes, gripping hard.

And then I sobbed my desperate words into his frame.

"I was starting to think . . . you weren't going to come this time."

13

GRIM

With those words, the essence of my soul, still gathered in my rib cage, shattered, the darkness splintering off to shoot down the lengths of my limbs, wrapping my bones to the tips of my fingers and toes.

The flesh I didn't currently have wanted to take a breath, to gasp and expand with the overwhelming influx of whatever sensation this was.

This mixture of emotions, never mind their inexplicable potency, made no sense to me.

Still, these . . . *feelings* fought to take a more definite shape.

Most prominently, something that resembled guilt but wasn't—not exactly—echoed through me. Rage toward Cedric boiled in the mix, too, but that had been there before. Now that I'd ensured her safety, my wrath slithered to the background of my being, sated if not slaked.

An unexpected possessiveness swirled in me as well, fueled by the weight of the librarian in my grasp—stoked, too, by the warmth that radiated from her, and the way she clung to me.

Mysterious pain enwrapped it all, an unfamiliar brand hammered into me by the thudding of her heart, the muscle that pounded against the cold bone barrier to where mine might have dwelled, as if calling—*pleading*—for an answer.

I needed to sever our connection, release her. That would stop this barrage. It had to.

This embrace, after all, must be the catalyst for my . . . discomfort.

Because I'd never held anyone before. Not that I could remember.

Maybe I had once, during the life I'd led, but I kept those memories at a greater distance than anything or anyone.

I'd certainly never held another soul like this since my rebirth as the usher of the dead.

The moment I let her go, these feelings *would* die, allowing me to once more be what I was: the impartial hand of death.

Having won the battle against Helena's Beetle, the bus shoved the car out into traffic before swerving off somewhere. More horns blared and shouts rose on the chilled wind that assailed us, sending the tattered hems of my garments into a dance around both our legs.

Shivering from the cold, fear, or both, Helena kept her face buried against my shoulder as if the world had become too much for her. No doubt, with Cedric's macabre interference, it had.

I sank slowly to the asphalt, all too cognizant that the danger for the librarian had not passed. Yet I couldn't transport Helena elsewhere with my powers, not so long as her spirit remained attached to her body.

But then . . . there were other, more worldly means of transportation at my disposal.

The soles of my boots rejoined the pavement half a beat before Helena's feet reconnected, and the instant she had the earth beneath her again, I released her.

She unwound herself from me with a reluctance I was sure I imagined, and freed, I brushed past her.

While I waited for—and willed—the mire of emotions her touch had inflicted upon me to depart, the infection remained. Worse, with every step I took away from her, the madness—I didn't know what else to call it—intensified. As if our embrace, born out of necessity alone, had branded me.

Only now it was the *absence* of her heat that blazed even hotter.

Which wasn't fucking good.

Somewhere in the distance but growing nearer, an engine growled. Then, at the far end of the alley, a sports car appeared, its high beams slicing their way through the night to bathe us both in their eye-searing light.

"Please," Helena called after me, her voice shaky and desperate. "Where are you going?"

Did she think I would leave her here to deal with this mess on her own? *My* mess?

Why did that thought piss me off?

I tossed my scythe aside, sending it unfurling into the Netherworld ether that remained ever at my command. With my other hand, I summoned forth the means of our extraction from Cedric's cat-and-mouse shit show game.

My car.

14

HELENA

He smelled of wood fire, oakmoss, and vetiver—an ethereal yet earthy essence that evoked visions of long-neglected cemeteries, old tomes, apothecaries, and bonfires.

Though he took that otherworldly aroma with him the moment he departed from me, the impression of those ribs digging into mine and that bone arm cinching me to him remained.

Bereft of that scent that, like his presence, I shouldn't have found comforting, I wrapped my arms around my shuddering body.

A Supra at the end of the alley revved, ready to mow me down.

Just when I feared Reaper Man would vanish as quickly as he'd appeared, he pointed a bone finger at a second car—one that materialized from nothing. The car's sleek and shining contours emerged from the gray-and-black fog he could apparently conjure things from as well as dispel them into.

As obsidian as everything else about him, the vintage vehicle roared to life, its grumbly voice not too dissimilar to that of the being who had commanded it forth.

Did the Grim Reaper seriously drive a muscle car?

Correction: Did he seriously *drive*?

"Get in," Reaper Man growled in that dreaded demon's voice that never, no matter the circumstances, failed to . . . *do* things to me.

Having learned my lesson about deliberating on his commands, I scuttled to obey.

Reaper Man followed after to shut my door the moment I fell into the bucket seat.

Lightning fast, he dematerialized in a swirl of more black smoke before *re*materializing next to me in the driver's seat amid more plumes.

Tires squealed behind us. They screamed beneath us, too, and I slammed backward against the black leather upholstery as we went careening down the alley.

"*Seat belt*," he barked.

"S-seat belt," I agreed. Because *wow* we were going fast.

My heart racing, my gaze flitting between the whirring alley walls and the rear window, I groped near the shoulder of my seat for the belt, but then, as we catapulted out onto Third Street, straight into oncoming traffic that he swerved to avoid, those smoky tendrils that fumed around him swept in to buckle the lap seat belt *for* me—because, oh yeah, *vintage* car.

"Oh," I said, looking down at my lap. "Nice . . . trick."

What *else* could his misty essence do besides open elevator doors and buckle seat belts? Throttle enemies?

Potentially . . . entertain . . . not enemies?

Really, Helena. Is this the time?

Jerked back into the moment when, lucky for us, the tailing Supra got taken out by an SUV with another teeth-jarring smash of glass and metal, I cringed. Still, we barreled on, ripping down the road, the angry snarl of this grumpy entity's grumpy beast of a car reverberating through me.

The world outside blurred on either side of us, becoming a smear of night streaked through with lights. The numbness of shock settled in, too, as my gaze fell to the skeleton's hand maneuvering the stick shift.

"Wh-where's yours?" I asked him.

And how wrong was it that, in this moment of being both chased and rescued by death, I was still stuck on his misty powers and the lingering sensation of those featherlight smoke twists as they'd swept in to buckle me?

"My what?"

"S-seat belt," I said. "Everyone needs a seat belt."

"I don't."

"Because you've got . . . smoke skills." I wiggled my fingers at him.

I should shut up.

Maui had been right. I *was* obsessing.

"That thing," said Reaper Man, his head swiveling away from the rearview mirror, his focus returning to the road. "How fast can it go?"

Thing? What thing?

I twisted in my seat, craning my neck to peer again out the rear window.

Oh. *That* thing.

"That's . . . the children's bookmobile," I said, pointing at the colossal flat-faced bus that had drifted out of nowhere to chase us.

"No shit," he replied, gunning the gas. "I'm more concerned with the fact that it happens to be gaining on us."

He had a point. The bus loomed so close its windshield reflected the muscle car's slim spoiler. The engine rumbled, reverberated just loud enough to be heard over Reaper Man's growling hot rod.

Already, we had to be doing fifty.

"It never *needs* to go fast," I said as the monstrous bus edged even closer, riding our rear as we shot through a red light. "I hate taking it on the expressway and don't if I can avoid it."

"*You* drive that eyesore?"

I blinked at him. "I'm the children's librarian."

"How fast can it fucking go, Helena?"

Oh, wow. He said my name. With that *voice.*

And he had a potty mouth.

The way I felt about that was . . . interesting.

"Um," I said, glancing back down at his bone hand, wringing the strap of my purse with both of my own while I squished my knees together, "the speedometer goes up to a hundred?"

"Fuck."

I frowned. "We . . . can't outrun it?"

It did seem odd to me that, so far, he'd avoided weaving in and out of traffic, choosing instead to take turns and blow through lights, switching lanes only when the bus had enough room to do so, too. He wasn't trying to lose this thing. Instead, he seemed to just want to stay ahead of it.

"I'm not worried about us," he said. "If I don't get it off the side streets, that motherfucker is going to kill everyone, and right now, I've got enough to do."

He swerved again, right onto a curving on-ramp, and I yelped, the centrifugal force sending me leaning his way, far enough that I again caught a whiff of that oaken, earthy, yet otherworldly scent.

The bookmobile thundered after us, its massive dark, blank, and driverless face somehow seeming to scowl. Still, even as we shot onto the expressway, seamlessly merging with traffic, the behemoth gained on us—its lumbering mass integrating with the flow of cars *less* seamlessly.

Horns again blared as unsuspecting drivers swerved to make way.

"How is this better?" I asked as he shifted us into a higher gear, his foot slamming the gas. As we rocketed forward, I blasted back in my seat, the vibrating sides of which I clenched, fingernails digging in.

"I'm open to constructive criticism," he snarled between his teeth as we revved on, bordering on entering hyperspace.

"There *was* an overpass back on Wimberly it can't fit under."

"Now you tell me!"

"Well . . . do you have anything like . . . a rocket launcher?"

"I'm not Batman," he snapped.

"There *are* some similarities," I observed.

He aimed a skeletal thumb toward the back window. "Isn't that thing for the kids?"

"The admins *really* need to purchase a new one," I said, speaking loudly to be heard over the ripping engine as we veered into the fast lane, "but they're not listening. Even on its best behavior, that thing is a death trap. Also, it's a *total* beater and older than the pyramids." I pried my hands up from the seat to start ticking off shaking fingers. "No heat, no air, and I took the stairs off last summer when I made too sharp a turn. Believe it or not, *I* was the one who got written up for that even though it was Trevor who forgot to fold them in."

"Your point?" he demanded as the bus's lights blazed once more into being behind us, washing all in its eye-searing white light.

"Point is, at this stage, that monster *needs* to be put down."

"What?"

I huffed a sigh.

"They keep telling me a new bus isn't in the budget, but then they go and buy a bunch of telescopes for the new branch out in the ritzy east end, so I know it's a lie. The kids deserve so much better, and I'm just saying that if you torched that one, I bet you anything we *would* get a new one in time for summer reading. I wouldn't be sad, either. Or mad. If . . . you had a rocket launcher. But you don't. So, the subject is moot."

He got quiet and, for a long moment, just roared on down the interstate, like I hadn't said anything helpful at all. And maybe I hadn't since he wasn't, like he'd said, Batman.

"It does have an emergency break," I offered.

"Where?"

"Um. There's a handbrake lever between the driver's and front passenger seats—mounted on the floor. You just pull up on it. But engaging it would require someone to—"

He grabbed my left hand in his skeletal grip, then positioned it on the steering wheel.

"What are you doing?" I shrieked.

He didn't answer but vanished, unfurling into wisps of smoke, leaving me barreling down the highway on my own, presumably so he could go do something about Gus the Bus.

"I'm gonna die, I'm gonna die!" I squealed as I did my best to guide the steering wheel to keep us, or rather me, hurtling on our side of the dotted white line, off the shoulder, and zooming straight on till morning.

Tires squealed behind, the bus's and those of a few cars. The horn of a semi blared, and I joined in with a scream of my own.

Then, just when I had my belt unbuckled and my knee halfway onto the driver's seat, my hooded chauffeur rematerialized in a swirl of smoke, his hands taking over the wheel while misty tendrils nudged me back into my seat before rebuckling my belt.

"Right," I whimpered, "seat belt."

"I took care of it," he grunted.

Oh. My God.

I should *not* start panting.

I swallowed hard, forcing my eyes away from him to the dark, whirring road. "What happened?" I spared a glance behind at the bus he'd somehow managed to pull off to the side, halt, and, apparently, disable.

"Hit the brakes, threw the emergency lever, disconnected the battery. There's books everywhere."

"So, it lives another day," I murmured, not certain how I felt about that. I had good memories with Gus, even if the library *did* need to replace him. But how could I possibly forgive him for killing Daisy, my Beetle?

God. That was right. I didn't have a car anymore. And after its run-in with the Very Hungry Bookmobile, my Bug *had* to be totaled.

But then, I currently had bigger problems than a busted Beetle, didn't I?

"Who was that back there?" I asked him. "The blond man. He came back, but I saw you kill him."

"He can't die."

Wait, what? "So he's a zombie?"

"Something like that."

An infuriating response that gave me zero insight into this reoccurring nightmare that had, since meeting him, taken over my life. My potentially fleeting life . . .

"What does that have to do with me?" I asked, bristling, my nerves finally catching up with me, panic over my fate sinking in at last. "What does *any* of this have to do with me?"

"Oh, come the fuck on," he grumbled, but before I could open my mouth and chastise him for his rudeness, the swirl of red and blue lights and the wail of a siren corrected the thought he'd been responding to *me.*

Though I braced myself for another high-speed chase, he actually started to slow down.

"You're pulling over?" I asked. Because how was *that* going to work?

"Let me do the talking," he said, like he'd been in this situation before and knew the ropes. Like he wasn't a literal walking, talking skeleton wrapped in vaporous death robes.

"Are you sure that's a good idea?" I checked the rear windshield again, squinting against the spinning blue and red lights of the cruiser that pulled us over.

"Not a word," Reaper Man said as he threw the car into park, switched off the ignition, and cranked down his window.

15

HELENA

"Sir." The gum-chomping officer, a thirtysomething man with close-cropped dark hair and the barest dusting of a five-o'clock shadow, leaned down to scrutinize us through the driver's-side window, his flashlight raised in one fist. When he aimed it at us—at Reaper Man—I said a silent prayer for the officer's soul. "Could you remove your hood for me, please?"

My eyes bugged at this request, and I *almost* told the officer to run, but then Reaper Man lifted hands—real flesh-and-blood hands covered once more in those black tattoos—to either side of his hood. Like if, instead of snatching the man's soul out of his chest before leaving him lifeless on the side of the interstate, he was actually going to do what the officer told him to.

Which, to my utter shock, he did.

I stopped breathing, my mouth falling open as, with long silver-ring-lined fingers, my until-now-faceless rescuer drew back that obscuring black hood to reveal dark and unruly chin-length hair. His choppy, careless, rock star cut struck through on the right with a single lock of shock white.

That ghostly strip wisped back from his forehead, comingling with ebony strands that curled around his pierced ear. A small silver loop glinted in his lobe, and another hugged the cartilage.

Now that his stately, nonskeletal, kind-of-really-hot profile had been revealed, I lost my ability to blink as well as breathe. I couldn't seem to tear my gaze away from that one visible cheekbone, either, as it actively competed with his jawline for the title of "sharpest plane" of his face. The shadows nesting below each did nothing to help me play the role of impartial judge, either.

But that wasn't all.

A straight prominent nose gave him an ultramasculine silhouette while his lips, full and shapely enough to make me jealous, parted to murmur the words "There a problem, Officer?"

With this utterance, I reared back in my seat, stunned at the change in his voice, which had gone from the deep register of the Keeper of the Gates of Hell to the brassier, warmer baritone of a jazz-lounge singer on his cigarette break.

Top it all off with broody brows and an ocean-blue gaze fixed in a scowl, because it wasn't like I wasn't already attracted to him as the skeletal harvester of dead souls.

"You ask like you don't know why I pulled you over," said the officer through a short huffing laugh.

"My plates aren't expired."

"Try eighty-five in a sixty-five zone."

"There was some trouble on the road," said Reaper Man. "Some kind of bus swerving in and out of traffic. I've got a car with horsepower, so I used it to extract myself and my date from the situation."

"Bus, huh?" said the officer, but *I* was still stuck on the word "date."

"It pulled off to the side about ten or so miles back," said Reaper Man. "The driver seemed to be having issues. Either way, my goal was to slow down after I'd put enough distance between us."

"I'll call it in," said the cop. "But where are you two headed?"

"Costume party," Reaper Man said without missing a beat.

"Figured given your getup," said the cop. "But can you even see with that hood on?"

This time, Reaper Man didn't answer. Instead, he slowly turned his head to regard the officer. "Are you issuing me a ticket?"

"That depends," said the cop, "on whether your bus story checks out. In the meantime, I'll take your license, registration, and proof of insurance."

Reaper Man's scowl deepened as he reached across to the glove box. I scooted my knees to one side, though due to my shortness, they weren't really in his way.

Still gaping, I traded my attention between his tattooed hand and that stern and very human profile. After forking over his paperwork to the cop, Reaper Man then tugged a wallet—of all things—from an inside pocket of his robes.

He flipped the billfold open and pulled out an ID before surrendering that, too.

"Wait here while I run your plates," said the cop before pivoting to march back toward his cruiser, leaving us alone again.

"Are you okay?" Reaper Man asked after a long beat of silence, and the question popped the shell of my shock like a soap bubble.

"I don't know," I said, my voice quiet even to my own ears, "am I?"

For the first time, his gaze flicked my way. He still wore that scowl, one eye half lost behind the all-black portion of his hair.

"Did the blond man say anything to you?" he asked, completely ignoring my question.

"Why wouldn't you ever talk to me when you called?" I countered.

Jaw jutting, hands gripping the steering wheel, he snapped his head forward as if I'd just slapped him, an action that confirmed once and for all the identity of my "Unknown" caller. Not that I'd ever really doubted he'd been the one behind the calls.

"Soon as I get rid of Dudley Do-Right, I'm taking you home."

"I can't go home," I said, the words falling out of my mouth the exact moment they occurred to me. "Please, not yet. I . . . I don't even know what's going on, or who—or what—you really are. Or who that man was. And what he wants. What *you* want—"

"I don't want anything," he snapped, his anger flaring, though it didn't necessarily seem aimed at me.

"I'm . . . supposed to die, aren't I?" I asked him after another long beat, but he didn't get a chance to answer, because our policeman returned, offering Reaper Man's paperwork back to him, which he accepted before handing the bundle off to me.

"Sorry about that, sir," said the cop. "You're free to go."

I did a double take between Reaper Man's driver's license and the cop, who I must have misheard.

"Have a good night," said Reaper Man.

"Happy Halloween," said the police officer as he turned and walked off.

"What . . . just happened?" I asked.

"I have diplomatic immunity," he replied.

"The government knows about you?"

"Not exactly," he said. "Basically, I'm just listed in the system as someone not to fuck with. Because, when it comes down to it, I'm not."

Hard to argue with that.

He restarted the car, and I took the opportunity to peer from his driver's license to him and back again. He didn't smile in his picture, which made me wonder if . . . he ever did.

"Your name is seriously Richard McDead?" I asked.

"What?" That scowl snapped toward me, his glare falling to the paperwork still in my hands. "No, my name's not *Dick McDead*," he snarled, snatching up his ID, which he scrutinized before tossing the card into the back seat. "Fuck, it is."

"It . . . is?" I asked, more confused now than ever.

"Fuck no," he said. "Fuckin' . . . Flora did that. She was in charge of getting all our paperwork settled, and I just didn't notice until now because I never use mine. *Ever*."

"Flora?" I probed as he cranked his window closed. And who did he mean by "our"?

"She's . . . Never mind," he said, seizing and toggling the stick shift. "I don't have a name."

"Everyone has a—"

"I don't!" The growling bite in this, his "normal" voice, silenced me.

"So . . . then what do I call you?" I asked as, when a break in traffic came, he guided the car back onto the highway.

"Not that you need to worry about that," he said, these words frightening me more than any other he'd uttered to me thus far, "but Grim."

"Where are you taking me now, Grim?" I asked as the car rumbled.

"I told you. Home."

"Which means you know where I live," I said. "That blond man who tried to kill me. Does . . . does he know where I live, too?"

Reaper Man's—or Grim's—hands tightened on the wheel, knuckles going white.

"Fine," he said. "I guess . . . we do need to talk."

"Can we do that at the next exit?" I nodded toward the interstate sign sporting all the logos for the approaching chain restaurants. "I really did mean it when I said I wasn't ready to go home. Also, I haven't eaten since noon, and your fake last name made me remember how hungry I am."

"What?" he snapped, glancing between me and the road.

But I just pointed to the upcoming off-ramp. "We get off here and take a right at the light."

16

GRIM

She insisted on going in. Inside the restaurant.

The eye-searingly bright and blasphemously well-lit *McDonald's* restaurant.

And "insisted" as in the moment I parked, she said, "Thank God, I'm starving," got out of The Judge, shut the door behind her, and, without a backward glance, walked toward the garish, french fry–scented electric bonfire of glowing yellow and red.

I gritted my teeth, mentally berating myself for letting her talk me into bringing her here when I really should have taken her home. Except she'd made a point.

If Cedric could find her at the library, he could find her in her apartment. I had no doubt he already knew where she lived. Maybe he was even there now, waiting for her.

Unless he'd followed us . . .

Muttering a curse under my breath, I got out of the car, slamming the door shut behind me.

"Wait," I called to her from across the parking lot as she grabbed the door handle.

Helena turned to me, arching a questioning brow as, still garbed in my sweeping black robes, I cut across the asphalt to the sidewalk.

Taking my human form contained my soul, so its smoky essence no longer tailed me or wafted around my frame. Assuming my human form brought complications, too.

Maybe, if I was lucky, this pit stop would be a quick one.

Though I admittedly didn't know where to go from here. Where to take her . . .

"A-are you hungry?" she asked when I stopped beside her. She tried to open the door, but I shoved—and held—it shut, peering in through the window, searching for any evidence of Cedric or his wizard's work.

Most of the booths and tables sat empty. The place had just a couple of diners—a beefy guy in a ball cap chowing down on a burger and an elderly couple eating soft serve. Quiet pop music played muffled through the glass.

No sign of Cedric. But that didn't mean he wasn't lurking about.

Maybe I shouldn't have hacked his soul off like that when he'd come snooping around the library. Just something about his wanting to get into that elevator, confirm Helena's death, had . . . triggered me.

Apparently into a murderous rage.

Maybe I was cracking up. Finally cracking up.

I'd been at this game long enough . . .

I couldn't deny, though, how that event—scything Cedric—and my knee-jerk need to retaliate had led to tonight's debacle. Which I still couldn't be sure was over.

"I can get you something," Helena said as I opened the door for her, surveying the parking lot next. "Goodness knows it's the least I can do."

I peered back down to her. What was she saying to me now? Half of what came out of her mouth struck me as absurd. Not so much the things she said, but more so that she said them . . . to me.

"You know," she elaborated, "for saving me? That's three times now. I'd say you deserve a treat for that."

She slipped into the restaurant while I gave the parking lot one final sweep before backing in after her.

Blinking against the glaring fluorescents that seared my retinas, burned my brain, and scorched my nocturnal, light-averse, subterranean-dwelling soul, I followed on her heels as she made a beeline for the counter, behind which stood a kid, his curly hair cinched under the band of his visor.

"Cool costumes," said the teen as he assessed us. "Bryce," his name tag read.

"Oh, I'm not—" Helena caught herself. She gave my black-clad form a once-over and then cleared her throat. "I mean, thanks." She issued the tiniest of curtsies before aiming a thumb at me. "He's the Grim Reaper, and I'm a children's librarian."

Helena gave a nervous, high-pitched titter, sharing the inside joke with herself alone.

Bryce nodded appreciatively. "Talk about the ultimate power couple."

Power couple?

I shot him a glare, and he gulped.

"Yeah, so, wh-what can I get you?" he asked, retraining his focus on his computer screen.

Helena sized me up with an admonishing frown, then turned to Bryce—whose hand shook as it hovered over the touchscreen.

"Chicken nugget Happy Mean—I mean Meal," Helena said. "Meal, not Mean. *Happy* Meal. Not Mean Meal." She popped her pumpkin-shaped purse onto the counter. "With a chocolate milkshake. And . . ." She gestured to me. "Whatever my . . . date wants."

I glowered down at her while Bryce arched both brows at me.

Like he was silently asking himself—*and* me—how I'd gotten to be such a lucky bastard.

But she was just trying to make us seem more natural. Like I'd done with the cop.

Also, did she seriously just order herself a kid's meal? And just a second ago, was that a Freudian slip? Did she really think I was mean?

I wasn't being mean to the kid. Then again, maybe I could be nicer.

But if we were supposed to be on a date—fake or otherwise—why the hell was she digging in her purse?

"Small coffee," I told the kid. "Black."

"That's not a treat," muttered Helena, sounding disappointed as, with trembling fingers, she unearthed her wallet.

My scowl, which I kept aimed at Helena, deepened as I extracted my billfold and then a twenty, which I handed to Bryce before Helena could wrestle free a ten.

"Keep the change," I told the kid as he rang in the cash.

"Seriously?" asked Bryce, brightening.

I shifted my glare to him, and he ducked his head, eyes vanishing behind the visor of his hat, his smile falling as he worked to break the bill.

"*Very* seriously," he murmured under his breath.

And here it was—one of the too-numerous-to-count reasons I never took my human form. I didn't fit in. I couldn't. And trying always made everyone, including me, uncomfortable as fuck.

"Thank you," Helena whispered my way as she slid down to where another staff member deposited an honest-to-God plastic jack-o'-lantern bucket and the paper cup with her milkshake. My coffee followed. "You didn't have to do that. I would have bought your coffee, but sidenote, that twenty you gave him totally looked like it came from the nineties."

Because it probably did since that was likely the last time I'd taken this form and, consequently, needed cash for anything.

"Does that mean you come from old money?" she asked, then laughed up at me, her smile—unexpected as it came—shattering something within me.

I looked away because, deprived of the obscuring sanctity of my hood, I couldn't just stand there staring at that smile like I had when she'd flashed it my way the first time. The last time . . .

We'd been on that balcony then—the site of her demise. The death that had never occurred because I hadn't let it. Because I'd *stopped* it.

That smile. It had done something to me then, and it was doing something to me now.

Except that wasn't supposed to happen. I certainly wasn't supposed to let it.

"S-sorry," Helena said before brushing past me, "I make jokes like that when I'm nervous. And . . . when I'm not. I'll . . . just grab us a table. Look, there's one that lights up."

Great. More lights. Just what I needed.

I grabbed my coffee and followed Helena to the long flat white table, which indeed displayed a grid of circular lights that changed colors and shifted patterns.

Because of course it did.

Helena, who'd slid into the booth, had already set up camp by extracting everything within the little plastic bucket, so I took the seat across from her, the one that gave me a clear view of the door we'd entered through.

I set my coffee down—dealing with the distracting light show in between monitoring the door behind her and the one behind me.

Sitting between two public entrances at a light-up table in the middle of a fast-food restaurant?

Why don't I just send up a flare for Cedric while I'm at it?

"They respond to touch," said Helena, poking at the circular lights with one hand while, in the other, she held aloft a golden, roughly boot-shaped chicken nugget. "That's too neat. I wonder who makes these. This would be so much fun in the activity area of the children's department."

"You're *not* okay," I said. "Are you."

"No," she said, a tear falling out of nowhere, "I'm not. But . . . that's okay."

She crunched into the nugget and chewed while tapping the table, the lights of which flashed yellow.

Everything I'd put her through—it *wasn't* okay. Nothing about this situation—our situation—was. A long beat elapsed in which I tried to figure out what to say—where to begin with how we'd gotten here. Did I even know myself?

Helena stole a sip of her milkshake and resumed poking at the table, her touch shifting the yellow lights to blue. "It's just that . . . I don't really want to die."

No one ever does.

"But I'm starting to think I'm going to anyway."

I come for everyone eventually.

"But I'm confused, too."

You're not the only one.

"Because you're supposed to reap souls."

I'm supposed to.

"Not save lives. And yet . . . you keep saving mine. *Why?*"

She wiped away that lone tear with the cuff of the sleeve of her jack-o'-lantern sweatshirt, then she popped the rest of the half-eaten nugget into her mouth and chewed.

I shifted, sitting back in the booth, glaring at the coffee.

Owning up to this being all my fault wasn't the most comfortable place to start, but all things considered, it was probably as good a place as any.

"I fucked up," I told her after a beat.

"With my life," she said after swallowing.

"With your death," I corrected.

Those eyes flashed up to me again, terrified—and tired. An odd and haunted hollowness emanated from them. She'd been through so much. And not just tonight. I'd brought it all down upon her. She'd asked me why, but even I wasn't sure.

"You were there to get me that night," she guessed. "At the party. Is . . . that what happened?"

"Normally people don't see me," I said. "You did, though. And that . . . complicated things."

"You're saying this is all *my* fault?" she asked, aiming a fry at herself.

I scowled at her. Because where had she gotten *that*? "Of course it's not your fault. I *just* told you I fucked up."

"By saving me." She popped the fry into her mouth.

"Yes."

Helena's scowl deepened to a glower as she chewed. Then she aimed another fry at me. "You are not good at answering questions, are you?"

"I'm not used to needing to."

She threw up her hands like I'd just proved her point. And . . . perhaps I had.

I never talked to anyone. I tried not to. I was better off keeping my own counsel. That way, I never got fucked. Until that plan backfired and, apparently, I did.

"Look," I said, because maybe it was best to just lay it all out. "I was supposed to collect your soul. I didn't. So I came up short with my delivery."

"Delivery," she repeated in a deadpan voice.

"Somebody important noticed there was a soul missing," I said. "They don't know it was yours. Not yet at least. But just because your arrival was delayed, that doesn't stop fate."

"Hold it right there," she said, flashing a palm. "You said 'arrival.' Arrival *where* exactly?"

"I don't know."

"You don't *know*?" she asked, her chin jutting forward, her tone incredulous. "You're the Grim Reaper! How do you not know where my soul's supposed to go?"

I sent a paranoid glance around the dining area. The beefy guy had left, but the elderly couple gave us frightened looks.

"Above my pay grade," I snarled through gritted teeth.

"Unreal," she said, grabbing her milkshake and thudding back in her seat, her stare going glassy as she trained it on the table, the lights of which flashed red. "'Fate,' you said. Meaning I'm doomed. Is that what happened today, though? The balcony and the elevator, yeah. But today didn't feel like 'fate.'"

"There are some . . . office politics at play," I said, which earned me a bug-eyed stare, but that was the only way I knew how to put it.

"Politics," she echoed. "At the *office*. Meaning the Grim Reaper has . . . an office. Does that mean that's a company car out there?" She aimed a thumb toward the parking lot.

"The Judge is mine," I informed her.

"You named your car?"

"That's the model," I corrected. "1969 Pontiac GTO Judge, Starlight Black. Limited production and that one's in survivor condition. Unrestored with factory paint, interior, and components still intact. Rare and collectible."

"You named your car," she concluded.

"Tell me you didn't name yours," I shot back.

"*I'm* not death personified!"

I clenched my jaw, holding my silence.

"Back to these 'office politics,'" she said. "*Please* tell me corporate gives you guys Tombstone pizza parties."

Now I leveled her with a baleful glare.

"Is there a customer service department?" she asked. "I have some feedback. Then again, maybe I should just go straight to Yelp." She waved her milkshake in the air between us. "'Doom can be hard, but these guys make it harder.'"

"That man who attacked you is named Cedric," I said. "He hates me, and the feeling is mutual. He also wants my job."

"Let me guess. The benefits are to die for."

"Is *everything* a joke to you?" I snipped.

"Why?" she asked, slamming her shake down. "Should I panic instead?"

"You haven't yet," I said, my tone quiet, calm, because I hadn't realized until now that she'd been using humor to cope. To deal with the sand in the hourglass that she'd already guessed was, for her, quickly running out. Though I guess it could be said she was borrowing time now. We both were.

Did she deserve to know why? Yeah.

Did I want to tell her? Fuck no.

"Why did you save me, Grim?" she asked.

"Because Cedric was trying to collect your soul, and if he does—"

"The first time," she said, cutting me off.

I went silent, snapping my mouth shut, my jaw hardening—ticking. "I don't know."

Those eyes, green as sunlit summer grass, flicked up to me. "You were going to take me home just now. Does that mean fate is *not* coming for me tonight?"

"I . . . don't know," I repeated before hurrying to add, "but I'll feel it if it does."

Like that was supposed to comfort her. But then . . . why did I want it to?

"Did you feel *it* tonight?" she asked.

"No," I admitted. "That's why I was . . . late. Cedric was trying to murder you so he could hand deliver your soul himself. Something that would implicate me and . . . get me fired."

"Sooo," Helena ventured, her words inflecting down, "you've been saving me to keep from getting fired."

"Essentially," I admitted, my eyes cutting away, toward the street and the switching stoplights, the lazy traffic that eased by. "Yes."

"I see."

I scowled at this response, that rush of guilt that had assailed me in the alley returning to flog me again.

"When fate *is* . . . activated and you do feel it," she said, "then what? You'll just come save me again?"

"Depends."

"Depends," she echoed, the softest catch in her voice. "On what exactly?"

I didn't get a chance to answer her.

Because just then, Cedric walked in.

17

GRIM

"*Get down*," I ordered, sliding out of the booth and rising, summoning my scythe to my grip in the same motion. When I glanced back at the table, I found Helena already hunkered beneath it, one hand scrounging for her jack-o'-lantern bucket, which she snagged and dragged after her.

I didn't have time to question why. Not with Cedric conjuring a vortex of green magic into one palm.

He blasted the sizzling energy my way, but I deflected the hex easily—too easily—with a spin of my scythe while the elderly couple, ducking and huddling together, hurried out the door behind the wizard.

Bryce bolted into the back, his visor toppling off.

Which thankfully left me with only one human to protect.

Except . . . where did she go?

Behind me, Helena yelped, and I whirled.

Cedric stood before the other door, too, the one Helena had tried to slip out without either of us noticing, the pumpkin bucket dangling from one fist.

"You didn't tell me he had a twin!" Helena snapped, abandoning her plan to escape on her own to scuttle my way again, putting her back to mine as we squared off with the doppelgangers.

"One is fake," I said. "Or possibly both. He's a wizard."

"Wizards aren't real!" she squealed.

Because this, apparently, was the one moment out of the night that triggered her skepticism.

"Happy Halloween, Grim," said the first Cedric, that smug glare leveled at me.

"More parlor tricks?" I growled.

"Parlor tricks?" mused Cedric One with a tilt of that haughty blond head.

"Come now," added Cedric Two, "I paid a hefty price for this magic."

"Stopped just shy of bartering off my soul," added Cedric One.

"So we'll thank you to at least *pretend* to be impressed," the twins said in unison.

"Well, you know what they say," I snarled back. "You get what you pay for."

One of them scoffed. The other rolled his eyes.

"How many rules have you broken now, Grim?" asked Cedric One. "It's got to be at least twenty."

"You might have bent a few yourself." My gaze bounced from one Cedric to the other and back again. I could attack and was probably going to have to, but I *had* to choose correctly. If one of these *was* the real Cedric and I went after the decoy, that could grant the true Cedric the in he needed to kill Helena right here and now. I could attack both simultaneously, but that might be what he wanted. To distract from a possible third incarnation that I couldn't see. "You need to back off."

"Or what?" challenged Cedric Two. "You going to tattle to White? I think we're both past the point of snitching without recourse. Which levels the playing field. And the two of us—we've been overdue for a showdown, wouldn't you agree?"

"You big bully!" Helena shouted at Cedric Two. "It's your fault my car got smashed. And I *almost* had it paid off!"

Helena tossed her bucket at Cedric Two—who she managed to clock squarely in the face. With a cry of shock, he winced and braced a gloved hand on his forehead, a reaction that identified him as the genuine article.

Which was all I needed.

Shoving Helena behind me, I stormed toward Cedric—the real one. Fear flashed in the wizard's winter gaze as I swept my now-glowing scythe downward, missing him by inches when he managed to backpedal out of my weapon's reach. He split as he did, more versions of himself peeling off to either side, like a deck of cards spilling.

"Coward!" I bellowed as he darted into the crowd he'd created.

"Sticks and stones may break my bones," chanted the small but growing mob, their words creating an eerie drone, "but . . . you still can't kill me."

That was true. But it also wasn't. I took a swipe at the wall of figures, my blade dispersing them into green mist as it sailed through. A glance over my shoulder showed Helena swinging at the doubles with her pumpkin-shaped purse.

"How about some whack-a-wizard?" Helena shouted, huffing between swings while, in the distance, sirens wailed.

I had to get Helena out of here, and there was no way I could take her home now. But then, where else was there?

Only one other place I could think of. The last place she *should* go.

"Let her go," I commanded the rows of Cedrics before me. "We both know this is between you and me."

"Are you saying you want to negotiate?" asked one of the Cedrics. "You have something I want. And now . . . Well, could it be I have something *you* want? The lady . . . exactly how much is she worth to you, Grim? From what I gather, our bargain could see her free of *her* situation, too, could it not?"

"What's he talking about?" asked Helena.

My rage boiled hotter that Cedric would take this angle. Get

Helena's hopes up *while* insulting my intelligence. "Like I'd ever trust you to hold up your side of any bargain."

"Snuff her out," another Cedric said as he held out one gloved hand as though to weigh the option. "Pay you off by buying her life," he droned while he held out the other. "Either way, I get what *I* want."

"Helena doesn't have anything to do with this."

"Mm, she has a name," said a Cedric to my left an instant before I turned to slice the mirage to nothing.

"Names make things personal, don't they?" taunted another double from behind me, which had me swinging that way next, cutting upward with the blade this time, rending another Cedric to green mist.

"That's why you hate names," jeered another Cedric, "isn't it?"

"What does he mean I could be set free?" Helena asked even as she kept swinging her purse at the Cedrics. Though this time, a gloved hand shot out to catch it.

"Let go, you platinum brat!" she yelled, tugging.

"*Helena!*" I shouted—but my warning for her to release her hold on the purse came too late.

Cedric—the corporeal one—yanked Helena toward him, straight into his grip. Again, she cried out as the wizard ripped her purse from her before flinging it aside. Whirling her around, he pulled her against him. After drawing a dagger, he held the blade to her throat.

I glared hard into her terrified stare, the guts I wasn't used to having twisting with the familiar sensation of rage, and the less familiar but just as potent emotion . . . of fear.

For her.

"I know what you hate more than names, though," Cedric goaded. "*Mirrors.*"

This last word he whispered into Helena's ear as, one by one, his doubles shifted shape, each morphing into someone else entirely.

Into identical versions . . . of me.

18

HELENA

Grim's expression, so hard and impervious before now, faltered under the scrutiny of his own repeated glare.

Hadn't I also experienced the trepidation that gaze instilled?

Even poor Bryce had almost imploded under that terrifying stare.

Apparently (and paradoxically), Grim himself wasn't immune to its effects.

While I yanked at the arm that imprisoned me—an arm belonging to a bona fide *wizard*—Grim peered from left to right and back again as the crowd of imitators closed in, their glowers bearing down on him from all sides, something about their stares putting an unmistakable crack in his previously impenetrable demeanor.

That collage of unblinking gazes drove his to the floor, as if they radiated some truth—some condemnation—he couldn't face.

I didn't know how to help him. I didn't know how to help *me*.

"Do you have *any* idea how long it takes to extract oneself from a body bag and *then* a morgue drawer?" asked Cedric. "My powers took *just* long enough to start recirculating with my blood that I almost asphyxiated first."

"Tell me you saved the toe tag," snarled Grim as he gripped his scythe between both hands. "Suddenly, I have the urge to start a collection with your name on it."

I blinked at this because, for someone who'd judged me for joking my way through a life-and-death situation, he certainly seemed to possess the talent himself.

"You think you're funny," said one of Grim's doubles, mimicking his low and smoky voice.

"And you are," grunted another, "but not the way you think."

"What are you doing?" I asked, yanking again at Cedric's unyielding arm.

"Torture, of course," muttered that sly voice, a grin implied in his tone.

"You fucked up," said another of Grim's doubles. "Again."

"But you keep fighting the consequences," said another, their verbal onslaughts piling on faster now.

"Your deficits will catch up to you soon, though," said another.

"You descend on everyone eventually," said another.

"Why would it be any different when it comes to you?" challenged yet another.

"And then."

"Everything."

"Will."

"Fade."

"To."

"Black."

"*Enough!*" roared Grim as he sliced through one group of doubles, dispersing them before turning his scythe—and fury—on another. All while Cedric laughed softly in my ear.

Despite Grim's efforts, the green smoke regathered, *more* doubles taking shape and splitting off from one another, their black-clad forms cramming the emptied restaurant.

Above us, the lights flickered while, outside, the wailing sirens screamed nearer—close to closing in on us.

"*Phineas*," hissed one of the doubles before the same name fell hushed from the lips of another—and then another.

Grim flinched, his distress growing as the room filled with whispers, enough that the name itself became lost—indiscernible in the rushing and unrelenting hush of sibilant syllables.

"Stop it!" I demanded, wrenching in Cedric's grasp again, trying to get to Grim, who, grimacing, braced his free hand on his brow, eyes screwing shut like the voices had invaded his head now. "Why is this hurting him? Who or what is Phineas?"

"Must admit I haven't the slightest," said Cedric, whose grip loosened by a fraction, the blade of his dagger no longer threatening to break skin. "My minions are mirror chimeras, capable only of reflecting what they're fed by the subject they're instructed to torment. I've . . . never seen him like this."

Torment. Torture.

Though I'd been Cedric's target earlier, everything he'd done since entering had been enacted with the aim of hurting Grim. Including, I now suspected, threatening me.

Maybe I couldn't save Grim like he'd saved me. Maybe I had no more power to stop a wizard than I did death. But I could, if I was lucky, bring the reaper back to himself and remind him . . . of how *he* could.

"Grim!" I called, and as if my voice had somehow broken through all the others, he opened his eyes, head snapping my way.

His gaze locked with mine as I bore down on the wizard's immovable arm, fingernails digging into the fabric of his sleeve. "I think Cedric could *really* use a seat belt."

The barrage of whispers ceased. Grim's expression changed, the heat of his anger giving way to a much colder—and more frightening—rage as the fumes that had wafted about him returned. The wisps swelled to sweep his hood up and over his head, securing his face once more behind the darkest mask of black shadow—but not before I caught a glimpse of the transformation that, in one fell swoop, overtook him.

Just as his eyes vanished into darkness, the flesh of his jaw and chin evaporated to reveal a skeleton's grin. In that split second, I had my answer to what he looked like in *this* form—even if I'd already assumed.

"*Shit*," said Cedric.

After that, everything happened too fast to track. A legion of hissing vaporous vines shot forward like striking vipers.

A sickening snap of bone—loud in the ear Cedric had whispered into—froze the blood in my veins.

The wizard's grip on me fell limp. His dagger went crashing to the floor—followed by his body.

Then those dark smoke tentacles had ahold of *me*. Cold but also dry, like the breath of a ghost, they wrapped my wrists, my arms, my waist, giving me no choice but to surrender as they drew me to him.

As sirens howled in the parking lot, red and blue lights flashing through the big windows, Grim swept me up in bony arms while those tendrils loosened their grips to gather and, as one, dive into my chest.

His invasion didn't hurt. On the contrary, the sensation that filled my rib cage could have been likened to drinking fresh water on a blistering summer's day.

I . . . liked it.

I liked him, too, and even as a strange drowsiness stole over me, I still found strength to loop my arms around his shoulders, literally holding on to him for dear life. Or so I figured . . .

"Is this it?" I murmured, overcome enough by the sudden onslaught of lethargy to rest my head on his shoulder. "Are you taking me now?"

"I'm not your fate," he said in that dark voice that hummed through me, igniting a flare of heat, that odd desire he'd stoked in me before. Though, perhaps not so odd?

His words invoked a rueful ache in my spirit, too—one that echoed on as I faded out, compelled into oblivion by his cold caressing of my soul.

He'd said he wasn't my fate.

But those words did nothing to stop the strange longing that, in a different world, another time, another life . . . he could have been.

19

GRIM

At this point, I could stop pretending that a way to unfuck myself was going to magically appear. Which was why I took Helena home.

To *my* home.

"Crivvens!" cried Flora when I entered the Basins from the hall, her voice echoing in the cavernous chamber. "What in the name of the wee hours of Allhallowmas do you think you're doing, Grim?"

"Grim's home," said Pluto, who once again rested on his perch. "He caught a bird."

I didn't reply. I just moved in silence toward my statue, carrying Helena's slumbering form to the only place in this realm or any other that I knew for certain Cedric, once he again reanimated, could not get to.

"Are you off your ever-lovin' bone head?" Flora yelled, and the quick scamper of bare feet forewarned me of her sudden appearance in my path.

"Pretty bird!" announced Pluto with a flap of his great wings, his voice, like Flora's, echoing in the enormous chamber.

"Who is that?" the fairy demanded, arms spread wide, like that could really stop me—like she could. "And what in the dancing devils is she doing *here*?"

I had my back to Johann. He'd looked up from his scribbling when I'd come in, and his face had hardened with concern. And possibly condemnation. He hadn't said anything, though. Yet.

"Move," I told Flora.

"Like hell, you crabbit," she snapped, crossing her arms. "Is *this* what the row with Cedric is about? A lass?"

"Cedric's dead," I said. "I killed him."

"Deadric Cedric," said Pluto. "Lost his headric."

"Again?" cried Flora, throwing her arms up and letting them flop to her sides in exasperation. "Oy, I can't believe this! Where'd you put his soul *this* time?"

"His scar will cry," added Pluto, "though no one knows why."

"Left it. Now kindly move the fuck out of my way before he comes back."

In the restaurant, I hadn't had time to mess with Cedric's soul. Not with the police surrounding the place—Helena couldn't be seen. Neither could I.

Aside from that, I'd just wanted to get out of there. I'd wanted to get *her* out of there.

Flora blinked in shock. She tilted her head at me, miffed, perplexed, and still, I could tell, horrified over Helena's presence here.

Humans—living humans—weren't allowed in the Hallowed Halls. No one was, aside from us. And, of course, The Few.

I seldom cursed directly at Flora, either. In her vicinity? Yes. At her . . . Rarely.

But I needed her to not interfere with me. Not tonight.

"Grim, are you daft—?" Flora started, but much to my surprise, Johann interrupted.

"Let him pass, Flora," said the old man.

"If it's all the same to you, Johann, I'd like answers out of him fir—"

"I said, let him pass."

Flora frowned and peered up at me. Then she quirked a brow. "She's the soul, isn't she?"

I didn't respond. I didn't have to. The answer was obvious. Flora was just digging, trying to find out what had driven me to this desperate move. She and Johann knew me better than anyone—and as well as anyone could. Both understood I wasn't the desperate sort.

Yet here I was. Nailing my own coffin shut and inviting them to a front-row viewing of my soon-to-be-flaming pyre.

"Flora," grunted Johann, an uncharacteristic note of warning in his weathered voice.

Finally, with a scowl, Flora made peace with the fact that she wasn't going to get anything out of me, and doing as Johann instructed, she stepped aside.

Johann wasn't exactly the "boss" of the Hallowed Halls—we didn't have one of those. But out of the four of us, he presented as the oldest. He *was* the wisest. And the authority his perceived seniority instilled in him was one we all respected—and heeded.

Most of the time at least.

I hadn't lately. I'd betrayed his trust, too. Flora's as well. So maybe the only reason Johann wasn't giving me shit about this forbidden act was because he'd already given up on me. Knew my time was limited now, just as Cedric had said.

Maybe he even *wanted* Cedric to take my place.

I didn't blame Johann for that stance. Couldn't.

Didn't mean his indifference didn't sting.

I carried Helena to my statue, into the designated hand of which I called forth my scythe. The weapon materialized out of the ether, triggering the mechanisms that revealed the descending spiral staircase to my underground quarters.

"I found out the way," Flora called to me—words that had me pausing halfway down the secret passage and glancing back to her.

By "the way" she must mean she'd done what I'd requested and found an alternate route into the realm of the White Basin—one that bypassed the Basin itself.

"I appreciate your efforts," I told her, "but . . . it's too late now. I'll talk to White myself when he comes."

"Too late?" said Flora, her small shoulders dropping, voice sinking with an unexpected sadness. "Because of that dunderhead Cedric?"

"Flora," called Johann. "Leave Grim to his business and come here. I wish to speak to you."

Flora opened her mouth to say something back to Johann, but then, thinking better of it, she snapped her teeth shut and started reluctantly away.

Then, with Helena cradled in my dead arms, I descended the corkscrew stairs into the pure and all-encompassing blackness of my abode.

20

HELENA

It was the silence that woke me.

Absolute and enveloping, it swelled around me, devoid of even the faintest ticking of a clock, hum of a fridge, murmur of wind, or rush of rain.

I opened my eyes slowly, disturbed even more by the absence of the background noises that usually swirled around my apartment complex—the swishing of traffic, the occasional blare of a horn or the moan of a siren, the trundling of a train . . .

"*Mmph.*" The murmur escaped me as I batted tired lids, eyes met with a blaze of crimson, cheek cushioned by plush softness.

But . . . I certainly didn't own any velvet upholstered furniture. And even if I had, it wouldn't have been the bright and unmistakable hue of fresh blood.

Slowly, the soreness in my limbs waking up right along with me, I pushed myself up from the huge Gothic-style couch someone had laid me on. Straight across from me, my pumpkin purse (looking rather worse for wear given that I'd used it as a weapon) sat in the center of a black and low-to-the-floor coffee table.

Where was I?

As I peered groggily around the huge room, I fought the impulse to assume.

My surroundings didn't seem to fit the description of either heaven *or* hell, and if I wasn't dead, that only left one place.

"Holy haunted bachelor pad," I murmured, taking in the high, dark wood ceiling and the gallery balcony that chased the second floor of the square Gothic chamber, its railing made of black metal scrollwork.

A candlelit chandelier hovered overhead while matching sconces threw shadows across the crimson wallpaper and gleaming wood paneling. Small lamps sat atop end tables, adding more low light to the red-themed room that could have belonged to a vampire's castle, or some huge manor house designed expressly for the use of some dark-agenda secret society.

Twisting, I peered behind the couch to find a desk laden with books and papers and decorated only with a Jack Skellington snow globe that sat on one corner.

Behind the desk hung an enormous, vertical, and silver-framed painting of a full silver moon suspended over dark ocean waters.

Three of the room's four corners hosted a slim and open archway, each leading into a hall. A small metal spiral staircase occupied the fourth, more decorative metal scrollwork corkscrewing up to the matching balcony above.

Shadows and low light fought for dominance while that scent—his—lingered everywhere.

One thing this place lacked entirely, though, was windows.

I swung my bare feet off the couch and wiggled my sparkly toes, newly painted in "Pumpkin Patch" orange, against the plush oriental carpet. Someone had removed my shoes. They sat on the floor, half tucked under the coffee table where I'd be sure to find them. I reached to gather my purse and search for my phone, but I halted, my hand diverting to the note pinned beneath the bag.

Neat, tight, and black cursive handwriting adorned the plain white stationery that sported neither header nor monogram, just a slim black border.

Had to go to work. I'll be back.

You're safe here.

Grim

Except where was *here*?

"Well, it's a good thing I have today off," I murmured to myself as I dug through my purse, already aware I wouldn't find my phone since I'd dropped it outside the library.

Had someone found it? God, did everyone think I'd had a breakdown before running off with the bookmobile?

There wasn't any way to know *what* had happened since the incident at the library, or even what time it was.

I was stuck here. And apparently at the mercy of the Grim Reaper himself.

But then, that part at least had been true well before now.

Should I be freaking out? I probably *should* be.

But . . . I still wasn't afraid of him. Well, not completely.

He'd only protected me so far. Even if that *was* just because of his job.

I frowned, my heart sinking all over again. Could be, when he came back, he'd talk me through the process of having my soul forcibly severed. And what came after. Whatever any of that looked like . . .

Maybe I had to sign something . . .

God, I wasn't making any sense.

Blinking several times, I tried to rid myself of the lethargy that made my mind extra foggy. Dizziness had me rethinking trying to rise yet.

Then, the final moments before I'd passed out came rushing back to me, prompting me to press fingers to my sternum.

Grim had . . . done something to me, reached into me with that dark essence, touched and wound his smoky wisps around some inner part of me.

Those constricting tendrils had since fled, but a small . . . twinge of sorts remained. Not painful so much as it was regretful, the soreness more emotional than physical. Almost like I'd needed that squeezing of my spirit, that soul-deep touch that had stirred and sung to me an instant before sending me into oblivion.

As if, with that intrusion, he'd . . . *fixed* something I hadn't known was broken, and now whatever that something was longed to be fixed, adjusted . . . again.

21
GRIM

This whole situation kept getting worse and worse. Worse still? I kept doing shit I shouldn't fucking do.

I glared hard through the motes and flotsam as I drifted deep in midnight waters half a world away from where Helena waited for my return, the glow of the souls in my hourglass, clipped to my belt, haloing me in murky, parti-colored light.

What was she doing right now? Cursing me, most likely . . .

While I didn't like to think I'd made her my prisoner, there was no denying that detaining her—a delicate way of putting it—was exactly what I was doing.

Was she awake yet? She had to be pissed. More pissed.

She had a right to be.

I hadn't exactly asked her if she wanted to come to the Netherworld and crash on my couch. Nor had I stuck around to explain myself.

A note hardly counted.

Guilt tore through me—though it warred with the conflicting peace of mind that came with knowing that, at the very least, Helena was out of Cedric's reach.

No measure of magic would allow him entry into my corner

of the Hallowed Halls. And no measure of ingenuity would allow Helena out, either, since the door moved only for me.

While the four luminous souls of those who had lost their lives during that morning's storm floated above the wreckage of a sunken fishing boat, I surveyed the scattered debris.

In the hours that had passed since the squall, the sea had calmed, and the deep had mostly cleared—not that either storm or lack of visibility would have impeded me or my work if I'd made it here earlier, at the time of death.

My intervention on Helena's behalf had set my schedule back by several hours—and several souls—however.

Though it could be argued I no longer needed to care half so much about the call of the deceased since I would soon have my title, powers, *and* soul stripped from me . . . I still did. The dead did not stop dying without me, and these waters presented a cold and lonely purgatory.

Aside from that, the necessity of carrying on with my duties gave me the excuse I'd desperately needed to leave Helena's presence.

After making contact with her soul, brushing my darkness against her light, wrapping her warmth with my frigidity and getting singed like that—like I'd dared to touch the fucking sun—I needed distance.

My goal had been to shift her spirit off its axis by the tiniest degree. So long as I had her soul in my grip, I could physically transport her out of her world and into mine without her presence being detected by one—or all—of The Few. And a slight loosening of her essence was enough to do the trick without unbinding it from her body.

If altering the fate of a soul was forbidden, an even more egregious crime was to tamper with one directly. Killing Cedric—twice now—almost didn't count because he had no fate waiting in the hereafter. At least none that he hadn't subverted through his own hubris and hunger for immortality.

Meddling with Helena's soul, however, had produced a few unexpected . . . side effects.

For me.

I drifted forward through the water, drawn by the glow of the souls.

With my free hand, I took hold of the first, and like plucking an apple from a tree, I freed it from its invisible tether.

If left to their own devices for too long, souls separated themselves from their vessels. Without my intervention—or Flora's—they would remain anchored to their earthly figures. Unless the souls jumped to new anchors—places, objects, and sometimes even people. If a spirit's desire to remain was strong enough, Flora and I would arrive to find empty vessels. Sometimes we could locate the renegade spirits, and sometimes they snuck through the cracks.

Either way, the living called those wayward spirits ghosts.

Some ghosts I came across would go with me. A few rare ones . . . would not.

Tonight's shipwrecked souls presented no challenge.

I let my scythe hang in the water while, with care, I secured the soul—a red one—in my hourglass. Then I descended to collect the next soul—pink in hue.

That soul would go into the White Basin—same as Helena's.

Helena's had been a rare yellow—the same bold shade as daffodils, those little flowers that so defiantly confronted the lingering breath of winter in those first days of spring.

I collected yellow souls perhaps once in a century—they were always Fated, and always, they went to White.

I'd not *seen* Helena's color so much as I'd felt it—perceived it—sensing it similarly to how one might taste brightness in food. Yellow might not have a taste, but pineapple did, and Helena's soul had felt like that, too—sweet in essence but also sharp enough at its core to sting.

I'd enjoyed that faint burn too much, and the resulting steam had not been expected, either.

While Helena's beauty had been something I'd noted nearly the moment I'd set eyes on her, I hadn't dwelled on it or even paid her appearance a second thought.

I encountered beautiful women every day, on the hour even, and I'd secured the souls of too many to count.

Helena hadn't been any different. Not until she'd spoken to me . . .

That fucking smile was why I was where I was now—why she was where she was.

In my house. On my couch. Safe but still doomed.

That night on the balcony, she hadn't seen my face. Didn't know that I looked like every man does when he's been dead for long enough. Yet she'd still expressed interest in me.

True, she hadn't realized I was an entity of literal death, but then, for all she'd known, I could have been anyone.

She'd still smiled at me.

Asked me out . . .

It hadn't helped, either, that everything she'd said had resonated—that, even if in her mind she'd been joking, so many of her words about who and what I was still rang true.

She had not seen me. But, at the same time, she also had . . .

I secured the final soul, but I lingered in the depths, my normally empty skull full of brine—and thoughts.

Of her.

And that was why I couldn't yet bring myself to return to her.

After laying her on the couch, I'd watched her sleep for far too long, my gaze tracing the curve of her cheek, dwelling on the shape of her lips before following the swell of her hip.

I was quite literally a monster, and my thoughts had no business trespassing on the reprehensible territory they now dared to venture into.

I'd taken an oath not to interfere—in any way—with the lives of the living.

Aside from that, my soul, which belonged entirely to my station and to the Hallowed Halls, certainly had no right to yearn for another taste of hers.

Hadn't I horrified the poor woman enough already?

Our relationship was strictly one of business—because it had to be.

I was not human and had not been for a very long time.

Therefore, I could no longer permit myself to take my human form in her presence—or even at all. Doing so only enticed me to behave like a human—to think like one.

Desire like one.

And neither Helena nor I needed the torment that would bring.

My priority must be to see her soul to safety, whatever that looked like.

And when I returned to my quarters after depositing today's souls in the Basins, I *would* do what I must. Because of the threat Cedric posed, I now had to. I would summon Sir White and confess to my list of crimes directly. I wasn't willing to risk the fate of Helena's soul any more than I already had. Aside from that, I'd likely fare better after admitting my guilt than waiting for Cedric to accuse me.

Most importantly of all, if I spoke one-on-one with Sir White, I would remove Cedric's motivation to kill Helena.

That could not save her—just like *I* could not save her.

But it would ensure Helena herself did not suffer any consequences. Any *more* consequences.

Helena would still die. That was out of my hands. In truth, that outcome had never truly been something I held any real capacity to change. I could still protect her spirit by fessing up and making it clear she had no hand in or influence upon my actions. Aside from that, I could implicate Cedric before he could incriminate me, which would disqualify him as my replacement. And hopefully get him booted from the Hallowed Halls as well.

Why, though, even with my own soul on the line, did facing one of The Few still feel easier than facing her again?

22

HELENA

Normally, I wouldn't stoop to snooping. In this situation, however, there'd been no stopping myself.

What *else* was I going to do after being abducted *Phantom of the Opera*–style and deposited into a special supernatural episode of *Cribs*?

Though I helped myself to a self-guided tour of the sprawling apartment—which spanned about twice the size of mine—I did resist the urge to open any drawers or peek into any cabinets, not that there were many.

Unsurprisingly, the bloodred-meets-ink-black *Addams Family* aesthetic continued throughout with more soaring, coffered ceilings, dark wood paneling, parquet floors, sconces, chandeliers, and refined antique furniture.

Overall, my expedition of the Grim Reaper's chambers yielded only a few new bits of information about him.

In addition to being partial to Gothic décor, he was, apparently, a musician.

Something we had in common. Though I'd only been playing the uke for a few years and mostly just strummed what I called "sunshine songs" for storytime.

In his music room (because why wouldn't he have one of those?), several electric guitars hung along one wall—including a deep purple one signed by Prince that I dared not touch.

Grim also owned a vintage stereo console and a large (not to mention impressive) collection of vinyl that stuffed the shelved walls. And these I *did* riffle through.

I shouldn't have been surprised to discover he had an eclectic taste in music, though I was. Perhaps because that (along with his possession of a lint roller covered—oddly—in glitter) made him seem, well, more human than . . . whatever he was.

This array of diverse genres and the general setup of the space bemused me, too, because I tried to picture him extracting the black discs from their sleeves, setting the needle in place with those bony hands, kicking back in the nearby armchair with a bourbon, and relaxing to the dulcet screams of the metal band Live Briefly and Fail while perusing the tracks on the back of a Tom Waits album.

But the spectrum of what he considered ear candy stretched even further than metal and Waitsian.

In addition to hundreds of titles and categories, I found Vivaldi, albums by a slew of metal bands, every Metallica album ever produced, Smashing Pumpkins, Radiohead, Billie Eilish, Tool, Depeche Mode, Evanescence, Muse, the Cure, and—as Hunter would have been delighted to see—My Chemical Romance, just to name a few.

Would Grim notice if I slipped in a Taylor Swift album?

Would I survive his wrath when he did?

I giggled—albeit nervously—at the image of him irritably yanking Taylor's *1989* (one of my favorites) off the shelf before engulfing it in hellfire.

And *why* did I find that image kind of . . . cute?

After exiting into the hall, which wrapped the exterior of the central balcony room I'd awakened in, I walked its perimeters again. This loop confirmed that Grim had no bedroom or bed. He did oddly, though thankfully, have a restroom.

Relishing the opportunity to freshen up, I washed my hands and face in the gorgeous black marble sink. I tried to tidy my hair, but without the help of a mirror, I couldn't be sure I accomplished much. He possessed just as many of those as he did windows, a detail that suggested Cedric had been right about Grim's aversion to them.

That aversion made little sense to me, because that face, the one I'd seen, certainly got *my* blood pumping. Maybe he merely found mirrors useless because he only managed to steam them up whenever he encountered one. Learning that was the case would not have shocked me half as much as his affinity for music.

Grim also possessed a scythe room—I wasn't sure what else to call it—and I tried not to be disconcerted upon entering the slim walkway flanked by two rows of differently styled scythes. The master of these implements had filed this array of tools in two lines, the handles clenched by skeletal-hand-shaped holders that extended from the walls. The blades faced away from the long stretch of polished wooden floor, making the trek to the door that waited at the end of the corridor—as red as everything else in this odd apartment—seem a touch less ominous.

I made my way past their ranks, drawn by that door whose knob took the shape of yet another skeletal hand—this one empty and open, a handshake waiting to happen.

When I gripped that frigid metal palm, it proved unyielding, refusing to twist one way or the other, or to lift or lower—yet there didn't seem to be a latch or a slot for a key. At least not on this side.

There had to be an answer to this riddle, though, and since this was the only door in a dwelling filled with unimpeded archways, I could only conclude this *was* the exit.

Exit to where?

As I glanced between the nearest scythe, held by a closed hand, and the open hand of the door, thoughts *did* occur to me. Interesting ones that asked if it might be worth it to try playing Pass the Pointy.

I gave the handle of the scythe closest to me a tentative touch, peering up at the massive black serrated blade fashioned into the shape of a raven's wing.

"Fancy," I whispered.

Maybe, since I now knew fate had it out for me, I shouldn't be playing with sharp objects. But then, if I was going to perish by way of toppling scythe, wouldn't I have fallen prey to one of the hundred I'd passed on my way to this one?

I grasped the handle and gently tugged. Then, with a yip of surprise, I rushed to brace the scythe with my other hand as the skeletal one snapped open, releasing the tool to me.

"Whoa, Nelly," I half muttered, half grunted, stumbling back a step as I marveled up at the beautiful—and lethal—blade, galled by how heavy the thing actually was. Seriously, this bad boy would take major muscles to hold upright, let alone wield with any precision.

Grim didn't have muscles—at least not in his Reaper Man form. He had, however, displayed impressive strength, both the physical and mental sort, in the face of danger.

He'd only faltered once that *I'd* witnessed, and that had been at the whispered name of Phineas.

I still didn't know who Phineas was. It wasn't my place to ask, and given Grim's response to the whispers from those mirror wraiths, there likely wasn't any wisdom to uttering the name in his presence at all. Not that I had the guts to dare. Despite the rescues and our interactions, and all I'd learned about him, there were still aspects of him that terrified me . . .

Apparently, not enough for me to be a good Helena, sit tight, wait for him, and not tinker with his important, highly dangerous, work-related stuff.

Carefully, moving slowly, I half shifted, half dragged the scythe over to the empty skeletal hand, which, with the same ferocity as the one that had released the weapon, clasped it.

The door popped open, and I jumped back as it swung wide, revealing a rectangle of the purest blackness I'd ever encountered.

"Holy smokes," I whispered, "it worked."

I gave myself a small and quiet round of applause for figuring out the trick, but then my trepidation returned.

While I wanted to leave, to explore, a small inner voice warned me to stay put, where Grim had said it was "safe."

But then strange voices filtered down to me. Muffled and echoed, they came from above—one male, one female, both heavily accented.

Their words came garbled—at least until I drifted to stand at the brink of the darkness.

"—certainly wasn't something I expected to happen this century," said the female voice, her Scottish accent thick, lilting, and musical. "A right turnup for the books."

"The good news is, we've done what we can for now," replied the man, and I placed his accent as German. "Perhaps when he returns and we tell him what we've done, we will get answers. It's entirely likely, though, that he'll confess nothing and insist on continuing with whatever plan he has devised in that bone head of his."

"Hardheaded Grim," lilted a third voice, also male. "Wouldn't want to be him."

"Always a damn lone wolf," grumbled the woman—the girl?

"Bound and determined to be an island unto himself," agreed the first male voice.

"If only we could talk to the lass."

By "lass," she had to mean me.

"Grim Grim found a pretty bird," sang the third voice.

Finding my courage, I extended a trembling hand into the darkness and sucked in a short sharp breath when my fingers encountered a stone wall. Then, growing braver still, I explored with my foot until I discovered the tread of a stone step.

"I admit, I'm curious as well," said the man with the German accent. "This turn of events is as unexpected as it is unprecedented. Especially when it comes to Grim."

"You're telling me!" exclaimed the girl, though they both fell quiet as I started to climb, their conversation interrupted by the low sliding of stone.

"Johann, look!" piped the girl as, above, a shaft of light ripped through the gloom, revealing the spiral stone staircase I now ascended. "I thought you said Grim left."

"He did," said the man. "You see his scythe is missing from the statue's grasp."

"Hello?" I called as I reached the top of the stairs, just before I poked my head into the enormous domed room that, at its center, hosted a little old man at a scribe's desk wearing a familiar McDonald's visor, an enormous and glorious raven perched on his shoulder. Next to him stood a barefooted, redhaired, and pointy-eared preteen in a fairy costume. An old-fashioned lantern sat at her feet, its panes lit with bright green light, which sparked and flared at my appearance. Though the lantern rocked and rattled, neither the girl nor the man nor the bird paid it any mind.

Instead, they gaped at me.

"Losh!" The girl put her hands on her hips. "You *are* a bonnie one, aren't ya?"

"Told you," said the bird as he ticked his head at me, revealing himself as the source of the third voice. "Grim Grim caught a pretty bird. Strangest thing we've ever heard."

"I'm . . . Helena," I said, which made the girl smirk.

"Welcome, Helena," said the man, his voice echoing faintly in the enormous chamber. "To the Hallowed Halls."

23

GRIM

A peal of laughter cleaved through the quiet as I stalked down the hall leading to the Basins, the high and light sound setting me on alert.

I unfurled, then re-formed in a swirl of black fog in the Basins chamber, my gaze at once finding the owner of that laugh—who was exactly the woman I suspected.

Helena.

Startled by my arrival, Pluto cawed and lifted off from his perch in a panicked flutter. He flew past Helena, who stood bold as daylight in the center of the room with Flora and Johann—the only one among the three who didn't lose his smile at my sudden appearance.

"Ah, Grim," said Johann, "we've been waiting on you."

Waiting . . . on me?

After circling the room once, Pluto rounded his way back to Johann before landing on his shoulder. "Grim's home. This time he's alone."

My gaze bounced between them while I tried to cobble together an answer for this assembly. How had Helena gotten out of my apartment? What were they all talking about together like this, as if they were having a fucking faculty meeting? And why was she just standing out here in the open? What if Cedric came back?

And Johann . . .

"Where did you get that hat?" I growled, pointing with a skeletal finger.

The visor he wore—I'd seen it yesterday. On Bryce's head.

"Flora brought it to me from Mickey D's," said Johann. He pointed to the hat's emblem. "One would think the yellow *M* would give it away. She also brought me a McFlurry."

"Had to make it meself," said Flora, "since there wasn't any staff about. You and Cedric did a right good job of clearing out the place."

Again, my gaze ricocheted between them, going from Johann, to Flora, to Helena, and then down to Flora's lantern, which flared bright green. It shuddered and shook, creating a racket against the marble floor, a clangor that echoed up through the dome and down again—until Flora gave the lantern a kick.

"Pipe down, you slippery radge," grumbled the fairy—an unusual response to her normally tender tenants. Whose soul did she hold in that lantern now? It wasn't a child's. Their souls were smaller, like lightning bugs.

"What is this?" I demanded, even though I already had an inkling. "What is going on?"

"Helena's come up with a plan," said Flora, hands going to her hips Peter Pan–style.

A plan? What kind of plan? For what?

"I think . . . it's a good plan," said Helena, her words shocking me. "If . . . I'm allowed to say so."

She wasn't angry. A moment ago, she'd even laughed.

That made no sense. *She* made no sense.

"How did you get out?" I asked her, glancing back toward the open passageway to my domain, my words coming out gruffer than I'd intended.

"I . . . figured out the lock," she said.

The lock? She must mean she'd moved one of my scythes, an action that had apparently triggered the door. I hadn't factored for that possibility. How could I have when, until now, I'd always been the only one capable of entering my quarters in the first place? *Or* handling my scythes.

Apparently, while others could not enter, they could exit.

Or was it possible that Helena was somehow . . . unique?

"Cedric is hunting her." I blurted this out to Johann. Perhaps I was appealing to him to help me—to help Helena.

Before, I'd been so sure I'd stoked his anger by acting on my impulses—and telling him off. Maybe he wasn't angry anymore. Maybe he'd never been. Sometimes, he was harder to read even than me. Whatever the case, I needed him to hear me on this. Flora, too.

Helena couldn't be anywhere near Cedric, who was bound to return at any moment.

Unless . . .

"Relax," Flora said before Johann could reply. "Pluto and I took a field trip to your McD's and picked up the meddling tyrant."

"We put the fries in the bag," said the bird.

Flora raised the lantern, which swung on its hinge, the green light within crackling as though with displeasure and, likely, rage, confirming my suspicions about the lantern's lone occupant. "Picked up a new chapeau for Johann while I was at it."

"So oft is he perfectly coiffed," added Pluto.

"The lady." Johann paused to gesture to Helena. "She emerged from your chambers less than an hour ago. But that was enough time for her to explain what I already suspected. That Cedric's behavior has become . . . ungentlemanly."

"Putting it mildly," said Helena through a snort, which she stifled the moment she regained my attention.

"It was Johann's idea to park him for a spell," said Flora as she plopped the lantern back down again—roughly. "When you said you killed Cedric and left him, Johann sent us to catch his soul before it could return to his body. Had to chase him around a bit, and he put up a fight for sure, but Pluto helped me get him wrangled. Managed the task just as they were zipping the body bag."

Flora had secured Cedric's soul? The fight at the restaurant must have weakened the wizard somehow. Or else Johann's bird was stronger than he seemed. Sometimes that bird made me wonder . . .

Whatever the case, I was glad her pursuit had kept Cedric too busy to rejoin his earthly form.

Which meant, at that moment, Cedric's corpse was probably right back in a morgue drawer. Possibly even the same morgue or even the same drawer. The authorities would want to assume their John Doe had an identical twin, but that would be hard to conclude with the original body now missing. From what I understood, Cedric also had a fair number of identifying scars, including that brutal one on his neck.

How many fires could I set and leave roaring until another of The Few showed up to take names and crack skulls? *My* skull.

"You'll be glad to know Lady Helena understands the finer details of her situation now," said Johann. "Flora and I took the liberty of elaborating on what a Fated Soul is. She mentioned how your conversation on the topic was . . . interrupted by our resident wizard."

"Resident bampot more like," added Flora under her breath.

Helena offered me a weak smile, but this did nothing to alleviate my growing confusion. *Or* anxiety.

"Johann and I guessed at what you must've been thinking when you brought the lass here," said Flora, her own expression sobering. "That you assumed you'd both fare best if you contacted Sir White directly now and owned up to this guddle before it got worse. But Helena thought it might be better to let the situation . . . play out. Without, of course, Cedric's meddling."

Flora gave the lantern another nudge with her toe, inciting the green orb within to once again flare and flash in agitation.

"In the meantime," said Johann, "Cedric can enjoy a much-needed . . . er . . . time-out here in the Hallows."

"You're going to keep him captive?" I asked.

"I think we'd better," said Johann. "You said yourself you didn't think it was a bad idea. Actually, to quote you directly, you said you didn't think it was a 'bad fucking idea,' and after learning more about the situation, I must say I've come to agree."

Flora's mouth dropped into an *O*, her eyes rounding as they flashed my way, her expression half scandalized, half delighted since Johann rarely cursed.

"So long as he has designs on hurting this charming young lady," said Johann, "what other choice has Cedric left us?"

Helena smiled at Johann, though her expression faltered when she again glanced to me, almost as if she assumed I had to be scowling within my hood, and that I was aiming my disapproval at her.

She must think I was agitated by this turn of events, and my friends' intervention. By her, too. Maybe I hadn't exactly given her a different impression.

"If White finds out," I argued, "if any of The Few find out—"

"No one's going to find out," said Johann. "And I'll tell you why."

I shook my head, because I didn't like where this was going. I was the one who'd broken the rules. In fact, I wasn't sure at this stage if there were many that I'd left *unbroken*. Johann and Flora had to understand I wasn't about to let them go down with me.

"This isn't—"

"Shut up, Grim," said Johann. And because it was Johann, and only because it was Johann . . . I did. It was Flora, though, who picked up on providing the explanation for the bizarre scenario I'd walked in on.

"We explained to your lass what you were trying to tell her—how she's fated to move on and go into the White Basin. She told us how you saved her on that balcony, something that put a wrench in our works here."

"Putting it mildly," mumbled Johann with a short and wry huff of a laugh, his words earning him a slight smile from Helena, who in my absence had apparently—though unsurprisingly—endeared herself to both my cohorts.

How could she still smile while we were all casually discussing her impending departure from this life?

"After finding out about Cedric's . . . incapacitation," Flora continued, "Helena thought it might be a good idea for her to return home and, well, let fate do its job."

"Not exactly a delicate way of putting things," I snapped at Flora, who blinked at me, taken aback. Then she scowled, her cheeks flushing red—never a good sign.

"Well, I'm not the coldhearted numpty who told her the only reason I was saving her was to keep my bony ass from getting sacked!"

"That *was* the only reason I was saving her!" I roared.

Like yelling it would make it true.

"You're a right fibber and a big ugly mood killer," she said, crossing her arms as she glared up at me. "And you've got zero game, Grim."

Helena giggled and my head snapped her way. Again, she stifled her mirth, mistaking my sudden attention—my utter shock at her reaction—for reproach. Was that because she still thought of me as mean?

I couldn't blame her. It wasn't like I had a face she could read.

Or maybe I *was* mean.

I hadn't meant to be. Not to her.

Taking a step toward me, Helena spoke up at last. "It's okay, Grim. What Flora, Johann, and I came up with was this. Basically, I go back home, return to life, and . . . well . . . wait for you."

My soul contracted, clenching into a tight iron ball of pain.

Wait for her death to occur was what she meant.

"Then," Helena continued, "you can take the hidden method Flora has found to infiltrate the realm of the White Basin, smuggling my soul in so that no one will know I was ever missing. When I'm accounted for and sent on my way, you can release Cedric."

Flora must have told her I'd asked about entering the White Basin covertly. Did she think of me as a coward?

Why did being banished to the Black Basin seem preferable to that?

"Cedric won't be able to do anything of consequence at that point," observed Johann as he stroked his beard. "Even if he went to tattle to Sir White, he wouldn't have any evidence, would he?"

This was a bad idea.

"C'mon," said Flora, as if she'd been able to read my thoughts. "This is a banger of an idea. And what's more, your hen's the one who thought it up."

Why did Flora keep doing that? Referring to Helena as "my" anything.

She was my guest. Our guest, technically. That was it.

"It makes sense," said Helena, who approached me. "And it gives me time, too. To . . . say goodbye. I mean, I know I'm not allowed to tell anyone I'm going to die. Johann explained how that will only make things harder on everyone when I am gone."

Gone?

That sharp contraction of my soul—it happened again.

I'd known Helena for less than a month, and I could hardly fathom a world without her.

She didn't know what she was talking about, either. She didn't understand. Once she got back home, there would be ramifications. She'd have to sit with the problem of her own mortality staring her in the face. Doom would lurk around every corner. Death *would* come to get her. And then so would I.

But then . . . how exactly was that different from before?

Cedric had been one thing. A force that could be stopped. A force *I* could stop.

He was not Helena's fate. No more than I was.

But I couldn't keep stopping elevators. The longer I kept intervening, too, the more likely Helena's demise was to be grisly—*grislier.* I couldn't stand for that.

Something had to be done.

If I summoned Sir White, owned up to my deeds, Helena wouldn't suffer. Or maybe, possibly, after dealing with me, White would simply send her back home anyway. And there, she would again await her doom and the collection of her soul—which, in my absence, still could be delegated to Cedric . . .

"Grim," said Helena, and she put her hand on my upper arm.

The smallest gasp escaped Flora, who like Johann and Cedric had never dared to touch me. It was one of my unspoken rules, which Helena had just unwittingly broken.

"It's okay," she said. "And . . . more importantly, it's what I want."

"You want to die?" I snarled at her, irate.

"Of course not," she said, replying with a softness I wouldn't have gotten from anyone else. A softness I certainly didn't deserve. "But . . . I understand now how you can't keep stopping that. It's going to happen. And I'm not the first or the last person in the world who it's going to happen to. I think you know that probably better than anyone."

Impossibly, my soul cinched itself tighter, constricting to the size of a pebble.

"I don't want you to get in trouble, either," she said. "Any of you. Especially not on account of me—"

"This was *my* doing," I told her.

"And I'm glad you did it," she said, shocking me. "If you hadn't—saved me on that balcony, I mean—I wouldn't have gotten this extra time. And . . . I wouldn't have gotten to know you." Helena's pained smile faltered, as if she hadn't meant to say that out loud. Flustered, she gestured to Flora and Johann. "A-any of you. Besides, what other option is there?"

The other option—the only other *feasible* option—was to turn myself in, an action that would, if nothing else, ensure the delivery of Helena's soul would be someone else's responsibility.

I didn't want to take Helena's soul. But then . . . I didn't want anyone else to, either.

Accepting this offer, agreeing to this plan—it seemed like the decision had already been made *for* me.

But then . . . was this decision even mine to make?

Helena said this was what she wanted, and maybe it was, but having gotten to know her even this little bit, I wouldn't put it past her to agree to something because she thought doing so would be in the best interest of others. In this instance, Johann, Flora . . . and me.

"I would like a word with my companions," I told her.

"Companions," she echoed softly as she stepped back from me. "*They* said they were your family."

I dared not move. I couldn't let anyone see. How helpless I felt.

Or guess how much I needed them all.

Wearing a wistful smile, as if she alone could sense the impending implosion within me, Helena started away, moving in the direction of the entrance to my chambers. And it spoke volumes that she was willing to return to the cage I'd put her in. Trust that I wouldn't imprison her—try to imprison her—a second time.

"Oy, Helena," Flora called, and the librarian stopped, peering back over her shoulder toward the fairy. "What's it like down there? Grim never has any of us over. *Ever.*"

"It's nice," Helena said. "A little scary, but also . . . beautiful inside."

Flora smirked and nodded. "I'd say that's on brand."

My head whipped back toward the fairy, who winked up at me.

When I glanced in Helena's direction again, she'd already descended the corkscrew stairs.

"Good night, bright light," said Pluto, the bird's words almost doing the trick of unraveling me.

Steeling myself, trying to play it off like I wasn't officially a flaming wreck, I left my scythe in its freestanding position and moved toward the Basins.

"Grim," said Johann, following after. "You may not know this, but there was a woman in my past, too."

"It's not like that with Helena," I lied. Sort of lied.

"Listen to me," said Johann. "My biggest regrets, they all tie back . . . to *her.* And I can't tell you what I'd give to have even one more day with her. I was so shortsighted. And hopelessly selfish. I should have realized what I had. By that time, I'd already sold my soul. Perhaps I wasn't in the same position as you, but . . . Marguerite . . . Because of what I'd done, she and I were also destined to be parted forever. Point is . . . I should have . . . What I'm trying to say is that you should, while you can . . . I don't know. Consider spending some time with Helena?"

Was he hearing himself? That was a disastrous idea. Spending time with Helena had so far only turned me into an obsessive, reckless-driving, kidnapping murderer with an insatiable and newly acquired appetite for her immortal soul.

Fuck me. Maybe vampires *were* misunderstood.

"Johann's just saying that you should think about taking her out somewhere," offered Flora. "Somewhere nice. Last I checked, Mr. McDead still had the company card."

"Hey." I whirled to aim a finger at her. "Speaking of, you're on my shit list for that."

Flora only grinned. "Took you decades to notice."

"There's bound to be some nice restaurants in the city where she lives," mused Johann, which had me whirling on him next.

Was this really happening? Were they both seriously trying to talk me into taking Helena out? As in . . . on a *date*?

"Did you two half-wits forget *none* of us are supposed to involve ourselves in the lives of the living?" I railed at them.

"At this point," said Johann with a wave of one gnarled hand, "I'd say it's in for a penny, in for a pound."

"What the fuck is *that* supposed to mean?"

"It means *we're* not going to tell anyone if you had some designs to go against the grain and live a little." Flora folded her arms with a satisfied smirk.

"Make the date while fate is late," chanted Pluto.

"She doesn't like me like that!" I snapped at the three of them.

And why would she? I was a fucking *dead-ass skeleton.*

More or less.

"Personally," said Flora, shifting her weight to one foot, "I think it's her skeleton in the closet that she does."

"She *did* mention being impressed by your powers," said Johann.

"'Smoke skills,' she called them," said Flora.

"Grim and Helena, sitting in some trees," sang Pluto, "trying to figure out the birds and the bees."

I flicked off the raven. "Keep talking, beak brain. This place *needs* a new feather duster."

The bird puffed. "Grim's just mad 'cause he's got it bad."

Damn. Bird.

"The three of you are full of shit," I mumbled, turning back to the Basins.

"Just . . . think about it," said Johann. "I personally don't see the harm. And that's coming from me. Someone who understands the ramifications of breaking the rules, perhaps, better than anyone."

"Like you said before," I muttered, unhooking the hourglass from my belt. "We all broke the rules in some capacity. That's why we're here. The idea is not to break them again. Mostly because none of us can afford to."

"You didn't break any rules, Grim," said Johann, his voice uncharacteristically gentle—and his words had me pausing before tipping the White Basin's souls into the vat. "Well, at least not until recently. Until you met Fräulein Hart."

"How do you know?" I barked.

I hadn't told him what happened to me. Even if I didn't remember what I did, I *would* remember telling him. The events of my human life were what remained at the outskirts of my memory, not those I had experienced in my current form.

"I know," Johann assured me. "At least now I do. But . . . we can worry about that later. For now, we have a librarian to help, and some tracks to cover."

"They're my tracks to cover." I shifted next to the Blue Basin.

"They were," Johann conceded. "But Flora and I, we've thrown our hats into your ring. And, thanks to Flora, I at least have plenty more to throw besides."

"I didn't ask you to do that."

"And we knew you wouldn't," said Johann. "Which is precisely why . . . we did."

Silently, I finished delivering souls to the remaining Basins, grateful I didn't have one for the Black again.

"I'm not agreeing to this," I said, retracing my steps to snatch up my scythe.

"Is it really up to you?" asked Flora, her voice soft, the question tender and probing when I would have preferred her anger.

"It's always up to me." I swung away, an invisible force tearing at the tight bulb of my soul, claws ripping up tendrils, shredding the core of me—because that was a lie, and we all knew it.

"Grim," called Flora, but I didn't pause or turn back. I just kept marching for my statue and the entrance to my quarters, a place I normally found much-needed respite and solitude.

Neither of those things would greet me there this night. The trade-off was that Helena would.

"Grim," said Flora again.

I halted next to the stairs, glaring back at her. She was trying to do me a favor—she *had* done me a favor. Helena, too. Like Johann, she didn't deserve my anger.

"What?" I growled at her all the same.

"For what it's worth," she said, "I'm . . . really sorry."

To this, I didn't say anything. There was nothing to say. Not when she'd seen through me—and Johann had, too.

They both understood what I hadn't fully until now. That it was too late.

That officially . . . Helena was someone I fucking cared about.

24

HELENA

"That painting," I said when Grim emerged from the doorway to the left of the desk and the picture in question, which I pointed to. "It changed. Twice."

"What?" he asked with his dark voice, which still scared me a little—but not totally in a bad way. Maybe, possibly, even in a good way. But I wasn't going to go there because I was not supposed to have a thing for death.

He was a very busy shadow-skeleton man, and meeting his family had made the importance and sanctity of his role here all the clearer.

"Earlier," I said, "that painting showed moonlit waters in the middle of an ocean—no land in sight. Just a moment ago, before you came down, it showed the big room upstairs with the magical cauldron thingies. Now it shows *this* room. Look."

He hesitated, then he drifted forward, his fuming form coming to stand next to me, though he left ample room between us.

"This is how it always looks," he said.

"It showed moonlit waters before," I insisted. "You believe me . . . don't you?"

He tilted his head at the painting. "You said an ocean?"

"Yeah," I said. "With a huge full silver moon."

"These quarters," he said after a beat, "are . . . linked to my essence. In addition to taking the form I prefer, it seems they also have the capacity to display my whereabouts. Something I never knew . . . until now."

"Omigosh," I said with a smile, my heart leaping since I'd been the one to make the discovery, and because talk about *cool*. "This is too neat! And it makes sense. You only see this version of the painting because that's all you *can* see since the painting always reflects wherever *you* are. Which means you were near an ocean before?"

"In it," he said.

"*In* it?" I piped. "Why would you be . . ."

I trailed off before uttering a small "Oh." Because, for an instant, I'd forgotten what he did. What he was. *Who* he was . . .

Flustered, I shook my head to sweep away the giant elephant in the room that was my certain death and turned toward him, seizing him by one bony arm.

"Go into another room," I said, shoving him lightly in the direction he'd entered from. "This is Disney World Haunted Mansion–level epic. I-I just want to see something."

He actually went, to my surprise.

"Go try your music room," I said, pointing down the hall before skipping back to the painting to see if it had changed already. It hadn't.

"You were in my music room?" he asked, and my heart clutched.

"Um," I said through a cringe-smile. "Nice Metallica collection?"

He didn't reply, but swept out of sight, down the hall, and I squealed when the painting changed before my eyes, melding to show the corridor instead of this same room. A beat later, the painting changed again, becoming Grim's music room. There were all his guitars, including the purple one.

"It shows where you are!" I called after him. Then, excited, I went in search of him, swinging around the corner and then another until

I returned to his side. "I can't believe you never knew this whole time that the painting showed where you are. How come no one ever told you?"

He didn't answer. But in the silence, Flora's response from earlier returned to tickle my brain. How she'd said something about Grim never having anyone over.

Was it possible I was his first . . . houseguest?

"I should have brought you a plant or something," I blurted out.

"What?" he barked.

I shook my head, because of course there'd been no way for him to follow that train of thought.

"I mean, since you never have company. I should have brought you a houseplant or some other housewarming gift since you've probably . . . never had one. But you don't have any windows, so a houseplant wouldn't be the best."

"I outright abducted you, and you're brainstorming housewarming gifts?"

I scoffed a laugh and waved him off. "You didn't *abduct* me. You just . . . borrowed me. Like a library book. But don't ask me where my RFID tag is, I'm not telling." I laughed. "And come on, you *totally* need a little gift. Do you drink wine?" My hands went to my lips. "I'm sorry. Maybe that's an offensive question. I . . . should think before I speak, but then . . . why start now, right?"

I laughed again, nervously this time.

"Why do you do that?" he asked.

"Sorry," I said quickly. "I won't do it anymore. But . . . what do you mean?"

"You just did it again," he observed.

"Oops. Um . . . did what?"

"You . . . stop yourself," he said. "And then you apologize for it."

"I'm . . ." I stalled, subduing the urge to apologize again. "I guess it's just . . . habit."

"Picked up from where?"

"Oh," I said with a shrug, "I don't know. Life, I guess. But then, that might be one less thing I'll be worrying about soon."

"Don't talk like that." The command in his voice had me snapping my jaw shut.

Silence surrounded us and, with each passing second, swelled big and loud.

"It bothers you when I joke about it," I said, "but considering it's you . . . I don't know why."

"Are you ready to go home?" he asked.

Home. Life.

Given that tomorrow was Saturday (I'd asked Johann what day it was) and I had to work, I'd better get back to the literal land of the living.

"Ready," I echoed. "I'm not sure that's the word I'd use."

More silence. And then he broke it.

"Because you know what's coming."

"Because I *don't* know what's coming," I said, turning to face him. "And if you want to get technical about it, neither, really . . . do you."

"We both know what's coming," he corrected.

"Who knows?" I put my hands on my hips. "Maybe we don't. Maybe fate got fed up with trying to find me and moved on. Maybe we're fretting about a storm that's already passed. Maybe I'm going to be okay after all, and I'll live until I'm a hundred and eight. Like I tell my patrons all the time. *Anything* is possible."

"I have to loosen your soul again to take you out of here," he said. "Here as in . . . the Netherworld."

"Is *that* what you did before?"

"I can't move your physical form through a portal unless I have your soul in hand. I would have asked permission before," he said, "but there was no time."

"It's fine," I told him. "I . . . trust you."

He shifted next to me, as if my words made him uncomfortable. But his disquietude didn't make my statements any less true.

"You have things to do," I said, "don't you? I understand. I do, too. Affairs to put in order and business to finish up. I work in the morning . . . though I guess I'm not sure yet how I'll get there. My car . . ."

Fiddling with my fingernails, I trailed off, because he'd been there. He knew.

"You're still going to go to work?" he asked.

I frowned and fidgeted with one jack-o'-lantern earring. Because I could see his point. Why go back to work when I wasn't going to need the money? Except, depending on how long it took for my projected fate to arrive, I low-key *was* going to need to keep the lights on.

Sure, I could max out my credit cards checking off items on my bucket list, but then . . . what if I really did have hope I might somehow be in the clear? Or that I still could be?

"My work comforts me," I said, which wasn't a lie. "Being busy will take my mind off things until I decide if I want to do something different. Until . . . I see you again. Because I probably *won't* see you again until it's time. Right?"

He didn't answer. Which was answer enough. He was the Grim Reaper, and now that there was a plan for me in place, he had bigger fish to fry than babysitting a children's librarian.

"I retrieved your phone," he said at last. "From outside the library."

My eyes bugged. "Y-you did?"

"It's . . . damaged."

"But it works?"

"Your mom has been texting you."

Mom. I sighed inwardly.

"And someone named Peter."

I scoffed. "What does *he* want?"

Grim turned that shadowed gaze down on me. "I didn't read your texts. I just saw the names. Is Peter your boss?"

"Ha!"

He tilted his head at me.

I coughed and lowered my voice. "I mean no. Peter is a tool. But you don't need to know about all of that. I have to ask, though. Since . . . you're taking me home, does that mean you're agreeing to the plan?"

For a long time, he didn't say anything.

But then, at last, he spoke.

"Can you drive a stick shift?"

25

GRIM

I led Helena out of the Hallowed Halls and guided her through the Netherworld Forest.

As soon as we entered the murky woods, the faintest of auras appeared around her, a subtle luminescence that she didn't seem to notice at all, even though it illuminated our path the way the soft glow of a lantern might.

I kept glancing her way, mystified and fascinated by the phenomenon, which I'd never observed in anyone before. Then again, no other living human had visited the Netherworld.

A thin and encompassing halo, the aura shifted hues, changing tones from pale pink to sky blue in a slow bleed, like the northern lights.

Maybe the colors reflected her mood?

Blue, I suspected, would be melancholy.

She stayed quiet as we walked together down the worn, gray, tunnellike alley between craggy trees, her gaze flitting here and there, scanning the tangled and vacant black-limbed branches, the formless gray skies, and our mist-shrouded surroundings.

She had no jokes now. Probably because I'd admonished her dark humor. But . . . I hadn't meant to silence her.

Her normal chatter. Perhaps I could coax it—her—back out of hiding.

"I come and go from your world by way of Netherworld portals," I told her, breaking the silence.

Normally, soundlessness never bothered me. Always, quietude had been my lone companion in these woods and in much of my work. But Helena's sudden muteness needled me—tied my thoughts into knots of concern. For her . . .

The threat Cedric posed might have been neutralized for now, but ultimately, his removal from the equation only delayed the inevitable—an early exit from life that Helena was now acutely aware of.

The sands would run out for her soon—perhaps even within the day. Possibly within the hour . . .

That had to be a difficult truth to digest, so perhaps I was giving myself too much credit in thinking her uncharacteristic pensiveness could be owed to anything *I* had said.

Whatever the reason for her contemplativeness, I still didn't want her to feel alone, even though in so many ways . . . she was.

Death was like that. I was there when it happened, yeah. But when the lights went out, it was still just you and yourself. At least, it was as far as I knew.

And this walk with me back to her world—how could it not, for her, feel like a trek to the gallows?

Then there was the matter of our impending reconnection.

Despite the heaviness of this pilgrimage, the anticipation for that delicious rejoining of our spirits buzzed in me—though it shouldn't have.

Was *she* dreading it?

"Then once you're through the portal," she said, speaking up at last, "in this world or the other, mine, you just . . . swirly twirl wherever you want to go?"

I did a double take her way. Because . . . *swirly twirl*?

That wasn't how I would have referred to my preferred method of travel, but Helena had her intrinsic view of things, and who was I to not let her have it? Aside from that, I wasn't about to correct her by saying I "smoke-shifted" or "mist-moved"—both of which struck me as equally stupid sounding.

"More or less," I muttered.

Helena kept her gaze downcast on the trail, and she took care to sidestep the knobby knees of tree roots that jutted up in her path.

"And you feel a tug," she said, "when it's . . . time for someone to die? You said before that . . . you didn't come to find me right away because you didn't feel the pull to get my soul."

I slowed my walk as we neared the portal, which loomed ahead, an open mouth back to Helena's realm, back to her life—which had no room in it for me.

"For the Fated," I said, "the pull comes shortly before death. For all other souls, I feel the pull after."

"Hmm," she mused. "That's interesting, don't you think? That you're called to the Fated just *before* death. I wonder why that is. Probably it's got something to do with there being some kind of . . . schedule. Like, the Fated Souls have somewhere to be?"

I didn't know for sure, but that had always been my assumption.

"Makes me feel important in a way," Helena added, her chattiness revived. "Like a VIFS. As in a Very Important Fated S—"

"This time, it might be uncomfortable for you," I blurted out. "*More* uncomfortable . . ."

Arriving at the open archway embedded in a freestanding stone wall, a seeming entrance to a missing castle courtyard, I stopped. Though the doorway framed more mist-shrouded trees, promising a continuation of our path, the facade was just that.

"'It might,' you said. What do you mean by 'it'?"

What did she mean what did I mean? What *else* could I be talking about?

"My . . . influence," I clarified, since she was apparently going to make me say it out loud.

She touched her heart. "You mean . . . when you reached into me like that. Like the claw on one of those teddy-picker arcade games. I'm pretty good at those, by the way. It's all in the timing."

She made her hand into a claw before she mimed snagging my heart. "You just line 'em up and then yoink!"

I just stared at her. Sometimes I couldn't think of what to say back when I was with her.

She perplexed me. The way a searching bumblebee must perplex a drab and colorless mushroom.

"Also," she said, "what you did. It wasn't uncomfortable. At all."

I turned toward her. Because *what*?

"It didn't hurt," she said. "It . . . was the opposite, in fact. Like a blast of air-conditioning on a hot day."

She had seared me. Like a bolt of lightning to a frigid, dark wasteland that, before that instant, had never known either light *or* warmth.

My soul could have devoured hers whole, and this next taste of her was going to be brutal. But only because it was bound to be my last. And from then on, well, I'd know what hell was, wouldn't I?

"Since you know it's coming this time," I said, "your soul will likely resist."

She smirked, her inherent lightness reinfusing her mien as she put her hands on her hips. "How do you know?"

I fought the urge to tilt my head at her. The last thing I'd expected from her at this moment was playfulness. Or could the sudden shift in her demeanor be owed to . . . something else?

"I've had to loosen souls from bodies before," I told her—a morbid truth, but a truth all the same. But then, weren't all my truths morbid to some degree? Just like all of hers had some shade of light to them, like she truly happened to be a walking prism . . .

"You mean I'm not your first?" She offered me a small smile.

Fuck me. What?

No. She didn't know what she was saying. I was reading into

things. Because there was no way in Hades's hot hell she was flirting with me. *Salaciously* flirting with me.

She didn't know how what she'd said sounded. Or that my dirty mind apparently wanted to read into her words.

"Typically," I said, speaking slow, trying not to seem taken off guard, even though I was, "forcible extraction is only required with reluctant souls. Those who do not wish to abandon their vessels."

"There's a choice?"

"No," I said. "But I sometimes encounter . . . strong attachments. My scythe will always do the trick of severing ties, but souls can cling to their bodies, or even to objects and places. Since you are alive, though, your soul will likely attempt to defend itself."

"It . . . didn't before," she offered.

"It had never been attacked before."

"You weren't attacking me," she said.

"Your soul doesn't know that."

She shook her head at me, her hair shifting in a way that made me long to touch it. "What if . . . it does?"

What was her angle? Maybe she just needed to tease and make light of the situation to feel safer in my presence. Probably she was just stalling.

"It'll only hurt for a moment," I said. "Then you'll fall unconscious again."

"Wait," she said, "then how am I going to get home?"

"The portal will take me straight into your apartment."

"O-oh." She blinked, a blush creeping up her cheeks, painting them the shade of hot-pink roses. "It's . . . kind of a mess in there."

"I promise I've seen worse."

She gave a nervous laugh. "I bet you have, though I don't think I want to know in what ways."

She was right. She didn't want to know.

Death could be quiet. It could be peaceful. But it could be many other things, too.

"You have to promise not to judge me," she said. "My apartment isn't huge. It's just me, and I rarely have company."

Outside of the pineapple.

"And lately," she prattled on, "I've been kind of . . . living out loud in there. But then, I guess it's only fair I let you into my place after I went galivanting around in yours. There is one thing I don't understand, though. Are you saying there are portals in and out of the Netherworld everywhere? Like, apparently, my apartment and the Lyndon McDonald's?"

I gestured to the portal that waited for us. "The ones in the Netherworld are stationary and fixed, with one positioned at each of the four corners of this realm. When I'm in your world, however, I can access them at will from anywhere."

"So *that's* how we got out of the McDonald's," she said.

"Outsiders are forbidden to enter the Netherworld," I explained. "Transporting you here was . . . a last resort to keep you out of Cedric's reach. I had every intention of reporting myself to The Few after informing you of the finer details of the situation. The only reason The Few have not automatically been alerted to your presence is because I . . . smuggled you in by shifting your soul into my grip. So they never received the alert that you were here. That's why I have to repeat the process on the way out."

"You camouflaged me," she said, wringing the crossbody strap of her pumpkin purse with both hands. "Makes sense this place would be high security. No wonder you guys don't get any tourism down here. Too bad." She scanned our surroundings, shrugging. "There's plenty of space for a resort. Lots of misty woods for Halloween hiking. And who wouldn't want to visit the edge of death and meet Faust himself?"

I snapped my head her way. "Who told you about Johann?"

She frowned, confused, and blinked up at me. "No one. I . . . just thought it was obvious who he was. Wizened man in Renaissance robes named Johann with a German accent with the title of doctor?

I'm familiar with the story, of course, and the legend *was* said to have been based off a real man."

With her being a librarian, I could see how she'd know of the legend of Faust, the fifteenth-century German scholar and alchemist who sold his soul to the devil in return for riches, power, and knowledge. Johann's story had endured through the ages, inspiring countless books, movies—a famed opera. But for Helena to have put two and two together with only the few clues she'd mentioned?

I'd known Helena was well read, but until now, I hadn't realized just how perceptive she was.

"You didn't call him by that name, did you?" I asked her.

"N-no," she said. "And something tells me it's a good thing I didn't ask about his history?"

"He's sensitive about his past," I said. "He rarely talks of it."

Something true for all of us.

"If Faust is real," she ventured, glancing back down the way we'd come while lowering her voice, as if already taking my cautions to heart, fearful she might be heard even from a distance, "does that mean his, uh . . . nefarious, er . . . *friend* is, too?"

"You're asking about the demon," I said. "And it's even wiser not to utter *his* name. At least not anywhere other than here."

"So . . . demons are real, too," she murmured, now white-knuckling the strap of her purse.

Probably not the best time to admit vampires were as well. Right along with a few other . . . "mythological" beings.

"Have . . . *you* met him?" she asked.

By "him," she meant the infamous Mephistopheles—the demon Faust originally summoned. A devil charged with seeing to the fulfillment of the doctor's every whim. But also, upon Johann's death, to the procurement of the soul the old man had sold in exchange for the services of his diabolical manservant. A soul he has, through the ages, managed to keep by remaining here in the Netherworld, a realm that cannot be reached by that demon or any other.

If nothing else, Johann *was* clever.

But so was Mephistopheles.

"I've had a run-in or two," I admitted. "He's always looking for Johann, and someone gave him a lead—a *correct* lead—that I happened to know where he can be found."

"Holy granola," Helena said, her eyes popping.

"You could say I . . . put him off," I said, "and he hasn't bothered me since. Though he'll still hassle Flora from time to time."

"So he knows," said Helena, "where Johann is?"

"It seems he heavily suspects," I replied. "But he'd have to convince someone to try to bring him Johann's soul since he can't come here, and I think our last encounter taught him not to try that angle again."

"Goodness," she whispered. "Could Cedric have spilled the beans?"

"It's not unthinkable he was the one who did," I said. "But, while I wouldn't put anything past Cedric, he doesn't have any real power here. He's more of a refugee than an official. For the time being, I also think it's worth more to him to have Johann in the Halls. And even Cedric probably knows better than to strike a deal with a demon."

"I don't understand," she said. "If he's such a troublemaker, couldn't the three of you . . . kick him out?"

"Cedric, like the rest of us, is here by the benevolence of The Few," I said. "He'd have to piss them off to get booted. I'm the only one who sees through his bullshit. Flora is tenderhearted—and misguided—enough to believe we can change him, while Johann sees too much of himself in Cedric."

"I see," said Helena. "You all . . . really care about each other, don't you? Even Cedric?"

"Cedric can rot," I snarled.

Helena folded her arms and smirked at me. "Spoken like a true big brother."

I grunted. "Not you, too."

"Sorry," she said with a sheepish, one-shouldered shrug. "I guess I . . . want to see the best in people. Even someone like Cedric.

Maybe I'm just in the club of everyone who, for your sake, wishes he could be different."

"He tried to hurt you," I blurted out.

Helena's eyes flitted up to me, wide and questioning.

"It's become all too clear that he wants to destroy me," I said, trying to cover for the moment. "That's why he targeted you. I might have cut him slack in the past, but now? Officially, when it comes to Cedric, for me . . . all bets are off."

"Because his taking me to The Few would get you fired," she said, her tone matter of fact, assured. Was she trying to reassure herself I *hadn't* started to care for her?

Because the idea understandably repulsed or frightened her? Or both.

I went silent. Maybe getting me fired had been Cedric's aim initially, but there were other reasons now why hurting Helena would mess with me. He'd already guessed as much, too, or else he wouldn't have tried to bargain with me in the McDonald's.

Shit. The worst had happened.

I *was* a creep.

Because I liked her. A fucking lot.

Something I'd made painfully plain to Cedric after going full-on murder mode and felling him at the library when I would have done better to feign indifference.

Feigning anything around Helena was getting progressively harder to do. Though, apparently, I was still the last one to figure all this the fuck out.

Well. Maybe I wasn't the *very* last one.

I didn't want Helena to suspect how I felt, but . . . so what if she did?

In a few minutes, the two of us would be parting ways anyway, so who would be around for me to feel embarrassed in front of?

She probably had tons of admirers. Maybe it wouldn't surprise her to have a monster among them.

Helena still didn't understand what getting fired really looked like for me, either. And maybe that's why she thought of Cedric as the wayward-black-sheep type rather than the snake he'd revealed himself to be. But I didn't want Helena to know Cedric's victory meant my demise and damnation, either. She had enough to worry about.

"Don't let on to Johann that you know who he is," I said, deflecting, "and whatever you do, don't mention Mephistopheles."

Helena's expression sobered, and she nodded, a clear indication she took my warning to heart. "Spoken as if you think I'll see him again. Johann, I mean."

In all likelihood, she would not.

"I won't pretend to know what will happen from here out," I said, deflecting yet again, hoping for the hundredth time to spare her any measure of fear she wasn't already contending with. "But I do know it is time for you to go home."

"Home," she repeated, before adding with a sigh, "Right. Um. I just . . . have one more question. If . . . you don't mind."

I waved an inviting hand with a hunch about what she would ask—one that proved true.

"Back at the restaurant," Helena said, "Cedric tried to . . . negotiate with you."

My soul contracted around my bones, constricting with reluctance.

"He alluded to there being a way to . . . avoid my death. At least, that's how I took it."

Fucking Cedric.

I hadn't wanted to have this conversation with her. It would only bring pain—for the both of us.

Still, she deserved an explanation.

"My role," I said, "is one that is traditionally passed along voluntarily. A human must willingly agree to assume the current reaper's place by taking an oath. In exchange, the new reaper can, during the course of his career, elect to spare a single life—even a Fated."

"Johann," said Helena, "gasped when I mentioned Cedric offered to barter with you for my life. He said something like 'I understand now.' Does . . . that mean anything to you?"

No. But only because I didn't remember my own past. I only knew the facts of my current reality.

Maybe Johann figured something out about me—which would make his earlier comments make more sense. Not what he'd meant, but the fact that he'd uttered them at all.

He could figure shit out about me all he wanted. So long as he left *me* blissfully unaware.

"Cedric," I said, "I assume, found out about this detail of my position. I'm guessing he wants me to voluntarily surrender my role to him with the understanding he would grant his one life to you. Making such a bargain with him would require me to trust that he would follow through on that. Given that the life would, at that point, be his to grant, however, and not mine, I—"

"That's why you said you wouldn't trust him to hold up his side of the bargain."

I remained silent. Because that was correct.

"But . . ." she ventured, a small smile touching her lips, "that means that, even for a second, you actually considered it. Negotiating with him."

Was that true? God . . . was it?

"I don't understand, though," she said. "What would happen to *you* in that scenario?"

"I would move on," I answered quickly.

"You mean you'd go into one of those cauldron thingies. Meaning . . . you'd die? Um. For good?"

"Yeah," I said, hoping we could just leave it—this whole conversation—at that.

"You don't want that," she guessed.

"I like my job," I said. "All things considered."

That wasn't a lie. Though "like" felt like a stretch.

She nodded like that made sense to her, and she cast her gaze to the ground.

"Helena," I said, and she looked up, her eyes misty now, though I couldn't be certain of why. Not that she didn't have plenty of reasons to be upset. "That one life . . . I don't remember the details but . . . I know I already granted mine. At least, I know I don't have it—if I ever did."

She nodded some more. "I thought that's what Johann must have concluded. That you gave it to someone already."

"If I hadn't," I said, "and if I still had it . . . please know I *would* grant it to you. After everything . . . well, that would be the least I could do."

She flushed, a tear falling, though she wiped it away quickly before waving me off with the same hand, suddenly flustered. "That's . . . sweet."

Sweet? Until now, no one had ever called me *that*.

Though I had meant what I said. I would have given it to her.

And God only knows what I would do if I thought Cedric *could* be trusted to keep his word . . .

He was a rat, though. And I was—and would be—the Grim Reaper for eternity.

Which meant I had to get Helena home, my fucking ducks in a row, and my skull back in the game.

"Are you ready now?" I asked her.

Again, she nodded. Then she released her stranglehold on the crossbody strap of her battered pumpkin purse before letting her arms fall to her sides. Before presenting herself like a sacrifice . . . "So, should I just . . . stand here?"

More silence passed between us. I didn't want to tell her yes or no. In truth, she didn't have to do a thing. But I couldn't be cold to her in this moment, not as I had been before. Flora, perhaps, had a point about my behavior.

So I lifted a skeletal hand, beckoning Helena with a finger, keeping my voice as soft as I could make it. "Come here."

I'd meant for her to step toward me, to deplete the distance it would take for me to reach her, to eliminate the need for me to catch and draw her to me as I'd done before like a spider callously snatching up its prey. Instead, Helena rushed me as she had in that alley behind the library, again wrapping her arms around my shoulders, as if the impulse to embrace me was something she had, until this moment, been trying to rein in.

I swept her up into my own arms, and in the same motion, I plunged my dark, cool essence into her chest and seized that sunshine soul, wispy tendrils lashing and wrapping her pale gold essence, tongues of darkness tasting—relishing—the heat of her.

"Grim, I—"

She didn't get a chance to finish before I shifted her soul that small degree, loosening it just a bit, just enough.

The resistance I'd expected, warned her about, didn't occur.

She surrendered to me, body *and* soul. I held her just like that for a moment, overcome by a debilitating feast of foreign sensations. Her warm body weighing hardly anything in my cold bony arms, her softness killing me by fitting itself between my ribs. That searing liquid-gold soul molten and malleable in the desolate, ravenous grips of mine.

I could have remained with her like this forever. Lost in the scent of her skin. Beguiled and bewitched by the gentle weight of her. Drunk on her scalding spirit, the heat of which burned simultaneously too hot and not hot enough.

I'd never let another human touch me before, but I suspected no other would have made me *feel* the way she had. Almost as if she'd dragged life into the quiet rot where I belonged.

That was a dangerous thought, and the temptation to keep her with me—held this way, like she was *mine*—forever would consume me if I let it.

She was not mine to hold on to. And could not be.

I *had* to let her go. In every sense of the phrase. I had to.

So I forced myself through the portal, gliding into her living room, the invisible membrane separating our worlds rippling away behind us.

I had to halt when, unexpectedly, her soul grew tendrils of its own. Like new shoots on a tender vine, those wisps began to wrap and creep along the invading tentacles of mine—heightening everything.

God, this intoxicating creature.

The spiritual taste of her alone, bright and sweet, simultaneously petal soft and biting, crisp as white wine yet hot as molten honey, forbade me from releasing her. To have her winding me like this had me again questioning the need to let her go, even though I should have released her spirit the instant I had her safely through the portal.

Instead, while I once again moved through her home, I caved to the overpowering urge to keep her in my grasp, giving in to her hold on me. Drugged and addled, yearning for an even deeper draft of her, all but wrecked by the sensation of her gentle and curious searing spirit climbing and coiling around mine, I fought the impulse to return her wanderings.

With enormous effort, I denied this hunger, this thirst. Already, I'd done enough to disturb her peace.

Helena's head lay on my shoulder as I carried her through her living room with its cream walls and yellow-upholstered furniture.

Unlike the last time I'd been here, clutter covered most surfaces, including the floor.

A testament, no doubt, to how out of control she must feel.

Her smiling stuffed pineapple now lay on the floor next to a fuzzy blanket she must have kicked off at some point. Empty mugs littered the surface of her coffee table along with several books and a few food wrappers. Stacks of novels and picture books lay strewn across the floor around the table along with a small collection of hand puppets.

A bra dotted with lemons draped the back of the couch.

Lost in the bliss of her, I only loosely took in the details of our surroundings as I turned a corner—passing photos on the walls, a pile of mail on the kitchen counter, sunflower notepads scrawled with looping, bubbly handwriting.

In moments, I *was* going to have to release her. Then I was going to have to leave. And not come back until this was over.

Next time I did see her, I would also have to do what I should have from the start.

My job.

Inside her bedroom, pink and purple lights hung along her walls and mapped her ceiling, casting all in a pearly, pastel glow not unlike her own. Bohemian-style pillows piled a queen-sized bed.

Gently, I laid her on the busy yellow-and-blue paisley quilt comforter.

Helena murmured, lids fluttering, her fingers curling into the fabric of my cloak, signs that told me she remained awake. Yet another surprise.

Though I extracted my arms from her, relinquishing her to the mattress, she clung to me, hands slipping to grip the collar of my robes, tendrils of her soul constricting around the dark limbs of mine.

Her essence spiked mine with more of that summer burn, thawing and searing me, like I'd frozen to death eons ago and forgotten what it was like to step into warm waters.

Fuck, she felt good—like a tropical breeze laced with pure morphine.

Heaven, if it existed, wasn't a realm I ever planned on experiencing, but damn if this didn't come close.

Helena.

Desperate to end this before I gave in and forked my spirit over to hers, I rasped her name with my soul, which I loosened from hers—tentatively. My hope was that she'd show me mercy, that hers would follow suit and loosen in turn. It did the opposite, tightening and tugging on mine, the true devourer.

Her spirit proved strong, and something akin to a gasp escaped me as I caught and braced myself above her with skeletal hands as she clung to me with both body and spirit, our souls entangled in a way that threatened to unravel me. Then that yellow essence of hers began to heat and temper mine, bringing a fever infused with her emotions: hope, sadness, fondness, and, yes, fear.

That fear, though, it wasn't the kind she *should* have been entertaining—the one surrounding the dark unknown. Instead, as I read her spirit's inherent nakedness with mine, unwilling to rip free of her, I identified a trepidation that fascinated me and scalded me with its potency. One surrounding her last wishes.

Sometimes, when I took souls, they echoed with their final desires—always unfulfilled.

Normally, time was out when they entered my grips.

That was not the case with Helena.

Her last wishes floated through me like gentle echoes. A day with her best friend. A visit with her parents. Strawberry shortcake.

And a kiss . . . with *me*.

The fear I'd picked up on, unfathomably, it surrounded not her death, or the thought that she wouldn't get any of her wishes, but my reaction to them. Her last one.

She feared my rejection.

She had no way of knowing that, if I was ever granted a final wish, I'd want the same. *From her.*

So I did the last thing I should have done and I surrendered when, despite that inconceivable fear, one of her hands released its hold on my collar to enter the darkness of my hood. Her palm, warm, found the cheek I did not possess while, with her other hand—still fastened tight around my collar—she drew me down to her.

Like the pull of death itself, I couldn't have denied her even if I'd wanted to.

Still, nothing could have prepared me, either.

In kissing me, pressing her soft lips to the bare bones of my teeth, she detonated my soul, ruining it—and me—for all the rest of time. And I let her. Welcomed the complete annihilation of the being I had been up until this point. A compromise to what I wanted to do in return—which was to retake my human form and kiss her back, show her just how sweet death could taste.

I'd already sworn to myself I wouldn't dare.

The repercussions from *this* kiss, the knowledge that there would never be another, would haunt me enough through eternity.

My now-trembling soul thudded in the simultaneously cruel and benevolent grips of hers, mimicking a phantom heartbeat, like her touch had the opposite power of mine—to restore life to the ravaged rather than to sweep up after the desolation of death.

No entity in either heaven *or* hell could ever have destroyed me more thoroughly.

After this latest forbidden action, the *most* forbidden of all I'd taken or allowed up to this point, I couldn't see her again. Not until it was time. Or dare to do more . . . I would.

So I reciprocated this unearned affection, this humbling last wish, by kissing her back with my soul instead, sending nearly the whole of my essence rushing into her, my freezing spirit scouring her suddenly scorching one, enwrapping it, braiding with it, piercing it, entangling with it, clenching it tight.

With this invasion, the softest and most enticing murmur of pleasure escaped my librarian.

And that subtle and breathy moan did me in, eliciting from my entire being something I had not experienced ever. At least not in this incarnation.

In that instant, Helena awakened a slumbering part of me, a dead corner of my former and long-forgotten humanness.

She did the impossible, the unforgivable. The undoable.

By, among so many other things, turning me the fuck *on*.

26

HELENA

I awoke with a gasp, sitting bolt upright in my bed, my chest heaving, my heart revved to top speed, thundering like I'd just been jolted back to life with a supercharged defibrillator.

No doctors or nurse staff surrounded me, and no bright surgical lights beamed down on me. Instead, my fairy lights alone brought relief to the darkness of the night that had settled again.

While I sat there with my hand on my sternum, like that might keep my heart from winning the battering-ram battle against the bone, I waited for understanding to return.

Grim. I'd been with Grim. And everything we'd been through together must have really happened, because I still had on my Halloween earrings, my purse, my jack-o'-lantern sweater.

"Oh my God," I said as, one after the other, I took the earrings out.

"Oh. My God," I repeated as I laid the plastic pumpkins on my Ikea bedside table.

"Oh my God, I kissed him." I turned this proclamation on my piles of pillows, none of which had anything to say. My heart, though, did an extra-jumpy triple step, pure terror pumping through my veins. My hand abandoned my heart to touch my lips—the same lips I'd dared to lay on *the* Grim Reaper.

"Oh my God, I kissed him," I repeated, a strange transmutation alchemizing my fear into something less mortified and more . . . giddy?

"Oh, wow," I said, scooting to the edge of my bed, slinging off my purse along the way.

That kiss. I scarcely recalled it because I'd been under the influence of his spirit. That freezing essence had seized my soul, giving it an uprooting tug that hadn't hurt at all.

On the contrary, I'd again had some trouble with sensations of the opposite sort.

Polar opposite.

He'd made me . . . drunk somehow. Infused me with a bliss-inducing balm I hadn't wanted to let go of.

Did that mean I could blame what I'd done on some otherworldly version of liquid courage?

"Oh, I really did that," I mumbled as I pushed off the bed to stand on wobbly legs.

What did he think of me? He must think I was utterly bonkers.

Then again, he *had* responded, his freezing essence pouring into mine, twisting and winding me up.

Wait a second. Had we . . . made out?

I'd certainly been ready to very literally jump his bones . . .

I still kept fingertips pressed to my lips as I marched out of my bedroom and into my disaster area of a living room.

"Oh, *goodnight moon*," I growled as I spotted my flipping *bra* just hanging out—flopped across the back of the couch, right where I'd thrown it the other night when the girls had needed a breather.

Heat rushed to overtake my face as I made a beeline to the garment and snatched it up, like it made any difference now.

"I can't believe . . ."

What, Helena? You can't believe what? That, while in a soul-wringing stupor, you kissed death on the teeth? Or that the sender of souls had gotten a gander at your fruit-themed underthings?

What had I been thinking? That was just it. I hadn't been thinking. Except . . . I also had.

Caution was so much easier to throw to the wind when you knew you didn't need it—when you understood that playing it safe ultimately wouldn't do you any good. And with my number being up, I suppose I thought I'd live a little by giving the Grim Reaper a smooch.

"Right on the lips," I whispered as I started to pace, even though, technically speaking, he didn't really have lips. At least, he hadn't had them at the time of my forwardness.

At the same time, he'd sure blown all the dud-muffins I'd ever kissed before out of the water.

Cover to cover, that kiss had been as *hot* as his soul was cold.

And those unyielding teeth under my lips—they hadn't moved, but they'd still sent one hell of a zing through me. Just like the rest of his teasy, deep freeze-y, scorched-earth, end-of-the-world essence.

Talk about a wild ride.

"I cannot *believe* I made out with death," I mumbled, pacing again before tossing my bra back onto the couch.

Apparently, I hadn't been able to help myself after spending half the night *flirting* with him. Flirting with him *again*.

"I hit on death," I muttered, heading straight for my kitchen. Because I needed tea. No, coffee. "I straight up hit on death. *Then* I made a move on him."

Had he made a move back? I still couldn't say.

Well, if my history with guys had taught me anything: If he hadn't already stopped calling, he certainly would now, wouldn't he?

Speaking of now, what time was it anyway? Heck, what day was it?

"Oh, shoot," I said, glancing at the oven clock, which read 6:28.

God help me, I hoped that meant 6:28 in the morning, and that I hadn't slept through work. My shift started at eight, and the library opened at nine.

My phone. I needed my phone.

I hurried back into my room, tripping over my unicorn house slippers along the way. I scoured my pumpkin purse but found nothing. But Grim had given me back my phone . . . hadn't he?

Maybe I *had* somehow dreamed the whole thing. The whole night. Except that couldn't be.

As I left my room again, I once more pressed my fingers to my lips, the sensation of that death's-head grin still inscribed there. As I stared out into space, I shifted my hand once again back to my heart, which had yet to settle, because it remembered things, too.

The way he'd flooded me like that, his whole spirit descending upon me, doing things to me—to mine.

My cheeks flared anew at the memory, the way his ice had clashed with my fire, the two of us, I was pretty sure, spiritually sprinting to second base.

Now my hand went to my brow because *what*?

I could hardly understand what had happened—only that he hadn't recoiled in disgust or affront when I'd done what I had, which is exactly what I'd feared would happen. I hadn't expected him to return my gesture. Was that what he'd done?

He'd certainly done *something*. And I'd certainly enjoyed all of it—the way those tendrils had infiltrated and wound me, cooled and teased me, scoured me in a way I wasn't sure I could go without.

That thought brought more heat to my face, my cheeks flaming now.

What, exactly, had we done? And why, if I had to die, couldn't I pick the method?

I'd choose him and our shadow-and-sunshine tango for sure. And if he were here right now, I wasn't sure I'd be able to hold back from telling him as much.

"Omigod," I muttered to myself, tempted to start pacing again, "I have a crush on him."

Maybe that was an understatement at this stage. Because, if I was being honest with myself, I'd had a crush on him on that damn balcony. The elevator episode had given me palpitations in more ways than one, and then when he'd cursed at me like that while pushing ninety?

Well, that had been the nail in the coffin I apparently wanted to roll around with him in.

"This can't be a healthy reaction to knowing you're going to die," I whispered to myself, once more going in search of coffee. But then, maybe I still had some vodka in the freezer? Because if I was still going to make it into work and wasn't fired as well as being on death row, I'd have to call an Uber anyway.

Somewhere nearby, my phone alarm went off.

I jumped with a yelp, my eyes flying to the little table stationed next to the door to my apartment.

My phone. It sat there, plugged into the wall—because it must have needed charging.

Except *I* hadn't plugged it in. I hadn't set my alarm for six thirty, either.

But . . . someone had.

After only a beat of hesitation, I hurried over, skirting my couch until I arrived at the table, which, in addition to my phone, held a strange set . . . of keys.

"Oh," I whispered, my hand bypassing my phone to clasp the silver metal keys looped by a simple key ring.

When I'd complained about my car, Grim had asked me if I could drive a stick.

I'd told him yes. Years ago, when I'd been in high school, my father had taught me to drive the family truck so I could take myself to Friday-night book club. That way he wouldn't miss any football or March Madness games on TV . . .

Carefully, I scooped up the car keys—the *vintage* car keys—letting the phone alarm pulse while I examined them.

Grim couldn't seriously have lent me his car, though . . . could he?

Keys clenched hard in my fist, I abandoned the table and my phone, cutting a path straight across my apartment to the window overlooking the parking lot.

Sweeping aside the curtain, I peered down on the slowly brightening world, the sherbert horizon letting me know I'd reawakened to morning, and I found my parking spot.

My Bug wasn't there, and I hadn't expected it to be.

But neither had I anticipated seeing . . . The Judge.

27

GRIM

After cleaning up after myself—and Cedric—I went to retrieve the asshole's body from the morgue. Not because I gave a damn about what happened to it, what happened to him.

I did, however, care about the particulars of the shit shows at the library and, later, at the McDonald's getting back to The Few.

A body disappearing from the morgue only to show up again would already raise enough red flags with the human authorities, and those of us who had dealings behind the veil and in the alternate dimensions all had our mortal-world contacts. Grapevines existed, too, and the last thing I needed at that moment with so much hanging in the balance was for someone to go snitching about Cedric's ass sitting in a drawer.

There was also the episode with the self-driving cars and the runaway bookmobile I'd needed to cover up.

I'd already erased Helena's involvement by retrieving her phone and removing her mangled Beetle from the scene.

Now I had Cedric, still in a body bag, laid out on the enormous oak desk in his pretentious, dark-academia-style yuppie office tucked away in the rear of the sprawling oval library of the Hallowed Halls.

Flora had deposited his soul here, too, setting the lantern that held his wretched spirit upon a nearby shelf crammed with Cedric's books on magic and necromancy.

Back at the morgue, I'd unzipped the bag partially to make triple sure I had the right asswipe.

I did.

I'd left the bag that way, and glaring down at Cedric's dead face with those chilling and now-sightless and unblinking ice-chip eyes, I frowned at catching something odd. Something I hadn't noticed before.

A dark line, illuminated by the glow of Cedric's own soul, marked his throat.

Indicating his decapitation scar . . . had bled.

Which must have happened in the restaurant. Or before. He'd been clothed then, of course. In a high-collared coat, which would have hidden the phenomenon. And to show signs of being bloody now, postmortem, the scar had to have reopened before death. His latest death.

All of this pointed to the idea that something had . . . upset him.

"You bled," I said, trying not to sound startled as I peered up at the lantern. "Bet *that* wound confused the fuck out of the coroner."

Uncharacteristically, the soul within that lantern hadn't stirred when I'd entered with its usual vessel, though it had brightened with interest. Now, as I turned away to pace in the office, it dimmed again, waiting no doubt for me to state my business.

And I did have business.

"Don't think this means I give a rat's ass what happens to you," I growled, just to dispel any illusions he might be laboring under. "I'd throw your carcass in a wood chipper myself if I didn't need to put you—all of you—somewhere where I can keep a watch on you."

The soul didn't respond, but it had to be listening.

"Was this your doing?" I held up a slip of torn parchment between two skeletal fingers, the note I'd taken along with the book I'd found in Helena's apartment. The small volume had caught my eye after she'd fallen asleep, her soul at last disentangling from mine, and I'd snagged the book from her nightstand before going to plug in her phone and leave my keys so she'd have a relatively safe way to get to work.

I didn't want her walking or taking public transport—not with her life dangling by a thread. Maybe, with the Fated mark on her soul, The Judge wasn't any safer than the rest of the world, but lending it to her made me feel better. And in this situation, false comfort was still better than no comfort, wasn't it?

False or not, that comfort had been short-lived. Because of this note. The one that said "Yes, Helena, he's real" in scripty blue handwriting I'd never seen before. But just because it didn't match Cedric's tight cursive didn't mean it wasn't his. If he could enchant a bookmobile to go rogue, he could forge a note in Swahili if he wanted.

"Found this in a book," I grumbled. "About me. Someone had to have planted it there knowing she'd go looking for answers."

With my hooded mug on the cover of that volume, which Helena had bookmarked with what had to be a hundred tropical-flower-speckled page flags, what else could that note mean?

"Then again," I muttered, "who else could have planted this for her to find?"

The glow from the lantern increased, the aura from Cedric's noxious green soul washing all in an eerie light and casting his pale face a sickly hue.

"I guess the real question is why you did it. Obviously, you've been following me. You must have been there that night I met her on that balcony. You saw then what I did—didn't do."

Cedric's soul flickered. Did that mean I was on the money? Or out in left field . . .

No. I was onto him. I had to be.

"Was that how you knew where to leave the note?" I asked. "That would also explain how you knew to look for her at the library after the incident with the elevator."

I stopped pacing to turn toward Cedric's body, which lay between me and the glowing lantern.

Dark wood-paneled walls surrounded us. Above, from a ceiling enchanted to display the night sky and its star systems, hung a magic-suspended mobile of the planets and their current alignment.

"The question is why?" I said. "If you knew she was the missing soul right from the beginning, why wouldn't you try to take her sooner? Unless . . . the elevator was *your* doing."

Rage boiled up inside me, born from the idea that Cedric would have sought to hurt Helena right from the start. I rounded the desk, went to the shelf, and seized the lantern, bringing it close for inspection.

The soul bobbed around inside, banging against the glass panes as though startled.

He *should* be afraid.

Even *I* didn't know what I was capable of these days.

This accusation, however, that Cedric had triggered the elevator's failure made little sense. Because, in that instance, I'd again felt the pull for Helena's soul.

Even if Cedric *had* rigged the elevator, that didn't explain the note in the book about me. Helena didn't need to be tipped off that I happened to be real for Cedric's plans to undermine me to work. In fact, her doubts would only have served his purpose.

So why eliminate her suspicions?

"Why leave her the note?" I demanded. "Why tell her about me if you were just there to finish her off—or to ensure she was dead—just so you could nab her soul and rat me out to White?"

The light in the lantern sparked and flashed, flickering and sizzling—probably telling me off in spirit speak.

"You were waiting for me to slip up, weren't you?" I asked. "Following me around and biding your time for the moment I screwed up badly enough. But you needed insurance. You needed me to be invested. You knew I'd save her again to cover my ass. And you thought you'd get her involved and asking questions . . . Is that it?"

That seemed like a stretch, too. The Few might have forgiven my initial slip, but they wouldn't have tolerated my bid to cover up my part in a missing Fated.

To get what he wanted, Cedric had never needed me to become interested in a human.

To care about one . . .

All he would have had to do to put my ass in a vise was to secure Helena's soul himself and deliver it to Sir White.

At the end of the day, did it matter what Cedric hoped to accomplish with the note?

"Maybe I fucked up," I told him as I carried the lantern to the desk. "But you fucked up worse. By screwing with me every chance you got. If you hadn't hounded me so much, followed me around like a sniveling dumpster rat, right at this moment, I *might* be tempted to believe you'd really grant the life you'd get by taking up my scythe to Helena. Too bad I know you. And how you'd sooner snatch her spirit out of her first thing while I watched . . . right before sending *me* to hell."

The light from Cedric's soul died down to a soft glow, the orb inside going still.

But maybe he wasn't throwing a fit because he understood—finally—there wasn't any use.

I opened a drawer, shoved the lantern inside, then shut it sharply, sealing Cedric away in the dark, too wary he'd find a way to tip himself over, bust out of the lantern, and rejoin his form. Go after Helena again . . .

I certainly wasn't willing to risk rejoining his serpent's soul to his physical form just to interrogate him. Especially not when I was unlikely to get honest answers anyway.

At the same time, I needed to park him here just in case he *was* working with someone else. Like Mephistopheles. Or another bad actor he might have made an alliance with.

Johann never hazarded to leave the Netherworld, and only Flora, Cedric, and I had clearance to come and go. So now, if Cedric did have an accomplice, at the very least, they wouldn't be able to get to him.

The only problem was, if there *was* a coconspirator, or even a separate conspirator independent of Cedric, then Helena was still at risk.

Clenching the note tight in my hand, I swept from the office and through the cavernous, dimly lit library with its towering book-lined walls and rounded, balcony-lined floors that climbed to oblivion. Halls of more books connected to the main chamber, a good portion of their numbers readable only by The Few.

Could the book Helena had in her possession have come from this same chamber, pulled and planted by Cedric himself? Or had someone else placed it for her to find?

The only other being who could have planted the book was Flora. Unless the book *hadn't* come from the Hallowed Halls.

Flora wasn't the clandestine sort. She spoke her mind, and the two of us trusted one another because we had to. There was nothing I could conceive of for her to gain from such an action, either.

No matter the case, something was afoot, and the only person who could provide me with any answers to help clarify what that was just so happened to be the one being, the one woman, I'd already sworn to myself I would stay away from.

I kept forbidding myself from doing things regarding Helena. Those promises—the ones that tied back to the *oath* I'd taken—kept flying out the damn window every time I interacted with her.

But I had to know where she had gotten that book. Because she would have said something before now if Cedric had been the one to hand it to her.

Maybe none of this mattered. Maybe I should let sleeping dogs lie.

The Jenga tower currently stood, after all, and we—me, Helena, Flora, and Johann—were just waiting for the trigger event to occur so we could all play our parts in a controlled demolition. So it wouldn't do well for me to go mucking about trying to get answers to a mystery that was likely not a current problem.

Unless it was . . .

Until this latest discovery, it hadn't occurred to me that there could be additional enemies at play. Perhaps even a broader conspiracy to subvert and depose all three of us.

Or, at the very least . . . me.

If silence and solitude were my main companions in this role, paranoia was too often a special guest. But what was that old saying?

You're not paranoid if they really are out to get you . . .

Helena could clear this up in one conversation. By approaching her again, I'd only be tying up a loose end. Or else discovering a new proverbial bomb to dismantle.

Maybe I was just looking for an excuse to see her again, speak to her.

Ask her why she'd done what she had. Kissed me like that . . .

Then again, this whole note thing wasn't a stone I could afford to leave unturned. Not if Mephistopheles or another entity happened to be pulling strings.

Not when it was more than just Helena's life on the line. Her soul had become caught in a trap—one that looked more and more as though it had been designed to bait *me.*

Flora and Johann could be just as compromised as her. And those factors left me with no choice.

I would ask her where she'd gotten the book—that was all—and just consider getting to see her a secret silver lining to a visit that I would keep professional.

That's what I told myself, anyway.

28

HELENA

It had been three days since my . . . interlude with Grim. To say I was experiencing reaper withdrawal would be an understatement.

There was something so comforting about him. Not to mention alluring . . .

I'd learned so many unexpected things about him, like his love for music, that he *played* music, where he "lived," and how he conducted, well, business. I'd met his adorable family. Learned how much they cared for him . . .

I could certainly see why.

But . . . each of those things, illuminating as they had been, had only brought more burning questions about who he truly was—and why our souls seemed to sing to one another this way.

Did his soar the way mine did when we'd intertwined like that?

Exiting the director's office after delivering our department's finalized summer-reading-program plans to his desk, I headed for the stairwell, today's shift officially over.

Yesterday, the director had smiled so big when he told me the "stolen" bookmobile—which the police had recovered—would be repaired and operational again within the month. I'd smiled back despite my disappointment that we wouldn't be getting a replacement, and I'd be spending another frigid winter ushering bundled school kids into Gus the Bus, who'd already tried to kill me once. Something told me he'd probably be the way I was going to go out after all . . .

Then again, maybe I'd go out in a more dignified way, like choking on a taco or slipping on a rubber duck.

The good news was that no one seemed to know of my involvement in the Halloween-night events. My car had vanished entirely, which told me Grim had done something with her.

I wasn't complaining. At least, in the fleeting time I had left—however long that turned out to be—I wouldn't be fielding questions from the police or having to make up believable excuses for how and why my car had been turned into an accordion by the library's hijacked bookmobile.

With a sigh, I paused at the entrance to the stairwell, my gaze going to the silver elevator doors cordoned off with yellow caution tape. Repairs were still underway and likely would be for the rest of the year. Was it bad, though, that I wished I could, right at that moment, climb aboard again?

It wasn't that I had a death wish—I didn't. I loved my life, my job, my family, my patrons . . .

I just . . . longed to see Grim.

Shoot. Maybe I *did* have a death wish.

If I wanted to be super honest with myself, it wasn't just to *see* him, either.

Would we have *time* for another soul-shaking make-out session when my proverbial library card finally got scanned in for the last time?

Maybe he'd just been humoring me . . . Giving me a little thrill before my spirit got weeded from the shelves of life, stamped with a mystical "WITHDRAWN," and chucked into the great recycling bin beyond.

We'd agreed he wouldn't stop my fate from unfolding again, and why would he when, with Cedric in check and a covert way to the White Basin uncovered, the need no longer existed?

At the same time, I still wanted to believe he'd once again find a way to get me off another haywire elevator.

Maybe that was wishful thinking, but then the stars had written hope into the job description of my entire being. Hope could be a beautiful thing, too, a lifeline and a friend—something to hold on to even as your grip on what you held most dear, or even everything . . . slipped.

I took the stairs to the first floor, then nodded to Sam, the afternoon security officer, as I exited through the main entrance. From there, as the late-afternoon sun took on a more golden hue, I started down the white stone steps of the library.

I had to pause as I neared the book drop.

Peter stood there, leaning against one of the giant metal bins, hands shoved in the pockets of his sophisticated black double-breasted peacoat. He wore a gray scarf that complemented those silver eyes, but not enough for the Grim-thoughts-induced butterflies in my stomach to do anything other than fall dead to the floor of my being.

"Helena," he said as I neared him, headed toward the parking lot.

"Peter." Since we worked together, I almost had to keep the interaction cordial, even though there were any number of colorful things I'd like to call him at that moment. Names I'd picked up from my favorite storytime crew like "poop head," "stupid face," and the perennial favorite, "doo-doo brain."

"Where are you going?" he asked as I strode straight past him. "And why did you block me?"

Peter had left me a string of texts after Halloween night asking me if I wanted to talk, if he could bring me a cup of coffee at work, and finally, if he could take me out. I'd ignored him and, with that last text, blocked him.

Apparently, hitting that block button was the only thing I'd ever needed to do to get his full and undivided attention.

Once again, joke's on me . . .

"Now you're giving me the silent treatment?" he asked as he kept pace with me to the parking lot.

"Do you have a work-related question?" I asked him.

"Helena," he said, and it was the wounded tone in his voice that had me stopping at last to wheel on him. "What is it?" he pressed, spreading his arms. "What's happened? Are you still angry about that day on the elevator?"

The day I'd nearly died, he meant. The day I'd nearly died *again.*

Had he really forgotten everything that had happened after he'd gotten off that elevator?

Leave it to Peter to assume my reaction had everything to do with him, and nothing to do with the fact that I didn't have time to waste on him anymore. In truth, I never did.

"We're at work," I reminded him, picking up my stride again, shouldering the yellow and lived-in boho patchwork purse I'd returned to after ditching the beat-up pumpkin number.

"Neither of us are on the clock," he countered as he hurried to catch up with me.

"I've got somewhere to be," I said—which wasn't entirely a fib. My plan was to take myself to see a movie, and to buy a treat. Lately, the walls of my apartment had seemed to squeeze me, its emptiness reminding me of how much I'd missed out on by chasing the wrong things.

Sure, I had a good job, and I adored my family, but I had never gotten to meet my person. And it was looking more and more like . . . I never would.

I blamed myself for spending time chasing men who hadn't been playing for keeps—men who were not interested in finding their soulmate. Men like Peter.

"Where are you headed?" he asked. "Can I come with . . . you . . ."

He trailed off as we neared The Judge, a scowl clouding those handsome features as I pulled free Grim's jingling keys.

"What in the devil is *that*?" he asked, his gaze bouncing between me and Grim's monster car.

"Mine's in the shop," I said—slinging out a full-on fib this time. I followed that up with the truth, though. For some reason, I still felt obliged to offer Peter particulars that were really none of his business. "I'm . . . borrowing it."

"From whom? Mad Max?" he demanded, his voice pitching upward, a look of abject disgust crossing his features as he rounded the black-as-night vehicle, peering over the rims of his glasses the way a food critic would regard a moldy hot dog.

His scrutiny of The Judge stoked my anger, though I couldn't exactly say why. Regardless, I turned toward him, chin lifted and shoulders thrown back.

"My boyfriend," I said, a bald-faced lie—one blurted out with the hopes he would shut up and get lost, leave me alone for the remainder of my short life, and take his pompous pride with him while he was at it.

And the stricken look on his face—it was beyond worth the twinge of guilt my deception evoked. He stared hard at me, incredulous.

"*Your boyfriend?*" he repeated, like he couldn't believe such a word could ever be paired with someone like me.

That hurt, though it shouldn't have.

"Yes," I said, shoving the key into the driver's-side door.

"Since when do you have a boyfriend? Wait a second. Is *that* who you had in your apartment with you the other night?"

Again, the night I'd nearly died, he meant.

But could this seriously be ruffling his feathers?

Wasn't he seeing Cleo?

"I'm not comfortable discussing my personal life with work colleagues," I shot back, my anger rising.

"Really," he snipped, his tone wry as he pointed to himself. "Well, it wasn't so long ago that you felt comfortable doing quite a bit more with *this* work colleague."

For that, I should slap him. His words, sharper than any he'd ever thrown at me, sharper than I deserved, cut me to the quick and left me reeling.

Tears threatening, I opened the driver's-side door of The Judge, wrangling the keys free again. I froze with a gasp when, with the shifting of the car's side mirror, a familiar figure—and face—snapped into view within its reflection.

I swung around, the dead butterflies in my stomach revived in an instant, all of them taking wing all at once, their sudden flight relieving me of my ability to breathe.

Objects in mirror were indeed closer than they appeared . . .

He stood there in human form, dressed like a metalhead dream in torn jeans, half-laced boots, and leather jacket, black tattoos crawling out of the collar of his Metallica T-shirt to map his neck.

"Grim," I somehow managed to utter.

But that hardened blue gaze didn't even flicker my way. It instead remained unblinkingly trained on the man behind me—Peter.

29

GRIM

Looked like Helena had a friend. A friend who was making her very unhappy.

And that was making *me* pissed as fuck.

Hopefully, for his sake, this dipshit had good insurance.

Helena gaped at me as I approached, chains clinking, boots scuffing pavement. I spared her only a half-second glance as I moved to take the open car door from her and put myself between her and whoever this fuckwit was.

Since I'd only just arrived, I hadn't caught their conversation. But this jack nut's pointed glower combined with the devastation on Helena's face had my right hand twitching to become a fist.

"Is this him?" the man asked, gesturing toward me, his British accent—too much like Cedric's—irking the fuck out of me.

"This dickhead bothering you?" I asked Helena, peering down at her at last, our eyes meeting full-on for the first time since my arrival, the connection sending a shock wave of memory through my system—a distant and booming echo of that mind-altering kiss she'd planted on me. Not to mention my subsequent and scandalous scouring of her eternal being with the remnants of my tattered-ass soul.

"Um," she said, my keys tangled up between her delicate fingers, the nails of which she'd painted posy pink, a single shade darker than the natural hue of those perfect lips. Lips I could still feel the burn of . . .

Fuck, she was beautiful in the full light of day, the waning sunlight giving her the aura of a goddess with a glow that tried hard to mimic the gold of her hair.

"If you don't mind, we were talking," said ponytail boy, his words summoning back the scowl I'd forgotten to keep in place—right along with my glare. "I'd like to finish having a word with her."

Looked to me like this asshole had said—and done—enough already.

"Let me guess," I said, gesturing toward him. "This is Peter."

"Are you serious?" snapped Ponytail, speaking to Helena. "You talked to your boyfriend about me?"

Boyfriend?

My head snapped back to Helena, who peered up at me with saucer eyes, her expression terror-stricken. She death-gripped the keys, beaming a plea at me to forgive her for one of the hundreds of crimes she thought she'd committed just by existing. And in that frightened gaze, I got my answer.

Before I'd gotten here, she must have been trying to shake this loser, who'd probably asked her about the car. And, as many a woman had done before her, she'd made up a story about having a boyfriend just so she could escape the unwanted ardors of an overzealous prick who couldn't take a hint.

Got it, I tried to convey with my own gaze. *Assignment fucking accepted.*

Gently, I closed my hand around Helena's, capturing the keys to The Judge. Despite her fear, she relinquished them to me without the barest resistance, just as she had her soul when I'd tugged it from her grasp. I could still taste it, too. That lemonade sting, that hot-honey heat.

How bad of an idea was coming to see her again? Didn't matter now, did it?

"I *said* I wanted a word," Dick Stick called—to me.

"Yeah, well," I grumbled, "you know what they say about people in hell. Helena, get in the car."

I nodded her toward the passenger's side.

"I don't care who you are," said Asswipe as Helena rounded the rear of The Judge to get to the other side, "you don't get to tell her what to do."

"Relax," I told him, "she likes it."

That sure got his goat. Steering away from me, a glower overtaking his face, he hurried to intercept Helena. An action that ensured he was about to have a very, *very* bad day.

And given that he worked for a nonprofit, his insurance was probably shit.

Oh well.

Play stupid games . . .

"Give me another chance, Leaflet," he said, ignoring me as I stalked around The Judge's grille on my way to more formally introduce myself. Which was okay. He wouldn't be the first—or the last for that matter—to receive a heaping helping of find out after fucking around in my vicinity.

"Does Cleo know you're looking to date around?" Helena asked him.

"Cleo?" he echoed, fighting hard to keep the surprise out of his voice and his expression. By that time, I had him by the scruff of his stuffy-ass coat, and it didn't take much to fling him away from Helena and send him backpedaling.

He'd just *had* to use a nickname. And now I was probably going to kill him.

Insurance issue solved.

"How dare you put your hands on me?" he snarled after getting his feet under himself again.

I spread my arms, a gesture that asked him what he was going to do about it.

He started toward me.

Making my fucking day.

"Grim," Helena called to me from behind, her voice soft, frightened. "Don't hurt him, Grim, please."

Damnit.

Pete the Treat took a swing, which I dodged. His second fist, I caught.

I'd had tussles with literal demons and, once, a drunken banshee. *This* twig-in-the-mud was fucked.

Or he would have been.

I squeezed his hand in mine, silver rings digging into his flesh, and that expression of rage cracked, betraying pain. But Helena had asked me not to hurt the son of a bitch, so I wouldn't.

Very much.

I flung his arm aside, caught him by the collar of his coat, then shoved him backward, taking care to give his soul a little love jolt in the process.

He hit the side of a Camry hard before crumpling witless to the ground. Though he probably hadn't felt the impact because of my hard reset of his life, I took solace in the fact that he felt the effects now—and would for at least a week.

Nothing like a Control-Alt-Delete to recalibrate a bitch.

While Helena's ex or whatever sat on the pavement trying to remember his name, take stock of his glasses, and account for his nonexistent 'nads, I stalked back to the car.

Stunned, Helena traded her attention between the two of us until the instinct to run to Professor Punk Ass had her starting forward.

"Car," I said, pointing her toward the passenger door, and she obeyed, getting in before fastening her seat belt.

After removing the book I'd swiped from Helena's apartment from my back jeans pocket and tossing the volume into the rear seat, I slid into the driver's side, then turned the ignition. The Judge flared to life with a snarling roar.

Pete got to his feet. Then he got the finger.

Then, because Helena and I had things to talk about, shit that actually mattered, I peeled the fuck out.

30

HELENA

I should not be turned on by any of what had just happened. At all.

But *God* I was.

As Grim drove down Third Street, The Judge's now-familiar rumble reverberating through me, I gripped the sides of the leather seat and tried like heck to ignore the subtle vibrations of the vehicle, the gentle tremoring of that powerful engine as it rattled up my bones and teased all the parts of me that he'd just lit up like bumpers in a pinball machine.

"Peter . . . seemed okay, but I . . . he . . ." I shook my head, rephrasing the question. "Did . . . you kill him?"

"Just for a second," he grumbled.

I gaped at him—*and* at myself, galled. Because why was *that* hot, too?

"Can't you get in trouble for that?" I asked.

"At this point," he muttered, "it's in for a penny, in for a pound, Hart."

Hart?

That was new. And more distant than I liked.

He kept his eyes on the road, that white patch of hair swept back above his pierced ear, darker strands teasing the collar of his bad-boy jacket. The aroma of him, filling the cab, had my memories bouncing from one moment of closeness to the next and back again.

I'd never been high in my life. Never until now. And oh my God, this *car*.

The ceaseless rumbling of my seat made it all the harder to wrangle my imagination away from wandering beneath his clothes. And picturing those strong and sinewy, ring-lined hands all over me.

I cleared my throat when a sobering thought allowed me to get a handle on myself.

"Is this . . . a business call?" I asked him. "Reaper Man?" I added after a beat. He did a double take at me, and I shrugged because turnabout was fair play. "That's what I called you in my head before I knew your real not-real name."

"I'm not here for your soul, if that's what you're asking," he replied, which had me relaxing a little. "I think you'd know if I was."

He had a point. This was the first time he'd come to find me in my world ahead of any disastrous event. It was also the first time he'd approached me in his burn-the-world-down-and-me-with-it, hot-as-magma, sizzler human form.

I should roll down the window. Maybe I had a mint.

Who was I kidding? Neither of those things was going to help.

"I thought . . . I wouldn't see you again until it was time," I whispered.

"Yeah," he mumbled, "I thought so, too. Who the fuck was that piece of shit?"

"I work with Peter," I said. "We have . . . a history. I shouldn't have told him you were my boyfriend. I'm . . . sorry. It was the first thing that popped into my head when he asked about the car, and . . ."

And maybe I wished it was true.

"He's not going to try bothering you again," Grim assured me.

"Is . . . he going to be okay?"

"You told me not to hurt him," Grim said.

"Right before you slammed him into a Toyota and rubber-band snapped his soul."

"He's fine."

Fine? I didn't think so. But maybe I also, just this once . . . didn't care.

Peter had behaved poorly enough to deserve stern words at least.

I'd gotten a few from Grim myself . . .

And a few more interesting ones said *about* me.

Relax, she likes it.

As Grim's rebuttal from earlier swirled through my mind, I shoved my knees together, gripping the seat even harder. Because he was right. I *did* like it. And I'd liked it even more when he'd told Peter I liked it—being told what to do. Bossed around. By him . . .

"What's the matter?" asked Grim, oblivious to my current struggles, my mounting strife. My boiling blood. Would he notice if I turned on the AC? "You want me to slow down or something?"

Yes. No . . .

"Why are you gripping the seat like that?" he demanded. "Are you afraid?"

No.

Yes . . .

"Where . . . where are we going?" I asked.

"I'm only taking you home," he said. "I just . . . needed to ask you something. I thought the parking lot at your work would be a neutral space."

"You have my phone number," I said as he pulled to a stop at a red light, my words earning a scalding glare from him.

"Look," he grumbled, "I didn't mean to scare you by showing up."

"I'm not scared," I murmured. "I'm just . . . curious. About what made you decide to stop by in person."

"Yeah," he said, "well, I'm curious about a few things, too."

Oh, so he was going to avoid the question, huh? Interesting . . .

"Like . . . ?" I probed.

"For starters?" he asked. "Why would someone like you ever waste your time on a guy like that? Was that the dipshit you went to the costume party with? You said you work with him, but I don't get it. Is he your ex or what? And did he fucking call you *Leaflet*?"

My face burned and I sank in the seat a bit. Because it was a cringey pet name, wasn't it?

The light turned green, and he hit the gas again—clearly bothered.

A small smile touched my lips, and then I turned my attention forward, eyes on the familiar roads as he took every turn like he'd driven this route to my apartment a hundred times.

Like he really was my boyfriend . . .

Was Grim interested in my relationship with Peter because he was genuinely curious . . . or could it be he was jealous? Why did I want to pretend it was the latter . . . ?

"Peter and I were together . . . yes," I said. "We weren't official for very long before he called it off. I found out recently that he lied and possibly, I'm still not sure, cheated. There were red flags but . . . I overlooked them. I guess I wanted to believe in my idea of Peter instead of the person he kept showing me he really was."

"Why?" he asked again.

"Because I'm starting to realize—too late, I think—that I have a bad habit of believing the best of people."

Grim got quiet. Then, without warning, he pulled off into a strip mall, and then into a parking spot in a deserted patch of the lot.

"That's not a bad habit," he said before throwing the car into park and killing the engine.

"Why are we stopped?" I asked him in the swelling silence.

For a long time, he didn't say anything, and my anxiety grew. Especially when he just kept staring forward like that.

"That guy back there," he said at last. "Is *he* the reason you stop yourself from smiling sometimes? Or why you're always apologizing for nothing?"

I frowned, a zing of fear shooting through my heart. At being seen. Especially by him.

I opened my mouth to answer but my voice, as it so often did when I seemed to need it most, fled.

"Is he?" Grim pressed, turning to look at me, those eyes cold in hue but not angry, or judging. Instead, he seemed again to be sincere in his curiosity.

"I . . ." Gosh. What could I say? Maybe I didn't even know the answer. Peter had made me feel small more than once, but . . . he wasn't the only one. I was a lot for some people. Most people, it seemed. Except for the kids.

"I scare off most guys," I blurted out.

Grim's brow furrowed even more, his confusion deepening.

Up came my hands to help me explain. "I just say things sometimes, and I'm also a little clumsy but, well, you knew that. And I make jokes that people groan at. But . . . you knew that, too. I like weird, off-putting things like bright colors and big earrings that match but don't—like a soda and popcorn, or a flower and a bumblebee? I make voices for all the characters when I do storytime—accents and everything. That can be a lot—*I* can be a lot—and I guess I just don't want to make anyone uncomfortable or mad or both, but no matter what I do, I just . . . seem to do that without trying anyway. If . . . that makes sense."

He turned his gaze forward again, eyeing the strip mall across from us.

After another several seconds, he spoke.

"You ever think that might be a them problem and not a you problem?"

I blinked at him.

"I don't run into many people like you," he added when I didn't answer—because I was still considering the possibility of what he'd said. "Which, if you think about it, is saying something. You . . . give off this energy. Even the fucking *bird* sees it."

"Pluto?" I asked, perking up. "And what do you mean? What did he see?"

"Your . . . light," he said, summoning another blush to my cheeks. "But it's not just the fact that you . . . *glow.* I don't know how else to describe it. Being around you. It's . . . like when you hear a song that's really good. A song that you can't deny is good. And if people don't like it—or say they don't or pretend not to or whatever while they try to turn it down or off—it's not because the song is bad. Deep down they're just pissed it's good. And because it's not *their* song. It's yours. And listening to it reminds them of how their own song can't compare. Or outright sucks. Because *they* suck."

A small smile touched my lips. Dare I call him sweet again?

"I think I get on *some* people's nerves," I said. "And if I'm a song, I'm not for everyone."

"See," he said, leaning back in his seat, an arm draped over the steering wheel, "I think they get on their own fucking nerves. And being around you just reminds them of that. So they shoot the messenger, try to contain you by dumping their shit on you instead of following your lead and figuring out how to play their own song better. My advice? When it comes to your song, turn that shit up for the people who *do* like it. And everyone else? Fuck 'em."

My heart swelled and I had to fight the urge to launch myself at him—for, like, the tenth time. More than that, I wanted so badly to believe him. That there wasn't anything wrong with me, and that I wasn't the one messing everything up all the time by being too much. By being . . . me.

"E-even if my song is like . . . a Taylor Swift song?" I asked.

His gaze remained forward, though those deep blues narrowed.

I gritted my teeth and cringed internally, waiting for the fallout. But then he said, "Honestly, she's got a few good ones."

Gasping, I clasped my hands together, joy lighting up my face.

"I said a *few*," he grumbled, leveling me with a "don't get excited" glare.

I giggled, clapped, and pattered my feet on the floor mat, delighted that he liked at least three of her songs. That's what "a few" roughly translated to, right?

In response, the tiniest of amused smiles tugged at one corner of his lips, but he banished it before glaring forward again.

An emotion I couldn't quite name, some mix of gratitude and affection, whisked through me all the same, and I opened my mouth to thank him for, if nothing else, the food for thought. But then he spoke again.

"Look," he said, "I need to ask you about something."

"Something good?" I asked with a hopeful upward inflection.

Grim didn't answer but twisted toward me, reaching into the rear seat in a way that exposed and brought his collar close to me—an action that had me actually licking my lips.

For the briefest of moments, I got a closer look at those black tattoos, too. Roughly silver dollar sized, they all took different shapes, each of which fit perfectly around the others, like stickers in a sticker book.

A raven like Pluto, a crescent moon, a grape leaf, a star . . .

I wanted to ask about them so badly—what they represented, because they had to signify something important. He was covered in them.

A short gasp escaped me, though, when, returning to his seat fully, he flashed a familiar book between us—the one about him.

That must have been what he'd tossed in the back seat.

"Saw this on your bedside table," he said, "and found the note inside. I need to know where you got this—who you got it from."

I took the book from him. "After our first encounter, I did what any librarian would do. Research." Opening the back cover, I showed him the RFID tag pasted on the inside. "This copy belongs to the main branch, and—sidenote—you'll be pleased to know that the book correctly designates you as a psychopomp."

"A psycho *what*?" he growled.

"A psychopomp," I repeated, my lids fluttering in surprise, because I couldn't be the first one to mention this to him, could I? Then again, he *was* a tad . . . antisocial. "It comes from the Greek word 'psychopompos.'"

"I am not a pompous psycho."

I snort-laughed but quickly sobered when he failed to crack a smile. Then I cleared my throat.

"A psychopomp," I said, "is an usher or guide to the dead, a supernatural being whose role is to escort the souls of the living to the afterlife. A nonjudgmental conductor instead of death itself. Like Hermes, Anubis, or Azrael. So, I was right about that—and so is the book. You're a psychopomp."

"If you say so," he allowed. "What can you tell me about the note?"

"Nothing, unfortunately," I replied. "I found the note inside. I don't know anything about who put it there but . . . I know someone who does."

I wasn't sure I should drag one of my coworkers, especially Hunter, into any of this. Even at eighteen, he was still a kid. And he'd just been doing his job of shelving returns when he'd had his run-in with whoever—or whatever—he'd encountered in the stacks before I'd arrived on the scene. But I did trust Grim. And the note—I could see why he'd want to know more about its origins.

"The book wasn't on the shelf even though the system showed it as being in," I continued. "Someone had pulled it right before I got there—someone who must have known I would come looking for it and find the note inside."

"Any idea what this person looked like?"

"You're worried about this," I said after a beat. "*That's* why you came back."

And that was the only reason he'd come back.

My heart sank while my throat tightened. Normally, embarrassment made me flush, but in this instance, my mortification had the blood draining from my face. The truth was he didn't like me back. Not *that* way. How could he? If nothing else, he wasn't allowed to.

And, oh yeah, I was supposed to bite the dust any day now anyway. Even if there had been some mutual attraction between us, which was still debatable, at least on his part, by default, we weren't compatible.

"It could have been Cedric who left the note," he said, that gaze remaining ever forward, his jaw tight. "But, as you know, I can't exactly ask him right now."

"My coworker friend said someone came in looking for the book just before me," I explained. "He said the guy was 'weird,' but . . . I didn't get a descriptor other than that. Now, though, it's more obvious than ever that whoever planted that note knew what was going on with us and, for whatever reason, wanted me to find it."

And to know Grim was real.

"I need to talk to this coworker friend," said Grim, a predictable response.

"He works tomorrow," I said. "He's there late afternoon. You could come in around four or so, and I could introduce you. Actually . . . he's into heavy metal, too."

Grim looked my way again. "I have more enemies than just Cedric," he said, "and you already know Johann's and Flora's enemies are mine as much as they are theirs."

"Package deal," I said with a nod. "Families are like that."

"So is the Mafia," he grumped as he restarted the car.

I swallowed hard, my heart leaping into panic mode, thrumming with the fear of parting ways with him again.

"You have to go back to work," I guessed, "is that it?"

"What?" he asked, which was becoming a common response from him. Perhaps a sign that I did, at least in some capacity, rattle him. "There's always work, but no pull for any Fated Souls."

"So you don't *have* to go? And speaking of the Fated, do . . . you retrieve them often?"

"I don't really pay that much attention," he said, "but maybe a few times a year."

"Wow." I got quiet, because that was somewhat of a bombshell, wasn't it? Here I'd been thinking one in ten people must be a Fated Soul. Apparently, they were much rarer than that. No wonder there was so much hubbub around me. I wanted to know more. I wanted to know everything. Maybe there would be comfort in knowing.

"Listen," I said, "if you're not pressed for time, would you want to get something to eat? I mean . . . *do* you eat? Sorry, again, if that's an offensive question."

"Why would that be offensive?"

"I don't know." Again, I started talking with my hands, my own telltale sign of nervousness. "You never touched your coffee and, well, if you didn't because you're unable, then it's kind of like asking someone who can't swim if they want to go deep-sea diving."

"It's been a long time," he said.

"Since you've deep-sea dived?" I asked. "I thought you went just the other d—"

"What do you want?" he half asked, half barked.

I shut my mouth and turned to stare forward. Now heat did crawl up my neck.

Of course I was wasting his time, and he could see straight through me, too. He was the Grim Reaper—ageless and important. He wanted me to tell him what I was after so he could ditch me and get on with his unlife while he waited for mine to expire.

On any given night, he saw—and handled—innumerable souls. Why wouldn't mine be just another number to him?

"To eat, Helena," he clarified, the words sending my startled gaze straight back to him—because he must have read the hurt in my expression. Did the softening in his tone mean he cared about that? "There's a Chinese place right there." He pointed to the strip mall. "Do you like egg rolls?"

I smirked—lopsidedly, my heart buoyed again.

"I do," I allowed, "but . . . to be honest, I could go for something a bit more substantial than a snack."

"Are you calling me a cheapskate?"

I blinked at him, taken aback, but I recovered quickly—*and* smoothly. "Well . . . you *did* take me to McDonald's on our last date."

"Hey," he said, turning to hold up a finger between us, "that shit's expensive now."

A broad grin spread onto my face—impossible to suppress or subdue. "Did . . . you just make a joke?"

Another joke?

"I don't joke," he said, shifting the car into gear, and when he pulled out of the parking lot again, rejoining traffic, I didn't bother asking him where we were going a second time.

So long as I was with him . . . I didn't care.

31

GRIM

I didn't know what the fuck I was doing.

She was so gorgeous in that black plaid skirt and white silk blouse with her hair in a ponytail, and here I was in jacked jeans, faded band T-shirt, and half-laced shitkickers.

Still, I couldn't just take her anywhere. After her McDonald's dig, I had to redeem myself, especially since she'd referred to that outing as our "last date."

It hadn't been a date. We both knew that. As well as we knew this wasn't a date.

But here we were, seated in a booth at a joint called the Hidden Gem, a 1920s speakeasy-themed restaurant in the heart of the downtown restaurant district near the river.

Johann and Flora had said I should take Helena somewhere "nice." This place fit the bill. But to say I was woefully underdressed would be an understatement. Then again, I didn't do ties anyway.

"How did you know about this place?" Helena asked in a hushed tone after our waiter brought our drinks—straight whiskey for me and Chardonnay for her.

"I didn't," I said, going ahead and tossing back half the amber liquid, which burned hot and bright in the back of my throat, like

I'd swallowed a star. It had been lifetimes since I'd imbibed anything. Still, the sensation *was* familiar. And oddly, in more ways than one . . .

Helena's eyes bugged as she watched me, questions brimming in that gaze. And of course they would. Most of the time we'd been together, I'd been a fucking skeleton. Now here I was shooting high-end bourbon served neat.

Did I have the balls to tell her that was largely because tossing back this searing sweet liquid fire was probably the only thing that rivaled the act of tasting her soul with mine?

Nope. But I could think it.

Thankfully, I'd ordered a double and I had one more swig left to get me through a dinner where I had little interest in the food.

I was going to have to order—and consume—something, though.

Like I'd told Helena, it had been a while. Long enough that I couldn't remember what I'd tasted last. I never took this form anymore. It took too much out of me. Simultaneously, assuming this long-since-shed guise burdened me with far more than I cared to shoulder.

But sitting with her made the slow creeping-in of my murky memory worth it. At least that's what I told myself while the shadows of the past remained at bay.

Maybe she was keeping those shadows away, too.

Sources of light did that.

"You just picked this place at random, you mean?" she asked.

I glanced away from the menu that, sparse as it was, still overwhelmed me, and scanned the darkly lit and windowless dining area.

Booths with shining burgundy studded leather seating lined the bare brick walls while matching fringed art deco lampshades hovered above each. Nearby, a bartender garbed in Prohibition-era attire, complete with bow tie and handlebar mustache, mixed cocktails at a varnished bar.

Old-school, *Gatsby*-style jazz played softly over some unseen sound system.

"It looked classier than a fast-food joint," I said, "so I thought I'd give it a try."

"Well, it really *is* a hidden gem, isn't it?" she asked.

I didn't answer. Because, if you asked me, the gem wasn't the joint.

The waiter came back, and when Helena smiled at him, I had to resist the urge to give him a little flick of the soul, too.

Wouldn't be doing myself any favors if I went around spiritually tasing people because I'd caught some feelings for a Fated that I couldn't seem to fucking regulate.

I was in enough shit.

"I'll have a small margherita pizza," she said, then glanced my way.

Frowning, I peered down at the menu again because now the waiter was looking at me.

My turn, I guess. It was just that, in the last however many decades—centuries—food had become such a foreign concept to me. I didn't know what anything on this menu was except for the oysters, and I'd had enough of the ocean as of late.

"Do you need another moment, sir?" asked Mr. Helpful.

Lost, I peered back up at Helena, who once again fluttered her lids at me, emerald eyes searching. Then, seeming to pick up on my ineptitude, she shot them toward the waiter.

"Make that a large pizza," she said. "We'll share it."

"Of course," said the guy before hurrying off, his steps fast like he couldn't wait to get away from us. Or, rather, me.

Death had an aura most humans recognized—even if only on a subconscious level. And I could look, act, drink, and eat like a human all day. But that didn't change the fact that there was obviously something off about me. And the only living, breathing human I'd ever encountered who had not been repelled by that currently sat straight across from me.

"Before, in the car," she said, her voice soft, "you meant it's been a long time since you've eaten, didn't you?"

"I sort of hope I remember how," I mumbled, which made Helena laugh outright again—bright and happy in a way that made her cover her mouth quickly.

I hadn't meant to be funny, but something warm unfolded within me at the knowledge I'd made her laugh—even if she was laughing at me.

"I'm sorry," she said. "Sometimes I think you're joking and . . . you're not."

"I don't joke," I repeated, which wasn't so true. But I had an image and a reputation to uphold. Even in front of her. Maybe especially in front of her.

"I hope you like pizza," she said. "Have . . . you ever had it?"

"Not that I can remember," I said.

"Remember," she echoed while I stole another glance around the room, still on alert for danger even if Cedric happened to be in a drawer—another drawer. Even without Cedric parading around with his magic, Helena was still a Fated Soul. Granted, being who and what I was, I ought to feel the tug of her spirit before any catastrophic event, but that didn't stop me from keeping an eye out. Especially not while we still had no real answer regarding the origins of the note.

"Grim, what *do* you remember?" The question drew my attention back to her. "I mean . . . if you don't mind my asking."

"About?"

"Um," she said, "about . . . before. Meaning . . . before you were Grim. When we were in the Netherworld Forest, you mentioned that . . . there *was* a before."

"The answer is nothing," I said truthfully. "I remember nothing." Well . . . that was mostly truthful. "Very little is what I remember. And that's how I prefer it."

Helena tilted her head at me, curious. She opened her mouth and then closed it, then opened it again, as if selecting, dismissing, and reselecting her words. "Do . . . you remember what happened when Cedric attacked us in the restaurant?"

"I snapped his neck," I said.

Now it was Helena's turn to shoot a glance around us, probably hoping no one had overheard me.

"Um," she amended, "I mean . . . right before that."

I frowned at my rocks-less rocks glass, tempted to shoot the rest of the whiskey but hesitant since that would also mean I wouldn't have any left. I could always order more, and the liquor wasn't going to do anything to me since my blood burned through the stuff before it could hit the brain I did currently possess—along with a pulse that, for whatever reason, started to race.

"Cedric fucked with me," I answered, "and I fucked with him back."

"You . . ." She trailed off, studying her wineglass while she rotated it by the stem with both hands. "You said someone's name. At least . . . your doubles did. I asked Cedric who it was, but he said he didn't know. He said the doubles were 'mirror chimeras,' and that they could only reflect what their target presented them with."

A name? They'd said a name . . .

Maybe I did remember that. Vaguely.

The best thing about assuming my other form was that the empty skull left no room for the memories that belonged to the life I'd led in *this* body.

"Please don't say the name," I whispered. "I don't remember . . . but I know I don't want to, either."

Helena's eyes fell. "I'm sorry."

"Don't be," I jumped to say. "For anything."

"I didn't mean to overstep—"

"You didn't," I said. "And you haven't."

"I . . . haven't?" Those eyes, timid, lifted to find mine again. "At all?"

Now she had me looking down, staring into my whiskey yet again as the sensation of that kiss returned to haunt my entire being. "No."

Silence overtook the table—uncomfortable but simultaneously loaded with heat and pressure, the consuming kind of burn that comes right before the wood in a bonfire breaks and embers go spilling.

"Grim," she said, severing the silence that otherwise might have devoured us both. "Don't you think it's odd that, well, nothing's happened yet? In . . . the last few days, I mean. Because if I'm a Fated Soul and already overdue for the White Basin . . . shouldn't that hurry things along?"

"Not necessarily," I said.

"Oh?" she probed.

"I don't know," I amended, grabbing the whiskey glass, my hand tight on the tumbler. "This has never happened before, so in this instance, it can't be said I know what I'm talking about. So, maybe it is odd. I guess I just don't like it, and I want to pretend the delay is perpetual."

"Don't like what?" she pressed.

I threw back the rest of the whiskey before setting the glass down too hard. "I don't want to do it."

Those lids fluttered again. Confusion flittered across her features while she tried to interpret my blunt but still-obtuse response.

"You should get to stay," I clarified. "Here, I mean. You're doing stuff. Good stuff. You smile and shit—that's getting rarer than you think. I guess that's why I saved you on that balcony. You didn't even know what I looked like, and you were hitting on me. Who does that?"

"My offer would have stood even if I *had* known what you looked like," she said tentatively, and why did I believe her? Maybe because she'd kissed my teeth, embraced my bones, run straight into my fleshless arms instead of away . . .

"I should talk to White," I said, eyes shooting askance because sometimes it hurt to look at her knowing she was going to die. The pain got worse with the knowledge I'd be there to see it. How was I supposed to just let it happen? I hadn't that night on the balcony when I'd known her for less than ten minutes. Now I knew what it felt like to hold her. And I knew myself, too. Plan or no plan, I wasn't going to stand by any other time.

And didn't that make me just as doomed as her?

"You can't talk to White," she cautioned as the waiter returned, bringing the pizza, which did smell good, though I still couldn't be bothered to be hungry. For food. "Flora and Johann are looking out for you. They want to protect you, and you have to let them. That's the deal."

"Are you trying to tell me what to do?" I asked her.

"Relax," she said with a wink as she used the serving spatula to slide a slice of pizza onto one of the small plates before setting it in front of me, "you like it."

That wasn't all I liked.

Fuck, I knew I shouldn't have come back.

I'd gone centuries untouched. And entirely unbothered by it.

Somehow, she'd now rendered me a touch-starved fool.

"Do you want Parmesan?" she asked as she wiggled a little jar full of powdery white cheese at me.

Want?

What I *wanted* was to save her life—for real and for good, not just temporarily. I wanted to protect that light that had been bright and powerful enough to blast me through again and again. I wanted to leave her be and let her grow like the wild rose she was. I wanted to return to her decades from now, after she'd already gotten everything she'd ever wanted out of life and was *ready* for a new fate.

I wanted other things, too. Things I shouldn't want.

Days with her.

Nights with her . . .

I wanted this pizza with her to not be our last as well as our first.

But the odds of getting any of that were nowhere near being in my favor.

So, for the moment, I just said, "Sure."

32

HELENA

Grim took me home after dinner—which he again refused to let me pay for.

Instead, more vintage cash came out of his wallet and went into the bill presenter, but the waiter didn't say anything. His lack of comment combined with the fact that he never asked if we wanted dessert gave away our server's eagerness to be rid of us. Or, rather, Grim—who (this time at least) wasn't *unfriendly*.

He did, however, exude a certain . . . aura.

One that promised to end everything you held dear. That aura, though—it hit differently for me. *Much* differently.

Like I couldn't *wait* to be drawn into his event horizon and crushed by that black hole pull . . .

If only I could be so lucky.

After parking The Judge in my usual spot outside my building, Grim escorted me up to my apartment door. We took the stairs instead of the elevator, because I guess neither of us wanted to play with fire any more than we already were.

"Do you want to come in?" I asked him. "I have some ice cream in the freezer."

"There's strawberry shortcake in your fridge, too," he said, his deadpan bluntness along with the statement itself shocking me.

I squinted at him, perplexed. "Wh—how did you—?"

"Don't worry about it."

"Wait a second," I said, hands going to my hips. "Not so fast. You're saying you've been *back* in my apartment?"

"It's from that bakery close to the library."

He wouldn't meet my gaze, but that didn't keep me from blinking up at him, floored. Right before I sucked in a huge, loud gasp, a major revelation crashing over me. "Oh my God, it was *you*."

"I didn't do anything."

"You did too!"

"Where *else* was I going to stash it?" he asked.

"No!" I piped. "*You* fixed my string!"

"I don't know what you're talking about," he said, his voice gruffer than before.

But he wasn't getting off the hook that easily.

"You fibber, it *was* you!" I narrowed my eyes at him. "How many times have you been in my apartment?"

"Am I in trouble?"

"Were you checking on me?"

He didn't answer. Which was answer enough.

"I never saw you," I said. "So it must have been after I went to bed."

He swallowed hard. "You going to tell me off?"

"Well," I said, folding my arms, "I *can* if you want to come in and have some stalker-berry shortcake with me."

"I don't think that's a good idea." He refused to meet my gaze again, that faint odd growl back in his voice as he extended the car keys to me.

Did he think I really *was* mad? Or that I would bite? In his defense, if given the chance, I just might . . .

Dare I tell him that?

No. Dying from embarrassment was something I hoped to avoid.

I opened my hand and Grim dropped his keys into my palm—like he didn't want to touch me. I gripped them hard, waiting to feel grounded by the burn of the cold metal.

"You're not still thinking of going to talk to the higher-ups about me . . . are you?" I probed.

"I go back and forth," he admitted, his voice still tight with some emotion I couldn't pinpoint, "on whether or not it would do any good . . . for you."

"Do . . . I get a last wish?" I asked him.

His eyes snapped up to mine, and a scowl darkened his expression. This time, I didn't back down. It wasn't that his (literal) death stare didn't faze me anymore. Oddly enough, I'd just developed a tolerance to its gut-piercing, soul-skewering effect.

"I want you to go forward with the plan to wait," I said. "I want you to do what's best for you."

"I'm not sure I can do that," he said, his jaw tightening as he looked away, down the hall where the elevator dinged and opened for my elderly neighbor, Ms. Lynn. I waved as she turned around after boarding. She waved back half-heartedly, her wide-eyed attention, shielded by gaudy, rhinestone-encrusted cat-eye glasses, fixed on Grim—at least until the doors closed.

"It . . . will be okay," I assured him. "And . . . if it's me you're worried about? Well, *I* will be okay."

"No, you won't," he snapped, that gaze shooting back to capture mine, sharper than ever. "Do you even know what you're saying?"

"I know what I have control over," I told him with a shrug, "and . . . I know what I don't. Fate, by its very definition, does what it wants, doesn't it?"

"So do I," he said.

I tilted my head at him, unable to help a small, bemused smile. "Are we having our first fight right now?"

"I don't understand," he growled, ignoring my teasing, his agitation growing. "Why aren't you afraid?"

"Who says I'm not?" I asked. "But even if I am—and I am—that doesn't change anything."

To that, he offered no reply. After a shaky breath, I spoke again.

"Are you coming into the library tomorrow to talk to Hunter? That's my coworker friend."

"I'll think about it," he grumbled before turning and walking away, back in the direction we'd come.

I stood there and gaped after him until he vanished into the stairwell, at a loss for what I'd said, what I'd done, to chase him off after such a nice night—though maybe I shouldn't have been.

Maybe his abrupt exit just meant he'd gotten a call for another Fated. Maybe I should be glad that, for the moment, I wasn't on his list of tonight's pickups.

I wasn't glad, and in his absence, only sadness emerged.

I opened my apartment door and stepped inside, dropping the mail I'd stopped to collect on the way in on the little hall table.

The energy bill sat on top. Should I even bother paying it?

Sighing loudly, I kicked off my flats and scanned the darkened apartment, which I had cleaned and tidied since Grim's last visit. In vain, it seemed. Maybe I'd secretly been hoping he *would* stop by. On the flip side, a part of me had worried about him having to step over clutter on his way to get to my soul if I happened to bite it here at home somehow.

I dropped my purse and the keys on the table next, ignoring the oppressive loneliness that closed in on me—right along with that hounding fear I'd just confessed to him that, despite all my jokes and dismissive comments, I *did* feel. Acutely.

At least—ironically—whenever I wasn't with him.

I threw the deadbolt and put the latch on the door, my heart in shambles now that I was officially alone, left to my own company and once more saddled with the crushing reminder that every second

I continued to breathe was borrowed—bought by a being, a man, who had never meant to sell himself out for my sake.

Like so much else in life—and death—it had just . . . happened.

Now it was time to accept that, even if he did care about me, I was still just a mistake he needed to rectify.

Not an easy task since reaching that level of acceptance required me to skip all the other stages of grief.

How many of them were there again?

Right at this moment, they seemed to all be coming for me at once.

Every night until tonight, I'd done an okay job of avoiding my deeper feelings, right along with the full weight of what my death really meant. What it would mean for others . . .

I'd done all the things, of course. All those things that 90 percent of people never got to do. I'd FaceTimed with my parents, for instance, and met up with Brooke at a local orchard for wine tasting and tipsy apple picking. The two of us had laughed so hard over old times, and for a few hours, I forgot about my predicament. Yesterday, I'd called my other friends to catch up, pretending the whole time that nothing was the matter when, in reality, *everything* was the matter.

Tonight, though, I didn't want to talk to anyone. No one but him.

Since I wasn't going to get to do that, I could try my usual trick of marathoning musicals or glutting myself on romance novels, but the problem was those things didn't make me feel alive. In the days since I'd left the Hallowed Halls, all my pastimes had come to feel like diversions I couldn't afford. Not that I had the bandwidth to concentrate on them anyway.

Instead, I was caught in this weird state of in-between, simultaneously wishing for a miracle and that the other shoe would go ahead and finally drop—if for no other reason than for a release from the pain of being locked in limbo like this.

I pressed a hand to the door and leaned my forehead against the cool surface, pining for my soul's undertaker more than I had for anyone or anything after learning I was staring down the barrel of a proverbial and inescapable gun.

On the one hand, my longing for him made no sense. On the other hand, considering the way he made me feel, that finding love *was* possible, my desires made all the sense in the world.

But then, Grim hadn't returned my advances or flirted back—no matter how bold the knowledge of my impending demise made me. He was still a pipe dream. *We* were a pipe dream. And I didn't have time for those anymore.

"I wish it wasn't so," I whispered, pushing away from the door, ready to end the night with a good and long ugly cry now that reality had finally seen fit to slam into me, totaling my already teetering world.

When I turned around again, though, I jumped to find him standing in front of me, all six foot whatever of his sexy, doom-and-gloom self stationed between me and the rest of my empty apartment, a never-before-seen ferality in that icy gaze.

My breath caught while my heart launched into hyperdrive.

Glowering hard at me, tension knitting his entire frame, he closed the distance between us in two long strides.

He caught me with those tattooed hands.

Then his lips—warm and demanding—found mine an instant before he backed me into the door, pinning me there.

33

GRIM

To hell with hope—at least any I had for myself.

Maybe a taste of heaven was all someone like me needed.

Whatever inferno waited for me after all I'd done—and was about to do—could have me. Already, I could say with authority that the inevitable torment I would face for shirking my duties, ignoring my oath, crossing this boundary . . . with her . . . was worth it.

She tasted of cherries and vanilla, her subtle citrus-and-honeysuckle scent teasing up my memory of Halloween night when she'd flung her arms around me, her supple curves colliding with my unyielding bones.

As Helena kissed me back, her warm and soft hands framed my face, her lips answering the demands of mine. Her desire was unmasked now as she held me to her, her fervor dispelling all the doubts I'd entertained that she hadn't wanted me. Hadn't meant the things she'd said to me.

She had.

And that knowledge unleashed something ferocious inside me, a greedy craving that I'd been trying to hold at bay—one that now surged up out of my gutted and war-torn soul to infuse my blood and enflame my flesh.

Neglected and abandoned for so long, this suit of muscle and skin had become alien to me. In this moment, though, with Helena pressed against me, her heart banging out an SOS that I *itched* to answer—and assuage—I became irrevocably fused with my body again. With hers, too.

Her hands half fell, half slid to grip the collar of my jacket, and the act of those slim and delicate fingers curling around the stiff black leather had my tongue diving to taste hers.

A soft murmur escaped her as she met my invasion with an answering brush of her own tongue, and that eager caress combined with that small hum of pleasure sent ripples through me. The simple idea that I'd done anything she liked threatened to set me on fire.

I wanted more. I wanted too much.

To coax that murmur into a moan. To taste all the rest of her with both tongue *and* spirit.

I wanted her under me, naked, flushed, delirious.

Bracing one hand against the door, I cupped her face with the other, pressing into her as unadulterated *need* ripped through me. My muscles drew tight, and my blood rushed through my veins, making everything—my skin, my mind, my jeans—suddenly . . . cramped.

How long had it been since I'd wanted anything? Anything that mattered . . .

Helena mattered.

She made me feel shit I'd forgotten I had the capacity to feel. She yanked my whole fucking soul into the light where colors outside of black and white rampaged through a world I didn't—and couldn't—belong to.

I didn't care anymore. Not about what I was or wasn't supposed to do.

I just needed her.

Deepening the kiss, I made one daring promise after another to her mouth as she pushed my jacket down, the stiff leather sliding back. If she wanted it off, I wasn't going to argue. In that moment, if she'd asked for it, I'd have given her my soul.

The leather garment dissipated to smoke before it could hit her carpet.

Helena placed her hands to my chest, pushing me back as she broke the kiss.

Instead of being disturbed by my powers—this reminder that I was still, essentially, more of a what than a who—Helena brightened, and a strange interest colored by a keen hunger lit those already-luminous eyes.

I backtracked as she shoved, stopping only when those fingers burrowed beneath the hem of my T-shirt, gathering the material up to unveil my torso—a canvas of small and interlocking black tattoos etched over muscle.

At least, the emblems would look like tattoos to her. In reality, they were all scars.

Imprints—each left by the rarest of souls. Those who, upon my gathering of them, had stamped their mark on me, both figuratively *and* literally.

Helena wasn't nearly tall enough to pull my shirt free. So, as she lifted, I took the job from her, and the fabric evaporated in an instant.

She wanted to see. And *I* wanted her to have whatever the fuck she wanted.

Those eyes scoured my naked chest, scaling down the innumerable solid black symbols and shapes that wrapped my biceps, wound my forearms, and mapped my torso, the collage of symbols vanishing past the barrier of my belt.

Helena seemed to be noting and appreciating each one, and I waited while she took me in, my own breath nonexistent while she stood with chest heaving, trying to catch hers.

But I didn't want her to catch her breath. I wanted, instead, to hear her murmur and moan for me. I wanted my soul wrapped around hers again.

I wanted a few other things besides, and at this point, there was no hiding exactly what.

Helena had stopped, though. Maybe because she'd gotten ahold of herself. Realized what she was doing . . .

She didn't meet my gaze again. Instead, she stared hard at my chest. Several moments passed before, finally, she lifted timid and curious hands. They hovered in the air between us for an instant, and then her fingertips went to trail my stomach, bumping over muscles on their way down—and down.

Going rigid all over, I had to fight the urge to shut my eyes in bliss, if for no other reason than that looking away from her, even for a second, would have been too painful.

The sensation of her feathery and warm touch sent a surge of desire through me, my already-rigid cock going rock hard, making me *remember* in an instant what even centuries as a creature of the grave hadn't erased from my being. While also unlocking a part of me I doubted I'd ever known even in life, either. This yearning for another singular spirit, a longing to be entwined only with her.

I gritted my teeth, my need for her threatening to overtake me, and hands curling into fists at my sides, I went to war against the nearly overpowering urge to snatch her, draw her to me. I yearned to kiss her again. Steal those lips, claim them. Start down the long and delicious path of making her scream for me.

I didn't dare, though. Afraid any one of my movements would make her have second thoughts.

Maybe *she* was remembering I was a monster. A death wraith tasked with collecting her soul, ripping her light out of this world.

Or maybe I just wasn't her fucking type.

But then Helena did us both in by biting her bottom lip, hungry, bedroom eyes flicking up to me as she seized my belt.

I let her get as far as unfastening it.

34

HELENA

I'd never been so turned on in all my life—and so far, he'd hardly touched me.

That kiss, though. Why did I get the impression it had evolved into a preview of . . . other things?

His muscled arms and lean torso, defined and sculpted—positively ripped—had me all but salivating.

Apparently, wielding a scythe on the daily was a *great* workout.

But the tattoos . . .

Those gave me pause. Now wasn't the time for questions, though. I was satisfied with the chance to admire them—and him.

Everything I needed to know in this moment . . . I did.

He wanted me, too. That was evident in his ravenous gaze alone, but the sizable—perhaps even intimidating—bulge in his jeans erased all doubts.

My fingertips played over his warm skin, appreciating the pattern of shapes—a moth, a spider, a diamond, a dagger . . . Then my hands went rogue.

After that mind-melting kiss, I couldn't have hoped to stop them as they latched onto his belt, which I unfastened. I undid the button on his jeans, too, but that's when my fun ended.

Grim grabbed me, and I only gave the softest yelp when he picked me up and hoisted me over one shoulder before carting me off caveman-style to the bedroom.

I braced my hands against his muscled, tattoo-packed back, lifting my head. My ponytail bobbed in my face, and I blinked in shock while my living room and kitchen vanished.

Delirious, giddy, and maybe a little trepidatious, I had half a mind to wave the main room goodbye.

Then my fairy lights came into view.

God, I hoped there was more of this kind of brutish, reprehensible conduct coming.

I also hoped I was in trouble. A *lot* of trouble.

As if he'd read my mind, Grim half dropped, half deposited me on the bed, hard enough that I bounced on the mattress.

I'd been wet since the moment I'd laid eyes on him that day, but now I had to be drenched.

Was this really happening? Apparently, death wishes—all of them now—*did* come true.

The idea that I hadn't imagined Grim's affection for me, *or* his desire, had me soaring on the inside.

Terrified in the best way possible, like right before you get on the big looping, upside-down roller coaster, I sat up partway. Squishing my knees together, I gripped the comforter beneath me with both fists as my gaze traveled up those torn jeans, lingering on his unfastened belt and half-fallen zipper.

Lips parted in awe of his physique—and because I was already parched for another scorching kiss—I took a moment to appreciate the newly unveiled patch of tattoo-covered skin there, the V of his hips, and the faint impression of veins under taut skin before trailing my stare back up that chiseled and decorated chest.

I swallowed hard when some deeply felt instinct, perhaps a sliver of what others experienced around him, had me shifting and scooting back on the mattress. Maybe to get a better look at him. *Maybe* to put distance between us. But Grim put a stop to that quick.

"Don't move."

I froze. Then, finally, I found the courage again to meet that cool gaze.

Despite their icy hue, those eyes seared me with a heat that threatened to consume me from the inside out. But behind the roaring hell-flames of reckoning, there lurked something else. A glimmer of that depthless tenderness that, until now, had only been communicated through the comingling of our spirits.

"Your hair," he said, his voice rough like it took every ounce of self-control he possessed to curb whatever impulse currently knit him with barely contained tension. "Take it down."

I sat up slowly, lifting my hands to remove my hair tie, following this command as well.

He watched without blinking—not even once—as I sent blond waves tumbling around my shoulders.

He gritted his teeth, and something dangerous sparked in those eyes. A decadent promise of ruin.

No running now.

He proved that point in the next instant when he moved like he had in the elevator, too fast to track.

The slim distance between himself and me.

Gone. Just like that.

In the same blurred motion, he grabbed my ankle and yanked me toward him and the edge of the bed, eliciting a gasp from me, one that he stole and devoured by claiming my lips with his.

My heart launched itself to full speed as my soul exploded with an electrifying brand of terror I could *so* get used to. I braced my hands on his shoulders, gripping him hard, as keen as I was nervous over whatever he planned to do next. Which, apparently, was trailing one calloused palm along the outside of my thigh to hike up my skirt, curtaining it to my hip before gripping me there.

Another silent pledge.

I moaned into the kiss, the tease killing me.

With his free hand, Grim took hold of my chin. He broke the kiss, eyes fastened on my reaction, soaking in my pleading expression as he rerouted his other hand to the inside of my thigh, warm knuckles and freezing rings trailing the tender flesh as they neared the most heated part of me.

"Perfection," he murmured against my lips, eyes shutting as if it was the softness of my skin he was savoring. Then he opened his eyes again, pupils expanded as they drove that stare into me. "Pretty thing. I will have you."

That last set of words. His lips didn't move with *those.*

Instead, his dark voice came through him. Like an escaped thought.

I flushed, taken aback even as my arousal reached new head-spinning heights.

It was as if the man in him and the monster had, in that moment, reached some dark agreement about me, their commentary seemingly more for one another.

And tangling him up like this. Being the bait that had drawn this unhindered version of him out of hiding. I loved it. And I wanted to entice him from the shadows even more. Even if that meant getting *myself* dragged into them.

"How to take you," he mused with his human voice, thumb grazing my cheek. "Where to start."

He didn't wait for an answer. Not from *me*. His two sides had their own ideas.

Slowly, Grim guided me back, one knee braced on the mattress as he leaned over me. Then those roaming fingers stalled at the barrier of my panties, fingers contemplating.

"I think of you. All the damn time," he said.

Warmth spread through me at these words, my yearning for his soul mixing with my desire to be under his body.

"I will show you." Yet another solemn guarantee from him. "How you have consumed me. By returning . . . the favor."

His fingers ventured beyond the lace of my panties to tease my core.

I flung my head back, arching, helpless to subdue the moan that escaped me. Grim descended on me, inviting himself to my exposed throat, lips, tongue, and teeth assailing the tender skin there with caresses even as, with a low and relishing groan, he dragged fingers through my slickness.

Why did it feel like he was trying to figure out which part of me he was going to devour first?

All questions evaporated when two of his fingers slid into me, the cool metal of his bulky rings stinging my enflamed flesh. The gentle roughness of it had me surrendering to the bed. To him. Eyes rolling back, I pitched my head to one side, hands knotting in the blankets again, lips parted in a soundless *O*.

"All this for me?" he asked, his smoky voice rough but also low, controlled, contained.

Unlike me.

And he must be asking about the mess between my legs.

Like he didn't know the answer.

He tsked once when I didn't reply, as though in sympathy. Like I *was* in trouble.

"Delicious librarian," he said, his thumb exploring now as well as those fingers, creeping close to where I wanted it, but not nearly close enough. "I want your shirt off."

This man. Already, he had me teetering on the brink.

Grim lifted away, both hands retreating. An involuntary whine escaped me, even as those hands ganged up on my skirt to relieve me of the piece of clothing.

Which, good riddance.

"*Now*," he said.

Wait. What had he told me to do? My mind scrambled for the answer.

At that moment, I'd have given him anything. If only he'd just . . .

Oh. God. Right. My shirt.

Crossing my arms over my torso, I seized the hem of my blouse and lifted upward. When I got my head stuck in the material, he helped to free me, those big tattooed hands much gentler—much more patient—with the delicate fabric than mine.

"Stunning," he said. And under his raking gaze . . . I felt that I could be.

The way he admired me. It left me with no doubt that to him, I *was*.

The shirt went somewhere, leaving me there in my pink butterfly bra and not-matching-but-still-thankfully-cute sky-blue lace panties.

Well, at least until Grim knelt in front of me, drawing the latter of the two undergarments down, off, and away.

"Do you have any idea what I'm about to do to you?" he asked—again in that calm but darkly resolved voice. The one that sought to warn me of the retribution I was thankfully already condemned to.

I didn't have time to do or say anything more than prop myself up on my elbows as he hooked my right leg around his shoulder. And there was no bracing myself for impact, either, when his mouth collided with my core.

I cried out, falling back again as, in a brutal onslaught, he swept his tongue through me, dragging it from opening to clit.

"Oh, God, Grim!"

Merciless, his tongue assailed that small bead of pleasure. He moaned into me, low and raw, like the pleasure was truly his. That sent me careening straight toward the edge of climax. Until, cruelly, his tongue whisked away—right before plunging into me.

Arching, I wailed in surprise, my legs falling open of their own accord.

Back he came to kiss, tease, assail my clit, fingers returning out of nowhere to invade me a second time.

God, what was he doing to me?

My ears rang, blood rushing hot in my veins. Then he emerged to hover over me. This time, thumb taking the place of his tongue, he didn't leave me wanting.

With that intense gaze locked on me, he worked a steady rhythm, knuckles and rings—now heated almost to the temperature of my skin—brushing against tender flesh.

"Decadent creature," he said. "You taste as good as your soul. So, I think . . . I will just have all of you."

A small whimper escaped me when he moved again, a blur of shadow and smoke until he materialized beneath and behind me, capturing me in those muscled arms, my spine pressed to his chest, his long, jean-clad legs on either side of my open bare ones.

I tried to shift toward him, my knees coming together, but a hand seized me by the throat, holding me steady against him, rings digging softly into the delicate skin of my neck now.

"What do you think you're doing?" he asked, the fingers of his other ring-lined hand slow-creeping between my knees like a spider.

I didn't try to answer. I just brought my hands up to clasp the muscled, tattooed forearm of the hand that clutched me to him.

"I want you like *this* first," he rasped, burying his face in my neck, lips brushing skin, breath teasing me as he spoke. "You're wet, but I'm gonna need more."

If he kept talking to me this way, I might just come from that.

All my fantasies about him. I hadn't let myself fully indulge in them. Because I'd been trying not to want something I couldn't have. Someone who didn't like me back. Couldn't. Now he was hand-feeding my daydreams to me. More even than what I knew I'd wanted.

I trembled in his grip, trying not to fall apart just from words.

"Legs. Open," he grumbled.

Caught, helpless to make any other move, I parted my knees as he'd ordered, but only slightly, suddenly timid again. Or maybe I wanted to test him? Tease him back.

For fun.

What was one more death wish?

"Are you really still afraid of me?" he asked, flipping his hand over, rings and knuckles gliding down my inner thigh, the promise of their picking up where they left off coaxing my knees open farther.

"Yes," I murmured, which was true. But we both knew I also liked being a little—a lot?—afraid of him.

"Good answer," he murmured into me, "you should be."

Pinning me against him, tightening his grip on me, he flipped his hand again, fingertips trailing down, falling fast. I opened my legs for him a little more but then gasped when those fingers lost their warmth and softness along the way, turning to bone before he drove first and second into me.

I gasped—then moaned, legs collapsing open for him, fingernails of one hand digging into his arm while the other went to clasp him behind the neck.

His muscles tight, grip restricting, he disallowed me to watch while he laughed, that dark, soul-shaking voice taking over as he pumped those cold, hard digits into me before bringing them up to circle my clit.

I fell apart with a shriek as the orgasm that had been begging to rip through me came barreling down, merciless as him as it wrecked—wracked—my system.

With *this* dastardly ambush, there could have been no stopping it.

A low wail fell out of me while I quivered in his clutches, helpless but to submit to the pleasure as he ushered me through it, bone fingers prolonging the rippling aftershocks.

"Oh, it is *incredibly* fucking dangerous," he said, murmuring the words into my neck, "for me to know you were telling the truth about that." He meant what I'd said at dinner. About still asking him on a date if I knew what he looked like under that hood.

Did he think I would lie about wanting him in his darker form?

Maybe he just hadn't thought I'd meant it *that* way.

No secret now that I had.

Ooohhhhh well.

"Helena, Helena," he chuckled. "You're *fucked* now."

"*Oh*," I uttered, an involuntary sound as, while he continued to hold me in place with his human hand, his skeleton hand—and arm—traveled up my torso, fingertips clicking against one another before they snuck under my bra, bony palm sweeping up to engulf and grip the whole of my breast.

I squirmed, pressing myself into him, the impression of his erection pronounced against my lower back, his touch making me long for him to make good on his threat. His latest one.

"You perfect luscious thing," he groaned, his two voices mixing as if his control over them, over himself, had once again reached a critical point. His hard thumb brushed over my pebbled nipple, then wickedly back again, increasing my building want. "How shall I ravage you next?"

Again, he half unfurled, half shifted out from under me, his smoky essence catching me, guiding me back to the mattress.

Remaining corporeal amid the roughly human-shaped collection of smoke and shadows, his skeleton hand stole away my bra. Then, rematerializing on his knees in front of me in full human form, Grim tossed that last scrap of clothing away, as naked now as me. Something that had me staring wide-eyed at his daunting size.

"Um," I said.

Instinct—and *maybe* worry—had me sitting up. Or attempting to.

Placing his hand to my sternum, Grim shoved me flat onto my back again, leaving me no time to ask the question I already craved answering the hard way.

The question of whether he really was going to fit . . .

"Don't worry," he said, my misgivings obvious in my actions. "We'll take it slow," he assured me in his human voice, breath playing on my lips as he guided himself to my opening. "*Until you beg me for more*," vowed that darker voice as he kissed me, open and hungry, tongue seeking mine ahead of his lips, those last two ominous words emanating from his being rather than being formed by his otherwise-occupied mouth.

With another whimper, that buzzing voice sending my eyes rolling back again, I clutched him by the back of the neck, holding on to whatever I had left of my dear life as he pressed into me.

I hitched in pleasure—and in fear—as I took the first inch, eyes wide, lids fluttering. And even that much brought with it a delightful burn of pain-tinted pleasure.

"*Fuck*," he gasp-muttered, wincing, his voices twisting into one another again, arms trembling as they held him above me, the one on my right shifting to bones before, just as swiftly, morphing back again.

I took his face in my hands, relishing this deterioration of his command over himself, the little he'd been operating under until now.

I loved him in control. Telling me what to do. Warning me about what I was in for before following through on whatever he wanted to do to me. At the same time, the thought that I had him struggling this way, fighting his appetite, battling the buried parts of himself that must have lain dormant for so long, had me teetering again on the edge of ecstasy.

"You feel so fucking good," he growled between his teeth as we fast ran out of room. "I think this is going to kill me. But *fuck*, I've never been more ready to die."

He said this, but he wasn't really daunted.

"Please," I said, even if I wasn't sure what—exactly—I was begging for.

More. Everything. For this never to end.

"Breathe," he commanded. I did. He gave me a moment—just one—then, impossibly, between exhales, he continued his intrusion, *making* room.

"*God*," I managed when he just kept coming, stretching me, filling me.

I opened my legs wider for him, as wide as I could, determined to take all of him, the sharp burn consuming me in the best way possible. But just when I thought I *could* handle the rest, that's when he paused.

He drew back an inch. Panicked, I caught him around the shoulders before he could escape any farther.

"Grim . . . please."

"Please what?" The smallest smile ghosted across his face before he kissed me, like his name on my lips was something he wanted to catch the taste of.

"Please don't stop," I pleaded.

"Is it too much?" he asked, words cool as he traced my bottom lip with a once-more-skeletal thumb, his hair falling soft around us, tickling my cheeks. I moved under him—tried to—wanting to win back the lost ground, but his skeleton hand grabbed me behind one knee, his grip tight as he held me still.

Those lips shifted to the shell of my ear. "Answer me."

"I love it," I whispered.

He froze. Then he took in a shuddering breath as though I'd just seriously shaken his ability to hold himself at bay.

"That is *not* what I asked," he admonished, speaking slow. "I want to know if it's too much."

"*Yes*," I said honestly, my own voice tight with truth—and hope. "But I don't want you to stop."

An eternity seemed to pass before he replied, though it couldn't have been more than a few seconds.

"Good girl," he said, the words falling out of him like he already knew the answer anyway. Knew and agreed. "Because I'm not planning to stop until you're so wrecked you barely remember your own name."

He slammed into me, hips snapping against mine.

My mouth fell open again, wide in a silent scream the moment he bottomed out. My grip on him tightened—that of my hands *and* my body. My mind left me before I knew I'd even had it to begin with, and I came. Hard.

The waves of this orgasm rolled through me, tinged almost with an ache, the shock of its suddenness robbing me of awareness.

"Oh, fuck, Helena," he groaned. "Again already? Starting to wonder if there's going to be anything left of you."

God, I hope not.

"Mmm," he murmur-growled into me, nuzzling my neck while giving me another moment, perhaps, to adjust. "You're in a world of trouble, aren't you?"

Understatement. Had been for the both of us since the second that cold hand had caught me on that balcony. "Grim," I said again, pleading.

"Oh, I will," he promised with the next stroke, this one dragging and drawn out.

That bit of assurance, he'd uttered it like he understood my plight because it happened to be his, too. Like he was currently pacing himself in the act of killing us *both* but wanted to extend the sweet torture for as long as possible before annihilation.

I didn't want to think about how that wasn't so terribly far from the truth . . .

"It's just that you feel so fucking good," he said, his words frayed from restraint as he drove into me again, hips meeting once more. Sparks appeared in my vision. "Just . . . like . . . this." He drew in another shuddering breath—this one laced with a hiss that sometimes accompanied the rushing of his shadows. "And I'm *trying* not to swallow you whole. But." He stopped there, that bony hand hooked behind my knee tugging me to him, sending him in another impossible half inch.

A small "Ah" escaped me as he hit this new level of depth.

"That's not a battle I'm gonna win," he continued. "And . . . I am going to fuck you *hard* now. Your job is to take it and, when you're ready, come just like that again on my cock. Do you understand?"

God. I wanted him to talk this filthy to me every day.

"Do. You. Understand," he repeated, human voice grated and strained, like I had *better* answer him. For *both* our sakes.

I nodded, slow and deliberate.

"Just let me have you when it comes," he instructed. "Give me everything. All of it. All of you."

Anything.

The tremble in his form abating, he assailed me with a series of gentle, even, and measured strokes.

This time, his monster's voice moaned, the sound coming from nowhere and everywhere.

I keened, each entering plunge shattering my mind, every abandoning sending a sensation of electricity through my limbs.

Then his thrusts, like the pleasure, sharpened.

"*Fuck, Helena*," he rasped as he dealt me one hard, fast blow after another, his voice dipping, shredding as, in the rawness of his pleasure, it shed its humanness halfway through my name, defaulting again to his *other* voice. The one that belonged to the nameless, faceless, hooded figure with the scythe.

That voice thrummed through my chest and straight between my thighs. Twined with his punishing rhythm, the rumble of that dark resonance hurled me toward the edge of another climax.

I reached for him, but he caught me by the wrists and, with another growl, pinned them on either side of my head.

Again and again, his hips snapped against mine, his cock slamming into me, the friction intoxicating, the heady euphoria building in my depths heightened by those eyes that held me down, too, while he delivered each blissful assault.

The fingers of his left hand, the one that pinned my right, lost their warmth, going hard, bony, skeletal.

His pupils widened like they, too, now sought to devour me, obliterating his irises to the thinnest of halos.

Then wisps of gray-black smoke unfurled from his shoulders while dark hunger swirled in those eyes—the monster part of him fully unleashed.

Couldn't *this* be the way I went out?

Those wisps descended, tendrils driving into my chest, seizing my soul in their fierce, freezing, and greedy grip.

I arched as that dark essence came pouring into me, clashing with mine, each of our spirits searing and branding the other.

My thoughts splintered, scattering, my body robbed of any ability to respond—to do anything other than take him as he pumped into me.

While his soul knit itself with mine, icy vines piercing, winding, and threading through, more tendrils dove between us to assail my clit, wispy, ephemeral tongues taking turns lapping and teasing while that unrelenting steel shaft filled me again and again.

The tension in me wound tighter, building softly at first, and slowly, before blooming with the golden promise of total destruction.

Grim! I screamed, this time with my soul instead of my voice, the avalanche breaking within me, a flood of debilitating pleasure hollowing my entire system.

I cried out, overcome by the drugging wave that engulfed me and pulled me under to drown in its grip.

His lips crashed down on mine, tongue invading along with every other part of him.

As the purest ecstasy I'd ever known shattered me, I surrendered to the onslaught, becoming his and his shadows' to feast on as I spasmed around him, my core clenching, rippling, and constricting around his cock.

He came with a low and growling moan that manifested in a mix of both his voices.

My fairy lights flickered as I shook beneath him, already helpless and heaving when, out of nowhere, an unexpected echo of another orgasm came rushing to overtake and underscore the first, the sensation infused into my body and my soul by his spirit, as if he had to be sharing his own climax with me. As if he'd gotten a taste of mine, which had been the thing to trigger his.

As if we'd both just taken matters into our own hands and had gotten to heaven in our own way and on our own terms. If only for one evening.

I sobbed as my spirit, still hopelessly knotted in the unyielding clutches of his, sang along with my body.

He released one of my wrists, his hand going to my cheek as he kissed me, as though I really might be dying, and he wanted all the last of me.

"Beautiful soul," rumbled Grim, his dark voice reverberating through me.

I reached for him, my limbs heavy like my mind. My lids drowsy.

And though I fought the darkness, my eyes fell shut anyway.

Kissing me still, he released his spectral grip on me, his mouth evaporating under mine, becoming those teeth once more. And then, as the final throes of bliss ebbed into silence, he swept his essence out of me in a way that swung me into dizziness, giving me back the soul I would, in that moment, rather him have kept.

Just before my consciousness . . . abandoned me, too.

35

GRIM

Sorry, not fucking sorry.

Because what was *any* version of eternity compared with making Helena come like that?

Stalking down the ICU wing of a hospital somewhere in Idaho, concealing cloak in place and scythe in one hand, I kept my gaze forward even as images flashed in my skull like a slideshow.

My skeleton's hand wrapped around the plush flesh of one sumptuous breast, Helena's head thrown back that way, hair splayed around her head, my cock buried shaft deep in her, my essence scouring her, taking her soul for a ride at the same time I decimated her perfect body.

Currently, I didn't have eyes to roll to the back of my head, but I did take a moment to pause and press a skeletal palm to one bland white wall, my other constricting around the handle of my scythe.

Because *fuck*. As much as I'd always tried to convince myself otherwise, possessing a body *did* have its perks.

Helena, Helena, Helena . . .

You kinky minx. You loved every fucking second, didn't you?

Not as much as I did.

Not once during my time as this *thing* I'd become had I ever even thought about a woman like that. Like this. Never mind that I wasn't supposed to. I just didn't.

But Helena . . .

Those eyes. Her breath. Those lips forming *my* name.

Pulling those screams out of her—with my bone hands no less.

Then. When I'd been getting off on talking shit, fucking with her. And she said she loved taking my cock?

I'd almost shaken apart right then.

I hadn't exactly been with a woman before. At least not that I could remember. And not for a very, very, very, *very* fucking long time.

Through some absolute miracle, I'd held it together. Somehow. But I hadn't been okay.

Still wasn't. Probably wasn't ever going to be again.

Because the taste of her. Pure ambrosia.

I could dine on her, that soul, and her pleasure every day for the rest of eternity.

If only.

Fuck this job. I wanted *that* one.

I wanted her.

Overhead, the intercom cut on, a screech of feedback lancing through my renegade thoughts just before someone announced a code blue. An instant later, the scrubs-clad team rushed into action, several members hurrying past me, oblivious to my presence. Or to the fact that their efforts would be in vain, and it was already too late.

Today, I was picking up a Fated. *Another* Fated.

The tugging impulse had come to me while Helena slept, and I'd had to leave her there, passed out from getting fucked into oblivion—mind, body, *and* soul.

Maybe I should have gone easier on her. But it had been hard enough behaving myself when she'd been so absolutely *soaked* before I'd even touched her. When she'd been a gasoline-drenched powder keg I'd set off with a few teases. With my *bones.* Which she'd fucking loved. Something that had sent my damn ego into the fucking stratosphere—a place I couldn't seem to wrestle it back from.

My thoughts, too, ran rampant, wildly circling all the ways I wanted to fuck her delirious the next time.

Except there wasn't going to *be* a next time. Not for me.

I was done.

Just like this poor bastard I'd come to get, whoever he was.

I stopped in front of his room, the door to which stood open.

Inside, the code blue team stood gathered around the hospital bed, a huddle of controlled chaos, their shouts along with the one-note song of the heart monitor providing a soundtrack to the drama that, like a Shakespeare tragedy—spoiler alert—ended in certain death.

Normally, I would wait outside. Give the doctors time to make the call official.

But sometimes, on rare occasions, souls abandoned their vessels on their own and went wandering. On rarer occasions, I even found them fully formed, cognizant, and . . . waiting.

"You're looking for me, I think," said the spirit who stood in the stretch of hall I'd just passed through. The old man in the hospital gown—I must have missed him because . . . well, because I'd been distracted.

"This way," the bearded and gray-haired man said, turning to head down the hall, absolutely atom bombing my daydream to flaming bits with the sight of his bare and wrinkly ass, visible through the open back of the half-tied hospital gown.

My shoulders slumped.

Duty calls, I fucking guess.

And where the hell did he even think he was going?

The old man walked straight into—and through—the closed ICU door, out into the waiting area. Even souls who had managed to disengage from their physical forms early didn't typically know they were dead and could move through walls.

This was weird.

When it came to the Fated, though, things sometimes got weird.

Case in point: *Helena.*

I unfurled and reemerged on the other side of the ICU door, in the waiting room populated with people waiting—fretting.

Though I expected to have to track down Old Man Bare Ass, I found him seated in one of the chairs, his back to me, though he twisted around to address me.

"Over here."

Though it was rare for the living to see me, the dead almost always did. Ghosts at least.

Which was, technically speaking, what he currently was.

I stepped toward him, curious, because even the dead, those with enough sense to perceive me, feared me.

Unlike Flora, I didn't exactly give off comforting vibes.

This man only smiled at me before gesturing up at the TV with one weathered hand. "Have you seen this show before?"

Internally, I scowled, only offering the screen a short glance before returning my hooded stare to him.

The flat screen portrayed some kind of sitcom with a corny laugh track.

"I've seen this episode before," said the man, "but . . . I love it. When I was young, I wanted to be in pictures. Make people laugh like these two actors. Like them, I had a talent for it."

"You can't stay," I told him, my monster's voice rolling out of me, cold and inflectionless.

"Time to go, you mean," said the man, even as he gripped the armrests of the chair, the first sign of his fear showing.

"I'm not trying to rush you," I admitted. "It's just . . . you have somewhere to be."

"Somewhere to be," he echoed, that death grip on the armrests easing a bit. "Somewhere good?" he probed, hopeful.

"We'd both know by now if it was somewhere . . . not good," I allowed.

I'd meant to calm his fears but worry knit his brow as he glanced up at the TV again.

"You're not sure," he grunted after a beat, reading into my reply.

"Honestly," I said, "I wish I did know."

"Look," he said, still not tearing his gaze away from the TV, "I know you must be busy. Probably one of the busiest beings around. But . . . can you just . . . give me a few minutes? Long enough for this episode to end? It's almost over."

I deliberated, my hand flexing on the scythe that I wouldn't need in this situation. His spirit had wandered off from its vessel, his body, so like the shipwrecked souls floating in the ocean, I could just grab him.

When . . . he was ready.

"Why not," I said, taking a few steps toward him before settling into the seat next to his.

"Th-thanks," he said, like he really hadn't expected me to agree.

Lucky for him, I had my own reasons for wanting to procrastinate.

The sooner I got done here, the sooner I had to go back to grabbing other souls. And the sooner I got done with that, the sooner I had to return to the Hallowed Halls. Reentering the Hallowed Halls meant facing facts. And, like this guy, for the moment, I preferred to prolong the fantasy that, sooner or later, I wasn't going into a Basin.

"The chemistry between these two," he said, pointing at the TV, "is . . . *otherworldly*. Their characters—they really love each other."

This time, I didn't say anything but stared up at the couple arguing on the TV show, having it out with one another in the middle of a coffee shop, shouting each other down before, out of nowhere, the two rushed each other, crashing into a kiss.

Again, my mind went to Helena—the way we'd kissed in her apartment.

Moments before, out in the hall, she'd asked if we were arguing. I hadn't thought we were.

Maybe, though, we had been.

Next to me, the old man started to stand.

"You don't want to do that," I told him. "Trust me."

He didn't say anything but settled back into his chair.

"Thought you were distracted," he admitted.

I was.

"You're afraid," I guessed. "For a moment, I thought you might not be."

"You're carrying a scythe," he said. "I thought that was just . . . something from movies and books."

I sighed long and loud, taking on my human voice and skin again before tossing back my hood.

"Normally," I said, shooting him a side glance as he absorbed my appearance with new shock, "pickups don't see me."

"Ah," said the soul, "you're a young man. That surprises me."

"Older than I look," I grunted.

"Really?" he questioned. "And how old is old?"

Here I'd been calling *him* the old man when, really, that descriptor applied more aptly to me . . .

This role. I'd been in it for eons. Longer than either Flora or Johann had occupied the Hallowed Halls.

And, in the beginning, it had just been . . . me.

The beginning . . . I didn't want to think about that.

"Don't know, don't care," I said truthfully, gesturing to the TV screen, which now displayed rolling credits.

The man fell silent again.

Then, after several long beats, he spoke. "If I could go back and do it all again," he said, "I'd do it so much differently, you know?"

"I think everyone feels that way to a certain degree," I observed.

"But that's the trick, isn't it?" he said. "No one does get to go back and do it all differently. Even if we do come back or move on to something new. There is only one Cielo Bluford—*was*, I guess I should say—and as much as he wanted to, he never did pictures."

I peered his way again. "I'm sorry," I said, shocking myself because I actually meant it.

Helena's plight. The snipped fuse on her short life. It brought more awareness to what I did than I'd previously bothered with.

Until now, I'd just been the collector of souls. Neither good nor bad. Just, like death itself, an inescapable reality.

Death, like life, wasn't fair, though. And maybe, for as long as I'd been . . . *this*, I'd never really appreciated that.

He shrugged. "It's all okay, I think. Because even if it's over, and clearly it *is* over, it isn't really, is it? Or else . . . *you* wouldn't be here, would you? Who knows? Maybe wherever I'm going, people make pictures there, too. And whoever is in charge there, they're bound to understand that circumstances arise. Things happen. Life gets in the way." His voice dropped, taking on an oddly knowing tone. "*Death* gets in the way, too . . . doesn't it?"

I frowned, tilting my head at him. Instead of elaborating, he only offered me a weak smile.

"All right, copper." Palms up, he extended both wrists to me. "You got me."

My frown deepened into a scowl as I peered from his wrinkled, weathered face with its bright blue eyes and neatly trimmed white beard to the matching and liver-spotted hands he offered me.

"I promise it's not like that, Mr. Bluford," I said. "I'm not anything like a cop. There's no judgment. I'm just . . . the middleman."

"Please," he said, dropping one hand in lieu of extending only the other, like a friend or even a rival offering a shake. "Call me Cielo."

I took his hand, but instead of offering the name I didn't have back to him, I zapped his soul into its more transportable shape—a pale pastel-blue sphere.

"Nothing personal," I said to the soul, to Cielo. "Just . . . time's up is all."

Which was the truth. Also, caring about another Fated, at least beyond the capacity required by my station, was something I needed to avoid.

I only had a few heartstrings anyway, and Helena alone owned those.

Rising, I leaned my scythe against the desk of the nurses' station while I worked to secure the Fated in my hourglass.

Inside me, my spirit tightened at the fate of this soul, this Fated, who never got to do what he wanted. Who had been granted more time than Helena, too.

Helena . . .

Was there truly nothing I could do?

After leaving the hospital, I went to pick up all the souls I'd kept waiting while I'd been playing hooky with Helena. After that, I went to collect the fresher ones. There'd been plenty to keep me busy until nearly five. That was typically the time Helena went home. It was also an hour after she said her coworker friend, Hunter, came into work.

A time frame that would allow me to talk to him without her there.

Because, until I figured out what was going on and what I needed to do, I *had* to stay away from her.

If for no other reason than that I wouldn't be able to resist taking her like that again.

And right now, if I was going to save her life, preserve her soul in *this* world and existence—I needed to fucking *focus.*

36

HELENA

I awoke just before sunrise to find Grim gone. Rather, he wasn't with me.

After lying in bed for nearly a half hour while I waited for my entire being to reboot and enter recovery mode, I half fumbled, half fell off the mattress. From there, wrapped in a sheet, I went looking for him in case he *had* stuck around. Grim . . .

I found a note instead, which he'd scrawled onto my sunflower notepad in pink ink since that was the only color pen immediately available.

Called to a Fated.

G

After peeling the note free, I stood in my dining room/kitchen staring at the paper as though, if I waited long enough, more words *would* appear. Some kind of clue about when he'd be back, or even a winky face or a naughty promise—something, *anything*, to go on until I *did* see him again.

I hated having to fight the needling fear, too—the new fear—that this note carried a lie.

He'd already revealed how the Fated were rare. Relatively rare . . .

So maybe he'd just scratched out a convenient excuse.

Because maybe he hadn't wanted to be here when I woke up, and maybe he didn't want to come back, either.

In other words, maybe he was having regrets?

I wasn't. And never would . . .

While a warm shower helped me ease back into my body—maybe even literally—the soap and water did nothing to clean the lingering dirty thoughts from my mind.

What it would be like to take a shower with him . . .

What other parts of my apartment—or his—we could . . . enjoy.

Different ways I could . . . retaliate.

I supposed the silver lining of possibly not being long for this world (if there was one) was that I wasn't going to have to worry about my love life or how no future bedroom interludes were *ever* going to live up to *that* experience.

The man had given my *soul* an orgasm, one layered over the O he'd delivered to my body.

With the help of ethereal *tendrils.*

"I'm ruined," I murmured to myself, my voice echoing slightly in the cramped shower as the water rushed over me, swirling citrus shower gel and the remnants of all hope that I wouldn't fall for this forbidden being—that I hadn't already—down the drain. "I'm ruined, and all I want . . . is for him to do it to me again."

And always.

37

GRIM

"Can I . . . help you?" asked the boy as he dug an earbud out of one ear.

"Hunter," his name tag read.

I'd stood there, at the end of the aisle between the tall shelves, scowling at him for longer than I should have without saying anything. It was just that . . .

"She didn't tell me you were a kid," I said.

Now he dug out the other earbud. "Excuse you? I'm eighteen. And 'she' who? Who are you even talking about—and who *are* you for that matter?"

Eighteen? Technically, that *wasn't* a kid. But . . . it also kind of was.

Flora took the eighteen-year-olds. That was her cutoff age. Which was why he looked especially young to me since my pickup age started at nineteen.

Whatever. Not important. I wasn't here to get him or anybody—just to talk.

"Do you remember this?" I held up the gray Grim Reaper book I'd found in Helena's apartment.

"Where'd you get that?" the kid asked but almost like he didn't care. He even returned to shelving the books he pulled off the huge cart that stood in the aisle between us.

"Where do you think I got it?" I asked him. "Helena gave it to me."

"I don't know who the hell you are," he shot back. "What if you're a serial killer and you murdered her and stole it or something?"

"I'm not a serial killer," I snarled between my teeth, lowering the book.

"Well, you sure as shit look like one."

Was he serious? Maybe I should have come earlier—let Helena handle the talking here. And maybe I would have if I'd known this "coworker friend" was practically still in diapers.

"I'm her boyfriend," I said.

That got his attention. Slowly, he peered my way again, scowling at me in turn—narrowing that one visible eye, his other curtained behind loose black hair.

"She said she needed to pull the book for a *friend*," he said.

"She did," I snapped. "A *boy*friend."

"She's dating *you*?" He gave me a skeptical once-over before sliding another book into place. "Pull the other leg. It plays 'Jingle Bells.'"

This little fuckhead.

"I need to know about the weird guy you said had this before Helena came looking for it." I held the book up again.

"Prove it," said the kid, examining the spine of another book before sliding it onto the shelf between two others.

I frowned. "Prove what?"

"If you're Hart's boyfriend, prove it, and I'll tell you who had the book."

Prove it? "How the fuck am I supposed to do that?"

"Not my problem."

Not his . . . ?

I cricked my neck, the fingers of one hand curling into a fist and uncurling. I could give him a soul shakedown like I had the other library asshole, but he *was* still a kid and technically out of my jurisdiction anyway. Also, he was Helena's friend or whatever.

Astrally ass kicking an ex was one thing. Soul snapping a friend would probably be frowned upon.

"She's borrowing my car," I said.

"Oh," said Hunter, "so *that's* where she got the meathead mobile."

I took a step toward him, and he dropped his book, skittering back. "You stop right there," he said, pointing at me with one hand while he shoved his other into a back pocket and brought out his phone.

"What the fuck are you doing?" I asked, spreading my arms as he started to dial. "Are you seriously calling the cops?"

"Kind of," he said, lifting the phone to his ear.

I put my hands on my hips and waited, but then I caught a familiar voice on the other end saying, "Hello?"

Fuck. He called Helena.

"Hart, I need you in the stacks, stat. Eight hundreds. Your stalker—I mean boyfriend—is trying to bad-cop info out of me about that book you had me scare up. Speaking of scaring things up, he's sus as hell, and I need backup yesterday. Bring security."

"*What?*" came Helena's voice in a high-pitched buzz, which had me shutting my eyes. Because I'd been trying to do this without her. "I'll be right there. *Don't* let him leave—whatever you do."

Be right there? She wasn't supposed to be working.

"Um, yeah, about that," said Hunter into the phone as his eyes cut my way. "Can you just, uh, stay on the line with me? Your boy is a little too Blumhouse Productions for my comfort. Bottom line, the vibes are *way* off, and I really don't feel sa—"

He blinked at me, lowering the phone before swallowing hard and stating what I'd already gathered. "She hung up."

"She's not supposed to be working tonight," I said.

"You just keep saying creepy shit, don't you?" Hunter noted.

"Just tell me who asked for the book, and I'll leave," I said. "It's important."

"What's your problem, anyway, man?" asked Hunter, gesturing toward me. "How are you gonna wear a Dungeon Druids T-shirt same time as a Thornz on Fire shoulder patch on your jacket?"

Both were metal bands. Admittedly, I was impressed this kid knew of either of them.

The two groups had beef—a fierce and ongoing rivalry I didn't particularly give a fuck about. I just came for the music. And, when it was time, the souls.

"Guess you could say I'm no respecter of persons," I said.

And, as if on cue, a familiar figure popped into view between aisles. Not Helena, but Peter the Cheater.

"Listen, Hunter," he said, eyeing his own phone before glancing up, "I'm heading out for today but, tomorrow, do you think you could—"

He stopped dead when he saw me, his face draining of color while, same as yesterday, I stared him down. Eyes going wide, the kid, Hunter, peered between us.

At least until Peter backtracked, turned tail, and ran.

"Bruh," said Hunter, his focus returning to me while he aimed a thumb over his shoulder. "Wha'd you do to the archivist?"

"Love tap," I said.

Well, maybe more like a spiritual spinal tap, but . . . details.

"Uhhh," said Hunter, shuffling back another step from me. "I'm not gonna lie, I low-key kind of want my mom right now."

"To be honest," I droned, "if things went sideways for you, even if she was here, she wouldn't be able to do anything."

He gave a nervous laugh and took another step back.

But the last thing I wanted *him* to do was bail.

"Look," I said, blinking slowly. "Just tell me about the guy with the book and you'll never hear from me again. Or . . . at least you won't for a while. Hopefully, for your sake, a long while. But tell me quickly. Before Helena gets here."

Just then, Helena, breathless and beautiful, darted into view at the end of the aisle.

Damnit.

"Thank God you're here," said Hunter, shuffling to get behind her, and he peered left and right once he got to the endcaps. "Wait . . . where's security?"

"Grim," Helena said, breaking toward me, those incredible eyes searching my face.

A surge of longing rushed through me as she neared, and it took every ounce of restraint I possessed not to grab her and pull her toward me, wrap my arms around her, crush her against me, breathe her in.

"*Grim?*" said Hunter, making a face.

"It's . . . a nickname," Helena threw back at him, thinking quickly even as she continued her approach, a deep blush coloring her cheeks as she neared me.

"Kinky," said Hunter.

But he had no idea.

"So, wait," said the kid, gesturing toward me, "does that mean this guy really is your boyfriend?"

Helena whipped her head toward Hunter and then back at me, ponytail swishing. When she arched her brows at me, I only gave her a shrug.

She hurried to close the remaining distance between us, one hand catching me by the arm, like she thought I'd dissipate to smoke right then and there. Like she thought grabbing on to me would—could—stop that even if I did.

"Yes, of course," Helena said, tossing the response back Hunter's way.

My throat tightened with her corroboration of my lie. With an "of course" of all things.

Claiming me as hers. Just like that.

That hurt. Like fuck.

I wasn't her boyfriend. And couldn't be.

"Does your *My Little Pony* mug collection know?" Hunter asked, incredulous.

"You . . . were supposed to come earlier," said Helena, peering up at me.

"You know he scared the piss out of Winston just now," remarked Hunter. "And all he did was look at the guy. Though, honestly, it was . . . kind of badass now that I think about it."

"Why didn't you wait to let me introduce you?" Helena asked, her voice soft, uncertain, and only faintly accusatory, to my relief.

"I was trying to figure it out on my own," I said, going for honesty. "And I didn't think you'd still be here."

"I . . . had to stay late tonight," she said. "There was an emergency meeting. About . . . about the bookmobile."

Oh. Fuck. The bookmobile. I'd forgotten all about that thing.

I glanced away, eyes shooting to one side.

"What about the bookmobile?" asked Hunter. "Wait. Did they find out who stole it and took it for a joyride on 71? Dude, it took *forever* to put all those books back. Whoever that freak was, he needs to go away for life."

"Couldn't agree more," I muttered under my breath.

"No," said Helena, glancing between us. "Its transmission . . . died."

"Hold up," said Hunter. "Gus the Bus is dead? Jeez. About time, too. That thing was a flipping fossil."

When Helena peered back his way, Hunter's eyes bugged. "I mean . . . sorry for your loss?"

"No," said Helena through a short huffing laugh, "it's . . . a good thing. We're getting a new one before the New Year. Apparently, a few donors came through, and there was enough left in the budget for the rest. It'll have heating and air and new stairs, too. The kids . . . they're going to love it."

Helena eyed me while she spoke, but I couldn't bring myself to look at her. Aside from the fact that, with her standing this close,

I couldn't keep from picturing the way she'd arched, moaned, and shook beneath me less than twenty-four hours earlier, I didn't want her to guess I'd paid the beater bus a visit between pickup jobs the other night.

Buses didn't have souls, but like most things that ran on energy, they had a life force of sorts. And Gus *had* been old as shit.

She didn't need to be driving that thing right now, and aside from that, the kids didn't deserve to freeze this winter while trying to get books, either. And maybe I'd gambled with the fact that they may not get her a new one, but bottom line, I'd wanted to reduce the number of potential death traps in Helena's life—even if just by one.

"So, what's this all about anyway?" said Hunter. "Why did *I* get dragged into this episode of *How Molly Met Mosh Pit*? I didn't even know you had a boyfriend, Hart. Let alone one from the set of *The Lost Boys*."

"Good movie," I said. "Even if it is about vampires. Surprised you know it."

The boy scoffed, insulted. "I'd throw my gauntlet down over that one if, A, I had a gauntlet, and B, I had more confidence *you* didn't have one to throw back."

"Hunter," said Helena. "Grim, um, I mean *we* wanted to stop by and ask you about that guy you said asked you to pull the book before I came looking for it. We might know who it was, but we're not sure. You talked to him, right? And you said he seemed . . . weird?"

"Why?" asked the kid, eyeing me up and down again. "There a hit out on him or something?"

"I just want to talk to him," I said.

"Talk," repeated Hunter, his brows bouncing once. "You know, back in the day, they used terms like 'ice' and 'whack.' These days you hear 'merc' and 'cap,' but 'talk' is a new one."

"Grim's not going to *merc* anyone," Helena stressed. "He just . . . is looking to get a new tattoo. Of . . . his namesake. The Grim

Reaper. And . . . that guy could be the artist we're looking for. He . . . specializes in . . . reaper tattoos."

I scowled at Helena. Who was a terrible fucking liar.

"New tattoo," muttered Hunter, again squinting at me. "Where the hell are you going to put it?" Quickly, he held up a hand. "You know what? Don't answer that."

"Please, Hunter," said Helena, "it's pretty important we ID this guy. Just . . . if you could tell us what he looked like?"

"He looked normal," said Hunter. "Like a normal . . . old dude."

"Old dude?" asked Helena, glancing back to me before returning her attention to Hunter. "I . . . You said he was weird."

"Yeah," said Hunter. "Meaning he *acted* weird."

"Did he have a beard?" I asked, my mind going straight to Johann—the only "old guy" I happened to know. "A long one?"

"Like Gandalf long," Helena added.

"Nah," said the kid, "it was short. Like Obi-Wan Kenobi short."

I tilted my head at him, my frown deepening. There wasn't a soul—friend or foe—I knew that fit that description. At least . . . there hadn't been until that morning. That had to be just a coincidence, though.

"Did he say anything?" I asked.

"Anything out of the ordinary?" Helena chimed in.

"Yeah, that's what I'm saying," said Hunter. "He gave me the Dewey and asked me if I could pull the book. He said he needed it because he was going to die in Idaho."

"*What?*" I barked, an actual chill clambering up my spine.

"Hunter, that's crazy," said Helena. "Why didn't you go alert security?"

"Because!" he said, spreading his arms. "In case you forgot, this is the free *public* library. And need I remind you it's a bit hairier on the adult side of this book-paved hellscape. If I grabbed security for every weird thing a patron said to me, Rick would probably assign a personal guard to me, and I've got enough trouble with *him* breathing down my neck about earbuds, hours, micromanaging my shelving technique—yes, I have a technique—*and* his weird hairline envy."

"Honestly, that's fair," said Helena peering up at me. But my disquietude must have been written on my face, because she scowled in concern. "Grim?"

"I have to go," I told her, handing over the book, which she took.

"Wait," she said, "what? *Where?*"

Back to the Hallowed Halls with my haul of souls—one of which I was apparently going to have to pull out and find a way to interrogate. Because this made no sense.

I'd come here certain this Hunter would verify my suspicions—that the note had been planted by Cedric.

Instead, he'd confirmed my worst fear. That there *was* something more at play here.

That there *were* forces at work beyond my control. Beyond my current understanding.

That someone other than Cedric *was* fucking with me. And using Helena to do it.

"You're welcome, by the way," called Hunter as I stalked past him and out of the aisle.

"Grim, please," said Helena, hurrying after me. "Don't go. Or . . . let me come with you."

Halting, I turned back to her, grabbing her by the wrist. Then, spotting the door to the stairwell, I pushed through it, pulling her in after me.

There wasn't anyone on the stairs leading either up or down. Which, good.

While she blinked up at me, I guided her backward until her spine met with the wall. Then I kissed her like I had last night. Like I never would get to again.

Helena murmured in surprise and bliss, her free hand going to cup my face.

But I grabbed it and pulled it back down before breaking the kiss and staring her dead in the eyes.

"I am never taking you with me again," I vowed through gritted teeth.

"Grim," she half pleaded, half cried, reaching for me.

But I stepped back from her.

And then, as she rushed after me, I dissipated—going to smoke and sweeping out of her sight and, officially, for certain this time . . . out of her life.

If I had anything to say about it, her *long* life.

Somewhere I was *never* meant to be in the first place.

38
GRIM

Usually, in any given situation, I was almost always the scariest person in the room.

Not so when I returned to the Basins.

Scythe clutched in one hand, my full-to-bursting hourglass in the other, I entered the chamber with a purposeful stride. But the moment I spotted *him*, I halted.

Sir White . . .

The foreman of The Few.

No one knew what they really were.

Johann speculated they were angels—some faction of them. Flora believed them to be a type of elemental or djinn. Cedric was certain they were Nephilim.

I didn't know what to think—and I tried not to, either.

Whatever they were, my MO had always been to stay the fuck out of their way.

Hard to do on those rare occasions when one happened to stop by.

"Grim," said Johann, his voice tense as he looked up from his writing, a Wolseley pith, safari-style hat strapped to his head, "welcome back. As you can see . . . we have a guest."

"Guess who, one of The Few," said Pluto, who sat perched on Johann's shoulder.

Garbed from head to foot in hooded white robes, that "guest" sat in a gold-trimmed white throne-like chair near the White Basin. Like all The Few, Sir White wore a full-faced metal mask.

Silver like the embroidered embellishments on his robe, the mask had the impression of a nose, though it lacked a mouth. While long and silken silvery-white hair poured out of the hood and down his shoulders, a pair of glowing red lights peered out at me through the eyeholes of that mask.

Gauntlet-style gloves, metal as well, concealed his hands, the fingertips fitted with sharp silver claws.

Since I'd shed my human form on my way here in favor of my own black robes, I didn't have the equipment to gulp—but a trepidation close to what that Hunter kid must have felt when *I'd* shown up in his aisle swept through me.

"Greetings, Grim," said Sir White, his voice gravelly and grated—but in a different way than mine. His register was more tenor than baritone, and the "filter" of his cadence hit somehow alien, like Morgan Freeman talking into a fan but . . . scarier. "I've been waiting for you."

I clenched my jaw, taking in the short table at his side, which, like the chair, he must have conjured. Someone had laid out a small silver tea set and tray, but no one held any of the teacups—including Sir White, who didn't have a mouth to drink with anyway. At least, not one readily accessible.

"Waiting for me," I echoed while my thoughts raced, going to all the worst-case scenarios first. The very worst being that he knew not only that I'd saved the missing Fated Soul multiple times but that I'd illegally transported her to and from the Netherworld.

Kissed her.

Slept with her . . .

The oath that came with this role included a vow—made to The Few—not to interfere in any way with the lives of the living.

I had sure as fuck done some flagrant interfering as of late.

But.

I wasn't stupid enough not to act stupid.

"There a problem?" I asked, scanning the room in search of Flora—who wasn't here. Hopefully she was stashing Cedric's body somewhere less conspicuous than his desk. I hoped even more that she'd done so before any potential tour Sir White might have taken of the premises.

"No problem," said Sir White, who tilted his masked head at me, an odd *click* accompanying the motion. Something that chilled my bones. "At least . . . none other than that of the still-missing Fated. Which is partially the reason for this . . . follow-up visit."

"Partially," I again echoed, glancing to Johann, who had returned to his scribbling, though he peeked up at me between jotting down names and notes, his stare a pointed one of both fear and warning.

God help us all if he hadn't debriefed that loudmouthed bird of his on the fine art of keeping his beak shut.

"There is another Fated due tonight," said Sir White. "Which is why I have been waiting for you."

And there went my damn plan to get Flora to help me separate out the soul from the others and try shoving him into Cedric just long enough to get answers.

"Johann insists that the issue must be on my end," said Sir White. "And, at this point, I must agree. For a Fated left to this world would surely have met their end and been delivered by now. I thought, however, if I oversaw your delivery of *this* Fated, I could observe its entry into the Basin and, from there, detect any abnormalities in its path. Perhaps, for instance, this Fated might go on a similar detour and, thus, lead me to the missing soul."

I wasn't going to get to talk to Idaho. Not if I wanted to keep my ass covered and out of the Black Basin.

Which I needed to do. At least until I could figure out who was trying to get to me through Helena.

Who *else* . . .

"Makes sense," I remarked as I left my scythe freestanding in the middle of the room to march toward him and the White Basin, feigning nonchalance, pretending to be completely unbothered and unfazed. Pretending as well that I wasn't pissed to my limits I wasn't going to find out how and why another Fated had left that note to Helena. What he knew about Helena's status, and if Cedric had somehow enlisted him.

"I got it right here," I said, holding up the hourglass.

Sir White said nothing. Instead, with more unsettling-as-fuck clicking, and an underlying hiss, like the far-off sizzle of the burning flesh of the damned, he lifted one of those metal-encased hands, unfurling silver claws toward the Basins—an invitation for me to do my job.

And I had to—unanswered questions be damned.

When I reached the White Basin, I unscrewed the lid of the hourglass with one skeletal hand.

The souls meant for the White Basin danced in a frenzy as I stood over the vat. Forcing myself to move, to do what I couldn't avoid, I tipped out the contents, and the top layer of souls went flowing out, the pastel orbs leaping into the swirling mixture.

Cielo's pale pastel-blue soul came out, and the old man's spirit splashed into the pearlescent waters.

He swirled away. My last hope for understanding gone.

"Something the matter, Grim?" asked Sir White, another low hiss and a barrage of clicks sounding as he rose.

"Nothing," I said. Even if the answer was the opposite.

"The Fated," said Sir White. "I must follow. Rest assured, I will report back."

"Of course," I managed.

"Perhaps Cedric will be about when I return," said Sir White. "A shame I missed him this time. He nearly always has something amusing to say."

With that, Sir White collapsed into a ball of pale white light—which then zipped into the White Basin with a soundless splash, his throne and table evaporating to mist.

I collapsed, bone knees hitting the marble floor as I hung my head.

Behind me, the scythe toppled as well, clattering loudly through the chamber of the Basins.

"Grim's hurt!" cried Pluto, taking wing. "Red alert."

"Grim!" called Johann, who hurried over to me. "What is it, Grim? What has happened? Are you all right? Speak to me."

"I . . . should have told him everything," I said. "But . . . I can't."

"No matter what happens, Grim," said Johann, "I will not let them send you to the Black Basin."

Spoken like he really could stop them . . .

"It's not the Black Basin anymore," I murmured. "*Fuck* the Black Basin."

Johann's bird fluttered to land on the marble floor in front of me, beady eyes blinking up into my hood. "Grim Grim. Someone help him."

"It's her, isn't it?" came a quiet, Scottish-accented voice from beside me as a pair of small bare feet stepped into view. Right before Flora laid a small hand on the jutting vertebrae of my spine. "Your wee lass."

Releasing my hold on the hourglass, I brought a shaking hand to the face I didn't have, covering the sockets in my skull because I couldn't currently close my eyes.

"I can't do this," I told them. "I *can't* let her die."

"Because you've come to care for the girl . . ." Johann said, his voice inflecting downward, both like he knew it to be true and, even worse . . . like he understood.

"Because," I corrected, the truth hitting me full-on in the same moment I spoke the words aloud, "I'm in love with her."

39

HELENA

This *always* happened. Every single time and without fail.

I should learn not to be surprised. It wasn't like I was a stranger to being ghosted—pun *not* intended.

This time, though . . .

The silence from Grim. Ironically, it threatened to kill me.

Three weeks. For *three weeks* I hadn't heard anything from him. No random midnight calls, no drop-ins. Not so much as a text. Though *did* he text?

Didn't matter. He knew how to find me.

When Thanksgiving arrived, I went home the Wednesday before, though I didn't dare fly.

Being a Fated meant that I was, well, *fated* to die. And I hadn't gotten a chance to ask Grim—not before he'd vanished from the stratosphere, my stratosphere at least—if that meant I could potentially put others at risk.

So far, my close calls had been solo events. All the same, I couldn't bring myself to board a plane or bus. Not without knowing for sure.

While I could have rented a car, I took The Judge. Somehow, though I wasn't sure quite how, I felt safer in it—even though I wasn't really.

Fate, if it truly was still on its way, would likely not care what space I occupied.

Or whose car . . .

Surely, Grim wouldn't have lent it to me in the first place if he was worried about his ride getting taken out with me. And maybe *that's* why I felt safer in The Judge.

During my three-day stay with my parents, my possession of the car (along with my more-somber-than-usual demeanor) had spurred a lot of questions, which I'd fielded okay.

My car? It just needed repairs—technically not a lie.

This car? Oh, I'd borrowed The Judge from a friend—no, he wasn't my boyfriend.

That part *was* just pretend . . . wasn't it?

Yes, the car was fine for a three-and-a-half-hour drive. Yes, both ways.

No, surprisingly it didn't guzzle as much gas as you'd think.

Yes, I was all right.

Yes, I was sure.

No, I didn't want more pie.

Of course everything was all right at work.

No, I wasn't seeing anyone.

No, I couldn't stay another night—tomorrow was my Saturday to work again.

Yes, I knew I'd be getting home late.

Yes, I'd be careful.

Yes, I promised.

Only when I arrived back in the city did I start missing my family all over again and wishing I'd taken an additional vacation day—or swapped Saturdays.

Because there was no telling when our latest "goodbye" would be our last . . .

Thankfully, traffic hadn't been so bad, and it looked like I was going to get home before midnight.

Not that I had anything or anyone waiting for me.

Grim had vanished after that last kiss. Like he'd never existed.

And the fact that there hadn't been any more balcony falls or elevator failures made me more worried than ever he'd done something rash.

It couldn't be a coincidence that death, in all aspects and manifestations, had left me entirely alone.

But after that soul-altering night we'd spent together, Grim's unceremonious—and gutting—exit from my life had to be owed to *something.*

For instance, Grim could have talked to Sir White after all—or one of the other "higher-ups." He could have successfully bartered for an extension on my life.

I feared for him, too. If he *had* asked, he could have gotten fired.

And what if the only reason I was still alive at all was because they were trying to fill Grim's position?

It was slowly destroying me not knowing where he was, what had become of him. Even more unbearable was the thought that I might *never* know.

I kept wishing Flora would show up, or even Johann. But no one came. No one called.

And life just . . . went on. Like none of this had ever happened. Like I hadn't been irrevocably changed. Like I hadn't fallen hopelessly—and perhaps pathetically—in love with a supernatural entity who might be, as the saying went, just not that into me.

Even after all those things he'd said.

Because if the world of dating had taught me one thing . . .

"If he wanted to, he would," I whispered to myself as I flicked on the turn signal, slowing down to take a left.

That was the social media mantra we'd all been taught to recite, right?

And it had to be true in this situation, too. Unless it wasn't—and Grim was somewhere horrible.

The longer I had his car, the more I was starting to think *that* was the truth.

Because if he really didn't care, wouldn't I wake up one day just to find The Judge missing?

But then, the idea of Grim being put away somewhere or punished assailed me with far more fear and grief than if he'd just . . . moved on.

Tears pricked my eyes as I took another turn on the deserted road, my vision going bleary as I checked for traffic even though there wasn't any.

Everybody else in the world, it seemed, had stayed home regardless of annoying family members and invasive questions to sleep off their food comas. And now, story of my life, it was just me, myself, Helena, and, I supposed, The Judge as we ambled over a set of train tracks.

Except the car stalled out the moment I found myself in the center of said tracks, headlights flickering out before going dark, grumbly engine sputtering and then dying.

"What?" I muttered, toggling the stick shift. Because unlike its owner, The Judge had never given me an ounce of trouble.

After hitting the brakes, I grabbed the key and twisted, but the car only whined, the engine refusing to turn over.

"Overdue fines and porcupines," I cursed, glancing left and then right before checking the rearview mirror.

A lime-green Mustang pulled up behind me—but it didn't slow down to idle in wait. Instead, the souped-up pony car veered around me, engine revving, red taillights flashing only once before the thing ripped out of sight, turning a sharp corner, its driver lost behind tinted windows.

"GRNQUEN," the splashy, lit-up vanity plate read.

Well. So much for being a girls' girl and helping me out . . .

Maybe whoever they were would have stopped if I'd put on my hazard lights. But . . . where was the button for those?

After locating the switch for the hazards on the steering column, I tried the engine again but stopped when a subtle rumble started beneath me, and a distant bright light appeared out of nowhere on my left.

"Oh," I said, "no," and twisted the key again.

The Judge just kept wheezing, and while it did, I trained my gaze on that approaching light, praying it didn't belong to what I feared it did—that I'd just glimpsed a stray high beam.

But they didn't make headlights that bright. That big.

What was more, typically, headlights came in pairs.

Only one glaring, flickering orb headed toward me now, though as it neared and the rumbling beneath me intensified, the eye-searing sphere evolved into five: one big one in the middle, two at the top of the train face, and two more flashing ones at the bottom.

"Son of a bookworm," I hissed, hands shaking, because it was happening again.

Abandoning the key, I grabbed the latch on the seat belt just as the warning bells for the crossing kicked on, red lights flashing as the gates lowered.

I whimpered when the button stuck, the latch on the lap belt refusing to give.

"S-seat belt," I sobbed. To no one.

When I looked up, the light blazed bright enough now to blot my vision—getting closer while the ground thundered beneath me, rattling the dash.

The train's horn blared, loud as a scream.

I wrenched up the door lock. Then, with one hand still trying to undo the belt, I grabbed the handle and yanked. Nothing budged. Nothing moved.

Nothing except the howling train that, despite the rising screech of its brakes, wasn't going to be able to stop in the next five seconds. Precious seconds that were bound to be my last.

I cried out, body tense, hands rushing to cover my eyes so that, at the very least, I wouldn't see my doom coming as the engine came bearing down on me.

In my last seconds, Grim filled my mind. If he was okay and not locked away in some prison cell for wayward wraiths or tied up somewhere being metaphysically waterboarded by the paranormal police, he'd be here any second—if he wasn't already.

Maybe this wouldn't hurt. Maybe it would be over quick.

Maybe, from here out, I wouldn't even know what happened until Grim took me wherever I was going.

"Take your foot off the break!" shouted a voice to my right—a dark and scary one that had become, for me, neither of those things.

As always, I did as it commanded, even if I couldn't bring myself to lower my hands from my eyes. Not with that blazing light shooting through them, that horn booming in my brain, the car rattling beneath me, shaken by the metal dinosaur that was about to flatten—and steamroll—us both.

All three of us?

We moved, The Judge and I propelled forward in a jolt by a silent force—one strong enough to send me slamming back in my seat.

Wood snapped and cracked.

The train blew again, long, loud, and angry—but now its bellowing came from behind, underscored by the alarm bells and the clattering and shrieking scrape of metal wheels on metal tracks.

That light had vanished, too. Still, my heart hammered in my chest, beating loud and hard enough to drown out my shuddering, gulping breaths.

"Stay there," said that voice.

Grim was here. Which meant he was okay. *Was* he okay?

Was I?

Somehow, the car went into park.

Moving on autopilot, I twisted for the door and groped for the handle, which at last gave. The door opened, and fighting nausea, I stumble-spilled out into the world as the train rushed by behind me.

The broken bits of the red-and-white gate lay scattered on the asphalt while, above, red lights continued to flash and flare, the warning bells ringing—banging—on and on.

Wooziness wafted around my temples as, numbly, I scanned my surroundings, trying to swallow against the bile that teased at the back of my throat.

Just then, a skeletal hand fell on my shoulder, and throwing him off, I turned toward him, wavering.

"Really, Grim!" I shouted up at him, into that concealing hood. Then I poked him, right in the sternum. "I can't *believe* you!"

He seemed taken aback. Hard to tell since he was drenched once more in a mixture of black, shadows, and black shadows.

"You are the worst!" I screamed as, finally, the roaring train rushed by, the clatter of metal wheels on steel tracks tapering away, leaving only the clangor of those warning bells. "And I am *so* angry at you right now."

"Get in the car," he said.

"Stuff your car!" I yelled, shoving past him while also irrationally trying not to worry about hurting The Judge's feelings. The car had been with me through some things recently when it felt like no one else—including Grim—had been there to help me cope, process, understand. Let go . . .

But then, The Judge *had* crapped out on me.

All because of fate. *My* fate.

Which Grim had again subverted.

In that way, hadn't *he* crapped out on me, too?

"Where are you going?" Grim asked as I just kept walking.

In truth, I didn't know the answer—which had me swinging back toward the passenger's side of the car since I'd left my purse in the seat there.

"Helena."

"I'm going to call an Uber!" I snapped at him.

"The hell you are," he growled. "Get in."

"Go away!" I railed at him as I grabbed my purse and hauled it out before slamming the door shut behind me—hard.

Grim rounded The Judge, stalking toward me, but I wasn't having it.

"*I'm* taking you home," he said, reopening the car door, but I brushed past him again.

"You're not, actually," I snarled over my shoulder. "Now leave me alone until you can do your job."

I trudged on while I dug in my purse for my phone, walking toward a crosswalk, my stride still unsteady, my pulse still racing, and my mind a mess. Tears started falling, too—though for a moment, I'd half forgotten they'd been there, left waiting, like me, in the wings.

A swirl of smoke and mist appeared ahead of me, the gray-black darkness gathering itself into that hooded shape.

I had half a mind to chuck my phone at him, and maybe I would have if I didn't need it to get myself out of here.

"You are reprehensible," I said, stalking straight up to him again since he was going to insist on blocking my path. "You ghost me with no word, and then you show up again just to delay things over your dumb collectible survivor-condition car, which I should *never* have agreed to borrow!"

"My car?" he repeated.

"Your stupid car!" I yelled. "I'm sorry, I know it's important to you, but I can't keep doing this, okay? On that note, I thought *you* couldn't, either. If for different reasons."

Since his Reaper Man form made him invisible to any passersby or window watchers, I had to look like a lunatic out here, screaming at no one on the sidewalk in the middle of the night.

"What are you talking about?" he demanded.

"The plan!" I screeched at him. "I'm talking about the plan, Grim. The one that we *all* agreed to—including you!"

I poked him again in the chest, but this time, he caught me by the wrist. I tried to yank away, but the man was the hand of death, and wasn't death known for having a grip that wouldn't let go?

When it came to me, unfortunately, that was true for him in more ways than one.

"You selfish creature," I growled between my teeth.

"You're mad at me," he said, that monster's voice low, even, and unaffected—infuriatingly so.

"What was your first clue!"

"Because I came back," he said, a flat statement he truly meant as a question.

"Yes!" I shouted. "No," I amended, somehow managing to wrestle my arm free, which I cradled against me even though he hadn't hurt me. At least not physically.

"You're upset about the train," he said. "I'm taking you home. I'll put you in the car if I have to."

"Over my supposed-to-be-dead body!" I snapped back before whirling again, walking in the other direction now. Except the sight of those train tracks, Grim's car, and that broken gate had me halting again and once more fighting a panic attack.

I wobbled, overcome all over again. Then my knees gave out.

He caught me. Of course he caught me.

"Put me down," I demanded, but I'd lost my ability to shout now. Grim wasn't listening anyway and wouldn't.

Instead, he carried me back to The Judge and placed me carefully in the front passenger's seat.

He slammed the door, probably just as irate as I was now—or even more so.

Then he dematerialized and rematerialized in the driver's seat.

Of course, when *he* turned the key, the car started.

Of. Course.

"You want to tell me why you're mad, or what?" he asked.

I spared a dazed glance his way, lost for how he couldn't understand why I was upset and even more confused at why he had me back in his car, and was bothering to, with those wispy tendrils, fasten my *flipping* seat belt.

Just like old times . . .

"I wouldn't have agreed to borrow your car if I'd known," I said.

"Known *what*?" He shifted The Judge into gear with one skeleton hand and started forward, down the deserted street to the next set of traffic lights, which flicked green.

"That it would stop you."

"That what would stop me?" he growled, frustration—the first scrap of emotion—at last entering his tone. "And stop me from what?"

"From taking my soul," I hissed.

"You're not making any damn sense."

"Your car," I said. "That's the only reason I can think of as to why you moved me out of the path of that train."

He hit the brakes, which screeched, and we came to a jarring halt halfway down the thankfully deserted road.

That hooded head snapped my way, and in the darkness within, I glimpsed a faint impression of his face—his real one, the one without flesh, the one of bone—the one that seemed to glower at me with hatred.

But he still didn't scare me.

Not because he wasn't scary. Once again, he was.

It was just that I was tired of being scared.

Scared of dying. Scared of how. Scared of what came next.

Scared of what had happened to him. Of what *would* happen to me.

Scared most of all that he wasn't going to come back.

And now that he had? Well, now I was scared that I loved someone who had, again, figured out too late that I was too much for them. Or not enough.

"You think," he began, "that I came back . . . for the car?"

"You were supposed to let me die this time," I said.

"You think," he said, anger infusing his tone now, "that I got you off those tracks . . . to save The Judge?"

I blinked at him. "It wasn't to save me. You weren't supposed to do that this time. That wasn't what we agreed on."

He snapped his focus forward, like I'd cussed him out. Like I'd slapped him.

And we sat like that for several long moments before, wordlessly, he shifted the car into gear again and, once more, we started moving.

40

GRIM

She was mad. And she had a right to be.

But not about what she was mad about.

At the same time, I couldn't seem to make myself talk again—to apologize for leaving her on her own without a word, a phone call, a drop-by check-in.

An explanation . . .

Because this, her reaction, was exactly what I'd been hoping for. That she'd assume the worst about me and dismiss me. I'd been gambling with the hope, too, that she'd been right about something she'd said. That maybe the fate that I'd explained to her was imminent, the certain death I'd told her *was* coming and the powers that be involved in it, had somehow changed their mind. Or even that, when I'd saved her the last two times, that had triggered a glitch in the "system," allowing her to skate free.

None of that had happened. Fate had called again, summoning me to her side.

And now I had her well-earned resentment on top of the knowledge her number was still up.

Gripping the steering wheel tight, I ground my teeth and forbade myself from setting her straight. While I'd expected her to be mad that I'd vanished from her life entirely, and even that she'd figured I had better things to do, never once had it ever crossed my mind she'd assume I would save her to preserve a possession. An object. A car.

I couldn't stand it. Even though, for her sake, I tried to.

"Grim," Helena said as I kept my gaze steady on the road, my name coming out as a soft sob. "I'm sorry. I'm . . . still angry, but I shouldn't have yelled at you like that. I'm . . . frustrated. I'm tired. Exhausted, actually. And, yeah, I'll admit it. I'm deeply hurt. That probably doesn't mean a lot to you. Who knows? Maybe I'm not even an anomaly. Maybe you have girls all over the world."

What the fuck?

"It's my fault for reading into things," she said. "I always do that. I *always* think things are way more serious than they are."

What was she talking about? How much more serious could you get than *death*?

"Especially when . . ." she said, hiccupping between those quiet little sobs. "After . . ."

She trailed off, and I let her. But I also passed up the entrance to her apartment complex.

Helena didn't say anything, the sobs turning into snuffles.

I kept driving, at war with myself over what to say, the heart I didn't have in flames. But why all the internal strife when I'd already decided what I was—or rather wasn't—going to do?

"Where are we going?" she asked at last. "Since I'm not dead, I have work tomorrow—and a big afternoon storytime. Families are still on vacation, and it's going to be packed. I have to get up early to get more glue sticks, too, for the craft."

I stayed quiet.

"Or do I have it wrong?" she asked, her voice dropping to a whisper. "Maybe . . . maybe you're tired, too."

Tired. I *was* tired. Until I met her.

"Before," Helena said after several beats, "when Cedric came to the library. You used your scythe on him. You could do that again and this would all be over. I know Cleo will cover the storytime—she knows how to work the popcorn machine, and I just saw my parents and my entire extended family, so that helps with timing."

This conversation—if you could call it that—kept delivering one more painful blow after another, each more brutal than the last. The worst part? Well, one of the worst parts. She thought these things about me not because of me, though my actions hadn't fucking helped. She thought them because of others. How they'd treated her. Those people who shriveled in her light. All those assholes she'd dated, making herself small for their comfort in the process.

How many of them had used her?

I wanted to kill them. All of them.

And what did it say about me that I *did* want to try to get some names out of her?

Probably a reaction to examine. Later.

"I don't deliver death," I reminded her. Maybe my murderous self, too.

"You don't save people, either," she said, "but here we are."

Ouch. Deserved . . . but ouch.

Spotting what I'd been hunting for, the entrance to an open cemetery, I turned off the main road and onto its drive.

"That what you *want* me to do?" I challenged.

Helena got quiet again, her face turned toward her window as we passed stone markers, gravestones, aboveground tombs, and sepulchers.

"What are we doing here?" she asked.

"I want to show you something."

"In a graveyard," she replied, her voice deadpan—like she didn't really care about the answer. Like she figured she'd inadvertently given me an idea, and that I *had* decided to scythe her.

"This place is ancient," she said. "They haven't buried anyone here in years."

"I know."

"You couldn't pick somewhere they're more likely to find my body *before* I turn into a moldy crouton?"

"I'm not scything you, Helena!"

She folded her arms. "Then what is this about?"

"You," I said as I neared the rear of the cemetery, a Victorian section with several elaborate and freestanding mausoleums. I slowed as we neared one that would do—an ornate and elegant hut-sized stone sepulcher.

Only when I put The Judge in park did Helena glance my way again, questions swirling in her red-rimmed but still gorgeous eyes.

"It'll only take a few minutes," I promised, killing the engine and yanking the keys free.

"What will?" she pressed.

"At this point," I said, dissipating into smoke, "what do you have to lose?"

I reappeared at the threshold of the mausoleum's iron doors, the lock of which I undid with vapors.

I glanced back at Helena once, then slipped inside.

41

HELENA

Maybe I would regret again following his command. But so far, when it came to Grim, I'd yet to truly regret doing anything he'd told me to do. Even now, with all this pain and uncertainty, I couldn't bring myself to wish I'd never met him. Never mistaken him for a fellow partygoer on that balcony . . .

He'd changed me. For the better.

If nothing else, he'd taught me it was wiser to take chances and to stop wasting time with waffly people and things. Also, to live in the moment instead of fretting over the future or ruminating on the past—realms that didn't really exist. Not like today did.

It was true what they said. Tomorrow *wasn't* promised. But when you had today in your hot little hand, it sure meant a lot more—became far more precious—when you thought there might not be another.

The irony was that I'd learned these lessons too late for my practical application of them. Couldn't do much more than make my last weeks—my last days—more interesting with a bit of flair here and there. Like splurging on the good wine. Going ahead and getting the mozzarella sticks. Using the good towels . . .

I would have to be satisfied with that.

I got out of The Judge and approached the mausoleum, which resembled a miniature Gothic castle. I slid through the metal door Grim had left ajar and into the quiet stone chamber. A single tomb dwelled in the center of the mausoleum, its flat stone lid bathed in the pearly light that streamed in through a tall Gothic stained glass window.

On one side of the tomb stood Grim.

Lifting a hand, he crooked a skeletal finger at me, beckoning me nearer.

"You're going to tell me what I already know," I said, "aren't you? That I'm not special. That what we had was fun, but it couldn't—and can't—last. Not just because of what you are, but what I am, too."

And wasn't that rundown a paranormal version of what every guy had ever told me?

Maybe it was even true this time.

"You're going to tell me I'm a nice girl, but that death is a deal-breaker—even for you. Especially for you. Also how, seeing as I'll soon be beyond the boundaries of space and time, you don't do long-distance relationships."

Even as I spoke, I went to him, and that beckoning skeleton's hand caught my chin when I came close enough.

"You read too fucking much," he said.

I might have laughed if my heart hadn't been so heavy.

"This soul," he said, pointing at the tomb with the index finger of his free hand. "I know I collected it, but I don't remember her."

"Great," I cut in. "You brought me in here to tell me you're not going to remember me because you collect so many souls. Everyone's. Basically, you're calling me a groupie. I feel better already."

"I didn't come back to rescue my car, Helena," he snapped. "And I didn't bring you in here to wax poetic about the futility of being together while breaking up with you."

"But you *are* breaking up with me."

God, I sounded so pitiful. Pathetic. The words had just leaped out of my mouth.

Embarrassment engulfed me, scalding my cheeks, which blazed against the November chill. I couldn't believe I'd said that when we'd never even been together. The word "boyfriend" had always been a cover for him. And what the hell was the Grim Reaper supposed to do with a girlfriend anyway?

Grim lifted skeletal hands to the hood of his cloak, which he drew back to reveal his human face.

"I don't remember this soul," he continued, "but I remember one from the same era. Her name was Rose."

Oh, jeez. He wasn't about to tell me about an ex, was he? *God.* Could it be this whole time I'd just been a rebound for some Victorian heartbreaker?

"She was nineteen when she died," said Grim. "She wasn't a Fated, in case you were wondering. She'd simply been thrown from a horse. When I came to get her, she refused to accompany me. Not until I agreed to take her to her 'one true love.'"

I frowned and tilted my head at this, glancing his way, though he kept his own stare down, on the stone lid of the tomb we stood next to.

"I wasn't about to let some headstrong, upstart soul tell me what to do," he said. "Aside from that, I had a schedule to keep. She wasn't the only soul I needed to see to, and I had to meet my quota for that day. Still, she insisted that I take her to see her beloved so that she could tell him goodbye. When she refused to come with me without my promise to help her, I cleaved her soul from her body with my scythe, but she was willful and would not be collected. I rarely encounter souls strong enough to withstand me. But . . . after all this time, you made me realize it wasn't her soul that gave her the strength to defy me. It was . . . the love between her and her young man. Who, much to my annoyance, I ultimately did take her to. He couldn't see her, but she spoke to him anyway, promising him that she would always love him, and . . . that she would be waiting for him in the hereafter. That they would reunite one day."

"That's . . . so incredibly sad," I said.

"She cried when I told her we had to leave. But she turned to face me, ready to go."

"Then what did she do?" I asked, curious to see where this story would go, and to find out what exactly Grim was trying to tell me. And why.

"Then she thanked me," said Grim. "I told her I hadn't done it because I wanted to. And because I was still annoyed, *more* annoyed, I also told her he hadn't heard her anyway. But she told me I was wrong, and that it didn't matter what I thought. Or what I thought I knew, for that matter. But then she took my hand and pressed it to her cheek—a show of gratitude despite my irritability. I took her soul after that and delivered her to the Blue Basin. You know I don't know what becomes of the souls, but the story of Rose doesn't end there."

Grim turned toward me, pulling up his sleeve with one skeletal hand to reveal that his other had reverted to flesh and blood. He bared his tattoo-covered forearm at me, and I couldn't help zeroing in on one of them. It was even one I'd admired before—a delicate rose.

"This showed up after my interaction with Rose," Grim said. "And I've had it ever since."

"Your tattoos," I ventured, curious and intrigued. "Are you saying that . . . all of them represent someone? A soul?"

"I've been doing this for a long time," said Grim. "Long enough that I don't remember when I started, or even really where I'm from, or who I was. But I remember certain souls. Those that have, for one reason or another, because of our interaction, left a mark upon me. It happens once every ten or twenty years. I will meet a soul that brands me irrevocably. A soul that alters mine—to the point that I am marked both physically and spiritually. Certain souls . . . they leave their scars. And I never understood Rose fully. Never until now. Because . . . I forgot my humanity. Something she was determined to appeal to anyway."

"Wh-why are you telling me this?" I asked him.

Grim didn't answer. Instead, he opened the collar of his robes, parting the mixture of black fabric and vapor with one flesh-and-blood hand and one skeletal hand.

And I had to suck in a gasp at what now occupied the center of his human chest—just over his heart.

Somehow, a bright yellow sun had appeared, shoving the other somber black tattoos that had been there aside to make room for the new cheerful symbol.

Unlike all the others on his form, this tattoo blazed with vibrant color. And thc sun, the happiest of yellows, beamed almost bright enough to exude real light.

"That wasn't there before," I said, my gaze snapping up to him. And it hadn't been. Because I'd gotten an excellent look at his chest—and many other parts of him besides.

"It wasn't," said Grim. "But it is now."

"You're saying it just showed up?" I asked, confused.

"I knew when I saw it," said Grim, "that it was too late for me. But I thought that if I stayed away from you, if I cut everything off cold turkey, you'd eventually . . . forget me."

"What?" I asked, shaking my head. "But—"

"You said it yourself," he explained. "Fate seemed to forget about you. Death, true death, never showed up to claim you. And I was starting to think, to hope, that your optimism could be founded. That you'd somehow slipped through the cracks and that you might get to go on with your life. Rose was right. I didn't—*don't*—know everything. So maybe if I backed off, I'd find out you were right, too, and that you'd get to have your life. If I cared for you, I needed to let you go so that you could live that life. And I do. And I did. But then, tonight . . . I felt the call."

I blinked at him, dumbfounded and a little lost. "You mean . . . it wasn't because of The Judge."

"Helena." He marveled at me, mystified. "How could you ever think I could hold *anything* as more precious than you? Let alone a fucking car."

His words speared me through the heart—and left me shaking. *Precious*, he'd said.

No man had ever called me that.

"But The Judge—"

"Fuck The Judge," he snapped. "And fuck fate, too."

"But—"

"I will come back a hundred—a thousand—times if I have to. I will stop fate every time. I don't care anymore."

"What . . . what about the plan—"

"Fuck the plan," he barked, turning toward me.

"But what about The Few?"

"Insert predictable foulmouthed response here," he said, which actually made me laugh—a little. Still, I was all but drowning in my own confusion.

"You came back to save . . . me?" I asked. "Again?"

"Of course I came back to save you," he said. "And I always will. Until they take me out."

"What?" I asked—borrowing *his* typical response. "No. You'll get fired. They'll take you away. And what about Cedric?"

"I'm tired of running," he said. "And it strikes me now that's all this job—if you can call it that—has ever been for me. An escape. At least . . . until now."

The tears returned to burn my eyes, their essence different now, infused with the happiness that came with the realization I'd had him all wrong. The truth of our situation soured that happiness, though. "Death is going to catch up to me. And The Few. They're going to catch up to you."

"Let them come," he said, his voice catching with emotion, and he swallowed, those blues searing into me. "Let all of it come. That's what life is anyway, isn't it? That's what death is, too. It comes when it wants. Ultimately, there's no stopping it. But the fucking dash that comes in between the dates on a tombstone? You made me realize, long or short, that's the part that matters."

"Oh, Grim." I lifted a hand to brush away my tears. "I . . . I don't know what to say. This . . . it all feels so impossible."

"Because it is," he half said, half growled. "*We* are. So let's just be impossible for as long as we can. Let the match burn down. It's fucking going to anyway at this point."

"I . . . I can't let you do that," I said.

"*Let* me?" he snarled, closing the distance between us, bringing that tattoo that, for me, dwelled right at eye level closer. "There isn't a force on this plane of existence, or any other for that matter, that could keep me away from you. Tell me to fuck off and I will still catch you from every fall, pull you off every elevator, sweep you out from under every train, walk you out of every fire, pull you out of every ocean. Maybe The Few will find out, but maybe they won't. When it comes down to it, I'm not going to be any worse off."

"You will be," I argued.

"You don't get to say that." He grabbed me, pulling me toward him. "Even if they send me to the depths of hell, I won't really be there, because I'll still have my memories of you. Aside from that, Rose was right about more than one thing. Say the worst happens and we *both* bite it. Get torn apart and tossed into other realms. I'll still fucking find you. Because I've seen it more than once. I've just never believed it until now."

"Believed what?"

"That nothing can sever love," he said. "Not even death."

I sucked in a sharp gasp—but that was it. No more air could reach my lungs.

Because had he just admitted to loving me?

"Being together," I said. "It . . . isn't sustainable."

"Neither is mindlessly collecting souls for the rest of eternity." He swung me toward the tomb, which he backed me against before leaning down, bringing his lips close to mine. "You don't want me around? Fine. Tell me to get lost. I'll leave you alone and just show up when I need to. You can even find somebody else, and I'll still—"

"Somebody else?" I interjected, cutting him off by placing my palm flat to that brightly colored tattoo. "You think I'll ever be able to love anyone else?"

"Then we're on the same fucking page, aren't we?"

He kissed me then, and I melted, unable to keep myself from throwing my arms around those strong shoulders.

The same page, he'd said.

Maybe we were there together. Even if the words written there didn't make sense.

Because there were so many variables, so much that could go so horribly wrong.

In all likelihood, death *would* find a way to claim me—a way Grim wasn't going to be able to stop. Maybe that would happen before The Few caught wise to Grim's involvement with me, and maybe not.

There was still the problem of Cedric, too.

Grim and his friends, his family, couldn't keep the wizard locked in a lantern for eternity . . . could they?

A mystery man had involved himself in our affairs, too.

I broke the kiss.

"What about the note?" I asked in a whisper. "Did you find out who left it?"

Grim pressed his forehead to mine, his hair brushing my cheek.

"Another Fated," he said, and I gasped again. "Sir White came to personally escort the soul, so I didn't get a chance to find out why. Cedric, the note, the involvement of another Fated—it's all tied together, though I can't figure out how. My guess is that someone's got it out for me—someone besides Cedric. But I don't know who, and I have no way of finding out. Not until whoever is responsible tries making another move. Seeing you again, though, holding you again, makes me realize . . . how much I don't care anymore. Not about anything I can't change anyway. My enemies are coming for me regardless. And now we know for sure, fate is coming for you, too. So all I can do anymore is hold us down until the worst."

"The worst," I repeated. "When you didn't come back, I thought the worst had happened—to you. I couldn't bear the thought you might be somewhere awful. At least that's what I thought when I wasn't thinking you just . . . didn't want me. Didn't care for me the way I'd come to care for you."

"I was trying to protect you," he said. "I never wanted to hurt you, Helena. I'd made such a mess by bringing this all down on you."

"Promise you won't do that again," I said. "Leave me to wonder."

"Whatever happens," he said, "wherever I am, I promise that no matter what, I love you. And will forever."

His way of softening the blow—of telling me he wasn't going to make vows he might not be able to keep. All while promising the most beautiful thing of all.

Then he kissed me again—before I could argue—and I found it harder to process everything he'd told me up to that point, or to think rationally about any of the problems that this change of plans, this total annihilation of our original plan, did nothing to solve.

Maybe, though, Grim was right. That we were trying to solve a conundrum that, because of how we felt about one another, had officially become *un*solvable.

No matter how you looked at it . . . it seemed there was no winning now. Not for either of us.

And the only thing left to do was to dance among the flames and in each other's arms, drinking one another up as much as we could while the world blazed around us, our enemies—whoever they were—closed in, and this doomed ship we occupied together gradually sank.

Even *I* had to admit how, when it came down to it . . . that approach was, like Grim himself—like *us*—pretty metal.

"Does this mean," I said as I again broke the kiss, tilting my head back while Grim assailed my throat next with trailing caresses, "that . . . you really *are* my boyfriend?"

"*Boyfriend*," he growled into me, a low, underscoring rumble of his monster's voice backing his human one. "I'm about to be your whole fucking world."

I sighed, a rush of euphoria sweeping over me, the sensation heightened and amplified by the press of his skeletal hand sweeping under my blouse and scaling up my rib cage before bypassing my bra entirely, burrowing underneath before clamping around my breast.

A needy moan escaped my lips the moment he squeezed, the soft cry echoing in our tight quarters.

"And you, librarian," he said, that thumb circling my hardening nipple, sending a rush of heat through my limbs—and between my legs, "are about to be *mine*."

42

GRIM

Three weeks away from her. That brief, agonizing scrap of time.

It made the centuries that had come before seem like a day.

The things she did to me. The way she dismantled and reorganized me, somehow making me simultaneously more human . . . *and* less.

When it came down to it, between the two of us, *I* was the one who was truly doomed.

Fated to adore her forever, whether she permitted me in her orbit or not.

For once in my afterlife, though, luck, even if fate had forsaken me, was on my side.

Helena loved me back.

That whole "meant to be" thing . . . It wasn't something we could ever aspire to.

Didn't matter. We were us regardless. Rewriting fate—*overwriting* it—to our liking.

At least until, one way or another, the powers that be ripped us apart.

Until then . . .

I scooped up my soft, sweet, delectable, *fuckable* librarian and seated her on the sarcophagus.

"Oh my God, Grim," she said, bracing her hands on my shoulders, squeezing muscles on one side, my exposed clavicle on the other. "What are—"

"I'm hungry," I rumbled in my reaper voice as I hiked up her skirt, hands—both skeletal now—gliding up her thighs.

Being this close to her, between her legs like this, hit by the heat of her, made it hard to figure out what the fuck I was. Good thing she liked my bones as much as my cock because trying to keep myself neatly filed into one form or the other certainly wasn't going to happen tonight.

"Are we supposed to be doing this in here?" she asked, her voice quiet and whispery—scandalized but tinged as well with hidden delight.

"I *promise* you she's not going to wake up," I said, the tips of my fingers finding the elastic lace of her panties, a garment she wasn't going to need.

I needed them, though. Which was why, after I drew them down, off, and away, I secured the hot-pink lace in a pocket of my robes.

"Shouldn't we—?"

I stopped her there, fleshless fingers clicking as I caught her chin with one hand, studying that strawberry-hued mouth that, even if I managed to keep us both out of the furnace for a thousand years, I'd never get enough of.

"Should," I said, "shouldn't. Supposed to. I don't think you understand how that all went out the window on that fucking balcony. Aside from that, you should have figured it out by now that I'll take you where I want."

Helena whimpered, like she hadn't known that's what she wanted—needed—to hear. I pushed her knees farther apart. As they had before, they fell open for me.

That had my hands itching for every part of her, bone fingers twitching.

Beneath my robes, my cock strained with its own need, the pain of its rigidness just as delicious as my prey. But the depraved monster part of me wanted in, too. And that's the part that came out first, wisps of smoke unfurling to catch Helena. I sent one vine winding up her body like a serpent. It shifted her bra aside as more vapors undid the clasps, unleashing her breasts in a spectacular display that made my dick throb. And she gave me no resistance as I bowed her backward over the cold stone sarcophagus. Which she *was* going to get fucked on.

Dinner at last.

The thought echoed through me as the moonlight bathed her glorious form in the floral pattern of the stained glass window—a fitting mosaic of gamboling roses and vines.

"Your string," I said, my dark voice reverberating around us in the tomb while my shadows caught her wrists, pinned them to the lid. "You should know I fixed it while you were in the shower."

"Wh-what?" she asked, trying to sit up, but I tightened my hold on her, smoke serpents constricting.

The pulse of her heart beat through my wispy black tentacles, building to a manic speed—something that had me relinquishing more control to the part of me that didn't think so much in words.

"You didn't know I was there," I said. Matter of fact.

Helena hitched a breath, like she liked that. Just like she liked this.

What else had I unknowingly done up to this point that she'd been into?

"The next time," I promised, "you will."

I obliterated the distance in a blink, diving in, assailing her exposed cunt open-mouthed and ravenous.

Helena arched on the tomb, as much as I let her, a wail escaping her, and as it reverberated around us, I lit up on the inside. The way flames did in a back draft.

Fuuuuck. How many times in the last three weeks had I thought about eating her alive like this? Having her come on my tongue this time. All while thinking I'd never get the chance again.

No wonder I couldn't keep my shit together.

Helena surrendered, her head falling back over the other side of the sarcophagus.

In reward, I sent my tongue wandering. Then I sent it plunging.

A sound I wasn't sure I'd ever made before came rolling out of me—a low guttural growl mixed with the hum of some happy, feasting carnivore. Helena writhed in my grip. I liked that, too, and she wanted one of her hands back, so benevolent wraith that I was, I gave it to her.

Apparently—for some reason, no guess as to why—she promptly forgot about all her shoulds and supposed tos, driving her fingers into my hair, palming the back of my head while I buried my face in her, dragging my tongue through her.

Gasping, like she was trying not to drown in pleasure, she fisted my hair, a signal that her stance on what *should* happen had recently fucking changed. That, combined with the decadent taste of her, had me funneling the whole of my concentration in on the new assignment.

Losing focus on maintaining my form, part of my lower face gave way to the hard bone of my working jaw.

"Oh . . . my . . . *God*," Helena panted, her breath coming fast.

I plunged my tongue into her again, but I lost control of that, too, heated flesh turning to wandering, invading shadows and maybe back again.

"Oh, fuck!" Helena's cry echoed in the tomb, and the darkest, most pitch-black laugh came rumbling out of my depths to rebound around us as she came with a violence that I went ahead and let myself be proud of.

Whimpering now as I returned to gently suck on her clit, cooling my assault while she still held me there, she trembled all over, like she might just break apart.

Poor thing. I *almost* felt bad for her.

I slid my lips along her inner thigh, giving the flesh there the softest sucking bite.

"Looks like I've been a bad influence," I said as, *somehow*, I managed to emerge from the heaven between her legs, one of my new favorite places.

Loosening the grips of my shadows on her, I gently drew her up into a sitting position again. Still reeling, gasping for breath, she fell against me.

Completely unaware how she was about to come again—even harder.

"Grim," she said, flushed, breathless, and desperate. "I'm . . . pretty sure . . . I have . . . a lot . . . more things . . . for you to fix."

"Oh, I *know* you do," I told her. "First thing's first, though."

I gave her another moment. Just one more to catch her breath. I gave myself the same moment to get myself together, wrangle myself into being human. Mostly.

"Look at me," I told her.

Helena took my face in shaking hands. Her eyes found mine, pupils blown wide so that only a slim ring of that summer-grass hue remained.

I lifted a skeletal hand to her cheek, thumb clearing tears. "You said a bad word."

She huffed a laugh, eyes averting from mine as she flushed to a brighter red.

"Afraid I can't let that slide."

She smiled, shy and embarrassed, and as obviously into the game as ever. Until my next words.

"Put my hood up," I told her.

She blinked only once as, slowly, that smile slid away, her gaze finding mine again, a dark hunger of her own replacing that shyness.

I waited. And Helena didn't disappoint. Her hands, shaking, went to either side of my head. As instructed, she gathered the material of my hood and slowly drew it up.

The familiar shadows fell over me. In the darkness I summoned my true face. The one that was no face at all.

Helena watched without fear, but she wouldn't see me. Not until I let her.

I had power over the translucency of my shadows—at least I did at the moment—and for right now, I just wanted her to see black. The color of doom.

And why did I love it so much that she liked me this way?

She was the only mortal being who ever had.

My form locked in this state—caught between being thing and man—I swept in on her, deleting the slim distance in a blink, straining cock now poised at her opening.

My turn to tremble, my whole being wavering, becoming less certain with the sensation of her scorching, velvety softness clenching me.

Helena's grip returned to my shoulders, one flesh, one bone. No. Both bone, both flesh.

Those curious eyes searched for my face.

Thinning the veil of shadows between us, I allowed her to see that it was *me* who wanted her this way, this time-torn being whose spirit she had resurrected. Then I grasped her by the hips, one hand skeletal, one hand not. Eyes locking with my empty sockets, Helena pressed a hand to my chest. And she didn't flinch this time when her delicate fingertips fell through the cage of my ribs as half my form faltered there. My grip on her tightened. I drew her to me, filling her to the brink in one go.

She took me with a soundless, open-mouthed, and breathless gasp.

Her shock. Her overwhelm. God, I fucking *loved* it.

I rocked into her again, and her jaw dropped open farther. Her free hand entering my hood, palm finding my hard cheekbone as my cock throbbed in the fierce grip of her divine body.

I withdrew, slowly, before plunging in yet again—all the way—what little mind I had left officially shattering at being sheathed to the hilt.

Helena kissed me, soft on the teeth. My own jaw fell open, like

I could kiss her back. Then, when her tongue darted between my teeth, something in me broke open.

I thrust into her sharp and hard, and Helena hissed with pleasure.

"Sweet . . . liiibrraariannn," moaned the creature part of me, officially in charge again as I hooked an arm, one of bone, one of flesh, under each knee, capturing her legs.

Knocked off-balance, Helena fell back on the tomb, though she caught herself with her palms so that she could remain upright.

So she could watch me as I drilled her.

I started fucking her hard. Helena braced herself, eagerly taking it, short, sharp gasps escaping her. I sent smoke snakes all over her, to lick and flick her nipples. More dove between us to have at her clit.

"Grim," she gasped. "God, Grim, I'm close."

Good to know.

My pace brutal, I sent my soul into her, seizing hers in a cruel grip.

Helena cried out. My invasion. Taking so much of me all at once. It had to be overpowering.

Good.

Come for me, Helena, my monster's voice urged through my soul, which twisted hers in its grip.

Her own soul, gentle as ever in return, even though it had once proved stronger than mine, sent shots of liquid gold to wind my darkness. Like her essence wanted me to crush it even harder—just as hard as I fucked her.

Now *I* was close. And when her soul gave mine the softest returning squeeze, I almost finished right there.

I held on, head tilted back, twisted toward the moonlight, which revealed more of my reaper's form to her, my white skeleton grin, my ribs and the shadows in between. The vines of smoke that surged to penetrate her more deeply, capturing her inner being, wringing her out—delivering a lick of death while soaking in the burn of her life.

All the way until Helena collapsed backward against the stone lid, her cunt spasming around me.

"*Fuck*," I choked out when she came, my soul seizing the pleasure that radiated through hers, my spirit swallowing her orgasm down whole, blissing out on it—and her. Right before, as I'd done the last time, sending the wave of ecstasy that came with my own release straight back into her. Brutalizing her all over again while she shrieked a second time.

Because I wasn't just a monster. I was *her* monster.

And I wasn't about to let her ever forget.

Our pleasure blurred together, the fallout prolonged, our climaxes trading echoes.

She shook against the tomb, demolished. Just the way I wanted her.

My shadows gathered her up, returning her to my arms.

I cradled her close.

Helena, knocked half unconscious again by the soul fucking I was seriously addicted to, slung one of her own arms around my shoulders.

"Grim, I love you," she managed, murmuring the words into my ribs.

I clutched her tight. Ripped to shreds.

Because . . . I fucking loved her, too.

43

HELENA

I didn't remember the car ride home. I just knew Grim was there. That, after securing my clothing back in place, he put me in The Judge.

Draped my coat over me.

Buckled my seat belt.

And knowing he was with me was enough to ease my mind because I fell asleep after that, and I only stirred again when he carried me into my apartment, which he let himself into with his misty powers.

"Smoke skills," I corrected myself aloud, murmuring the words into his leather jacket and once-more-human chest.

"That lady in 402," said Grim as he turned down the darkened back hall, not bothering to hit a single light switch. "The one with the rhinestone glasses?"

"Ms. Lynn."

"Pretty sure she hates my guts," Grim rumbled. "She grilled me pretty hard about why you were passed out. Couldn't tell her I literally boned you senseless in a mausoleum, and I didn't want her to call the cops, so I had to tell her you were drunk."

"Mmmmnot really a lie," I murmured when he bypassed my

bedroom, heading into the connecting bathroom. My insanely pink bathroom with flower decals on the wall.

Again, he forwent hitting the lights, which left us in the glow of the light-up, piña colada–scented, ukelele-shaped plug-in air freshener.

Gently, Grim set me down, the cold tiles stinging my bare feet, bringing me reluctantly back to life.

"Your shoes are in the living room," he said, though I hadn't been worried about them.

Woozy on my feet, in a good way, I smiled up at him. Grim's eyes traced my face, lingering on my lips before finding my gaze again.

Behind us, the shower clicked on.

"You're a dirty girl," he chided. "You know that?"

I put my hands on my hips. "Well, I wasn't before."

"You desecrated a tomb. What's wrong with you?"

"Grim!"

"Yeah, I know it's all my fault," he said, smiling to himself, *pleased* with himself, as he took hold of my shirt, which he gently lifted over my head. I let him have it. And my bra. "Still, no regrets."

He unfastened my skirt next, letting it fall.

My underwear? Still MIA. Had he put it in his pocket? I was pretty sure he had.

Hopefully we hadn't left it in the tomb . . .

Steam filled the small room, and Grim must have used his shadows to shift open the sliding door, because his hands—and eyes—never left me.

He guided me backward, into the hot stream that *did* feel blissful as it washed over me. I grabbed my yellow loofah, happy when Grim climbed in after me, his clothes evaporating as he came to stand in front of me, leaving the shower stream at my back.

"When you were here before," I said as he reached behind me to riffle through my shelf of products. "And I was in here. Did you think about me being in the shower?"

"No." His eyes cut back to mine. "You were singing. And I liked your voice. It's beautiful. Like you. That's what I thought about."

I smiled again as all the warm fuzzies came up to engulf my heart.

Grim shrugged, bringing a bottle of my citrus shower gel between us. "I didn't become a raging sex addict until *after* you kissed me. If that's what you're asking."

Still grinning, I looked away. "I thought for sure you thought I was out of my mind."

"Who kisses a skeleton?" he asked before answering himself in an ironic mumble. "Same type who fucks one, I guess."

"I *liked* kissing you," I admitted. "Besides, by that time, I'd had a crush on you for a while. Though I didn't think you liked me back."

A few beats of quiet passed before he spoke again.

"That night I fixed the uke," he said. "It was late, and the whole reason I came in at all was because I thought you were talking to some guy. I wanted to know who, and I was jealous as fuck for a second until I figured out it was a pineapple."

"You were spying on me?" I might have blushed—and furiously so—but I didn't really mind Grim knowing I talked to my stuff. Maui at least. "Through the window? And did you say you were jealous?"

"What *were* you talking to that thing about?"

"Maui's a she," I said as he opened the gel, giving it a sniff. "And I was probably ranting to her about you."

"Yeah, well," he said, pouring a generous amount of gel onto the loofah, "she didn't rat me out, so you won't have to worry about her going missing."

I laughed as Grim lathered up my loofah, tattooed hands working the yellow puff into a ball of fragrant suds before he applied it to my shoulders, gently washing me.

"This orange shit," he said. "You smell like it."

"You must like the stuff," I observed as he moved to wash my breasts.

"You kidding?" His eyes flicked between me and his task—which he seemed to be taking quite seriously. "I could fucking *drink* it."

I laughed again, my spirit beaming in his presence, my heart reveling in his undivided attention—his affection.

Grim continued to dote on me, washing me with reverence, like he really did think of me as precious. He even shampooed my hair and surprised me by following up with conditioner.

Relaxing fully, maybe for the first time in months, possibly even years, I let him take care of me, and fingers going to his chest, I traced the outline of his sun tattoo.

"You're not mad at me anymore," he asked, "are you?"

"No."

"Good," he said. "Next time you are, I know how to fix it."

That got a snort-laugh out of me. "Grim, you're joking again."

"That was abso-fucking-lutely not a joke."

He shut off the water, and when we got out of the shower and into towels, Grim brushed my hair. I let him do that, too. He even took the curl cream from me after he was done, insisting on applying that for me, too.

"I could get used to this," I said.

"Yeah, me too," he replied, the smallest catch in his voice. Enough of one to bring all my worries rushing back. I wouldn't dare let my heart sink under the weight of them. Not so long as I had him with me. Not when I wanted our time together, however long that happened to be, to be happy.

When he carried me to my bed, I held on to him extra tight.

"Don't tell me you have to go," I whisper-pleaded when he laid me on the covers.

"Not yet," he said. "Not if you don't want me to."

"Stay. Please."

He evaporated and re-formed on the bed next to me.

Unable to help myself, I all but attacked him, kissing him as I straddled him.

"We think the same, librarian," he said, his human voice rough with renewed desire as those tattooed, ring-lined hands, following my curves, fell down my body, which once again came alive under his touch.

Then I relished giving him a taste of his own shock-rock medicine when, guiding his hard shaft to my entrance, I lowered myself onto him, moaning as he again filled me to stretching.

His mouth fell open in awe before he seized my hips. I rode him with slow and even movements. For a little while, he even let me have control, his hands only encouraging my rhythm, deepening penetration.

Until he flipped me under him, taking over to make love to me again. Soft, slow, and human this time.

Which maybe, just like him . . . I needed.

44

GRIM

I only departed from Helena after she fell asleep, though I left her a note—again in fucking pink ink—that I'd be back the following night to take her out. Somewhere nice again. At eight.

Left a PS that she shouldn't wear anything she minded getting ripped off.

What could I say? I knew myself.

About an hour late delivering souls to the Basins but still within the expected time frame, I returned to the Hallowed Halls.

Johann wasn't at his desk. No bird in sight, either.

It was never my favorite thing to find the old man missing, but *I* was the one off schedule, so who was to say he wasn't just brewing a fresh pot of coffee in the apothecary?

Flora's statue had its eyes closed—so she was still out.

Hourglass in hand, still drunk on Helena, her scent clinging to me, I trudged toward the Basins.

As I neared the White Basin, I slowed, a sense of ill ease creeping over me—and not just because Johann wasn't here.

The sensation of eyes boring into my spine had me halting.

For a long moment, I stared forward, but then I swung around sharply, cloak, robes, and mist swirling behind me.

My soul withered, cramming itself into the shape of a human heart behind my sternum before giving one hard thud.

I clamped my hand more tightly around the handle of my scythe, having to fight back the surge of terror that banished, in its entirety, my lingering bliss.

A dark figure stood behind me, black robes spilling long around his form, an obsidian crown encircling his head, its clawlike spikes jutting toward the ceiling.

A featureless black mask, half hidden within the shadows of his hood, obscured his countenance.

Red glowing eyes gazed at me through two angry, downward-slanted slits, as though lit by the fires of hell.

Over the decades—the centuries—Lady Green, Lady Red, Sir Blue, and Sir White had all seen fit to drop in for some reason or another.

For as long as I'd been here, though, I'd never met *him*—Sir Black.

For a while, I'd even started to believe the Black Basin didn't have a guardian.

That it was just a lawless, prisonlike bog for the souls that settled like silt to the floor of depravity, vileness, and evil.

About that, I'd been wrong.

At least about there being no warden . . .

The entity, taller even than me, loomed at a distance, his hood cinched to his head by that menacing crown.

Within? Blackness and a face that was no face at all.

In that way, we two were alike.

Never before had I stopped to think about how terrifying it was for those who did glimpse me. To be faced with a horrific specter that had no features. None that could be discerned . . .

This must be what it was like. To stare into an abyss that stared back, knowing all the while that abyss was there to get you.

I stood frozen for a moment longer, waiting for this . . . guest to speak or move. To do anything other than lurk . . . and stare.

"You have business in the Hallowed Halls," I said at last, and it wasn't a question so much as it was a prompt. A plea for this being—whatever he was—to end this intolerable standoff.

To reveal what I already suspected his appearance pertained to.

He didn't answer. But still, an answer came when Cedric stepped out from behind the grim sentry, tugging his gloves more tightly into place like some pretentious asshole getting ready to take his Bentley on a summer drive through the countryside.

I should have known this was his doing . . .

"I assume no introduction is necessary," said Cedric, gesturing toward Sir Black as he eyed me darkly, those frozen blues promising retribution even as he offered a congenial smile.

"What have you done with Johann?" I asked. Not that I could do anything for the old man at this point—or anyone.

"Sent him on a goose chase," Cedric said. "Flora, too. I don't have anything against *them*."

I wanted to believe him.

"How the fuck did you even get out of that drawer?" I growled. Let alone Flora's lantern.

"Lady Red came looking for me," he replied. "Unbeknownst to you, she and I have been . . . *friendly* for some time now. I suppose I should thank *you* for introducing us."

Wait. Was he implying what I thought he was? That I wasn't the only one with a secret girlfriend?

He was seeing one of *The Few*?

Fuck me. Did that mean they *were* Nephilim?

And wasn't that what I got for shoving him into Basins whenever he happened to get his ass killed and I stumbled across him in the wild?

Unlike me, Cedric hadn't taken any sacred oaths forbidding such a union.

At least not yet.

Then again, mine included not dallying with *mortals*. The fine print? Well, it didn't say anything about entertaining one of The Few.

Suddenly, the Grim Reaper book on the library shelf and the note Helena had found inside made more sense . . .

As did the second Fated—Mr. Bluford.

Or, rather, Sir Blue.

Could it be . . . was it possible that getting rid of me had, somewhere along the way, become an inside job?

How many of The Few had Cedric enlisted against me?

Enough, it seemed, that the wizard was about to get his wish.

"I don't need to remind you," I said, "that you can't take the job if I don't pass it along."

"But I *can* apply if you're found derelict in your duties," countered Cedric through a bored sigh—like he was tired of thinking ahead of me. "Which you soon will be. Given that you're about to go quite . . . well . . . *missing*."

A beat passed in which my soul withered, wilting within me and sinking into my empty gut.

Cedric had me in checkmate. There was no denying that.

While I hadn't expected my stint in Elysium with Helena to last long, I hadn't foreseen it coming to a screeching halt quite this soon, either.

"Clearly," I said, glancing from Cedric to Sir Black and back again, "I'm leaving the Hallowed Halls regardless. But swear in front of The Few to leave Helena alone, to let her live, to grant her your credited life, and I'll make the bargain. I'll pass the scythe—and everything—to you of my own free will."

Cedric gave one short and scoffing laugh. Then he tilted his head at me, a look of dark bemusement crossing those features before they sobered back into veiled rage.

"Two things," he said. "Firstly, I think you can appreciate how well beyond the point of negotiations the two of us have now traveled. Secondly, since I've had my own plans for that life right from the start—something you guessed at, *correctly*—I can only promise you one thing. And that is, unlike you, when it comes to Helena, I *will* do my job."

Gripping my scythe between both hands, I started toward him, fully aware I wasn't going to get close enough to chop his block off *and* of the fact that, even if I did, it wouldn't change anything.

All the same, if I was going to go down, it *would* be swinging.

Every fucking time.

Cedric made no move to evade me. He didn't have to with Sir Black stepping forward.

Not caring anymore, I took my swing at him, but the angel, the devil—whatever he was—caught the scythe, which he ripped free of my grip like someone tearing a toy from the grasp of a child.

As he discarded the weapon, which misted to nothing, his other metal, black-clawed hand lashed out to snatch me by the throat.

Caught in his grip—more unrelenting even than mine—I pried at his fist with both of my skeletal hands as he hauled me toward his Basin, the entrance to *my* hell.

Helena. She'd be waiting for me again, and again I wouldn't show.

Would she think—even for one moment—that I'd lied about loving her?

Why did that strike me as the most horrifying part of this?

Sir Black dragged me to the Black Basin, which, as soon as we got close, loosed tendrils of ebony muck—oily whips that lashed me by the throat as well. They snagged me by the wrists, too—my ribs and spine, which cracked as my assailant bowed me backward over the hungry vat.

Helena, I'm sorry.

Helena, I love you.

"Farewell, Grim," said Cedric even as I still strained to escape. "You might not believe this, but I will miss you. It's nice, though, to see you at last heading somewhere where you're wanted."

I fought against Sir Black even as he bore down on me, shoving me into the Black Basin, which unleashed more tentacles, all of them finding bones to wind around and tug.

Together, they worked to loosen and unfurl me into spirit form, something I battled with every ounce of willpower I possessed.

That willpower lasted only long enough for me to give Cedric one skeletal middle finger.

And then, just like that, the Basin took me, and the reaper at last became the reaped.

45

HELENA

I wore a champagne-hued belted dress with tulip sleeves, but Grim never came to pick me up for our date.

At first, I waited for him on the couch with Maui, expecting him to materialize somewhere in my vicinity. At twenty minutes past eight, I went to stand at the window, where I peered out over the parking lot to see if he might be waiting next to The Judge.

"Where is he?" I asked Maui, grabbing the pineapple and hugging her close.

After an hour, I turned on the TV.

After two, I gave up, washed up, and went to bed.

Not that I got much sleep.

All over again, my mind went rampant. This time, instead of thinking the worst about him, I fretted that the worst had indeed happened to him.

He said he loved me. And that tattoo . . . Didn't it prove he held deeper feelings for me?

Grim didn't have a phone for me to call, and his family lived in a realm I couldn't reach on my own or communicate with.

Sunday crawled by, and I did a fair amount of pacing in my apartment. I couldn't even bring myself to make the grocery trip I desperately needed in case Grim *did* come looking for me—in case anyone from the Hallowed Halls did.

When Monday morning arrived, however, I had to leave for work.

I took The Judge to the library, where I hoped my anxiety would lessen. But work proved less of a time-passing distraction than a set of tasks I couldn't seem to focus on.

Something was wrong. It had to be.

But . . . what could *I* do about it?

When noon arrived, I gathered the day's selection of books and headed to the storytime corner, the area already packed with day care kids and afternoon regulars—moms and dads with their toddlers, grandparents with their grandkids.

Flustered, beside myself with worry, I sat down on my stool and tried to get a grip.

Today marked the first time I'd ever had to force a smile when faced with so many shining eyes and upturned and curious faces.

The kids, ranging in age from three to six, sat on brightly colored round cushions and, farther back, on carpeted risers. Behind them, a mural depicting storybook scenes and characters like Rapunzel in her tower and Anansi in his web provided a colorful backdrop.

Its cheer and whimsy couldn't spread to me today, and neither could the joy or the rapt attention of the children during our welcome song, which I strummed out on my ukelele while everyone followed along with the sign language I'd taught them.

Still, I kept my grin in place as I revealed our first book of the day—a classic and a personal favorite: *There's a Nightmare in My Closet* by Mercer Mayer.

The moment the nightmare creature started to cry, though, I found myself fighting tears, too.

Ramsey, one of my tried-and-true regulars, raised his hand. Blinking away the tears, I called on him, glad for the reprieve.

Maybe I shouldn't have picked out all monster books this morning . . .

Or brought my ukelele.

"Miss Hart," said the six-year-old, tilting his head while he blinked dark eyes at me. "Are you afraid of the monster?"

That. Well, that got a laugh out of me, which made my young patron smile.

"No," I assured him, "I'm not."

His frown returned. "Then what's the matter?"

"Oh, I don't know," I said, shaking my head. "I think maybe I'm afraid *for* the monster."

"I've read this one before," volunteered Maya, a five-year-old from Sunny Street Day Care. "The monster is okay at the end. Keep reading, you'll see."

I nodded, raising the book again. "That's a great idea."

I kept reading and turning pages, but I only partially recovered after my initial lapse.

Still, I got through the other books and, miraculously, a precarious rendition of "Head, Shoulders, Knees and Toes" before finally wrapping up.

Ramsey hurried over to me as I started packing my books back into my *Don't Let the Pigeon Drive the Bus!* tote that I'd purchased at an ALA conference a few years back.

"The monster turned out okay," said Ramsey. "Did you see?"

"I sure did," I replied, offering him the warmest smile I could conjure.

"All the monsters did," he added. "Even Grover."

"That Grover," I said, referring to the other classic I'd added in, *The Monster at the End of This Book* by Jon Stone and Mike Smollin. "He was worried about nothing, wasn't he?"

"He didn't know he was the monster," Ramsey observed. "But . . . he also didn't know that he wasn't."

I blinked at this and frowned. Then, finally, out of nowhere, some much-needed relief washed through me.

Children. In so many ways, they were so much wiser than adults. Always, they had been my best teachers.

"You know, Ramsey," I said, "you're right. Grover did all that fretting for nothing, didn't he? He was afraid of the monster because he didn't know *he* was the monster. At the same time, he didn't know that he wasn't really a monster at all. Not like he was thinking. Not like he feared."

"Yeah," said Ramsey. "So nobody got eaten or anything."

He patted my knee with one umber hand, a gesture that melted my entire heart—what was left of it at this point anyway.

"That's lucky," I replied with another short laugh that made Ramsey's smile broaden. "You know, Ramsey, you really helped me to see things more clearly."

And I wasn't just telling him that. He had.

Because his words served as a reminder that Grim wasn't a monster, either. Not really. And if he wasn't a monster, not the truly scary sort, then what did he have to fear?

The powers that be . . .

If they—The Few—cared enough about collecting human souls and seeing them to their various destinies, if they cared enough to give Faust, a man who had notoriously sold his soul to the devil, refuge from literal demons, then they couldn't be *all* bad.

And if they weren't all bad, Grim was likely . . . okay.

If they were looking out for Johann, Flora, and Cedric, they would look out for Grim, too.

Right?

"Don't worry, Miss Hart," said Ramsey as he rushed in to give me a hug. "The monsters all turned out fine."

"Thanks, Ramsey," I whispered, patting his back before he turned and hurried off to line up with his friends for craft time.

For a while after that sweet interaction, things got better. *I* got better.

I started to focus again. But then, when three o'clock rolled around, my terror came crashing down on me all over again when Hunter entered the children's department—something he never did.

Behind him, dressed in jeans, a Hello Kitty T-shirt, a spring-green raincoat, and a yellow beanie that hid her pointed ears, trailed a distraught and anxious Flora.

"*Flora*," I gasped, rising from my swivel chair behind the checkout counter. "Oh my God."

"Oh," said Hunter, folding his arms, "so you *do* know this pint-sized heathen."

"That's *Miss* Pint-Sized Heathen to you, you great boot-wearing goose."

Hunter blinked at me, unamused. "She was looking for you all through the stacks in the adult nonfiction, yelling your name like someone who, I don't know, has never been in a flipping *library* before."

"I have a library in me house the likes of which you've never even dreamed of," snapped Flora.

"I bet its two bookshelves filled with *Goosebumps* and YA trilogies."

"Try life records, forbidden magic, alchemy, and divination."

"Okay, *Merlin*."

"I know someone who knew him, you know," said Flora, hands going to her hips. "Taught me a hex or two he learned from his books. So, if'n you'd rather not find your elbows inverted in the mornin', you'd do well to remember your manners, Boot Boy."

"My name's *Hunter*."

"Well," said Flora, "at least you don't shame your own name. Did a fair job hunting down Helena, didn't you?" Abruptly, Flora turned to me. "But what are y'doin' all the way on this side of the building?"

"I'm . . . the children's librarian," I told her, gesturing to our more colorful surroundings. "The children's section is separate."

"Didn't know you worked with kids," said Flora. "You and I have something in common after all."

"How are you gonna say you work with kids?" challenged Hunter. "You *are* a kid."

Flora wheeled on him. "Well, if that ain't the wean calling the fairy a shrimp."

Hunter spread his arms. "What's with you people? I'm eighteen!"

"When I was eighteen," said Flora, "I was pulling pixie pranks on the countryfolk, not traipsing through a boring old library molding my brain on books."

"*What?*" Hunter squinted at Flora like he, too, had caught the barest of shimmers in the air at her back—her wings poking through whatever glamour she'd cast over herself.

"Flora," I said, drawing the fairy's attention back to me. "What is it? Is everything okay?"

Didn't I already know the answer, though? Why else would she be here?

"Och," said Flora, "it's all the exact opposite of okay."

"It's Grim," I guessed, "isn't it?"

"The kid knows Grim?" asked Hunter, aiming a thumb at Flora, who, arching her brows, aimed a thumb back at him before echoing the question.

"The kid knows Grim?"

"Um." I bit my bottom lip. Then I shook my head. "We . . . all know Grim. Hunter met him the other day when he stopped by to ask about—well, that's not important. Flora knows Grim because she's his . . . um."

I couldn't exactly say "coworker," could I?

"I'm his niece," said Flora.

"From Scotland," said Hunter, his gaze darting between us, more dubious now than ever.

"Twice removed," Flora added.

"Twice?" Hunter crinkled his nose. "But that would make his actual niece, like, ancient."

"How old *is* ancient?" asked Flora, turning the question on me. "Personally, I don't think I'm quite there yet."

"Okay," said Hunter, holding up both palms. "The math isn't

mathing here—on *any* level. But I don't think I super care about that. All I care about is that I *really* feel like you shouldn't be in the library unsupervised. Honestly, I don't think *I* should be in the library unsupervised, but I guess I keep holding out they'll eventually offer me hazard pay. Bottom line, are we good now? Can I foist this hobgoblin with her spectacular vernacular off on you, Hart, and go back to my Quasimodo bell tower—aka the nine hundreds?"

"You've never met a hobgoblin in your life, have you?" asked Flora. "I've half a mind to sneak one under your bed in the wee hours, I do. If for no other reason than to teach you a lesson about the fair folk."

"Whatever you do," Hunter said, shifting his focus back to me, "please don't marry into this family."

A furious blush heated my face. "Um . . . I've got it from here, Hunter, thanks."

"Then I'm out," Hunter said. "This place gives me hives. Too many colors. Deuces."

He threw up a sideways peace sign before swinging away and fast-walking out of the children's department—probably wanting to make himself scarce before someone under the age of ten saw his name badge and asked for help finding a book, logging on to a computer, or with tying a shoe.

"Look, lass," said Flora, concern knitting her expression, "I hate to bother you at work, but I didn't have much of a choice after what we found in the Hallowed Halls."

"No," I said, "it's okay. I've been worried sick about Grim. What is it? What's happened?"

"I was hoping—perhaps in vain—to find out you'd seen him in the last day or so."

"The last I saw him was Friday night," I said, blushing again—and hoping desperately Flora didn't ask for details.

"That's the night Johann found Grim's hourglass abandoned in the Basins chamber. I was out with Pluto, chasing Cedric's soul down—except we found out too late it was a clever decoy."

"Cedric?"

"Aye," said Flora. "He's loose—but I don't know how. Or, unfortunately, where."

"Oh no . . ."

I gave the children's department a scan. I swallowed hard, too, overcome with the need to get the heck out of here in case the wizard came to the library looking for me. To finish the job he hadn't been able to with the bookmobile.

Clearly, in his pursuit of ruining Grim, he didn't care who he hurt.

I couldn't be around my patrons.

"Johann was away in the Netherworld Forest," said Flora, "walking with Lady Red, who asked to speak with him about . . . Well, Johann has something like a stalker."

"I know who Johann is," I said.

"Grim told you?" She tilted her head, surprised.

"I . . . sort of guessed."

"Oh," said Flora. "It's a sensitive topic for Johann, which was why he followed Lady Red out to the forest. She wanted to ask him about the smashed-up Volkswagen parked near one of the larger portals—to see if its presence there meant anything to him. She thought it might mean the portals had been breached, and he—we—were compromised."

"That's . . . well, that was *my* car," I told her. "Grim probably took it to the Netherworld to hide it after Cedric demolished it trying to kill me. But, Flora, where's Grim? What's happened to him?"

"We don't know," she said. "But I do know souls are dogpiling. I'm making my deliveries, but the adult spirits are backing up. Grim's not doing his job. Usually, if one of us stays put for long enough, he and I can find each other's signature—but I can't feel him anywhere in the world."

This was terrible. Horrible. *Worse* than I'd imagined.

Clearly, something had happened to Grim. And Cedric was to blame.

"What about The Few?" I asked. "Have you spoken to any of them?"

"Johann has tried summoning Sir White, but he won't answer," Flora replied. "Neither will the others. And we've searched the Hallowed Halls from top to bottom for Grim. Everywhere but his chambers—but we can't get in. Johann and I both tried."

His chambers.

"Oh my God, Flora," I gasped, my eyes springing wide as they found hers. "I know how to find him. But I *need* to get into his apartment. I'll explain when we get there. But can . . . can you take me to the Netherworld?"

"How soon can we leave?" said Flora.

"We'll go now," I said, grabbing my yellow cardigan from the back of my swivel chair.

"That's what I was hopin' you'd say," said Flora, a flicker of relief registering on her young face.

46

HELENA

Flora had a different method for smuggling me into the Netherworld than Grim. Instead of taking hold of my soul, she masked me with a glamour similar to the one she'd used on herself, smothering my essence under fairy magic so we only registered as one being, one fairy—her—when we crossed the threshold.

From there, the two of us ran through the woods, all the way to the towering black cathedral-like citadel that loomed like a behemoth amid the craggy trees, which skirted its foundation, small as toys in the fortress's presence—just like us.

Together, we entered a long Gothic hall, and as we raced down the straight and unending corridor, I swore the green flames in their sconces whispered my name—like they knew me. Like this place did.

If Flora heard, she didn't let on.

Finally, we reached the familiar chamber of the Basins, where we found Johann pacing in front of his desk. Perched on the old man's shoulder, Pluto saw me first.

"Bright light!" the bird called, wings opening as though with excitement. "What a sight!"

"Helena!" Johann exclaimed, his frightened and surprised gaze darting between me and Flora.

"I had to bring her here," said Flora. "She says she knows how to find Grim."

"Grim Grim," said Pluto, "we miss him."

Johann frowned, his eyes suddenly so sad. "My greatest fear is that he's been arrested. Or even that he is on trial this very moment—facing judgment with The Few. Otherwise, with the backup of souls, why wouldn't they have answered my summons or come looking for him before now?"

I didn't say anything. I just hurried to Grim's statue, which did not hold its scythe.

I froze under that hooded stare, suddenly much less sure I could actually get in to view the painting that portrayed Grim's whereabouts.

Last time, I'd gotten out of his chambers by borrowing one of his scythes. This time, though, I had nothing to offer the statue.

Nothing, that was, except for myself.

Unsure of what else I could do, I gripped the stone reaper's awaiting hand with mine.

To our unanimous surprise, those fingers curled around mine. Stuck, I peered wide-eyed over my shoulder at Flora, Johann, and Pluto, who ticked his head at the phenomenon in wonder.

Maybe this was some kind of trap set by The Few?

That thought left me as the hooded statue lifted my hand to press its teeth—or rather, the lips it didn't possess—to my knuckles.

"Missing Grim," said Pluto, "kisses the miss."

The statue released me and, with a low *clunk*, began to move, its short plinth sliding to one side to reveal the spiral staircase down to Grim's lair.

Cradling my hand close, the one the statue had "kissed," I couldn't help a small smile—a small *hopeful* smile.

Surely, if Grim was somehow no more, this statue wouldn't have responded to me this way. And this sweet gesture from this inanimate eidolon. Did it somehow mean that holding the keys to Grim's heart was the same as holding keys to his place?

A question for another—and I hoped to God happier—time.

Without looking back, I plunged into the darkness, followed by Flora, whose wings fluttered as she flew down the channel.

Johann came, too, Pluto remaining perched on his shoulder as the three of us spilled into the long hall of scythes.

"Great gobs of bobs," marveled Flora, her voice breathless as she took in the collection of scythes. "I knew he had a few of these, but lord. He's got a right problem, I'd say."

"Fascinating," rasped Johann. "He's always scared me a little, you know. And this collection. It *does* make me feel more founded in that fear. Less guilty for harboring it."

"He's fickle with his sickles," said Pluto. "Every day it's trade a blade."

I rushed past the collection of scythes before taking a second hall. Then, I burst into the central room with the red couches, Grim's desk, and that painting.

I gaped at the portrait, which did not depict the interior of this room or any other. Neither did it show a moonlit ocean, or anywhere at all.

"Gods almighty," whispered Flora as she trailed in after me. "Who'd have guessed the bone brain's got *taste*?"

"Sharp objects," said Pluto, "sharp décor. Never been in here before."

"Oh," said Johann, pointing to the snow globe before smoothing his beard. "I gave that to him ages ago. For Christmas. Never thought he kept it."

"It's . . . black," I said as, with slow steps, I edged nearer, drawn by the nonimage that I willed to become something other than absolute nothing.

"That painting," said Johann. "You're saying it is of significance?"

"It shows where Grim is," I explained, my voice quavering as a terrible foreboding—worse even than before—stole over me. "*Wherever* he is. But . . . I don't understand."

I swung around to face them. "There's something wrong with it. Unless . . . unless either of you know of someplace he'd be that is . . . pitch black."

Flora gasped, both hands leaping to cover her mouth. "Gods."

Johann's expression went gray and graven. "It's worse even than I thought."

"W-worse?" I asked, my voice shaking. Because . . . were they saying he was somehow . . . dead?

"Where is he?" I demanded, taking a step toward them. "Tell me right now."

Neither answered, and both averted their gazes. Even Pluto refused to meet my eye.

"Is he gone?" I asked outright. "Did Sir White or one of the others take him away? Into one of the Basins?"

"He . . . his soul is in one of the Basins, aye," allowed Flora, a pair of tears cutting tracks down her face, both of which she quickly whisked away with the heel of her palm. "And no soul has ever come back from a Basin. Not ever. None but Cedric's. Basins won't have him 'cause he can't die. But Grim . . ."

My heart sank. Then it imploded.

But this . . . none of it was making sense.

If Grim was well and truly gone, why did the painting still show his whereabouts? Why had his statue responded to me the way it had, allowing me entry?

If he, his soul, was gone and he wasn't the Grim Reaper anymore, if he'd been replaced, then souls wouldn't be piling up in want of collecting.

"Flora," I said to the fairy, who had to battle away new streams of tears that, like her wings, sparkled with a strange iridescence. "Before, when we made the plan to smuggle my soul into the White Basin, you said you knew how Grim could get into that Basin undetected."

Flora's eyes widened, and she started to shake her head at me—slowly at first, then with rapid refusal.

"I know what you're thinking," said the fairy, "but you don't know what you're askin'."

"The Black Basin," said Johann as, hands clasped behind his back, he eyed me with curiosity and, I wanted to believe, new respect. "It won't keep Helena's soul."

"Johann!" piped Flora. "For her to go in at all, I'd have to remove her spirit from her body—which would *die*. Are y'both forgetting that the plan was only supposed to go into effect *after* Helena died?"

"She won't die if her soul exits her body willingly," said Johann. "At least . . . not right away. It will remain attached, in essence, to her physical form until that form perishes or until her soul is cleaved from it."

"And that's exactly what will happen the moment she goes into the Basin," said Flora. "She'll get cut off."

"Chop suey," said Pluto. "Ka-plooey. Light's out. Check, please."

"We don't know for sure," said Johann. "And as you said a moment ago, Cedric's soul always emerges from the Basins because they can't keep him. Because he's not dead."

"Cedric *can't* die!" exclaimed Flora. "He's hardly a good example of what's likely to happen to Helena. And when he has gone in in the past, his body at least has been dead—however temporarily."

"His body revives itself," argued Johann, "which draws his soul back. The case could be the same for Helena."

"Could be," stressed Flora with a growl. "It could also *not* be the case."

"I want to try," I said, my gaze bouncing between the two of them.

"You want to try dying?" challenged Flora.

"It's not like I haven't before," I said, exasperated. "Aside from that, aren't I destined to anyway?"

"Aren't we all?" mumbled Johann from beside us, drawing both our gazes.

"Aye," said Flora, "everyone except for you. And Cedric. And Grim."

"Just my point," said Johann. "Cedric, Grim, and I—we all sidestepped fate, did we not? I at least did not expect to. And aside from that, Flora, *you* are currently here and out of fairy prison because Grim asked for his duties to be split with another. He saved you. He's protected me—more than once, I can only assume. Here has arrived our chance to roll the dice again despite the odds and to strive to repay him."

Flora shook her head, more tears falling. "It's not that I don't want to save Grim. I'd go into that Basin meself if I could."

"You can't because you're not a spirit," I guessed.

"Johann and I," said Flora, "we're still in our physical vessels. To smuggle you into the White Basin, Grim was going to need to drink from the Basin's waters while carrying your soul in his hourglass. Presumably, the essence of that realm would have disguised his soul and cloaked yours long enough for Grim to carry you in. Once the waters wore off, the Basin would kick him back out—but The Few don't monitor souls coming out. Just those going in . . ."

I took a steadying breath and then asked the obvious question. "What happens if I drink from the Black Basin?"

"The answer to that," said Johann, his tone grave, "is . . . anyone's guess."

I turned and started for the door, but Flora's wings flittered, and she zipped ahead of me, blocking the exit with both arms.

"Grim wouldn't want this," she said. "He wouldn't want anything terrible to happen to you. He didn't want you to die."

"You're right," I said. "And Grim tried to stop my death from happening. He saved me . . . so many times. Now it's my turn to save him."

"*I'll* drink from the Basin," said Flora. "I'll go in to get him."

"In truth," said Johann, "I almost offered to do the same myself. But . . . none of us knows what lurks beyond the barrier of any of the Basins—let alone the Black. Flora and I—what if either of us is destined for it? Given our . . . histories, I cannot discount it. In that case, either of us could become trapped—and dead—as well. But Helena, we know, is a Fated. She is destined for the White Basin. So the Black. It *cannot* keep you."

"It has to be me," I agreed, already ten steps ahead of them on this. Not because I understood how the Basins worked, but because I understood . . . how Grim worked.

Who knows what state I would find him in? I did know, however, that he had come to recognize the feel, the shape, the light of my soul. If nothing else, he *would* recognize me. And I would recognize him. No matter what.

"Only the darkest souls go into the Black Basin," Flora warned, her voice dropping with dread. "Whatever happens in there, whoever—*whatever* you encounter. Johann and I won't be able to get you out."

"You can sit with my body," I said, "and protect it in case Cedric comes back."

"If you don't die the moment you go in that Basin!" she piped.

"Even if I do," I said, "I can still get Grim."

"He's going to be so mad," Flora said, her bottom lip trembling like she still hated this plan but also like she didn't want to fight my resolve anymore. Like she finally grasped what Johann had the moment I'd entered the Hallowed Halls tonight. That this, trying to convince me not to attempt to save the man I loved, was a losing battle.

"He might be mad," I said, stepping up to Flora, who, after lowering her arms in defeat, shifted aside to clear the way, "but even an eternity of his anger is still better than losing him to the Black Basin."

47
HELENA

Johann brought me a bejeweled, beautiful, and archaic-looking chalice from his chambers. He said he was told angels once drank a special and rare wine from it.

The silver goblet seemed a fitting vessel for my final drink if it indeed ended up costing me my life.

While Johann and Flora watched on, their expressions knit with anxiety, I approached the most ominous of the Basins.

Inside the vat, the smooth and shining blackness reflected my own wrought expression like a dark mirror.

I didn't have time to waste. Grim needed me. And never once had he hesitated to appear at *my* side when fate tugged at his soul. Fate, in a way, was tugging at mine now, and Johann was right. Fate *could* be changed.

His had changed. So, from what I understood, had Flora's. As had Cedric's.

The Hallowed Halls—how often had they facilitated those changes?

I dipped the chalice into the vat, breaking the smooth surface tension. The slow and thick consistency of chocolate syrup, the liquid flowed into the chalice.

Though I wasn't entirely sure how much I needed to imbibe, the information that Flora had shared about the effects of the potion eventually wearing off had me filling the cup to the brim.

I didn't want to gamble on the idea I might run out of time before I could reach Grim.

"Are you sure you want to do this?" asked Flora, still in denial that this truly was our *only* course of action. *My* only course.

Instead of answering, I gripped the Basin with one hand, and steadying myself, I brought the goblet to my lips and started to gulp down the liquid.

Behind me, Flora gasped. Johann remained silent.

"Finish the drink, you'll go in the sink," urged Pluto.

I drank and drank, ignoring the taste as best as I could—though it wasn't as bitter and vile as I'd been expecting. I'd braced myself for a muddy or even motor-oil flavor, but the waters of the Basin carried only the faint tang of fermented fruit and stale flowers.

Only after I finished the entirety of the chalice did I come up for air.

Dropping the goblet, which clanged on the marble floor, I gasped and coughed, bracing the back of my wrist to my nose as I slowly turned to face Johann and Flora.

Flora's eyes darted as they mapped my face, her fingers tangled up together as if she felt desperate to do something. Johann's expression remained both expectant and solemn, though he seemed to be holding his breath.

"The deed is done," said Pluto, blinking as he ticked his head at me, seemingly curious as well over what would become of me now.

"How . . . do you feel?" Johann asked, his voice rasped and low, edged with dread.

I blinked at them, waiting to feel something—anything.

For several long moments, nothing happened—nothing outside of my stomach giving a noisy slurp.

But then a lightheadedness stole over me. Dizziness tugged at my awareness, and a strange wooziness encroached on my senses.

"Nothing'sss haappening-ah," I said, my words slurring.

"Flora," said Johann as the man shuffled to stand behind me. "Give her soul a little nudge, would you? I'll catch her."

Flora frowned but then determination overtook her expression. "If Grim asks, I never did this."

The fairy padded up to me, and then lifting one hand, she gave my solar plexus a small shove.

I gasped, propelled backward from myself, light as a kite that had caught a breeze.

As I floated in reverse, my abandoned body collapsed—straight into Johann's waiting arms.

"Pretty bird!" cried Pluto, the glow from my spirit casting him in a pale yellow light that highlighted the iridescent sapphire, teal, and garnet undertones of his ebony feathers.

Gently, even as he peered up at my spirit form, squinting against the strange golden light that continued to bloom around us, the old man guided my limp and unconscious form to the floor.

"Gods, Helena," said Flora, her voice hushed and reverent as she shielded wide eyes from the light that radiated . . . from me?

Still suspended in midair, I peered from one arm to the other and then down at my legs, shocked at the way my transparent and translucent form, garbed in my work clothes—pencil skirt, flats, cardigan, and blouse—shone like a sunbeam.

My time to marvel at this strange spectacle, and to revel in this oddly euphoric sense of weightlessness and freedom, didn't last, though.

Like a spreading shadow, an obsidian stain flowed down my arms, coating and cloaking my luminous form, hiding the light I exuded from view by sheathing it—and all of me—in a subduing layer of black. One that transformed me into a librarian-shaped wraith.

"What's—?"

I didn't get a chance to finish asking my question because something caught me from behind—a lashing whip of freezing ebony, thicker, darker, and more viscous than Grim's smoke tendrils.

Another murky tentacle wrapped my leg. Two more caught me by the wrists.

Then everything zeroed down as I shrank into a tight ball of awareness. A sphere of darkness that, an instant later, got sucked into a devouring and all-encompassing pit of the same.

48

GRIM

Outside didn't seem to truly exist. Just me, the hut, and the small figure occupying the straw bed in the corner.

Every time I tried to leave the house, the hut's lone doorway would take me straight back in instead of out. It didn't matter how the dark outline of the forest waited at the edge of the farm, visible through the door's frame. Nor did it matter that the light of the shining full moon beamed through the open shutters of the only window.

I knew that small sleeping figure, that sick child—that boy. But at the same time, I didn't *want* to know him. Rather, I didn't want to remember him . . .

It hurt too much to remember him.

So I walked out the door again, straight into the cold and starry night.

Except that night morphed back into the interior of my simple house with its low, raftered ceiling and dirt floor.

The boy slept under the wool-filled blanket made by his mother—my sister.

My late sister . . .

Damnit.

I didn't want to remember her, either.

I didn't want to feel. *Any* of this.

Turning on my heel, I rushed out the door again, as though speed could somehow break me through a hidden barrier, whatever invisible veil existed that kept returning me to this house, that room.

To hell . . .

My hell.

My efforts failed me like they had before. Like they undoubtedly would again.

But then that now-familiar sensation of dread crept over me, soaking into my skin before whittling its way between my ribs.

Memory. That's right. I was in a memory. Stuck in a memory—and it was about to start. All over again.

I shook my head, tears burning in my eyes as I stared at that bed, and my nephew, whose breathing had turned unexpectedly shallow.

That afternoon, the boy, who had seen six winters with hardly a cough, had been fine. He'd helped me out in the field with the crops, and for the first day in weeks, he hadn't cried for his mother. Finally, he'd started to adjust to being away from the city. To being with me. A makeshift and ill-fitting parent, but the only scrap of family he had left.

Just as he was mine . . .

My throat closed up as I fought the draw of the memory, and I swallowed hard against my unshed tears, trying to force them back.

But then, like a drug-induced sleep, the memory took hold of me, overriding my awareness that I wasn't really here, and that I hadn't already relived this moment a thousand soul-shattering times already.

49

HELENA

I floated down and down, through an arid atmosphere of pure nothingness—like outer space but without a single twinge of light.

Keeping the urge to panic in check—as much as possible—I let myself sink through a soundless abyss absent of color and shape.

When I reached a certain depth, the sense of gravity grew stronger. My form stretched, elongating from an orb back into my normal, human-shaped spirit body. An instant later, my feet connected with solid ground, and the world gained shape, gray stone walls rushing in to meet with and join the matching floor.

A giant black throne—empty of any occupant—loomed ahead, flanked by Gothic wrought iron candelabras with onyx tapers lit by black flames.

The shadows this ominous candlelight threw galivanted along the rear wall, taking on phantasmal shapes that seemed to possess clawed hands, teeth, and eyes.

I swallowed down my building terror and peered behind me, searching for any sign of anyone or, perhaps more importantly, any way out of here. Wherever here was . . .

A slow look around confirmed what I already suspected. That no door or window interrupted the stone walls that now imprisoned me.

I did discover, however, that I had company.

An enormous crowned figure now occupied the throne, his black gauntleted hands gripping the armrests of the obsidian chair.

Glowing red eyes, a pair of angry slits, beamed at me from behind the mask lost within the darkness of a black hood.

"You do not belong here, soul," said the man—the entity—with a voice like an undead Gregorian monk, deep and melodious, but somehow corrupted, as if produced by tattered vocal cords.

"Um," I said, offering the tiniest of curtsies because, well, he *was* wearing a crown. "Hi. Uh, I'm here looking for someone. Are . . . are you like . . . the supernatural equivalent of a Walmart greeter? I'm sorry, I've never done this before." I cleared my throat. "Descended into an all-consuming void of dreadful nothingness, I mean . . ."

"You have no darkness that binds you here," said the man—the creature, who must be one of The Few. "You cannot be admitted."

Oh. Well. That sounded like a *good* thing. Sort of . . .

For me at least.

"I'm looking for my friend," I admitted. Honesty being the best policy and everything. "My boyfriend," I amended, then quickly added, "Actually, I'm . . . pretty sure he's . . . the love of my life."

"Love?" asked the figure. "Life? That cannot be. For *you* were not meant to find love in this life."

I stiffened and scowled, arms going rigid at my sides. "Who says?"

"Sir Black," replied the figure as he rose. "Ruler of this realm. Warden of Wraiths. Guardian of Shades—those souls whose darkness weighs them in regret and paints them in the impenetrable shadows of despair."

"Right. W-well," I replied, lifting my chin, refusing to shrink, Grim's words about turning up my song returning to strengthen me. "I'm Helena. Children's librarian. Avid reader. Musical fan. Pancake maker. Dad joke enthusiast. Unapologetic Swiftie. And girlfriend to the Grim Reaper."

Might as well give him the full rundown so long as we were comparing résumés.

"I know who you are," said the figure, Sir Black, as he started toward me with a slow and measured stride, armored boots clanking against the stone in a way that made me gulp.

He . . . did?

"Th-then you know I don't fit the description for tenants of your world. At all. So I don't see where you get off making judgments about me or declaring things over *my* life."

"But your friend," said Sir Black, coming to a halt right in front of me. "Does *he* fit the description?"

I frowned and tilted my head at this bleak sentinel, confused. My thoughts whirred as I tried to resist the nearly overpowering urge to step back from him and put distance between us again.

But now that I was here, what did I have to be afraid of? If the worst was going to happen, at this point there'd be no stopping it.

As Grim had said, in for a penny, in for a pound.

"I think that description *could* fit him," I allowed. "But I also think that, as would be true with anyone, it doesn't have to."

"That you know that," said Sir Black, peering at me through that mask embellished only by those two downward-aimed slits of glowing crimson, "underscores what I said before. That you do not belong here."

"But he does?"

"His darkness binds him. For him, there is no hope."

I shook my head. "What if I don't believe you?"

"That matters little," said Sir Black. "It only matters that *he* does."

"I . . . I want to see him," I said.

"Then you must go through me."

Well, that sounded iffy. Not to mention impossible.

He didn't exactly look ticklish.

Shoot. I *knew* I should have stayed in tae kwon do.

I might have even gone on to earn my orange belt if that one overly aggressive purple-belt lady hadn't kicked me in the boob so hard.

Maybe, if I was lucky, I could dart around him or even hit the dirt and scramble between his legs. And I might have even tried either one of those techniques if there'd only been an exit I could run *to*.

"Don't suppose you could be tempted to settle this with a game of rock, paper, scissors?" I asked.

"You must answer my riddle."

I released the ethereal breath I hadn't realized I'd been holding and braced a hand on my chest.

"That's *all*?" I asked. "Oh, this is just like Oedipus and the Sphinx, or Bilbo Baggins and Gollum. *Not* that I'm comparing you to Gollum. I have to say, though, riddle answering is *much* better than hand-to-claw combat. I've totally got this. Hold my beer." I gave a nervous laugh that tapered off when he just kept standing there, staring at me. "Um . . . I have to ask, though. What happens if I get it wrong?"

"I will hold you in my darkness forever."

I blinked, eyes bugging. "Sounds fair . . . Um. If I answer correctly?"

"You will be free to pass."

I frowned but nodded, ready. And if anyone could solve a riddle, wouldn't it be me? Was there one I hadn't heard before?

"Okay," I said, "hit me." Quickly, I held up a halting palm. "Figuratively, I mean. With . . . the riddle."

Sir Black didn't waste time.

"I am your dearest friend and your most ardent foe. Though you flee, I still will be wherever you go. I live in your shadow and dwell in glass. Armed with fear, I will never let you pass. If I am against you, you cannot prevail. But if I be for you, you ne'er shall fail. What . . . am . . . I?"

I gritted my teeth, my mind reeling anew with panic even as the cogs turned, working to produce an answer. The right answer.

I sort of forgot to ask how many guesses I got. Usually, this kind of test allowed for three, but Sir Black didn't seem like the generous sort.

So, one it was.

Except, I couldn't think of the answer.

Not until, as was true with most riddles, the solution surfaced—suddenly as obvious as daylight and bold as brass.

The riddle, though, was itself a riddle. In that it wasn't meant to help *me*.

Also, Sir Black had dropped plenty of clues before this moment—right from the start of our conversation.

"I know who you are," I told the ominous and intimidating figure.

"It makes sense that you would," said Sir Black, "given what I said before. That *you* do not belong here."

"Grim doesn't, either," I told him. "He just doesn't know it. And knowing it . . . really knowing it . . . well, *that's* what makes you free, isn't it?"

"Who am I, Helena?" asked the dark figure before me.

I smirked at him, my fear of him falling away in a rush as I lifted my hand to take hold of the edge of his mask.

"You are him," I said, "you are her. This one and that one. You are everyone. But the answer you are seeking is . . . that you . . . are 'me.'"

I pulled free the mask, which, like Grim's scythe had on occasion, misted away to nothing, revealing a face I would find in any reflective surface—in, as he'd said, glass. A familiar countenance that went everywhere with me because it belonged to me.

My best friend and my worst enemy. My supporter, my saboteur.

"You didn't mean what you said before," I whispered to him—to her, the woman who occupied that darkly cloaked and heavily armored form. "Did you? That I wasn't meant to find love in this life."

"Not if you don't believe me," Sir Black said, though he spoke now with *my* voice—right before he, she, *I* misted away, too, the entire being unraveling and dispelling to vapor.

A moment later, our surroundings did, too, the impenetrable walls unspooling to fog before evaporating, revealing a nighttime scene.

A strip of forest ran behind a small thatch-roofed hut stationed next to gardens planted with neat rows of cabbage.

A wooden cart filled with straw waited to be hitched again to a mare or donkey.

Weak candlelight the hue of tarnished gold flickered from the hut's lone window, drawing me toward it—toward the house. Right along with the low murmur of voices.

One of the voices belonged to Grim: his human form.

But then . . . the other voice belonged to him, too. That one to his monster form.

Drawing up to the window, I peered inside to find both versions of him present within the humble abode.

"Grim!" I shouted to him—to them. But as if they hadn't heard me at all, neither of them looked my way.

I almost shouted to them again, but I stopped, my breath catching when Grim's reaper form, scythe gripped in one hand, lifted a bony finger to point at the child sheened in sweat—the tiny boy I hadn't noticed until that moment.

The one breathing shallowly, his small hand draped across his belly.

The one sleeping, sick—and unaware of the conversation being held in his vicinity.

A conversation that continued to unfold.

One that pertained to him.

To the boy who could be only one person.

"*Phineas*," I whispered.

50

GRIM

"I'll not let you take him," I said, positioning myself in front of the fearsome wraith who had entered my home unannounced—uninvited.

"You should not see me," said the dark figure wrapped in black robes, his face concealed behind a veil of solid shadow.

"Leave now," I commanded, even though my voice shook. Not because I feared for myself, but because I knew who he was—what he was—and why he was here. "You're not welcome."

"I am your guest nonetheless," said the dark figure, his tenor low and raw, rough and ragged, that of a monster with no soul.

"You said you are death," I snarled, "but my nephew . . . he is not dead."

"I said I am the *hand* of death," corrected the monster. "And . . . he will be soon."

"He cannot die!" I snapped, trying—and failing—to keep my volume down so as not to wake Phineas. "Devil. I *order* you to leave."

"Send me away," said the ghoul, "but know that will change nothing. I will return for him later. I do not bring death. I am simply the courier."

"You lie."

"To what aim?"

"You cannot take him from me," I growled.

"I must."

"Can I not assume his place?" I asked, pleading now, for in truth, what could I, a mortal man, do to stop this creature? "Can't you leave him and take me instead?"

"It is not your time."

"He is but six and I am three and thirty," I argued. "My time should come before his."

"That's not how it works," said my oppressor, his tone infuriatingly gentle—like *I* was the true child in this situation.

"Then how *does* it work? Where will you take him? What is to become of him?"

"You ask me questions I cannot answer."

"Cannot," I challenged, "or will not?"

"The answers are mysteries to me as well," said the specter, spreading one skeletal hand, then the terrible figure took a step toward the bed. I darted to stand in his way, my arms out as if that could do anything to keep this nightmare at bay, or Phineas's spirit from his cold grip.

"Leave him be," I said. "I told you. I will take his place."

"There is no substitution. He is Fated."

Again, he started forward, that scythe blade gleaming, but I backpedaled, keeping myself between him and the bed, him and my poor nephew. "Fated for what?"

"You must see me," said the ghoul, "because of the child. So often they see me. As do those close enough to the young to truly understand them. A rare quality. Perhaps you are Fated, too . . ."

"Please?" I said, because begging was the only tactic I had left. "There is no way? I will do anything—perform any task, traverse any realm, perish myself—if you say it will spare him."

The specter lifted his head, peering at me through that darkness, his face hidden in the gloom but then, just for the scarcest moment, faintly visible.

"There is . . . *one* way," said the creature. "But I hesitate to offer it. Be your answer yes or no . . . the price merely to consider is high—let alone the payment to accept."

"What is it?" I insisted. "Tell me now."

"It lies within my power to grant you a life," said the monster. "One to spare. A single one—even a Fated—on the condition you agree . . . to take my place."

"Your place?" I half asked, half huffed, the idea as terrifying as it was unthinkable. At least for the span of one fleeting moment.

"I have offered this trade a handful of times before," said the wraith, "but no one has ever agreed. The burden of their refusal, what that refusal cost them, then became theirs to bear until their own deaths. So know that I do not offer lightly."

"If I take your place," I said, my heart hammering hard—too hard, catching wise, it seemed, to this sudden conspiracy being formed against it. For, if I understood correctly, the muscle would have to cease beating for me to become as this thing was—a shade of death. A courier, he'd said. Of souls . . . "If I agree, Phineas will live. Is that the trade?"

"The life would be yours to grant—or to hold—as you see fit," said the monster. "Should you bequeath that life to this child, it would grant him a long one but . . . know he will traverse that life without you. Never can he know what became of you. And then, decades from now, when the time comes, *you* will be the one to perform the task that you now seek to prevent me from completing."

So long as that moment remained far, far away from this one . . .

"He's clever," I said, my voice quavering, "and resourceful. He will find his way."

Though I forced myself to speak with conviction, I couldn't bring myself to feel it as wholly true. Phineas *was* all of those things—tenfold. But he was still just a boy.

How could I leave him utterly alone in this heartless world?

Yet I could not bear to let him go with this stranger. Especially now that I knew there *was* something I could do to stop that from happening.

"This world is harsh," said the monster, his words echoing my own thoughts. "It is my opinion that you deceive yourself into thinking *I* am the cruel one when, really, it is you. But in abandoning your nephew, you do *me* a kindness by releasing me from my duties and my oath, freeing this tired soul. Knowing you trade your soul, your life, your destiny for his, and that you will serve in this capacity and this role until the day you find someone to willingly change places with you . . . do you still wish to take up my scythe? My oath? My burden?"

"My destiny," I said, extending my hand for the scythe, "I face it now."

"Uncle Renwick?" came a small voice from behind us, and I turned my head to peer back at Phineas, who stirred on the mattress, eyes still thankfully shut, shadowed underneath by dark circles. "Who are you talking to?"

"No one," I told him. "Not a soul. You must have been dreaming. Go back to sleep."

The boy obeyed, most likely because he could not fight against the illness that lulled him back into the arms of sleep—that close cousin of death.

I would much sooner sleep have him than *this* dark relative.

"You are ready to take the oath?" asked that ominous figure, drawing my gaze back to the awful blackness within that hood.

"Quickly," I said. "Before he wakes again."

51

HELENA

Renwick.

It seemed a fitting name. Sharp and quick, but also lyrical and, in a way, elegant.

I let the scene unfold before me, in awe of this version of Grim that, from his dated attire, our rustic surroundings, and the absence of any of his tattoos, I could gather was a memory.

As the two figures spoke, making their deal, I held my breath as Grim, *my* Grim, took the scythe from his opponent.

The moment he did, the tool, the reaper, the former reaper, vanished, unfurling to mist and vapor just as Sir Black had done.

The boy turned his head away, resuming a previous position, and Grim seemed to wake up.

Frowning, tears burning his eyes, he peered at the boy, his nephew. Then, after raking a hand through his hair—which currently lacked its white streak—he hurried to the door, which he opened.

I rushed to meet him there, but the instant he stepped out, something strange—something *else* strange—happened.

Grim blipped out of existence before reappearing with his back to me, as though the threshold represented some invisible portal that sent him straight back into the house.

"No," he muttered, gripping his hair with both hands now.

"Grim," I said, "I'm here."

I surged forward, desperate to go to him, to embrace him, to let him know he wasn't alone anymore. And that I'd come to get him.

That invisible barrier worked the same way for me as it had for him, depositing me in a flash back into the darkness and the night instead of allowing me into the house.

I whirled to find him pacing now, anxiously glancing from the doorway he could not get through—that he could not see me standing in—and that small boy he'd been forced to abandon.

His pain—the anger he carried with him everywhere, and in every fiber of his person. It all made so much terrible sense.

Right along with why he didn't want to remember.

That one life Grim had been granted by the prior reaper—Johann must have realized right away when I'd told him about Cedric trying to barter with Grim for my life that Grim had used his own credit to save someone he loved. And how saving that life had led him to take up the scythe.

In saving Phineas, though, Grim had also left the boy behind.

And he'd spent all this time—centuries—blaming himself for that.

"Grim," I called again, tears burning my eyes, too, because I wanted so badly to put a stop to his angst, to this agony that worked to eat him alive.

When the figure of the Grim Reaper rematerialized in the far corner of the hut, unfurling from gray-black smoke and mist, my stomach plummeted.

The memory—it was about to begin again.

How many times had Grim already relived it in the hours—the *days*—since he'd been here, in the Black Basin?

"Grim!" I tried again as the door, moving on its own, slammed itself shut, sealing him in with what had to be his darkest moment.

Though I tried to shove the door open, it refused to budge, which sent me scrambling back to the window.

"Demon," said Grim, *my* Grim.

"I am but the hand of death," corrected the reaper, a response that had Grim whipping his head toward Phineas before, panic-stricken, glancing back to his unwelcome guest.

"I'll not let you take him."

And just like that, the memory began again, forcing Grim to participate, to revisit, to relive every excruciating second.

How could I stop it when he couldn't see or hear me?

When, to him, *I* was the phantom, and these shadows represented his current—and unending—reality?

This. Wasn't it the true riddle? Its answer much more difficult, much more elusive than the puzzle Sir Black had presented me with. But then, Sir Black had well and truly been *me*. Did that mean Grim had encountered his own Sir Black, too?

To be here, he must have. He did not grasp what was plain to me—that he did not have a prison guard here. None outside of himself.

This torture. Grim was doing it to himself.

Which meant I had no power to stop it. *He* would have to.

One thing I *could* do was to try to be a better mirror than the one he found himself staring into now. The distorted one he showed himself.

The one he could not escape. Because it was his only perspective.

With just a few words uttered to me in The Judge, hadn't Grim done the same for me? Adjusted my view. Shifted my soul. Just enough . . .

"You did everything you could, Grim," I said, calling to him from the window.

He didn't hear me. None of the figures within the hut did. Impervious to my efforts, the phantoms and my poor Grim carried out their play, their reenactment.

"You saved his life, Grim," I said. "Even if he never knew it, even if he thought the worst, that was still worth it . . . wasn't it?"

Grim again hurried to put himself between the reaper and the boy, spreading his arms as the dark figure started toward Phineas.

"You tried to do the same for me," I said. "Remember? Because you love me. I understand that now—even if I didn't before. And you loved Phineas, too. That's what matters. That's *all* that matters. That's all that matters now."

He didn't seem like he could hear me.

But then, a shaft of bright golden light shot out of me and into the hut, illuminating it.

I glanced down at myself to find the beam emanating from my heart. Another beam, born from my collar, joined the first.

Finally, I had Grim's attention.

He looked to the window, eyes widening on me.

But the only reason I'd caught his attention was because the draft of the Black Basin had begun to wear off.

There was no way to know how long I had—how long either of us had—before I got expelled and the two of us were separated forever. Or for at least as long as this fever dream of guilt decided to hold on to Grim.

"Grim," I called to him when he just kept staring at me like he didn't recognize me at all.

But then his expression broke, his eyes softening.

"Helena," he said. "It can't be you."

"It *is* me," I said, hope filling me to the brim, something that sent another shaft of light bursting through the flimsy shield the potion of the Black Basin had placed over my soul.

Pushing away from the window, I rushed to the door of the hut, which, this time, opened for me. I shoved my way through, stumbling into the sparse room, which dissipated the moment I entered, our surroundings reorganizing themselves into a certain nighttime balcony.

An autumnal breeze rushed between us, the air laced with the distant aroma of bonfire smoke.

Somehow, I'd been returned to my homemade costume of sunshine and rainbows.

Grim stood just as I'd found him that night, hooded and robed, solemn and alone with his scythe gripped in one hand.

I rushed over to him as more light broke through my being, casting our surroundings in a bright glow.

When I reached Grim, I grabbed his free skeletal hand, lacing my fingers through his bony ones.

"Helena," he said again, this time with his dark voice, which emanated from within the shadows of that concealing hood. "I failed you."

"No, of course not," I said, pressing his knuckles to my cheek, the bones of his hand clicking, the imprint of those bones cold against the "flesh" of my ethereal form.

"What are you doing here?" he asked.

"I came to get you," I said, lifting my hands to the hood of his cloak, gently guiding the fabric back to reveal the face I'd only glimpsed through shadows and partially in the moonlight before now.

A grimacing skull peered down on me with empty sockets. I pressed my hand to his bony cheek even as that hand went radiant, the glow of my being intensifying.

"To stop you from falling," I whispered wistfully, giving half a glance to the portion of the balcony that had crumbled that night when I'd tipped backward, when he'd reached for me.

"I . . . forgot all about him," Grim said, his voice originating from his skull now rather than that dark hood, though his jaw never moved. "I don't even remember getting him. And I made myself—*let* myself—forget. That was the only way I could . . ."

"You felt guilty," I said when he trailed off. "That's understandable. But . . . you shouldn't. You saved him."

"Did I?"

"He lived," I whispered.

"Without me."

"He would have been without you in death," I said.

Grim hung his head.

"You gave him a gift," I pressed. "Like you did me. A gift of time. Love. Life."

"I forgot him," he rasped. "On purpose."

"And now you remember him," I said. "Because now you can. And that's okay. And who knows, Grim? Maybe . . . sometimes the Fated . . . There's so much we don't know about how this all works. And, well, couldn't it be possible that sometimes the Fated are sent here to live instead of die?"

"Beautiful soul," Grim said, that skeleton's hand coming to my cheek.

Grabbing it, I squeezed and pressed it into my skin as more shafts of light broke through, shooting every which way, uncontainable.

"What has happened to you?" he asked. "Are you an angel now?"

I smirked, peering up at him. Then I smiled. "I'm not sure what I am now," I admitted. "If I'm dead or still alive. A ghost or even, like you say, an angel. The only thing I want to be, though . . . is yours. Your love. Your fate . . ."

Grim leaned down, placing his bone forehead to mine. "I'm stuck here."

"You were," I whispered. "Come with me, Grim."

"Where?"

"Home."

"The Hallowed Halls?" he asked.

"Your place or mine," I said with a wistful smile. "I'll totally let you pick."

"How?" he asked.

"Just hang on to me," I said, grabbing his hand and wrapping it in mine. "And whatever you do, don't let go."

Grim didn't answer. He did, however, release his hold on the dream scythe, which misted away like all the other elements of this strange realm, this Basin with no true warden or guardian. None but the one created by each of its tenants, all of whom had, like Grim, sentenced themselves here.

"Hold on," I repeated, "don't let go, and believe what I told you. That it wasn't your fault. That you did the best for him. And . . . that I love you."

Grim grabbed me and pulled me to him, crushing me against his skeleton's frame.

I wrapped my arms around his shoulders again as the last of the Black Basin potion wore off, my essence eating through the darkness, banishing it. Mine at least.

Some invisible force, too strong to fight, lifted me into the air, and because I kept Grim in my grasp, he went with me.

In an instant, we reentered that black nothingness. Instead of free-falling, though, I went sailing backward. This tore us apart.

Almost.

I kept one hand clenched around Grim's, drawing him after me, with me.

He gripped mine in return even as he peered up at me, those empty sockets seemingly full of uncertainty and fear—fear that he wouldn't be able to leave with me. That he shouldn't.

Ultimately, that choice would be up to him.

But me? I would never let go.

But just as the atmosphere began to thin, Grim's fingers seemed to lose strength.

"Grim," I said, my voice pulsing through my now-amorphous being. "Seat belt."

Right away, he unfurled to vapor. But those tendrils, still dark, wrapped and held on to me, clinging to me like vines around a sun-soaked trellis.

Then the two of us, together, broke the surface tension of liquid black, our entangled souls propelled upward, nearly to the pinnacle of the dome in the Basins' chamber.

I kept my hold on Grim's soul even as mine began to free-fall again, hurling back toward Johann, Flora, Pluto, and the body I hoped still breathed.

Grim went with me, and I prayed as we plummeted together that the Black Basin, or rather Grim's regret, his guilt, his pain, and his unhealed wounds, would not try to suck him back into his own imprisoning solitude.

But then, the colored and masked figures pluming into view, gathering around us in a circle, each expelled by one of the other Basins, told me that, even if his demons didn't try to reclaim him, we both still had more hell to pay.

52

GRIM

While Helena's soul fell straight back into her body, my smoky essence splattered against the cold stone floor, spreading out even as it regathered into my reaper form.

I lay face down on the floor, hood still thrown back, and I glowered into the black marble floor that reflected my human form. I pushed up, skeletal arms trembling, and I looked away from the man I had once been but could never be again, head twisting her way.

I waited, praying, hoping, *desperate* for her to awaken. To *live.*

Helena lay draped against Johann, who held her while Pluto, perched on his shoulder, cawed at The Few. Until Helena arched, taking a huge breath as that incredible soul of sun and light reconnected with and reanimated her physical vessel.

"Helena's wellena!" cried Pluto.

In this form, I had no capacity to shed tears. Relief, powerful and potent, flooded me anyway, and I sagged, hanging my bony head.

At least she was okay.

The Few. They'd materialized—all of them except for Sir Black—as we'd descended.

I'd glimpsed Cedric among them, too.

And though I wasn't foolish enough to believe they would not banish me back into the Black Basin or do something even worse with me now, I could at least take solace in the knowledge they would not condemn Helena.

Perhaps they would still try to take her life. Undoubtedly, they would let Cedric, who must be here to claim my role, do just that.

"Renwick Loxley," said Sir White, that strange name I had, until now, forgotten was mine echoing through the chamber of the Basins. "You have been found guilty of breaking your oath, betraying your sanctified station, grossly neglecting your duties, and egregiously tampering with the sacred order of the universe."

He forgot kissing the most divine creature on the planet. But then, maybe that crime was lumped somewhere in that list of grievances—right along with my salacious interludes with that same stunning woman.

My bone arms still trembling with the effort, I rose, pushing onto my feet.

"You, The Few, have conspired against me," I accused as I switched my gaze from figure to masked figure, my bravery bolstered by Helena's—by Johann's, too, who'd stood up to The Few well before I had. "You provoked Helena's interest in me, *using* her for your purpose. You plotted with that vile wizard to corner and condemn me."

I extended a skeletal hand toward Cedric, pointing at him with a bone finger while, with my other hand, I summoned my scythe.

"Vile, am I?" asked Cedric in a cool voice, a single brow bobbing. "I would have thought at some point you'd recognize I've been *trying* to do you a favor."

The Few surrounded me, Flora, Johann and Pluto, and Helena, who only now just began to regain her senses enough to sit up on her own and then, with Johann and Flora's help, climb to her feet.

Across from me stood Sir White. Between him and the masked woman draped in crimson—Lady Red—smirked Cedric, his arms crossed as if he'd already won.

Which, perhaps, he had.

Behind me stood Lady Green in robes of deep emerald, her mask silver like Sir White's. Beside her lurked Sir Blue, sapphire robes spilling down his tall form, glowing red eyes regarding me with what I could only assume was contempt.

"I will surrender my title," I announced, "my scythe, and my claim to this position willingly, and face whatever punishment The Few would decree, but *only* if Helena's soul be released from her role as a Fated."

"You attempt to bargain in vain," came Lady Green's cool and sultry voice, its essence faintly warbled, as though funneled through water. That weird hissing and clicking emanated from her, too, when she tilted her head at me. "You no longer have any right to hold the station or power that will, in moments, be stripped from you anyway."

"Then you deny it?" I gripped the staff of my scythe between both hands as I slid to stand before Helena and my friends—my family. "That you are culpable, too? Guilty yourselves of *orchestrating* my downfall—and using a Fated to do it! Tell me, who among us has truly tampered with the '*sacred* order of the universe'?"

Darting forward, Helena rushed to stand at my back.

"Grim," she whispered, clutching my robes as she pressed her forehead into my spine. "Don't make them angry. Angrier . . ."

I ignored her. If I was going to save her this time—this last time—I had to.

"I accept my sentence," I told The Few, shifting my focus between them, ignoring Cedric, who only held that infuriating smirk. "And my punishment—whatever it may be. But only if Helena is rewarded her life in exchange for being made your pawn."

"This is a right injustice!" snapped Flora, who hurried to my side to shake a fist at Sir White. "Entrapment."

"I agree that Grim cannot be held accountable," said Johann, who stepped to my other side. "He, like Helena, was manipulated. By you, The Few. And for what reason? To install a new reaper? Why? Cedric . . . why?"

"Don't worry, old man," said Cedric. "Grim, or should I say *Loxley*, has had this coming for a while—and you and Flora know it."

"You've betrayed one of our own!" Flora snapped at him. "And do you have mince for brains? If The Few sold out Grim, then it'll only be a matter of time before you're the one under the bus!"

"Grim might have taken an oath," said Helena, stepping out from behind me. I extended my free arm, holding her back—to keep her as safe as I could for the moment. "But he never did anything wrong to land himself in this role. He's not here because he's serving a sentence or working toward redemption. He took the oath willingly. It should count for something that . . . that he is the only one among the occupants of the Hallowed Halls who hasn't gotten his second chance."

I glanced her way, stunned. Because what she was saying . . . I wanted to believe it.

For so long, I'd blamed myself for abandoning Phineas. But in the Black Basin, Helena had made a point of how the alternative, the only other choice, would still have resulted in my nephew and me being torn apart.

I'd had no choice. The one I'd made . . . For me, it *had* been the only one.

I could regret the consequences without regretting the choice itself.

Helena had shown me that.

"How Grim came to be in his role is irrelevant," said Sir White, lifting a silver-clawed hand at me, that palm open. "It only matters to The Few that he broke that oath. We are in agreement, and our decision has been made. Renwick Loxley, you will now and forever be stripped of your title, your role, your scythe, and your place here in the Hallowed Halls."

One after the other, Sir Blue, Lady Red, and Lady Green lifted their palms as well, aiming those gauntleted hands at me as colored light swirled in those palms, the energy building, brightening, intensifying.

"No!" shrieked Helena as she flung her arms around me, like that could stop the blast—or save me from the rays that hit me from all sides.

Somewhere, Pluto started cawing again, panicked cries echoing above the sudden roar in my ears as the four energies, white, red, blue, and green, dove into me, swept through me and then—as one—out of me. The surge of power ripped free my robes, cloak, hood, scythe, and skeletal form, leaving me standing there in my human incarnation, garbed in boots, ripped jeans, leather jacket, and T-shirt.

The Few then shifted the aim of those hands and that energy toward Cedric, who welcomed the blast with open arms.

Gritting my teeth, I glared hatred at him as my former robes swathed him, fabric and mist dancing with the crackling green energy of his wizard's magic as they enwrapped him.

He grinned, then laughed darkly as my scythe materialized in his grasp the moment he, like I had done so many times before, called the tool—the weapon—forth from the ether. That laugh built in volume as green-tinted smoke enshrouded him, tattered robes flying out, his figure flickering between his human form and his new skeletal form.

Helena whimpered as she clung to me. Turning to her, I pulled her close, enfolding her in my arms. I squeezed her tight, all too cognizant of the fact that we were moments from—one way or another, or perhaps even all ways—being torn apart for good.

Cedric roared with laughter, the smoke of his own essence rising and winding about him, dancing with luminous, phosphorescent, poison-green magic that illuminated his now half-human, half-skeletal frame, transforming him into a terrifying figure with even more power than I had ever possessed.

While he reveled in his victory and this act of retribution, the first among the many he was now bound to claim and exact, the figures of The Few each contracted into colored orbs. One after the other, they shot back to their Basins, plunging into the waters—vanishing.

But where were they going?

That. It was a stupid question.

They were going back to their realms.

Because their work here was done.

My punishment? Helena's fate?

The Few—it seemed—had seen fit to leave those items in the now-highly-capable hands of the world's newest Grim Reaper.

A *true* pompous psycho.

53

HELENA

I could only gaze on in horror and in dread as Cedric basked in his victory, his dark cackle like that of the heinous wizard—and now hand of death—he had become.

Just as soon as they'd whipped up, though, the winds Cedric had conjured died.

His newly acquired robes of pure darkness settled around him, his form became fully human once again, and his magic calmed, too, the sparks and flares of lightning-like energy fizzling before, like his villain's laugh, abruptly ceasing the instant he brought the staff of his scythe down hard against the marble with a resounding *clack*.

A moment of pure silence passed in which all of us regarded him with skittish terror.

Then a more genuine grin than I'd seen on him before spread across his face.

"I've always wanted to do that—*with* legitimate reason," he purred.

I spun to put my back protectively to Grim, who, gripping me by the upper arms, whirled me to face him again before swinging me away from Cedric.

"What are you doing?" he demanded, peering down at me.

"Defending you," I replied. "And standing up to the bully."

"Let me talk to him," he rasped.

"No offense, Grim," I said, "but that's not going so well so far. Listen, I've got an idea."

"An idea?" he snarled. "What do you mean you have an idea?"

"Well, I was going to try to barter."

"With *what*? Library cards are already free."

"I know a lot of people with connections," I told him. "Rare-book people. He seems the type to—ah!"

I jumped to find Cedric at our side. Grim grabbed me and shoved me behind him.

"Are you two ready to go?" asked Cedric as he smirked at Grim, a renegade swoop of that white-blond hair half concealing one more-mischievous-even-than-usual eye.

"Helena's going home," Grim said. "And you're going to let her."

"I'm going to *escort* her," Cedric corrected. "You as well."

"I'm not going back into that Basin."

"Frankly," said Cedric, "thanks to Miss Hart, I'm not so sure it would have you anymore. But that's beside the point and not really my concern any longer. At least, not for a good long while."

"What are you yammering about?" snarled Grim.

"Oh, if I must explain it to you," said Cedric, rolling his eyes. "I've decided to punish you with something far worse than death—*life*. All the rest of the life you never got to live after you took on the cloak and the scythe."

"What?" barked Grim.

"The Few and I felt that would teach you," he said. "If you wanted so badly to meddle with the affairs of the living, then meddle you now shall—and must."

"You're not making any sense," Grim growled even while I tilted my head at this, hope springing in my chest, making my heart flutter.

"You're returning to the land of the living," said Cedric. "For the foreseeable future. Which means you have to get a new job. A life, while you're at it. God knows you've been in need of one of those for nigh on centuries now."

"This is a joke," said Grim, even though I was starting to think . . . it wasn't. "You're toying with me."

"Not anymore I'm not," said Cedric. "Just take the gift, Grim. Loxley. *Ren.* Can I call you Ren? Consider it something of a long-overdue tax refund, if that helps you to compute."

"I'm not going anywhere without Helena," he snapped.

"Which works out," said Cedric, "since I've been instructed to escort *you* out of the Hallowed Halls as well as her. Humans—*living* humans—aren't allowed here. You know that."

"Helena's a Fated," Grim argued. "If you think—"

"About that," said Cedric. "You were right when you accused me of following you to that party. Watching from a third-story window, I did indeed witness everything that happened on that balcony. Nothing short of astounded, I hurried back here and told Lady Red right away what I'd witnessed—a miracle of sorts. Someone, a human of all creatures, got through to you."

"What are you talking about?" demanded Grim.

"I strove to help you so many times," said Cedric. "No matter what angle I tried, though, I could never get close enough to even begin to reach you. That was *my* task, you see. In exchange for refuge in the Hallowed Halls, I agreed to try to talk you into moving on. The Few . . . they had no complaints against you. You did your job well. Too well. You became a machine, Grim. You forgot what it was like to live. And that made you an efficient agent of death. But it also transformed you into a, forgive the term, dead man walking. I never wanted to hurt you, but ultimately, Lady Red helped me to see how the rehabilitation of your immortal soul—and mine—was the true objective. And I eventually concluded I was not averse to playing the role of villain if that's what you needed. And when I followed you to that party that night, when I saw this woman do what I—or any one of us—had not been able to do, to touch your heart, I knew that would be the role I would have to play."

"I *knew* you fucking followed me," growled Grim, but I gripped his hand, squeezing, hoping to ground him and settle his temper. Cedric hadn't been trying to undermine him so much as he'd been trying to . . . what?

I couldn't say for sure. At least not yet.

"Did you know?" Grim asked, glancing toward Flora and then Johann. He even eyed the bird.

"They didn't know," said Cedric, speaking up before any of them could. "They couldn't. The bond the four of you share was too precious to tamper with. If *I* was to be your adversary, well, then you would certainly need friends."

Cedric smirked again, arrogant as ever.

"But why?" asked Grim. "All this just to take my place?"

"As I said," replied Cedric, "taking your place was and always has been secondary to the goal of saving your soul. *That's* what The Few tasked me with in exchange for asylum and potential release of my own soul. They were worried about you, too."

"Impossible," scoffed Grim.

"Yet true," Cedric rebutted. "And your stint in the Black Basin should tell you that."

"Why did they send me there?" roared Grim.

"*You* sent you there," said Cedric, his voice soft—even kind now. "The Black Basin, it has no true guardian. It's a place souls go when they are . . . damaged to the point of unrepair. But only because they refuse intervention. They go there because they cannot go anywhere else. The souls of the Black Basin. Within, they face no darkness but their own—but it is all by choice."

"I would have been stuck there if not for Helena," said Grim, still angry.

Several beats passed before Cedric answered. When he did, he spoke with a gentleness that I wouldn't have imagined him capable of. "My point entirely."

Grim looked away as though he'd taken a punch, like Cedric's compassion hurt worse than anything he'd done to Grim before, and now he refused to meet anyone's gaze—mine included.

"Helena *reached* you," Cedric stressed. "Obliterated in an instant the impenetrable barriers you'd erected around your soul—the ones *I* had spent years just trying to peek beyond."

"*She* wasn't trying to get under my skin," grumbled Grim.

"That's just it," said Cedric. "I wasn't trying, either. Like everybody else . . . I just did."

Grim's scowl deepened. He went silent yet again. Maybe because he was still mad. Or maybe because he was reflecting on that.

"You'll find it interesting," said Cedric, "that Lady Red, a romantic at heart, became particularly enthralled with the idea you might have feelings for someone. You know the rules as well as I do, though. True, you'd already broken them by the time I brought your would-be crime to the attention of The Few. But . . . no one wanted you fired so much as they wanted you . . . free. As you know, a swift firing *would* have sent you straight to the Black Basin, which you were always bound for. Not through any misdeed, mind you, but rather through the lack of grace you seemed—miraculously and despite your taciturn demeanor—to grant everyone else around you. Everyone aside from yourself. And, if I may say so . . . me. Perhaps because caring for me meant you would feel some responsibility toward me. And that prospect reminded you too much of your perceived failings. Regardless, who knows how long you would have insisted on staying in that Basin? If, however, you could be enticed to go a step or two further in your delinquencies—and perhaps, well, grow a little in the process—a more creative 'punishment' could be dealt."

"You played me?" snarled Grim, somewhat and endearingly missing the point. Or maybe just pretending to.

"I wasn't the only one," replied Cedric. "The Few . . . Well, at my behest, they might have orchestrated a few scenarios . . . manufacturing a call or two to Helena's soul by staging some . . . incidents. Lady Red with the elevator . . . Lady Green with the train. Sir Blue, as you have perhaps guessed, planted the note. Because the fact remained. No matter what, you still had to face your own shadow. And The Few—they agreed with me that Helena was the only person who could even begin to tempt you out of your own darkness. Because, until her, you could not see the light. Not even your own."

Grim's hand shot out to grab Cedric by the collar, and he seethed his next words between his teeth. "You tried to kill her with a fucking bookmobile!"

Cedric raised his gloved hands. "I just caused a small ruckus."

"Small!" roared Grim. "Third Street was a fucking *war zone*."

"Most of the cars were phantasms," said Cedric. "And I might have sent a few vehicles after her, including that colossal bus, but I had all the faith in the Netherworld that you would not let me—or any other force in existence—harm a hair on Helena's head. Including, as you say, a bookmobile."

"What about the damn McDonald's?" bellowed Grim.

Cedric scoffed. "*Please.* If I'd wanted to be a *genuine* menace, I'd have managed a better ambush than *that.* That whole debacle. I'll have you know, it hurt me more than it did you."

"In what fucking way?" Grim demanded.

"Aside from getting my neck snapped," he said, "I didn't know the mirror wraiths would do what they did. In that moment, because of my vast array of talents, I managed to keep my devilish mask in place, but . . . I didn't relish your obvious pain. Quite the opposite."

"*That's* not why your scar bled," said Grim, shoving Cedric back even as he released him.

I didn't know what scar he was talking about, but Cedric did. An uncomfortable smile flashed across the wizard's face as he cricked his neck.

"If I didn't care about you, Grim," said Cedric, "I wouldn't have tried to pretend to want to murder your lady love so voraciously."

"I should punch your damn lights out," muttered Grim, even as his anger, at last, began to abate.

"Ill-advised," said Cedric as he smoothed his robes. "Given that I now have access to your substantive music collection and coveted memorabilia."

Grim brandished a finger at him. "You'd better not touch that guitar."

"When you're settled," said Cedric, "and officially out of my hair, so to speak, I plan to hand deliver it. Until that time, you'll simply have to trust I will handle your effects with care."

"So . . . that's it?" I asked, again squeezing Grim's hand. "You're just . . . going to let us go? Grim, too?"

"You really have no choice," said Cedric. "I've already credited the life that assuming this role grants me . . . to you, Grim. I told you I had plans for it. That life, if my plan was going to work . . . I had to save it for you."

"This is really happening?" asked Grim as he glanced to Flora, who dabbed at her eyes with a leaf-embroidered handkerchief. Johann, in the meantime, smiled wistfully at Cedric—a bit like a proud grandfather.

"This," said Grim, swallowing hard, emotion straining his voice. "Why does it feel like another fucking bait and switch?"

"You," I said, interrupting Cedric before he could answer. "You love Grim, too, don't you?"

"Abrasive as he is," said Cedric, "he's a bit hard not to hold some affinity for, isn't he?"

A smile broke onto my face, and I beamed up at Grim, who could only look down in response.

"I always hated you," said Grim.

"See," said Cedric, "I don't think you did. Not truly. Even when you scythed me and snapped my neck. In fact, I would wager you've never hated a single soul in your entire existence. None, perhaps, but your own. But . . . Helena helped you with that, didn't she? And Flora and Johann, too. Maybe me as well, albeit backhandedly. You're welcome, by the way."

Grim didn't answer. Swallowing again, he just looked away.

"I'm free to leave and Helena, too?" he asked at last. "I'm not bound to my oath anymore, and Helena's no longer a Fated. Do I have that right?"

"She's still technically a Fated," said Cedric. "Though none but The Few know for what. Her fate, as everyone's in this room has for one reason or another, has simply . . . changed. Sir White made some adjustments, swayed by the realization she had far more important work to do here. *You* are her fate now, as I understand it . . . and she is yours. The rest? Well, that will come one day, won't it? When I do. In the meantime . . . I think you two have some particulars to sort out. By the way, I should probably let you know that you've also been left with a few of your . . . tricks. Being a wizard of my standing, I didn't need to take your powers. Also, The Few know you have enemies—Mephistopheles, for one. Rumor has it *he's* the one who gave you that striking white streak in your hair."

"Yeah, well," said Grim, "you should have seen *him*."

"Just like a demon to put flair in your hair," announced Pluto.

Goodness. *Mephistopheles* had put that shock of white in Grim's dark locks? *That* was certainly a story I was going to have to get out of him later.

"Aside from Johann's demon friend," added Cedric, "there's also a vampire or two in the mix from what I understand?"

I narrowed my eyes on Cedric. Because . . . did he seem anxious?

"Fuckin' *hate* vampires," muttered Grim through clenched teeth before tilting his head and rolling back a shoulder, as if the thought of them gave him the heebie-jeebies. Like *he* might have even been bitten once.

"Um," I ventured, suddenly nervous as I traded a terrified glance between the two of them. "V-vampires?"

"There's also that one witch from Florida, is there not?" asked Cedric.

"The fucking Sarasota Shrew," mumbled Grim, his gaze going distant and hollow, like he happened to be recalling a nightmare. "You're going to have to watch out for her. She's still pissed as hell over the cat incident."

"Um. Cat incident?" I couldn't help asking. "What happened? Did the cat . . . die?"

"No," said Grim. "But that witch's boyfriend did—and I got there just in time to keep her from stashing his soul in the neighbor's Siberian. I sort of get it now why she didn't want me to take him."

"You mentioned she was still angry," said Cedric, his tone now unmistakably daunted.

"Maybe don't go to the Keys alone," warned Grim.

"Mm," said Cedric with a frown. "Noted."

"Something tells me we should probably have a conversation about these . . . acquaintances of yours . . . later," I muttered to myself more than Grim. "Over some . . . drinks."

"Point is," said Cedric, "adversaries don't go away even when you get fired."

"Can't we just say he was laid off?" I asked.

"For my own sake," said Cedric, "let's go with 'deposed' since, to a certain degree, I'm inheriting Grim's track record with said enemies. Makes me sound formidable while also suggesting Grim himself won't be a satisfying target any longer—and it's true-ish. Anyway, what I was saying is that you've got the means to protect yourself—and this Fated—from harm. I mean . . . that's what those powers you have are for, right?"

Grim's gaze shot to mine, and I blushed even as I tried to look oblivious.

"I'm so sad I'm happy," whimpered Flora, her tears freely rolling down her cheeks now.

"I knew there was more to you than what you pretended to be," said Johann, speaking to Cedric. "Both of you," he added, turning to address Grim.

"Cedric's done pretending," said Pluto, "happy couple, happy ending."

"Invite me to the wedding?" asked Cedric through another surly, self-satisfied smirk.

"You could come to dinner, too," I said, my response drawing Grim's shocked gaze. But I just winked at him. "Flora and Johann as well. And Pluto, of course. Surely one of The Few could babysit the Hallowed Halls for a few hours. I make a mean lasagna."

"I could bring pastries from Paris," said Flora.

"I have an appetite I could bring," said Johann, patting his belly. "And I suppose I could pop out of hiding for a short spell so long as we're not in public. If it's cold, I'll wear the ushanka Flora got me from Siberia."

"Dinner at the Grims'," called Pluto.

"It's a date," said Cedric. "So long as Loxley agrees, of course."

Grim remained quiet, still processing the emotions that had to be warring for his attention, his mind, his heart—that dark soul that still needed to learn what it was like to fully embrace the light.

But then, I still had things to learn, too.

From and about myself as well as him.

Thanks to Grim, I now had the promise of a full life in which to do that.

"Yeah, fine," said Grim at last. "Just . . . don't touch my shit until I have a place to put it."

"I'm turning the furniture green at first opportunity," said Cedric.

"Prick," growled Grim.

To this, Cedric grinned, and stepping forward, he looped an arm around Grim's shoulders, guiding him—and by proxy me—toward the hall leading out of the Hallowed Halls.

"As the Americans say," replied Cedric, "I love you, too, man."

"Grim won't say it," said Pluto. "He won't use his breath. But I think it can be said, he loves you to death."

"We'll go with that," grumbled Grim.

I smiled at Flora and Johann, who, both sniffling now, followed us, no doubt wanting to see us off as Cedric escorted us to the nearest portal—the doorway that would not just take us home but return me and Grim to the greatest gift of all.

Life.

And not just any life—but one the two of us would get to spend . . . together.

EPILOGUE

HELENA

I wore a flower crown crafted from real, deep pink roses, yellow daisies, lavender, and baby's breath. And I *did* look queenly.

My new *killer*, smash-hit Halloween costume, a floor-length chiffon dress of a softer complementary pink, even had a short train.

Grim looked mouthwatering (as ever) in head-to-toe black and a spiky ebony crown. A sweeping black cloak, knee-high boots, and Gothic belt completed his own guise, and instead of his scythe, he now carried a dark staff topped by a crimson globe.

Hunter had come up with the idea for a couple's costume, but it had been *my* idea to dress as Hades and Persephone—perhaps the OG power couple.

I hadn't even had to convince Grim, either. He'd just said "sure" when I'd asked him if he wanted to attend the costume party with me—to return to the place we'd met roughly one year before.

Now, on Halloween night, we stood together amid the crowd of fellow partygoers, our contrasting figures bathed in the glow of colored lights, swirled in the mist of the fog machines, swathed in our faux finery, our hands linked.

"Do you ever miss it?" I asked him while spooky, techno-themed music pulsed and revelers frolicked on the dance floor, their costumes ranging from elegant to absurd, grotesque, and ironic.

"The job?" he guessed, glancing down at me, his tattoos poking through the sexy open collar of his tunic.

I gave him a soft smile. I'd asked him this question before and he'd given me a very Grim version of "no," but now he'd had some time away, some distance to think and reflect . . . more fully adjust.

"I think I miss it the way you do Gus the Bus," he said.

I snort-laughed, catching the unladylike sound in one hand. Then I grinned, basking in his attention and glowing under his ardent gaze.

He smiled, too—just a smirk. Grim rarely smiled big, but I *had* made him laugh, too.

Like when I'd stepped in the paint pan while helping him to redecorate his new apartment, the one he'd rented in my same complex.

We still spent most nights together, either Grim at my place, or me at his, but my apartment was small, and he hadn't wanted to cramp me by moving in while he, very literally, rejoined the land of the living.

He wouldn't have cramped me but since he lived only a few doors down (much to Ms. Lynn's dismay), I could let Grim do things his way without complaint.

In addition to getting to keep his misty shadow powers, his smoke skills, Grim, it turned out, got something of a pension. Enough to help him comfortably get on his feet in the "real" world, which he had through his music.

Understandably, practicing the modern guitar since the instrument's inception meant he had acquired a certain level of skill. And one afternoon, after hearing Grim play during a special teen program I'd roped him into, Hunter immediately lost all fear of him—and began hounding Grim to form a band with him and a few of his friends.

Now they were Death's Obsession, a metal band (of course) with an alternative rock flair.

Grim said he'd named the band after me—after us. Though Grim hadn't expected the band to go anywhere, Hunter's prowess with social media had ensured otherwise.

Now it seemed everyone knew him as "Grim." Except, of course, for the people who called about car insurance for The Judge, credit cards, and bogus extended warranties.

On paper (and his new driver's license), he was the man he'd once been, the man he'd spent time reconnecting with and remembering—Renwick Loxley.

I loved both versions of him equally and deeply.

"Oh my gosh," I said when the pumping music died out and the DJ filtered in a new song, slower and far more melodious than the techno. It was also a song I knew well—David Bowie's "As the World Falls Down" from the movie *Labyrinth*.

I seized Grim's arm, wrapping it with both of mine. "Can we dance?"

Grim only gestured to the dance floor with one sweep of his arm, inviting me to join him there just the way the king of the underworld would.

Giddy, I squeaked and stooped to gather my train while Grim propped his staff against the wall.

After securing the train to my wristlet, I looped one arm again through Grim's and let him lead me to the floor.

He grasped my hand, and I parked my free one on his shoulder as the warm palm of his other hand came to rest on my upper back.

As we started to dance, his gaze strayed to something over my shoulder—and narrowed.

"What is it?" I asked, checking—and glimpsing a strange man in a hooded black cloak, matching Renaissance regalia, and a Venetian Carnival-style red devil's half mask complete with horns just before he vanished behind a group of Nintendo characters. "Grim?"

"Sorry," he said, trading his attention between me and the figure as we turned again. "I thought . . . I saw someone."

"Someone?" I asked, my gaze bouncing back and forth, even though the devil man seemed to have disappeared.

"It's nothing," Grim said, shaking his head, his attention returning to me. "Just my mind playing tricks, I'm sure."

"Halloween does that," I said. "Plays tricks."

"So do I," he leaned down to whisper in my ear.

I giggled and pressed myself closer to him while we swayed to David Bowie's voice.

"Have you seen this movie?" I asked.

"Honestly, there are a few parts I'd like to *unsee*. If you know, you know."

Another peal of laughter broke forth from me as he turned me yet again, swaying me expertly as pale opalescent confetti rained over us, catching in his hair and on his robes.

"At least it's not glitter," he grunted as the lights chased one another, David's voice echoing around us, crooning about the stars, love, and a world undone.

"Flora told me about the glitter," I said, mildly chagrined but . . . not *really*. "Did you ever get it out of your robes?"

"Cedric's probably still sporting that shit right now," he said, and this time, we both laughed, a rare bright smile lighting his face, prompting me to touch his cheek, savor the image, the moment.

"I should also let you know," he said, "that a certain . . . garment of yours *was* still in one of the pockets."

My smile dropped, my face flaming bright red. "*No.*"

"Can't you see his face when he checked for loose change?"

I blanched. "God, I feel like I'm about to see him since I'm *this* close to dying of embarrassment!"

"You want me to ask for them back?"

"No!"

"Good," he said. "You don't need them anyway."

I shook my head, my smile fighting its way back onto my face. "Grim, I love you."

"That's good, considering," he said.

"Considering?" I tilted my head at him, but instead of answering, as the song faded into its final refrain, the garbled clock from the movie tolling thirteen in the background of the music, Grim took my hand and led me off and then away from the dance floor, the swirling lights, mist, and people.

From there, we entered the hall that ran parallel to the restored balcony.

"What are you doing?" I asked when Grim opened the sliding glass door, because this time there *was* a sign. Instead of warning partygoers away from the area, the fancy folding sign designated the balcony as "Reserved."

Grim placed a finger to his lips. Then, at my first shudder from the October cold, he swept his cloak from his shoulders before settling it around mine.

Taking my hand again, he led me out onto the balcony, to the site of our first meeting.

I hung back a little, gulping at the stretch of stone balcony that had so easily crumbled away last time.

"If you look hard enough," Grim said, tugging me closer still, all the way to the balcony, which he touched with one ring-lined, tattooed, flesh-and-blood hand, "you can see the cracks where they mended it."

I glanced over my shoulder, half expecting security to come rushing out after us because, if there hadn't been cameras installed before, after my incident here, they'd surely mounted at least one.

"I know the same could be said about me," said Grim, drawing my attention back to him just as he sank onto one knee before me, an open jewelry box proffered in one hand, a sun-shaped diamond ring embedded in the velvet. "But . . . I still hope you'll say yes."

My hands leaped to my mouth. Tears sprang to my eyes.

"Helena," said Grim, "will you marry me?"

My throat squeezed itself closed, allowing for no words to pass.

So I nodded, and nodded, until finally, after once again being able to draw breath, I could answer.

"Yes," I told him. "*Yes.*"

Grim rose, and he slid the ring onto my finger, the diamond surrounded by a halo of spiky gold, its band embedded with tiny stones that formed a rainbow.

"I bought a house, too," he said.

I gasped. "*What?*"

"That one you like on the hill. It has a library, by the way."

I beamed at him. "And a music room?"

"Different floors, I promise."

"Like that will muffle anything!" I shouted at him, laughing again as the tears streamed down my face—tears of joy. Overwhelmed in the best way possible, I launched myself at him, wrapping my arms around his shoulders as he lifted me and spun me.

My flower crown toppled free, flying over and off the balcony, down to the flagstones below, as though in commemoration of the death that never was.

Setting me on my feet again, Grim kissed me. Taking his face in my hands, I kissed him back, ready for this newest chapter of life, and fate, to unfold.

From here?

Well, we just had to set a date.

ACKNOWLEDGMENTS

Writing this book was such a wild and magical ride, and I can't express how much fun I've had with every phase of this project. Bringing this story to life has been a total dream come true, and I have so many wonderful people to thank.

This book would not exist without the invaluable guidance of my amazing agent, Jessica Watterson. Your suggestions during our brainstorming chat sent me searching for the right idea, and I was so excited when you loved the sample pages. I deeply appreciate your input, your cheerleading, your expertise, and your support.

While I was noodling on Jess's guidance and contemplating what direction to take, my nephew, Ethan Creagh (a straight A physics major—not that I'm bragging, but he totally is), stopped by for a visit. I shared some general parameters with him before asking what he thought. His response? A shrug paired with a nonchalant, "What about the Grim Reaper?" You're a genius, Skillet. Thank you for the lightning strike that sent me off to the races. Thank you as well for being a tester for my jokes, and, always, for keeping it real. I know you're proud of me. I'm super proud of you, too. But tread with caution while reading, dude. This book does contain what you might call some "zesty shit."

I am supremely grateful to my amazing editor, Ghjulia Romiti. During our initial call, when you asked if I'd be open to kicking it up a notch in the monster romance department, I knew we were already vibing and surfing the same spooky, skeleton-loving wavelength. Your ideas helped to sharpen and focus this story while enhancing the romance, and I loved that you were all-in for my crazy ideas, bookmobile antics, and Faustian lore drops. Thank you also for those extra pushes and for leading me to discover Pluto. I've had an absolute blast working together.

A deep heartfelt thank-you goes to Kimberly Laws for helping to tweak and refine this project leading up to production, and for guiding all those finishing touches that have helped to give this book as much sparkle as doom.

The Gallery team has spoiled me from day one, and I'm indebted to everyone who has helped to shine, polish, and fine-tune this project. Thank you to my copyeditor and proofreaders for those eagle-eye catches. Thank you as well to the marketing team for helping me build buzz and for the social media guidance. Thank you also to the design team for the interior design and the killer and super adorable, to-die-for cover. I am one lucky Gallerina.

April Cannon, your encouragement means the world to me—thanks for always hyping me up. Dayton Cannon? Dude, your suggestion for Grim's car was *perfect*. We wouldn't have The Judge without your input.

Because of Jeannine Storm, the Halloween of 2024 will be one I will always remember. It was a quiet one for us. We spent a long time at your kitchen table—hours, in fact. You listened to my ideas about this book and gave me so much great input. More than that, you listened to my ideas about all the things going on in my life. With your kind words and unique perspective, you also performed some gentle and much-needed chiropractic maneuvers on my soul. I walked out of your house that night with the wattage of the sun. Thank you, too, for what you said while we were checking out at

Target—that was another mind-expanding moment I needed. Thank you as well for always listening to my plot tirades in TJ Maxx, First Watch, Target, your car, my car, the movie theater before the latest new horror flick, and the arcade that one time when we annihilated those space alien punks who *all* had it coming. Most of all, thank you for always believing in me.

The brilliant Gina Possanza might also have listened to her fair share of plot tirades. Gina, thank you for being my sounding board. You've talked me through more than one pickle while reminding me, even when I doubt myself, how I "always" find the solution. Thank you also for the nuggets of research you text me and the fun names you find—including Mr. McDead's. Your old-money joke came in handy, too. Your help with marketing and making me fly graphics is also so much appreciated. Our Halloween escapade of 2025 will also be one for the books, won't it? Thanks for accompanying me on the Grim Trails haunted trail and putting up with me while I argued with that bridge troll. I didn't mean to spoil his entrance, and maybe my brain was still in editing mode, but I stand by my claim that he shouldn't have let us pass without a riddle. I am *not* sorry we both scared Ichabod Crane more than he scared us. Let's do it again this year. Maybe the eight-foot-tall Jabberwocky will want to hug me back this time . . . Like Grim, I'm *sure* he just needs love.

A huge thank you goes to my fellow writers and critique partners: Bill Wolfe, Colette Ballard, Kurt Hampe, Katie McGarry, and Bethany Griffin. Thank you for your invaluable input, your encouragement, and the years of memories and laughs. You have all helped me to become a stronger writer, and for that I am infinitely grateful.

My family has always served as a source of encouragement and inspiration, particularly my mom. Thank you, Mom, for offering your thoughts on plot points, suggesting jokes, and laughing at mine. I know you don't always dig the scary stuff and that you're *still* mad at me for turning Danny into a clock, but I'm glad you like Grim.

I'm appreciative as well to my brothers, Daniel, Michael, and Tom, whose antics also continue to inspire me. Tom, thanks additionally for your help with the haywire elevator scene—I can always count on the captain!

To Norah, Eilley, and Autumn—I love you girls, and thank you for the Grim Reaper drawings.

Most days, I go on a long walk. It's during these walks that I ponder my stories, gain insights, and, I feel, get those important "downloads" from the universe. Always, I thank God for His help with my creative pursuits, the gifts He's given me, and for sending me new inspiration each day.

And of course, many thanks go to my readers, whom I adore. I would not be here without you, and it is my pleasure and honor to write stories for you. Thanks for reading, recommending, reviewing, following me on social media, and for reaching out to let me know you enjoyed the adventure. I'm so glad I got to share this one with you, too—and I can't wait for what's next. Never forget, I love you all to death. ;)

ABOUT THE AUTHOR

© Gina Possanza

KELLY CREAGH is the critically acclaimed author of the *Nevermore* trilogy, *Phantom Heart*, and *Strange Unearthly Things*. She holds an MFA in writing from Spalding University and a BS in theatre arts from the University of Louisville. She lives in beautiful Louisville, Kentucky, with her rescue dogs. When not writing, she enjoys baking, gaming, daily walks, and teaching and performing belly dance. *A Date with Death* is her first adult novel. Visit her at KellyCreagh.com.